ACKNOWLEDGMENTS

Thanks to my loving husband for his continued encouragement, and to my family.

My appreciation goes to George Deeming, Curator of the Pennsylvania Railroad Museum, for his assistance. Thanks to my critique partners Mary Adair, Sandra Crowley, and Jeanmarie Hamilton, the Raven Mavens critique group, and to those member of North Texas Romance Writers, Dallas Area Romance Authors, and Yellow Rose Romance Writers who offered encouragement and support.

One

"Marry by my thirtieth birthday or lose this ranch to my worthless uncle?" Seething with rage and betrayal, Drake Kincaid stepped off the porch of his ranch house, glared back at his grandfather and cousin Lex. "How could my own flesh and blood put me in this position? All I've worked for hangs by a wedding ring and a noose of lace!"

Drake turned to gaze across the wide expanse of gently rolling range sloping to the Pedernales River. New leaf buds swelled on the branches of the cottonwoods and willows, promising the end of winter. Early bluebonnets would soon be joined by other wildflowers bursting in a riot of color.

The sight of this land usually filled him with pleasure. Today the threat of losing all he held dear blinded him to the rustic beauty. On horseback and on foot, he had covered every acre to tend cattle, horses, and the crops he grew. He knew each dip and rise better than the face of his closest friend or relative. This land was branded on his soul.

Dear Lord, how could I bear to lose this?

The thought staggered him and he shut his eyes against the pain. Without turning, Drake's attention reverted to his grandfather. Grandpa had been his ally against the follies of his ill-matched parents when they were alive, and acted in their place for most of Drake's life.

"Why didn't you talk them out of it, Grandpa?"

"I tried. You think they listened to me?" Grandpa put his hand on Drake's shoulder. "Be reasonable, son. You've known the conditions of your parents' will these twelve years since they died. Why hold me responsible now?"

Drake shrugged off his grandfather's hand and turned to face him. "You are responsible. Dammit, you're the famous Judge Robert Kincaid, aren't you? Instead of enforcing the marriage clause in that ridiculous will, you could help me break it."

He'd always believed his grandfather would do just that. For years Drake had pushed that absurd marriage clause to the back of his mind, never considered the will a threat. Until now.

His grandfather's craggy face broke into a scowl. The older man's faded blue eyes sparked beneath bushy white brows as he pointed a weathered finger at Drake.

"That's where you're wrong, son. If I don't enforce the law for my own family, how can I expect others to respect it? And just what makes you think your hard-nosed uncle Winston would stand for such a thing? You know him living in Massachusetts doesn't prevent him from keeping tabs on you and this ranch."

Drake turned on his cousin. "You're a lawyer. Why don't you help me?"

Lex shook his head. "They've got more lawyers in Boston than you could shake a stick at. Cuz, if you tried to break the terms of that will, Winston would be on you like a chicken on a June bug. You can bet good money that money-grubber is already counting the days 'til your birthday."

Lex walked over and slumped a lanky hip against the hitching rail. Wind ruffled his auburn hair and sunlight brought out the freckles splashed across his amiable face. If not for the concern in Lex's dark eyes, Drake might have thought him unaffected by all he heard.

Concern was well and good, but Lex wasn't the one who stood to lose everything. Drake shifted his gaze to the calming strength of the hand-hewn limestone blocks which formed his home, his haven. Built to withstand the onslaught of time, this house and the ranch had become a part of him. He couldn't give it up, couldn't tolerate another man—or woman—in charge of *his* ranch. His voice rose as he forked fingers through his hair.

"Look how Uncle Winston ruined that ranch he used to own East of town, before he had it fenced and sold off in parcels." Drake gestured to the land sloping to the river. "He'd do the same to this one, or worse, curse his ornery hide. Have you forgotten he actually threatened to run sheep on this place? They'd ruin the grazing land plus rile the other cattlemen so much there'd be outright range war. Sheep!"

He turned to face his grandfather eye to eye. "But damned if I'll marry some mindless skirt just so I can keep what's rightfully mine from passing into the hands of my useless uncle."

"You've found a reason to disqualify every woman in Kincaid County and all the counties around," his grandfather snapped, drawing himself up to his full six-foot-five height. "Facts be known, you don't want to settle down and raise a family."

Drake could not deny the charge, but he refused to admit it his grandfather. Plenty of marriageable women had paraded before him over the years. Some had even dared broach the subject of marriage when he failed to do so.

"I couldn't spare time from building this ranch to play courting games." He didn't add he had no wish to expose himself to the sorry ordeal he had watched his parents endure. Instead, he tried reasoning with his grandfather.

He walked a few feet from the shelter of the porch. "How would you have felt if you'd married someone you didn't love before you met Grandma?"

Dark clouds gathered overhead, darker ones in the Southwest. Drake faced the one spot of morning sun peeping through the thunderheads. The most dangerous storm building around him didn't come from the sky. This silly marriage business could wash out every dream he harbored for making this the best ranch in Texas.

"Grandpa, I don't want to *settle* for a wrong or even an *almost-right* woman. The true one and only one for me might be waiting just around the next bend."

Grandpa left the porch to stand beside Drake. "Then, son, you better round that bend and be gol' durned quick about it. If you don't catch you a bride by your thirtieth birthday, everything you've worked for will be gone and be damned. This ranch will revert to your mother's miserly brother, and you'll be looking for a job and a place to live."

"If I haven't found her in almost thirty years, how can I find her in a few weeks?" Desperation tinged his voice and he hated hearing it. He felt as hopeless as he sounded, but he faced his grandfather. "Be reasonable, will you?"

Anger flared in the older man's eyes and he used his hat to point at Drake. "Since none of the women of Kincaid County suits you, you'd best look around on your trip East to buy horses. Find yourself a good woman. And, son, I mean a *good* woman. Marry her by April tenth." Grandpa slapped his leg with the large-brimmed hat. "Otherwise, you'll be looking for a new place to live and your uncle Winston or his lackey will be living here."

Drake refused to lose land he had poured his life's blood into for twelve years. "I'm the one who made this ranch into a profitable business." His voice rose in pitch as his indignation grew. He gestured wildly. "How can you consider taking the ranch from me, your own grandson, your own flesh and blood? I've fought twelve hard years—"

His grandfather interrupted with a roar, "Don't you go bellyachin' about what you've done for this land. You think you're the first Kincaid who had a hard row to hoe?" He gave a derisive snort. "Didn't my own ancestors in Scotland lose all their family lands to the English? Didn't both my grandfathers beat the English in the Carolinas to carve out a place for themselves?"

He stepped closer to his grandson and pointed to the

ground. "Didn't I help wrench this very piece of land you're standing on from ol' Santa Anna and the Comanches? Even after that we had the devil of a time holdin' on to it through the War, and purt' near lost it afterward to that bunch of thievin' carpetbaggers. But we've kept it, by damn."

As long as he could remember, Drake had heard stories of Grandpa's early years in Texas and the struggles he faced. Drake hadn't meant to compare his own struggles with Grandpa's. Now the man was on a tear and Drake knew better than to interrupt him. But, damn, he had fought hard and long for this ranch too. His own sweat and toil had stamped his brand on this land whether Grandpa agreed or not.

Grandpa's eyes narrowed and pinned Drake where he stood. "That's the way of it, boy. Kincaids fight for what's ours, for our land. But what good is it unless we have sons and daughters to pass that land on to?" He punctuated his remarks by stabbing a gnarled finger at Drake.

No matter how much he loved and respected Grandpa, Drake refused to back down. "Do you think I don't know that? But why does it have to be right now? Why can't it be in my own time? Why can't you bend a little on this?"

Grandpa's voice softened, but he offered no hope. "Believe me, Drake, this is not easy for me. The law is the law, and it's supposed to be impartial. I'm pledged by oath to uphold it for you the same as for anyone else—even that fool Winston."

He clapped his hat on his head. "Now, I've said as much on this subject as I'm going to." Grandpa turned and stomped to his horse.

With a swiftness that belied his years he mounted and, half turning in the saddle, shouted, "By April tenth or you lose the whole shootin' match!"

Drake watched his grandfather ride away as if the hounds of hell were in pursuit. All Drake's hopes and dreams seemed doomed to hell as well. Lightning flashed and a great roll of thunder punctuated Grandpa's departure and his own mood.

Pacing, his cousin got the brunt of his complaints.

"You know how much time I've devoted to this ranch. How

could my own parents, and now Grandpa, hinge all those years and work on this one ridiculous clause? Marry or lose everything to pompous Uncle Winston, a man who cares nothing for ranching. After all, the man lives in Boston!"

Drake clenched his fists. "Winston doesn't give a hoot about the land or its people, only the profit to be made. The man's mean as a snake and twice as crooked. He'd have some manager do all the work for him and pay the hands only a pittance for hard labor."

"Winston wouldn't have the loyalty of his ranch hands that you do, that's for sure. Doubt he'd provide decent housing or pay them near as well."

"Probably wouldn't even visit the place, durn his blue-blooded, worthless hide."

A grin split Lex's face. "Remember when we first heard the terms of the will? We joked about the marriage clause."

"I was eighteen. Thirty seemed aeons away. I never dreamed Grandpa would enforce the stupid thing. He even joked with us."

Lex tugged at his ear lobe. "He's not laughing now."

"No, the old man's dead-level serious. And me planning this trip so close to my birthday sure put a burr under his saddle."

Drake stalked to a nearby stand of live oak trees, wondering how best to fight this battle. With the toe of his hand-tooled boot, he worked a rock loose from the soil. The wind buffeted against him in brisk gusts. A gyrating dust devil whirled along the wagon road.

He would take his fists to anyone who called him a romantic. Still, he had hoped one day to meet a woman and, well, just *know* she was the one for him. Evidently, real life didn't work that way. Not his.

"I've told Grandpa I'm perfectly capable of finding a wife for myself—when the right time comes. Now the old man's come up with this harebrained idea for a bride search. All I want is to look for a few thoroughbred mares. I refuse to be put out to stud like one of my own stallions."

He scooped up the stone and, with unerring precision,

threw the missile to thunk against the trunk of an ancient oak. From a branch above the target, a startled squirrel chattered angrily at the intrusion.

"Damn that will, and damn Grandpa's meddling."

Lex Tremont shifted his weight against the hitching post and waited patiently for his cousin to calm. He watched Drake's long fingers work forcefully through his thick hair and marveled no furrows were left in his cousin's scalp.

He sympathized with Drake and wondered about him giving in to their grandfather's edict. Drake and their grandfather were too much alike, each a remarkable man in his own way. Nose to nose a few moments ago, the two looked a picture of the same person at different ages.

Both tall, Drake's black hair hung longer than their grandfather's shaggy white mane. But they shared wide shoulders and amazing strength. Drake's eyes were a steel gray to their grandfather's pale blue, but one had only to see them together to know Kincaid blood ran true.

They shared more than looks. The same mile-wide streak of Kincaid stubbornness ran through both men. Lex counted himself lucky his affable Tremont blood tempered his obstinate Kincaid blood.

"To be truthful, Cuz, it was your own father and mother who put that clause in their will. Grandpa's just enforcing it—or reminding you to before we go East."

Drake turned. "I'm so riled I've let the morning get away from us. We were supposed to be on the road two hours ago. Now we've let a storm catch us. Though if you ask me, a blue norther would be more fitting with this marriage thing hanging over my head."

Giving his bay mare a pat on the nose and stepping clear of Drake's massive gelding, Lex left the hitching post and strode over to his cousin. "Calm down. A few more minutes' delay won't make a difference. Let's think this through."

Lex knew his cousin was more intelligent than he was, but Drake's temper sometimes caused his actions to bypass his brain. And that stubborn streak had landed him, and them, in more tight spots than either cared to remember.

"If I have to settle for a wife who's merely suitable, it'll be on *my* terms," Drake said as his boot worked at another stone. With his chin clamped in anger, his face looked carved from stone as well.

"You heard Grandpa, and you know how stubborn he is." Good Lord, who would know better, since Drake was exactly the same? "What do you figure on doing?"

Drake answered, "I'm going to do just what that old man asked."

"No." Lex gave a brief shake of his head and clamped on his hat. He adjusted the brim to shield his face. "I know you're too muleheaded to back down so easily."

He tilted his head upward to look closely at the man who topped his six feet by a good five inches. Though Drake now appeared relaxed, Lex recognized the steel behind that look. The little muscle tic at the corner of Drake's mouth gave him away.

"No," Lex repeated. "I know you too well to believe that. What is it you really have in mind?"

Drake scooped up another rock and hit the same trunk, sending the angry squirrel bounding to the next tree. "He wants me to go East. Find myself a wife. So that's just what I'll do."

Lex saw anger flash in his cousin's eyes as he faced him.

Drake said, "I give you my word, I intend to find the most disagreeable, the homeliest, absolutely the most unsuitable *virgin* I can and make her my *wife*." Drake spoke with such derision the words seemed a curse. "Let's just see how happy Grandpa is then."

Struggling to conceal his shock, Lex tried once again to reason with Drake. "That's cuttin' off your nose to spite your face. This is a bride you're talking about, not a hat or a brood mare. You're goin' to be married to her for a long, long time." He paused as the shock deepened. "Say, you don't plan to run her off or somethin' soon as you're married, do you?"

"Naw, nothing like that." Drake paused as if in thought,

then raised his ornery gaze to his cousin. "If I wanted a wife, it would be different. I don't, especially not like this. Don't have time for one, don't intend to live in the same house with the woman once I marry her."

Thunder rumbled across the rolling prairie. The approaching storm drove even the angry squirrel to cover. No birds sang or flew overhead. Cattle in the pasture bunched together with their backs to the wind.

Though he denied being superstitious, Lex knew that along with needed moisture, storms always brought trouble—even if it was only the extra work required for the ranch hands to calm the stock. The one headed this way looked to be a gully washer.

He gave one last look at the clouds before he stepped toward his cousin and placed a restraining hand on Drake's shoulder to repeat his earlier advice. "Calm down and think this through. How will that meet Grandpa's ultimatum or satisfy the will's conditions?"

Drake affected a shocked expression and clutched his chest. "How could I expect a genteel lady to live the rough life on the ranch anymore than my mother did? She can live in town—with the old man." He smiled. "Yeah. Let Grandpa see how well he likes having a woman forced on him."

Lex shook his head at his cousin's folly. "No woman will stand for that kind of marriage."

"If I have to marry, my wife will do as I say. She'll stay with Grandpa and Aunt Lily, and she'll like it."

Worry tugged at Lex. "Don't do this, Drake. Don't you want children, sons to carry on the ranch like Grandpa said?"

"Oh, I'll do my husbandly duty often enough for that." He stepped into the stirrups and mounted Midnight, the huge black gelding only he could ride. "You still game to go with me to buy horses—and join this search for the most unsuitable bride I can find?"

As Drake spoke, rain drops the size of quarters peppered the land. Not a good sign, to Lex's way of thinking, this storm launching their trip.

Lex donned his rain slicker and mounted his own horse. Drake and trouble were no strangers. This plan might make sense to Drake in his hardheaded, stubborn way of thinking, but it smelled of crisis to Lex.

He knew most of Drake's protests were out of frustration for the situation created by that ridiculous will. Once they were on the trip, Drake would calm down and rethink his position, probably wouldn't carry through on his threats. Lex hoped not.

No way around it, though. His cousin had to marry to save his ranch, and that meant finding a wife pronto. Knowing Drake's present state of mind begged for real trouble, he was certain to find it.

Lex turned up the collar of his oiled coat against the storm. Sure was a bad start for what promised to be an unusual adventure.

"Grandpa's let me off work, I told my folks goodbye last night, and my stuff's packed. Believe me, I wouldn't miss this for the world." He shook his head in disbelief, sending a trickle of cold rain down his neck. "Most unsuitable wife, indeed."

Piper's Hollow, Tennessee
Two weeks later.

Pearl Parker watched the sun send its first tentative fingers of light over the crest of hills framed perfectly in the cabin window. Early morning was her favorite time, full of promise and hope for a brand new day. Robins in the hawthorn bushes beneath the window called noisy greetings while a nearby cock crowed to herald the sunrise.

Inside the cabin, Pearl's workday had begun hours ago. Proof of that labor was the tempting yeasty scent of fresh-baked bread mingled with the tangy perfume of spiced fruit in warm pies. She turned as her half-sister slipped into the kitchen carrying a basket of eggs.

Sarah set the basket in the dry sink. "Looks like you're about ready for town." She cleaned her hands, and reached for a slice of warm bread. "There's a chill in the air this morning. Aren't you going to wear shoes?"

Pearl untied her apron and tugged at the neck of her faded brown dress. "No, you know I hate those stiff old clumping things. Lately they pinch my toes something awful." She brushed a hand over her sister's pale hair. "You've grown so over the winter. I hoped you'd be shorter than me, but I think I was about your height when I was thirteen."

The younger girl smiled, "I'd be pleased to be like you—in every way."

Sarah's eyes were a shade bluer and her hair a shade lighter blonde than Pearl's. Even with those differences, Pearl had to admit they looked a lot alike despite the twelve years separating them. Leaning against the kitchen table, she inhaled the aromas that surrounded her. She turned and spread butter on a slice of bread. Pearl took a bite and closed her eyes to savor the taste.

"Mmm, nothing better than fresh-baked bread and butter." When she had finished the treat, she took several sips of her coffee. "Now, I'd better get back to work."

Pearl and Sarah wrapped each loaf in a clean cloth made from flour sacking, working rapidly in a pattern learned from daily practice. Warm loaves were placed in neat rows in the lower part of the cart. Pies made from Pearl's cellar cache of apples and dried peaches were stacked on racks across the top. Eggs for the general store went into a special basket nestled securely in a corner slot.

Once all her wares were loaded to suit her, she tucked her most precious possession, her medical bag, safely inside the vehicle's wooden base. Though she loved baking, she loved healing more. Making people well, easing pain or helping birth new life gave satisfaction far beyond life's ordinary pleasures. It made a difference in the world. Only a few patients could pay her, but she called healing her true life's work.

The cart took up most of the open kitchen area in the large cabin and barely fit through the outer doorway. She hated having the thing inside, but knew no other way to protect it from the vicious vandals plaguing her family the past few weeks. The wheelbarrow-like conveyance served its purpose well as she made her daily deliveries of baked goods across the area. Her half-brother, Storm, had helped build it using pieces of planking and parts of broken machinery salvaged from the barn. She thought of it with pride. It was their most ingenious invention.

Sarah leaned forward to sniff a warm apple pie. She straightened and fussed, "I wish you didn't have to wear those hateful old dresses of Granny's. That one's been mended until I declare it's the ugliest thing I've ever seen."

Pearl fingered the unsightly hopsacking garment in question. "Yes, I hate this one even more than the others, but it serves its purpose to disguise my figure."

"But you work so hard and help so many people, you deserve pretty things. I hate to see you look so dowdy."

"If I don't look this way, some men might make improper remarks and propositions." Pearl twisted her face into a grimace while she wriggled and tugged the upper body wrap across her breasts into a more tolerable position.

"Is the binding on your bosom hurting?"

"Some, but I don't mind." She straightened and smiled at Sarah. "I don't mind the dresses, either, not if that's needed for us to stay in business. A housewife won't buy our baked goods if her husband gives the baker"—she fanned the voluminous skirts in a mock curtsy to her sister—"a second glance."

Storm strode in from feeding the animals and milking the cow. In one hand he carried a pail of fresh milk; in the other, a rifle. He set the pail beside the churn and leaned the rifle in the corner.

Sarah reached for another slice of the bread. "They'd give you more than a second glance if they saw how pretty you really are. They'd be chasing after you for sure."

"We have enough problems without men getting ideas into their heads about either of us." She thought of the troubles she had encountered over the past few years. A controversial lone woman acting as head of household could not be too careful, especially with two young people in her care. "All people need to see is we're clean, we're good cooks, I help sick folks, and we all three mind our own business."

Storm spread jam on the buttered slice of bread he held. "That's more than most of the people 'round here do."

His long black hair was clubbed behind him this morning. In a nut-brown face that confirmed his half-Cherokee heritage, his cobalt blue eyes explained his Cherokee name, Eyes Like Storm Cloud. Though he had turned fourteen last week, Pearl thought he looked several years younger, maybe even as young as eleven or twelve.

She caught the twinkle which sprang into his eyes as he watched her ritual.

"Getting all prettied up for the folks in town, I see."

She grinned at him, happy they shared the joke of conspiracy against the public. What would she do without him? His dry sense of humor and sharp mind bolstered her spirits as much as his helpful nature made her work easier. In fact, he helped her in many ways each day, and so did Sarah. Once again Pearl thanked God for sending them to her.

The two had come into her care at separate times when she was no more than a girl herself. Both were big responsibilities, but she couldn't love them more if they were her own children. She would never turn them over to someone else or abandon them, and she couldn't imagine her life without them in it.

Pearl skimmed her hand across the block of butter on the table and patted her oiled fingers to the front part of her hair. Then, she frizzed the hair around her face.

"Have to get into my wild woman look." She dipped her fingers into the flour and flicked it at her hair. "A little flour on the grease to make my hair look dull and listless." She cleaned her hands on a towel and stood as if for inspection.

"There, now my masquerade is complete. Am I frumpy enough?"

Sarah wrinkled her nose in disgust. Pearl gave her a smile. They went through this routine each morning. Sarah never approved, but Pearl knew her disguise helped insure their fragile existence.

In one fluid motion Pearl swung her braid behind her right shoulder and picked up her revolver. She slid the heavy Colt .44 into the special pocket of her dress and patted the weapon for reassurance. Drawing a blue shawl around her shoulders, she gave last-minute orders to her charges.

"Storm, bar the door behind me and stay inside the house. Sarah, please take care of our guest 'til I get back, you hear?"

Storm drew his thin frame to his full five feet. "I don't see why I have to stay here. Sarah can look after Belle. Let me help you." He rushed forward to open the door for Pearl.

Sarah nodded. "I don't mind staying with Belle while Storm goes with you."

"Those blasted Ainsworths were due out of jail yesterday evening. They'd just love to cause another ruckus, or come causing mischief around here." Pearl gave Storm's shoulder a pat. "I really need you stay home and keep a sharp eye out. Belle's not well enough to help Sarah fight them off if those two worthless brothers show up."

For a couple of months, Belle Renfro had worked at the local saloon, Roxie's Place. She had been brought to Pearl a week ago after a beating from a vicious customer. For the first two days they feared the woman would bleed to death from internal damage, yet she had gained a little strength each day.

Belle's presence in their home only added more conflict to their unsettled lives. The preacher and his cohorts would use Belle's presence as another lever to charge Pearl an unfit guardian for Storm and Sarah. Pearl knew the danger when she took Belle in, but she couldn't turn away anyone who needed her help, even if it meant more unpleasantness. And she wouldn't let anyone take Storm and Sarah from her, no matter what she had to do to prevent it.

Pushing her cart before her, Pearl cleared the sloping ramp from the front stoop. She paused, waiting to hear the bar slide into place on the door. She took a deep breath, filling her lungs with the clean, crisp morning air. With bare feet, free of the pinching shoes she hated, she scuffed little puffs of dust through the chill as she trudged the half mile to town and her first customer.

Her family's troubles burdened her thoughts. How were they to protect themselves against a multitude of trouble-makers?

Dear Lord, what's to become of my family and me?

Two

By the time Pete Hammonds unlocked the town's only store, Pearl had finished all her deliveries except those for the storekeeper. She parked her cart and gathered her remaining baked wares to carry inside.

Pete pulled the door open to admit her. "Mornin' Pearl." From the living quarters above, smells of Pete's breakfast sausage wafted down the stairs and into the merchandise area. "Got my cinnamon-apple pie this mornin'?"

"Right here, but your eggs are still in my cart." Pearl laid four loaves of bread and a plump pie on the counter. She handed Pete a list written on a small piece of foolscrap. "And here's the supplies I'll be needing today."

Pearl liked to visit Hammonds Mercantile. While the dapper shopkeeper filled her order, she strolled slowly between shelves stacked with clothes and household goods. Baskets hung from the beams. Dried herbs, vegetables, oil, and other smells blended with the odor of Pete's breakfast.

The sights and aromas kindled her imagination. What unseen hand made the overalls? Where had these buckets come from? What wonderful sights had the lanterns seen on the way to this small village? Pearl loved dreaming of places these things had traveled. Someday she'd leave this nowhere place and take her family to see a bit of the world for themselves.

Today her load would be heavier on her trip home than when she came into town. While the storekeeper carried sacks of flour and sugar and other supplies to her cart, she wandered the shop's aisles. How she would love to surprise her brother and sister with special treats, but she must save every penny. Well, maybe a few peppermints or some sticks of licorice wouldn't be too wasteful. She loved the smiles her brother and sister rewarded her with for even a small treat.

Lingering over a bolt of blue calico, she fingered the fabric longingly. What lovely dresses she could make for herself and Sarah, and maybe even a shirt for Storm from the red nearby. On a shelf overhead, a spool of sky-colored ribbon caught her eye and she brushed at the wisps of hair escaping her braid.

With a deep sigh, she put pretty dresses and hair ribbons from her mind. There would be time for such things later. At least, if her plans worked out.

By the time Pete loaded her purchases, other townspeople were about their daily chores. The steady clang of the blacksmith's hammer resonated from the smithy down the street. In the cottage nearby, old Mrs. Peabody wielded her broom to attack the dust on her front porch with a fury that defied her age. The woman must be close to one hundred.

From the west end of the village, two strangers rode slowly into town, dismounted and tied their horses in front of the jail. They were dressed differently from local men, more like pictures in the *penny dreadfuls* depicting men from the Wild West. She wondered if they were from California, or maybe Texas.

Would they be outlaws or cowboys or businessmen? Not many strangers came to Piper's Hollow. She memorized each detail of the men to relate to Storm and Sarah. At least today she would have something interesting to tell when she got home.

Both men wore waistcoats and wide-brimmed hats, and each had a rifle in the saddle scabbard. The taller of the two caught her attention as he leaned against the front of the jail, his gaze slowly roaming the town. He appeared relaxed until she noticed the way he stood, back to the wall, as his scrutiny took in each building along the short main street.

Oh, my. Just look at the man standing there like one of those Greek god drawings in Mrs. Cummins's books. Of course, the statues in the pictures didn't wear a western hat or boots. In fact, most times they didn't have anything on at all.

Unable to stop the images that leapt to her mind, she smiled. In spite of the clothes he wore, this man beat those pictures seven ways to Sunday for good looks. He stood tall, towering over her long frame, higher than any man she'd ever seen. Even she would feel dainty standing beside a man that size.

His long, dark hair hung almost to shoulders wide enough to furnish shade for three people. With a shrug, he rolled those massive shoulders as if to lessen their fatigue. Maybe this past night he'd slept on the ground instead of a fine feather bed like her own.

Though casually dressed, his clothes appeared of a quality superior to those of Piper's Hollow residents. The tan fabric of his pants fit taut across muscled thighs. One thumb hooked in his belt loop and pressed his dark brown jacket aside. From the wariness of his expression and his stance with one hand near his waist, she decided he must have a handgun tucked into his waistband. Smart man. Few would venture far without one and, clearly, this man had come from far away.

She wondered if he thought himself better than the people in a little hick village like this? Probably so. Most travelers who wandered through here had only criticism to offer for its lack of opportunity and unfriendly residents.

Under her lashes, she tried to appraise the other man. He wore his large hat at an angle. Though shorter than his companion, he would tower over anyone hereabouts. He wore his clothes well and his waistcoat looked to be made of cow's hide with the hair still on it, of all things. Dark pants of fine wool tucked into boots with fancy stitching on them.

Her gaze strayed back to the other man. His clothes were not so fancy as his friend's, but she figured they cost plenty. And didn't he look grand? Standing there like a king surveying his domain, he set her mind wandering to fanciful dreams.

How wonderful to have a man like that sweep her and her family away. His arms would be strong, his character stronger. They would be partners against all life's problems, share all of life's joys. Their romance would be as powerful as Anthony and Cleopatra, Romeo and Juliet, Lancelot and Guinevere.

With a start, she brought herself to task. Just look where romance and dreams got those couples. Disaster for all of them. Safety for her family lay in depending on no one but herself. Yet this man looked so handsome, so strong, so intelligent. At the very moment she decided he surpassed any man anywhere, his gaze swung her way.

His piercing stone-gray stare roamed up and down her form and a frown puckered his brow.

A frown?

Indignation boiled up from deep inside her, and she fought to keep from stamping her foot. How dare he? What gave him the right to gawk at her and frown, of all things?

The devil take the man, anyway.

She long ago grew tired of people treating her as if she were so much trash on the heap. Did that scowl mean he thought her worthless, too? Or maybe he thought her too tall and spindly?

She held herself as straight as she could while pushing her cart. With her haughtiest glare, she met his stare. She saw his surprise and could have sworn his mouth opened, as if he meant to speak.

Pleased with the unexpected reaction, she let her gaze assess him openly. Let him see how *he* liked being subjected to examination. Once again, she took in every detail of his clothing, from fancy boots to wide-brimmed hat.

What brought him here to a wide place in the road like Piper's Hollow? To her mind, only those who absolutely had no other choice would be anywhere in this county where more rocks than crops grew.

The other man appeared more polite. He smiled and tipped

his hat as she passed, revealing a shock of unruly auburn hair and a pleasant face sprinkled with freckles.

"Mornin', ma'am."

She watched the corners of his eyes crinkle and his smile shine out of sparkling cinnamon eyes.

"Good morning to you, sir." She spoke directly to him, pretending to ignore his glowering companion.

The taller man continued to gape at her. What on earth was wrong with him? Had he no manners at all?

Movement across the road caught her attention. She spotted the two worthless Ainsworths loitering about with that evil Jug Eggers. Inwardly she cringed, but kept herself straight and tall. She dared not let Jug know how he frightened her.

Pearl figured those three hooligans would make trouble for her, maybe even try to tip over her cart again. Well, she vowed to prevent that. Precious flour and sugar spilled across the road would do her no good.

She saw that stocky brute Jug nudge Willard Ainsworth before he yelled.

"Lookee here who's come to town all by herself, and her friend the sheriff ain't even around."

Willard moved his rotund form and stepped into the road. His brother Burris followed him. The two of them reminded Pearl of plump roosters. Burris's Adam's apple even looked like a wattle. Between them, she thought, they didn't have as much sense as one rooster.

"Let's just see what ol' Pine Tree Pearl, The Pig Girl, has for us this mornin'." Willard smacked his lips and ran his tongue over them before he repeated the tormenting rhyme they'd used most of her life.

"Pearl, Pearl, the tall pig girl,
Pine tree Pearl, the big pig girl."

"Maybe she's got a pie for us. I sure do like her pies," Burris said.

Jug slapped his leg and chortled, "I sure would like to sample me some of the pig girl's bacon—or grab me her pine cones."

Burris and Willard laughed as if stupid Jug had made clever remarks.

Pearl stopped her cart. Her right hand slipped into her pocket and gripped her pistol. She made a shooing gesture with her other hand.

"You three just get away and leave me alone. I'm warning you, now. Didn't sittin' in jail a few days teach you anything?"

"It made us awful lonesome, if'n you know what I mean. Oink, oink, you big ol' pig girl." Jug spoke as the three moved closer, spreading out as if to surround her.

He made a calling gesture with his broad hands. "Why don't you come with us? We'll just step over to my place and show you a good time. Even a pig girl needs some romancin' in her life."

"Ha." Withdrawing the revolver from her pocket, she motioned the three together. "You wouldn't know romance if it poleaxed you."

"We could teach you the ways of men and women. You'd be plum grateful to us 'fore we were through. You come with ol'e Jug and we'll get us a room over Roxie's Place."

"Even if I were that stupid, which would make me the stupidest woman in Tennessee, Roxie won't let you set foot in her place and you know it."

She almost shuddered at the thought of Jug's arms around her. Though no taller than she was, his huge arms dangled to his knees and reminded Pearl of the picture of a big ape she'd seen long ago in one of Mrs. Cummins's books.

Jug stretched a grimy finger toward her. "Why don't you share some of your Granny's gold with us and we could all go somewheres real nice? Wouldn't you like to go to New Orleans?"

With her free hand she pointed to herself and the faded and mended dress. "Can't you fools see the way I'm dressed? Do I look like I have a bunch of gold from my Granny? Dresses like this and our little plot of land are all she had to leave me."

She took a step toward the three men and waved the gun.

"Now you get away from here and let me alone or I'll shoot the three of you so full of holes, you'll leak water every time you take a drink."

Burris put up a hand and whined, his Adam's apple bobbling as he spoke, "Aw, Pearl, you don't want to be pointin' that there gun at us. We was just havin' some fun."

"Your last 'fun' near ruined me. You wasted a hard day's baking, and it took my brother a whole day to repair my cart. I hope the three of you rot in hell for the cowards you are."

Jug snorted. "Damn, I don't know why you call him your brother. Sonofabitch ain't nothin' but a half-breed, and a bastard at that."

"Ooh, that does it," she growled at them and cocked the gun. Jug's statement pushed her fury ahead of her caution. "Quit talkin' and start walkin'." She fired two shots into the street, one on each side of Jug's feet. He was the man nearest her and by far the most dangerous of the ruffians. Dust flew up, and the men turned and ran.

She yelled at their retreating backs, "Now you stay away from me, and don't you be goin' toward my place neither." None of the three even looked back when she yelled, but disappeared around the corner of the nearest building.

From her other pocket, she took two bullets. With shaking fingers, she replaced the spent cartridges. That done, she slid the pistol back inside her pocket, firmly grasped the handles of her cart, and walked away from town.

She refused a backward glance at the two men standing in front of the jail or the curious townspeople on the street. Her knees wobbled like jelly, and she trembled something fierce inside. Never would she let anyone in this stupid town know how terrified she felt right now, nor how often she felt that way.

Sheriff Evan Cummins tore around the corner of the store, yanking his suspenders up on his shoulders. He rasped out, "I heard shots! What was that ruckus about?" He must have run all the way from his house in the trees behind the store, for now the gasping man stopped and bent with his hands braced against his knees. "Are you okay, Fannie Pearl?"

He hadn't even combed his hair today, and his thin salt and pepper wisps blew in the light breeze. She must find a way to help herself and this dear man.

Pushing the fear deep inside her, she said. "I'm fine. It was only the Ainsworths and Jug making mischief again." She blinked to keep from crying and met his gaze. His brown eyes were level with hers and full of concern. "I—I'm sorry, Evan. I lost my temper and shot at their feet."

"You got to be careful, girl. You're just giving Higgins and the pastor more fuel against you when you do things like that."

"You're right." She sighed, then spoke with quiet desperation. "Lord help us, I've got to get away from here. And it has to be soon."

"I know, girl. I know."

She worried for the sheriff. His breath still came in puffs through lips tinged blue against the gray pallor of his face.

He gasped out, "Soon as I find out who's terrorizing you and threatening anyone who tries to buy your place, we can get you away."

She would never confess to Sheriff Cummins she thought him well past the ability to do any real peace keeping or detecting. He did his best, she knew, and he alone protected her and her family. Best to change the subject.

"You're taking the thornapple syrup I made for you, aren't you?" She frowned with concern. "Have you been taking it and drinking the tea?"

"Yes, yes, I'm doing just as you said." He waved a hand of dismissal. "Won't make me any younger, though. Get on home now, Pearl, and take care."

"I have a sick call to make first. Mr. Wilson hurt his arm real bad and the kids have the croup, but I'll get on home after that. You take care, too, Evan."

Pearl pushed her cart toward the edge of town, but paused at the corner to watch Evan greet the two strangers and take them into his office. As she turned, she saw that pompous Pastor Fayne Upperly and his bony stick of a wife, Dessie

Mae, storming down the opposite side of what passed for a street. The couple glared at Pearl as they drew even with her, but continued without speaking. They were probably on their way to complain about her again. More trouble for her, Sarah, and Storm. More bother for Evan.

Pearl regretted her earlier burst of temper, but she had to defend herself against idiots and ruffians. It seemed she couldn't control her temper lately. Her nerves were on edge since Granny died three weeks ago and all the extra meanness started. And Belle staying with her family only gave people like the Pastor more cause to condemn them. With a huge sigh of resignation, she started on her way, her cart rumbling.

I have to get my family away from this place. Soon.

Drake stood mesmerized by the sight of the woman's bold gaze as she passed him. A prickle of unknown origin raised hairs along the back of his neck. When she had boldly met his gaze, he felt thunderstruck.

She had violet eyes. They pierced right into a man, as if she saw deep into his soul.

Then he watched this lone woman face down three pole-cats. When Lex would have stepped to her assistance, Drake stayed him with a word and a hand to his shoulder. Drake had been set to rush to her aid himself—until he saw the pistol. It was then he decided to see what she would do.

That she had faced these same men many times in similar situations became obvious. Why hadn't some of the other people in town come forward to help her? To speak up for her? To her? Only the storekeeper and the sheriff even conversed with her. What kind of crazy place had he come to?

Damn. She had violet eyes.

Her sunkissed face provided a perfect contrast to her jewel-toned eyes. Dressed in a ragged brown sack of a dress far too large for her and pushing a strange cart full of packages, she was without doubt the most unusual woman he had ever seen.

The little toss she gave her head as she walked away sent

that thick plait swinging with a tantalizing swish back and forth across her hips. Sunlight turned the wisps of hair escaping her braid into a halo around her head. As regal as a queen in spite of her ragged dress and bare feet, she intrigued him beyond all reason.

Those men called her "pine tree" and "pig girl." Her height no doubt caused the reference to a tall, strong pine. She must be only two or three inches under six feet. But why the other? Not because of her looks. Her features certainly were not porcine. Maybe her family raised swine.

She had violet eyes. Imagine that!

Sheriff Evan Cummins saw the two men waiting outside his office in front of the jail. He suspected he knew the identity of at least one of them. Well, if so, they had arrived none too soon. He pulled out his keys and walked up the street toward the men.

When he reached the door, he fitted the key in the lock and gave it the extra jiggle it needed. "You may as well come inside to state your business." He pushed the door wide and motioned the men ahead of him.

The taller of the two swept off his hat and stuck out his hand. "Drake Kincaid, Sheriff. This is my cousin Alexon—uh, Lex Tremont."

Evan smiled with pleasure. "You'd be Rob Kincaid's grandsons then? I had a letter from your grandfather just a couple of days ago. Said you might be headin' this way. Real treat to meet you both. How in the world is that old renegade?"

Both men smiled broadly, and Drake answered, "Strong as an ox and mean as a bear with a sore paw. He asked us to stop by and pay our respects."

"And we wanted to offer our thanks to you, also." Lex nodded. "Grandpa often says we wouldn't be here, or anywhere else for that matter, if you hadn't saved his hide."

"Works both ways, boys. Many's the time he saved me, too. Lordy, but didn't we chase old Santa Anna out of Texas?"

He couldn't suppress a chuckle, though it made him cough. "Couple of wild ones, we were, young and feisty. It purely is a wonder we survived at all."

He addressed Drake as he looked him up and down. "I truly would like to see Rob again, but you look the spittin' image of the man I knew. Be patient while I tend to a few matters, then we can have us a good long yammer."

Evan poked the embers of the fire in the pot-bellied stove and added some coal before he started coffee.

"Though we haven't seen one another in a long time, Rob and I keep in touch with long letters. I feel like I know both you boys almost as well as I know my own daughter."

With a last poke at the coals, he turned to start his coffee. "I keep a pot going all day. Folks claim by evening the brew's so thick and strong a spoon will stand straight up in the cup. That's the way I like it. If a man wants water, he should drink water. If he drinks coffee then, by damn, it ought to taste like coffee."

No sooner was the pot brewing than the door slammed open. Fayne Upperly, Pastor of the Church of the Fount of the Blessed Word, ushered his wife inside. Thin as a rail, Dessie Mae Upperly made a perfect contrast to her husband's pot-bellied figure.

Evan thought Dessie Mae's mouse-brown hair looked pulled so tight into her bun her face must hurt. Could be that's why her sour expression matched that of her prune-faced husband. Evan sighed and resigned himself to another lecture on the sins of Pearl Parker.

"Sheriff, as God-fearing, law-abiding citizens, we are once again lodging a complaint against that Parker woman." Fayne pounded his fist into his hand as he spoke. "We just spoke to the mayor and he is in agreement with us."

Evan held up a hand. "Now, Pastor, you're not in the pulpit here. No need to preach at me."

Dessie Mae thrust a finger under Evan's nose. "Now that Nancy Parker is dead, those young people have only Nancy's lawless granddaughter to guide them. You saw her yourself, shooting off a firearm in the middle of town at eight in the morning. She shouldn't even carry a handgun. I ask you, what sort of example is a woman like that for young folks?"

The sheriff tried to quell his rising temper. "I'd say she's a good example, Dessie Mae. Nancy Parker never helped her granddaughter when she was alive. I'm sorry to say, I don't see how my cousin Nancy dyin' could do more than lighten Pearl's load."

He took a deep breath and continued. "Pearl Parker works hard to make a living for herself and those under her roof, she helps a lot of folks with her medicines, and she minds her own business."

He emphasized the last phrase, wishing he could say something terse. Being a public servant definitely had its disadvantages for putting people in their proper place.

Dessie Mae gasped. "Well, if you think practicing witchcraft and harboring a—a common harlot under her roof in sight of two youngsters and—and strutting around town toting a pistol and firing it at our citizens is setting a good example, then you are no better than she is."

"She has my permission to carry that gun. The woman travels alone all hours of the day and night to doctor folks. And helping people with herbs and such is not witchcraft. In case you've forgotten, Pearl learned her doctorin' from my own good wife. And a better woman never lived, may she rest in peace."

Dessie Mae screwed her face up like an apple left too long in the sun. "We haven't forgotten, Sheriff, nor have we forgotten the story of how that woman came to be named after your wife. She's not fit to raise young folks, I tell you."

In a perfect imitation of her husband, she pounded one gloved fist into her other hand. "The Higginses are willing to take Sarah and that Storm person into their home and give them a good Christian upbringing, even though the boy is a heathen."

Evan snorted in disgust. "The fact that Merline Higgins is ailin' and Billy Joe is just plain lazy wouldn't have anything to do with their so-called generosity, would it?" His temper bested him and his voice rose. "If you think those kids would have a decent life with the Higginses, you are sadly mistaken. In case you've forgotten, the slaves have been freed. Now get on back about your own business and leave enforcing the law to me." He waved a hand of dismissal at the pastor and his wife.

Fayne Upperly bristled with indignation and thrust his weak chin into the air. "It was only with a good many reservations I supported you in the last election. Now it's clear you are not fit for your job. I'll be speaking with the town council about recalling you from office."

"Suit yourself. Just leave me be now." He thrust a gnarled finger at the couple. "And you two best leave Pearl and those in her home alone. As long as I'm still sheriff here, I'll arrest anyone who bothers her or hers, and that includes you two."

After the angry couple left, Evan sank in his chair and put his hands on his desk. He sighed and, with his right hand, massaged the muscles over his chest. "Welcome to Piper's Hollow."

Drake sat in a chair near the wall. Lex pulled the one remaining chair near the desk and flopped more than sat, stretching his long legs out before him. He grinned and asked, "This just your usual day here?"

"I'm afraid so." Evan massaged his left shoulder and worked down his arm. Each time the pain went further along his arm and the tingling lasted longer.

Drake looked concerned. "Are you all right? Your color's downright gray."

Evan felt gray inside, too. "Give me a few minutes, and I'll be fine. Damn, but I'm gettin' too old for this job. I'd love to quit and move to Chattanooga. My daughter's been after me to come live with her."

He pinched the bridge of his nose and closed his eyes. "Lordy, but I'd love to have nothing more to do than sit on Mary Alice's front porch and rock while I spin yarns for my grandchildren." Just the thought cheered him.

Drake smiled. "Sounds like a great idea. What keeps you here?"

"You saw that incident out front, didn't you? I can't leave till I get that young woman and her family far away from here. I just haven't been able to think of a way, short of taking them to Chattanooga with me."

"Wouldn't that work, at least temporarily?" Lex asked.

Evan shook his head. "Mary Alice and her husband just barely have room for me. There's no place for Pearl's brood for more than a day or two. Then what would they do?"

He paused, trying to gather his thoughts and calm his breathing. "I guess I'm a little shaken by that encounter with the pastor. No doubt our town council members are already hearing the preacher's latest version about the need to replace me and get those two youngsters away from Pearl."

He saw the two younger men exchange concerned looks before Lex asked, "You mean everyone in town is like those two?"

"No, no. Some of the people hereabouts are good honest people. They mind their own business. But there's a few, like the so-called *good* pastor and his wife, who are spiteful and blind where Pearl's concerned."

Evan leaned back in his chair and looked from one man to the other. It was so good to have Rob's kin here, a relief to speak frankly for a change. "Damned if they don't take what's good about Pearl and twist it to make her look bad. Then they worry with it, like a dog with a bone, and get folks all riled up over nothing."

He rubbed again at muscles which betrayed him more and more often of late. No amount of rubbing could fix what was wrong inside, so he turned his attention back to Drake and Lex. "Well, boys, enough of my problems. Tell me about your grandfather and what brings you to Tennessee."

Three

Pearl settled her cart inside the kitchen and exhaled a weary sigh. Sarah closed the cabin door and the bar slid into place. Her sister slipped away and Pearl leaned against the cart, her mind clouded with worry. All the way home she had replayed the incident in town and speculated on the backlash sure to follow.

They must leave this place, and soon. For some time now she had plotted with Storm and Sarah for their escape. Never would she let them live with the Higginses.

She saw the looks Billy Joe gave Sarah when he thought no one else noticed, and she had no doubts as to his evil intentions. She would never let him get Sarah into his bed—or even under his roof. For most of their lives, Pearl had provided for Sarah and Storm. And now, at least for a while, she must provide for their new friend, Belle, too.

If only she could think of a way to get herself and her family away from here. If only she could start over in a place where no one knew—or cared—about the background of her or Sarah or Storm. If only her Granny really had left her gold instead of nothing but this house, land, and a legacy of bitterness. She sighed and admitted her life held too many "if onlys."

Sarah shared a gentle smile, then took the medical bag Pearl retrieved from the cart. Sarah might look almost her twin, but they were very different in nature.

Pearl considered herself stubborn and sturdy as a mule. She knew she was bossy, too apt to make decisions without consulting anyone. How could she be otherwise when she'd been sole provider for her family all these years? Shy Sarah was gentle as a dove. She never lost her temper or spoke out of turn.

Sarah put the bag away and said, "You're late. We ate lunch, but there's cornbread and beans if you're hungry."

Pearl shook her head. "Pete Hammonds told me the Wilsons asked for me, so I went over there. They gave me lunch after I dosed their children and stitched up Mr. Wilson's arm. Oh, Mr. Hammonds saved the newspaper a drummer left in his store. It's with the supplies."

"Oh, how nice. Something new to read." Sarah brought her a steaming cup. "I heard your cart and made you some chamomile tea."

"Thank you. What would I do without you?" She sipped at the liquid, letting the honeyed warmth slide down her throat. "How's Belle?"

"She's asleep now." Sarah darted a glance toward the bedroom housing their guest. "She still won't say who beat her. A little earlier today she was able to walk to the door and back to the bed."

"And the bleeding inside has stopped?" When her sister nodded, Pearl added, "I'll see to her in a few minutes."

Sarah said, "Walking tired her, so I gave her a dose of the laudanum and some tea. She's just drifted off to sleep. This time she's resting peacefully."

"That's good. Rest will help her recover faster." Pearl looked at the large range against the wall. "You've started dinner. It smells heavenly."

"Jim Mitchell brought us two hens to thank you for helping with his son's birthing. He even plucked them for us." Sarah frowned as she laid an arm across Pearl's shoulder. "You look worried. Was there trouble in town again?"

"Just the Ainsworths and Jug up to their usual tricks." Pearl patted her sister's hand before she stepped forward to draw the rocker nearer the warmth of the huge stone hearth. "I don't know how much longer Evan can go on as sheriff. He looked real bad today."

"I know he only stays because of us. He's been a good friend." Sarah worried with her apron, twisting it in her fingers.

"I must have caught a chill." Pearl shivered as she sank onto her rocking chair, pulling her shawl close before cradling her mug of tea. "I suppose I'll wear those blasted shoes tomorrow."

She sat lost in thought for a few moments, her feet toward the fire. Storm came in and helped himself to a large piece of cornbread and glass of milk. In spite of his small size, it seemed he never stopped eating. Pearl wondered where the boy put all that food.

"There were two strangers in town who looked like the western men in those papers Evan lends us. It looked as if they were waiting to see Evan."

Pearl let her head fall back against the chair. Oh, no, those men must have seen everything. In spite of the rude way the taller of the two stared at her, she hadn't been able to keep him out of her mind all day. Now he'd probably heard an earful of her faults from the pastor.

Without realizing she spoke aloud, she said, "I guess they were still in Evan's office when the Upperlys went to see him."

Fear darkened Sarah's lavender-blue eyes. "The Upperlys? Oh, no. Do you think the pastor complained about us again?"

Pearl nodded. "You can be certain of it. Oh, if only I hadn't lost my temper. I fired two shots at Jug's feet." She closed her eyes a moment as the scene replayed in her mind. "By now Pastor Upperly and his wife are probably riling people up again, trying to get Evan removed from office and you and Storm removed from my evil influence."

What on earth must the two strangers think of her? She couldn't say why it mattered, but it did. Her first impulse was to bury her head in her hands and cry. Instead, she gathered all her worries into a ball inside her, hidden from her sister.

Storm pulled another rocker near hers and sat down. "Tell

us about the strangers you saw in town." He leaned forward in the chair, eager for news.

In as much detail as she remembered, she described the men. She tried to recall every detail of their appearance. Why could she see the taller man so much more clearly in her mind?

"What about their horses?" Storm asked. "You said they rode into town."

"Trust you to ask that." Pearl tried to sound reproving, but ruined it when a smile broke across her face. "One was big and black. I think the other was a bay. I hardly remember, except they had big fancy saddles with big stirrups. You know, like the ones Evan described from Texas."

When she had answered all his questions, she remembered something more important. "I may have found us a wagon," she said, setting the rocker in motion again.

"From someone who would sell to us and not tell the pastor or those Higginses?" Storm asked.

"The Pinckneys over the ridge have two wagons and they'll sell one."

"Ha. How can we get it? We've got no horses or mules. It'll take most of our savings to buy the wagon and supplies." Then, as if his cynicism turned hopeful, he asked, "Did they make a fair price?"

"Yes, it's in line with what we agreed. I haven't quite figured it all out." She stopped rocking and stood. "You and Sarah won't be forced to live with the Higginses, though. I promise you that."

Sarah wrung her hands. "Why are people so mean? We'd do fine here as we are, if they would just leave us alone."

Storm's jaw jutted and his head came up in anger. "They hate us 'cause we're all different." He addressed Sarah, anger fueling his words and sparking from his dark blue eyes. "They'd run off Pearl and Belle, or worse, if Sheriff Evan didn't stop them. Then they'd force you and me to work for Billy Joe Higgins. He'd have me slavin' on his farm and you . . . well, never you mind his plans for you, 'cause it ain't never going to happen."

Pearl shuddered at the picture her brother painted, knowing it only too accurate. "We know we're family, but I have no legal papers to prove I have any rights to raise you. The good pastor and his crowd don't consider your mothers bringing you here enough."

Storm's blue eyes turned to ice. "The so-called good pastor wouldn't accept any papers from our mothers either, 'cause he don't approve of either woman. He believes himself equal to the Creator."

Pearl sighed, wishing she could contradict her brother. "Now that Granny's gone, they're saying I'm unfit to supervise two young people"—she lowered her voice—"especially now that Belle's here."

Storm snorted in derision. "As if your Granny ever helped. All she did is have you and Sarah slavin' for her all day."

Pearl watched a familiar look of pain cross his face before he continued.

"She wouldn't even speak to me 'cause I'm half Cherokee. Called me a heathen."

Pearl hated the pessimism in Storm's voice, sorrowed for all the experiences that caused him pain and taught him distrust of others. "Hush, now. It's not right to speak ill of the dead." *Even if they deserve it,* she added mentally. "You know that you're a wonderful and gifted young man, no matter what any small-minded people might say."

Thinking aloud, she added, "If anyone tries to take you two or Belle away, we'll have to get out of here fast."

The boy looked at the bedroom and shrugged. "How? Belle can't walk anywhere, no further than across the room."

"I remembered something I read." She nodded. "If we have to leave before we get a wagon and mules, Belle can ride in the cart. You and I can take turns pushing her. We can all carry food and a few things in packs on our back. I read where some people called Mormons moved halfway across the country that way."

A lifetime of living in fear of reprisal had sharpened her brother's innate senses. Seconds before Pearl heard hoof beats, Storm grabbed the rifle and rushed to a window. He peered between the parted curtains. She went to his side.

"Three men on horses. One looks like Sheriff Evan. Hey, the other two match your description of those strangers."

Pearl patted the gun in her pocket, then lifted the bar from the door.

Drake watched Evan as they rode. The sheriff looked terrible, probably his heart playing out on him. He wondered what would happen to Lex and him in this crazy place if the sheriff died while in their care. The older man rode slumped in the saddle, barely able to remain seated on his horse. Evan's gray face and blue-tinged lips were as worrisome as his difficulty breathing.

Lex and Drake flanked the ailing man, ready to catch him if he fell. They had wanted to take him back to town, but Evan insisted they continue. Through gasping breaths, Evan directed them here for help. Drake only hoped the man would last until they could get him inside and onto a bed.

The house looked large by local standards. Rather than the thin boards or rough logs Drake expected, the sturdy logs of the dwelling had been hand-hewn to square them. The pitch of a high roof indicated a loft or second floor. It looked as if the traditional dog run had been enclosed to make additional rooms.

When the door opened, the woman he'd seen in town stepped onto the porch, her hand in her pocket. Remembering the confrontation he'd seen earlier, he thought he knew what else she had in her pocket. He wanted no part of the business end of her pistol, so he called out to her.

"We've a sick man here, your friend the sheriff."

Lex braced the sheriff while Drake dismounted, then Drake slid the older man from his mount. He carried Evan forward while Lex dealt with the horses.

Pearl stepped backward, concern shadowing her face. "Bring him in. Gently, now, be careful with the man. Right this way."

They followed her as she moved ahead, around her cart, and to a room at the back of the house. She threw back the covers of the bed with a smooth motion. Drake laid Evan there as gently as possible.

"Careful now. He's not a sack of potatoes," she chided.

"Pearl . . . forgot . . . medicine," gasped the sheriff.

Drake's eyes met hers across the bed and he explained. "He had an upsetting confrontation in town earlier. Seemed all right after we'd sat and talked all morning. We were on our way to the Walker's when he got sick. Forgot to bring his medicine with him. He asked us to bring him here."

Lex came into the room as Pearl patted the sheriff's hand.

"It's all right, Evan. I'll get my bag and you'll be feeling better in no time. You'll have to stay here tonight."

She stepped out of the room and returned with a large satchel. "I started some new thornapple syrup for you, and Sarah just strained it up today."

From the bag she extracted a blue bottle and uncorked it. She poured the thick liquid into a spoon and fed it to Evan. Lovingly, she ran her hand over the man's forehead, then checked the pulse at his throat.

Without looking up, she said, "You gentlemen step back into the parlor. I'll be there in a bit and fix you some tea."

Drake's hackles rose at this bossy woman ordering him about. "If he's going to stay here, you'll want help getting his clothes and boots off."

Without even looking his way, she dismissed him with a wave. "He doesn't need to be jostled any more right now. My brother will help me later."

He and Lex nodded and left the room. When Pearl emerged from the bedroom, he and Lex stood by the fireplace. She acted all business in motion, but a smile lit her jewel-like eyes.

"He's sleeping now. Thank you for bringing him here. I'm Pearl Parker."

He stepped forward, hat in his hands. "Drake Kincaid, ma'am. This is my cousin, Lex Tremont. Our grandfather is an old friend of the sheriff's." He pointed toward Belle's room with his hat. "Um, ma'am, do you think you could tell who-ever's in that room to point that rifle somewhere else?"

She turned toward the room and called softly, "It's all right, Sarah. These are the men I told you I saw in town. They're friends of Evan's."

The tip of the rifle disappeared, and a pretty young woman poked her blonde head around the doorframe. After a glance and a shy smile, she retreated into the darkened room and closed the door. Pearl turned back toward them. "Sarah doesn't care much to be around people, especially strangers."

Lex stepped forward. "Look, Ma'am, we were on our way over to the Walker place, Oak something or other. If you don't need our help with the sheriff, can you tell us how to find the place?"

Pearl frowned. "Why would you be wantin' to go there?"

As if it was any of her business. Drake stepped in front of her and challenged, "Does it matter?"

"We're going to look at horses," Lex volunteered. "Evan said Walker has some good stock to sell."

A young boy stepped into the room, his rifle cradled in his arms and his finger on the trigger.

"It's all right." Pearl stepped to him and placed her arm around his shoulders. "Gentlemen, this is my brother, Storm. This is Mr. Kincaid and Mr. Tremont. They'd like you to show them the way to Oak Haven."

To Drake and Lex she added, "Don't say a word to anyone about the sheriff's illness. His safety, as well as that of others, depends on it. I must have your word on this."

Drake shrugged. "If you wish." Lot of good that would do. How could the locals not notice their sheriff was near death? "Can we get going now?"

Her brother said nothing, but walked to the door and opened it. His eyes shone in admiration when he glanced back over his shoulder before he sauntered to the rail. With only a pat and a word to the sheriff's horse, Storm concen-trated on the other two mounts.

"The bay is nice. Ahh, but this black is a beauty." He ran his hand down the horse's nose and spoke quietly to the large animal. Then, he slid his hand down the black's neck.

Drake watched, amazed at Midnight's response. The mighty horse trembled and his ears swiveled, but he made no move to harm the boy.

"Yours?" Storm asked Drake.

"Yes. You must have a gift with animals," he said with more than a little respect for Storm's ability. "Midnight doesn't like strangers."

A smile transformed the boy's face. "Neither do my sisters."

He moved in front of Midnight and slid under the hitching rail to loosen the reins of the sheriff's horse. "Come on, I'll show you the place you want."

With an agile leap into the saddle, the boy led them off the road and across the countryside. A path of sorts led through the trees, up ridges and down. Drake and Lex ducked tree limbs and dodged brush to keep up with the youngster.

When they came to a rail fence, Storm stopped and pointed. "Follow this fence West to the house. That is the home of the great Quinton Walkers. You'll like their horses very much."

"You won't continue with us, then?" Drake wondered why the boy accompanied them only this far.

He shook his head. "You'll get a better bargain without me. Tell them you heard in town they had horses. Don't mention me or my sisters."

He started to turn, then stopped and placed a hand on Drake's arm. "Please, sir, it's very important—don't tell anyone the sheriff is ill. *Not anyone*." With that, the boy turned the sheriff's horse and rode away.

Lex watched Storm's retreating figure, then turned to his cousin. "Damned odd. What do you make of that?"

"Don't know." Drake shrugged, then the two men urged their horses slowly forward. "Seems the lady Pearl doesn't have many friends except for the sheriff, doesn't it?"

His cousin nodded. "Pearl and her sister are honey-blondes. They look a lot alike, but their brother looks like a half-breed. And there must be a doxie we didn't see living there as well. Sheriff Cummins said Pearl takes care of her family. Strange family."

"Yep. Appears that way to me, too. But I guess she takes care of her own just like we do ours." Drake rode in silence, thinking of the home they just left.

What an odd woman, that Pearl. Those violet eyes captured his imagination. He sighed and shook his head. The oddity of this village must have put peculiar notions in his head. Yeah, that had to be it. He shook his head, as if he could shake away the curious atmosphere of the place and its effect on him.

Apparently Lex shared his opinion, because his cousin said, "This is a strange place we've stumbled into just to say hello to an old friend of Grandpa's. I can't put my finger on why, but it kind of makes my skin crawl."

"I agree. Be glad to see the last of Piper's Hollow."

At the crest of a small rise, they saw a huge white house. The rail fence bordered the drive, winding its way along a tree-lined paddock. A dozen or more fine looking horses grazed inside the enclosure.

They stopped a moment to admire the unexpected scene. Drake wondered if the plantation in front of them would vanish into thin air. "Can you believe this is even in the same state as that ramshackle town?"

His cousin shook his head. "You could fit the whole town on the front lawn."

"I'd think a set up like this would have suffered during the war. From here it looks prosperous."

"It does at that." Lex turned to him and asked, "You really planning to buy horses here?"

"If what Evan said is true. Can you imagine horses in this backwoods place that came from the same lineage as old Sam Houston's horse, Copper Bottom?"

"Hard to fathom, but stranger things have happened."

"Reckon I might find me another Copper Bottom or Steel Dust in the lot?" Drake chuckled at the thought of owning a horse even distantly kin to the one owned by the great Sam Houston.

"But what about the other matter? What about the wife? Time is running out and you haven't even courted a woman yet."

"Yes, have to do something about that, won't I?" A plan so ridiculous formed in his mind that he had to chuckle to himself. Drake touched his heels to Midnight's side and the horse broke into a smooth stride.

As they neared the house, the façade of prosperity vanished. Clearly, this home begged for care. Rotted boards at the eaves needed replacing and a corner of the porch sagged. In contrast, the horses they passed looked magnificent.

At the front door, a wizened old man dressed in threadbare gray livery greeted them. Drake stated their business, but they were allowed to cool their heels in the foyer until the butler returned. They were ushered into a small study as if being granted an audience with a king.

The dark wood paneling and bookcases all around cast the room in shadow. In the sparse furnishings, a large desk dominated the room. Light from the window behind the desk threw sunlight to burnish the dark blond head of the man seated there.

When Drake and Lex entered, the man rose to greet them. Tall, fortyish, he smiled and extended his hand. "Gentlemen, welcome. I'm Quinton Walker. My man tells me you're here to look at horses. You won't find better bloodlines in the country than right here on Oak Haven, don't you know?"

As he studied their host, Drake noticed gray laced the thick blond hair at Walker's temples. Something about the handsome man seemed familiar, yet Drake knew they had never met. He couldn't put his finger on it so he dismissed the thought. The oddity of this community must really be getting to him. With smile intact, he introduced himself and his cousin.

"We were headed for Kentucky and Virginia, but we heard in town you have stock as fine as any in the South."

"You heard right. Shall we go to the stables?"

A younger version of their host joined them in the hallway and the elder man paused. "Gentlemen, this is my son, Quin. He'd be about your age or a bit younger, don't you know?"

Drake thought the age might be near his and Lex's, but there the resemblance ended. Possibly he matched his father in height, but the slight paunch and slumped shoulders made him look ill-proportioned. Puffiness around bloodshot eyes spoke of a late night the previous night. In fact, Quin bore the indolent and pampered look of one who let others do his work for him. Drake had no use for idlers, and struggled to keep his face from revealing his opinion.

Quin stuck out his hand in a cheery greeting. "Say, where're you fellows from?"

"Texas," Drake said as his callused palm met the other man's soft, smooth hand. Only a few scabbed abrasions on the top of Quin's hand marred the perfect skin.

"Kincaid County, in the central Texas hill country," Lex said as he shook Quin's hand in turn.

Calculating looks flashed simultaneously across the faces of both the Walkers. The elder spoke to Drake. "Kincaid County, as in your last name?"

"Well, actually, as in our grandfather's name." Damn his cousin for supplying more information than necessary. Lex's gregarious nature sometimes caused his tongue to disconnect from his brain.

The elder Walker stroked his chin in thought. "Hmm, I believe I met your father or maybe an uncle once—many years ago. If my memory serves me correctly, it must have been when he stopped by to see Evan Cummins, don't you know? That'd be a few years after Evan came back from Texas."

Drake fingered the brim of the hat he held in his hand. "That's possible, I suppose, but I'm afraid it must have been before my time."

The senior Walker stroked his chin. "Yes, don't you see now, that would probably have been well over thirty years ago? I believe he was on his way back East."

Lex spoke up. "Say, Drake, that must have been when your father was on his way to Boston to marry your mother." There went his cousin's tongue wagging again.

Senior's mouth broke into a smile that never reached his eyes. "And how are your father and mother?"

"They died over ten years ago. My grandfather is still quite active, though." Drake clamped his hat onto his head. "Shall we have a look at those horses?"

The stables were magnificent in style though they, too, lacked recent paint or repair. Matching the architecture of the manor, they were built better by far than any of the buildings Drake saw in the village of Piper's Hollow. Two stable hands moved with deliberation, darting sidelong glances at the Walkers and their two guests but never meeting their gaze.

Damned if he wouldn't give the Walkers one thing. They had some fine looking horseflesh in addition to an amazing stable layout. He examined teeth, mouth, legs, and conformation to narrow his choice to half a dozen horses. After riding each of the six, Drake picked out two mares he wanted and selected another two if the price was right. He prided himself on driving a hard bargain and kept his enthusiasm hidden.

Quinton Walker was no easy mark. When they reached a tentative price for the four thoroughbreds, he invited the men back to the house to look at bloodline documents. Once again in his study, Walker produced the papers to prove his claims. The man knew horses. Unless his papers lied, two of the mares were linked to Sam Houston's Copper Bottom, and several other well-known steeds. As the deal was struck with a handshake, the elder Walker addressed Drake.

"Perhaps you two would join my son and me for dinner this evening to continue our discussion of horse breeding."

Drake stood, his fingers working the brim of his hat. "Thank you, but we have other obligations. We'll be back tomorrow for the horses. In the meantime, we have to arrange for their transport to Texas."

"I can't let you gentlemen leave without at least a little

celebration, don't you see now? How about joining me in the drawing room for a toast to seal the bargain?"

Quinton Walker led them out of the study and down the hall, his son trailing behind. As they entered the drawing room, both Drake and his cousin stopped dead in their tracks. There, over the fireplace mantle, hung a portrait of one of the most beautiful women Drake had ever seen.

Golden ringlets framed her face and she wore a lavender gown. She posed with a few white lilacs in her arms and her rosebud mouth beckoned with a warm, sweet smile. Most astonishing of all were her eyes.

Lex gained his voice first. "Imagine, a woman like that, here—"

Drake knew he stepped hard on his cousin's foot, but he had to stop Lex's comment before he insulted their host. "Yes, she's the most beautiful woman I've ever seen, too, Lex." He turned to his host. "Who is she?"

Both men beamed, but the elder also puffed out his chest with pride. "My mother, Elizabeth Piper Walker. Her father built this house and gave his name to the town of Piper's Hollow."

Drake realized Walker's coloring and facial features resembled those in the portrait. The eyes of the woman portrayed in oil haunted him. He tried to make sense of the eerie feeling they caused, but could not.

"Yes," Quinton continued, "that portrait and most of the objects of any value you see in this room were hidden by my son and me during the war. Like I told you outside, soldiers liked to have wiped us out."

"That must have been a feat. Where'd you hide?" Lex asked.

"A Cherokee family led us to a cave. You couldn't see the openin' 'til you were three feet from it. That cave opened onto a hidden valley with their garden and home. Said my grandfather gave it to their family to prevent the gov'ment finding and removin' them years before and it was time to repay the debt."

"You left this place all during the war?" Drake wondered the place hadn't been burned to the ground.

"No, no. We stayed here on and off, don't you know, and spent the other time hidden with the Cherokee man and his daughter. Had to check on things—make the soldiers believe they got all we had. We hid whatever of value we could carry. Told the soldiers others took everything, don't you see?"

Drake saw the flash of pain and anger on Quin's face and wondered about the cause. So many had painful memories of the war, he shrugged off the thought and examined the beautiful room.

"The house doesn't look badly damaged."

"The structure is sound, in spite of the repairs it needs. Still, that was a terrible time. The constant terror drove my poor wife out of her mind in '63. She jumped from the upper floor when she spied a band of roving soldiers."

Embarrassed at his uncharitable thoughts earlier, Drake could only apologize, "I'm sure sorry to hear that, Walker. That was a tough time for everyone."

Quinton Walker tossed back his drink and set down his glass. "That it was. All in all, this county escaped damage for the most part—too remote, don't you see now, to be on the way to any-where. But there's a lot of damage here we're still trying to repair." He pointed to a series of jagged scars on a wall. Each about shoulder high, they marred the otherwise perfect panels.

"Soldiers thought there might be a hidden storage area for treasures behind these walls. Like I said, I was able to hide five of my beautiful horses from those thievin' scoundrels but couldn't save my own wife." He stood silent for a moment with head bowed, as if lost in memories.

"Well, now," he continued with a start. "It took me ten years to rebuild the bloodlines to those beauties you see today."

After drinking the bourbon offered him, Drake once again begged off dinner. What he most needed was to get away from these people and think. At least Lex finally got the hint and kept his thoughts to himself.

"I'll walk our guests to their horses, Father." Quin trailed behind them down the wide steps of the home. As the two visitors gathered the reins of their horses, he addressed Drake and Lex in a hushed voice.

"Don't tell my father I told you so, but if you're looking for someone to help with the horses on the trip to your ranch, there's a boy who would do you proud. He lives in the next house from here toward town."

Lex looked at Drake but, for once, said nothing.

Drake spoke casually. "Oh? A boy, you say?"

"Yes. 'Bout thirteen, looks younger. He's a half-breed. Cherokee, you know. Got no real family and needs whatever money you could pay him. Don't know how you feel about injuns, but this one has a real gift with animals."

"The next house? What's his name?"

"Calls himself Storm Cloud. Lives at the Parker place just over the hill and 'round the bend. You passed it coming here. Be sure you take the right fork when the trail splits."

Drake mounted his horse. "Thanks. We'll look into it." He touched a finger to his hat brim. "See you tomorrow."

His senses sharpened and a chill slid down his spine. Why would Quin make certain his father didn't hear him speak about the boy? Why mention the boy at all?

Four

The two cousins rode swiftly in silence until they were out of sight of the Walker home, then slowed their horses.

"This is the craziest place I've ever been. By the way, thanks a lot for stomping on my foot. I think my toes are broken." Lex took off his hat and scratched his shock of dark red hair.

"I thought you were going to ask what a beautiful woman like that would be doing in this godforsaken place."

A blush spread across his cousin's face. "I guess I was at that." He smiled sheepishly. "Probably our host would have taken exception to a statement which insulted his home." A thoughtful expression settled on Lex's face. "You know, the woman in that portrait reminded me of someone. Can't think just who, but someone we've seen recently."

Drake shrugged off the comment. "Probably everyone we've met. I imagine most people in this isolated valley are related."

"Maybe, but I think it's the eyes. Yes, that's it. They remind me of that Pearl Parker's eyes. Never seen eyes that odd shade of blue before."

"Violet. Her eyes are violet."

Drake rode deep in thought, mulling possibilities over in his mind. "We've got to stop and see about the sheriff. Maybe we'll get some questions answered then."

He shrugged again, his mind made up on another issue. "There's one answer especially I intend to get before we leave."

With that said, Drake urged Midnight faster along the ruts that passed for a road.

Storm stepped out of the door as they dismounted in front of the Parker house—or Storm Cloud house—or whatever the hell place it was. The boy still carried his rifle, but now with the barrel down, using only one arm. This bunch trusted no one. Given the odd sequence of events Drake had witnessed since his arrival in Piper's Hollow, he thought maybe caution was a good thing here. Damn, but he hated this place, and he'd been here less than twenty-four hours.

As he examined the young man more closely, he realized Storm was older than he had at first thought, maybe as old as thirteen or fourteen. Except his eyes. They looked close to a hundred.

The stark look in the slightly built boy's gaze spoke of more than caution. Here stood a young man with the weight of the world on his shoulders. What troubles had placed a burden on a youngster and brought this small family to such wariness and distress?

As Drake stepped onto the porch, he smelled dinner cooking inside the house and his stomach gave a rolling growl, reminding him he'd missed lunch. If the aromas wafting from the kitchen were any indication, he and Lex made the right choice in a place to dine. Well, if they were invited, that is.

Pearl paced the small room. When she saw Evan rouse, she moved to his bedside and leaned over to check his pulse. "Your color's better. How do you feel?"

He gave her a weak smile but made no move to sit up. "I'll be fine in a bit."

"You need quiet and rest, but I need to talk to you." She glanced toward the open doorway, then resumed pacing. "There's not much time."

"Well, either sit down or go in the other room. You make a body plumb dizzy goin' back and forth."

She whipped a napkin off a bowl and sat near the bed to feed her patient. With a nod of her head she indicated those in the other room. "We talked something over while you were asleep."

Spooning chicken broth with chunks of breast meat into his mouth, she tried to think how best to word her notion. Her idea might be crazy, but she very much needed it to work.

"These men who brought you here. Are they really friends of yours?" She paused in her feeding to let him answer.

Evan pushed himself higher on the pillows. "Their grand-father. Told you 'bout Rob Kincaid."

She exhaled with a sigh of relief. "Oh, yes. Your good friend in Texas. I thought that must be the connection."

"Grandsons." He gasped, as if already exhausted from the dual effort of eating and talking.

"Just listen and let me feed you while I tell you our plan." She thrust another bite of the nourishing broth at him. "I have a little money saved. It might pay part of our fare to Texas. If one of these men would pay the other part plus our food, then I would work as a maid or cook or housekeeper until I re-paid it."

"Crazy." He shook his head. "Bachelors." A look of con-cern descended on his face, and then he raised his gaze to meet hers. "Rob might."

Those words were all the encouragement she needed. She knew her plan was crazy, improbable, but desperation drove her. "Then I would work for your friend, sort of as an inden-tured servant until I'd repaid him. We're going to ask this Drake and Lex to stay for supper. Then, after they've seen how Sarah and I cook, I'll ask them."

As she set aside the empty bowl and helped her old friend drink some tea, his eyes fluttered in fatigue. "Rest now. Likely they'll want to check in on you. I hear them coming inside now." What would these two strangers think, though? More important, what would Drake Kincaid think?

Evan grabbed her hand. "You—don't act so bossy."

Her face felt on fire and she knew a blush spread. Evan, and before him his late wife, had tried to train her to act like a lady. Many times they cautioned her against being so bossy. But how else was she to behave when everyone in her family waited for her to make decisions, when everyone's welfare depended on her alone? She could depend on no one else for their sustenance, had no partner to help her in times of trouble. No, she had to be in control to protect her family and herself.

"I'll try to be ladylike, but you know I can't help telling everyone what to do. I've had to do it too long to change overnight." She gave his hand a reassuring pat and left the bedroom.

From where she stood in the kitchen she heard Storm answer their questions about Evan. Sarah stood by the bedroom door, wringing her hands and chewing on her lower lip. Neither Sarah nor Storm quite approved of her decision, but neither had a better suggestion. Like her, they both felt desperate to leave this place as soon as possible. How on God's green earth could she broach the subject to a stranger?

"Hello again." The big man's confident baritone voice sent tingles down her spine.

His name's Drake, Drake Kincaid, she reminded herself. She struggled to get hold of herself before her fancies made her forget her purpose.

Drake took off his hat and used it to gesture to the bedroom where Evan lay. "Your brother said the sheriff's awake now. You think I could talk to him a bit?"

Pearl gulped and nodded. "Don't let him talk much, um, please," she added as an afterthought, remembering Evan's warning. "You do the talking and let him listen. He needs rest, lots of rest," she said to his back as he headed for Evan's room.

The man was so darned good-looking he left her almost speechless. She must be out of her mind to think a man like him would ever consider a plan that would throw the two of them together on a long trip. He wouldn't want even to be seen with the likes of her in tow. Already her nerves were taut as a banjo string, and the evening wasn't half over.

When the second man remained in the kitchen, she scooted a rocker around, practicing the good manners Mrs. Cummins had drilled into her so many years ago. "Won't you sit down, Mr. Tremont? Supper will be ready in just a few minutes. We hoped you'd stop back by and eat with us."

Lex dropped into the chair. "Please, call me Lex. That's a powerful good smell you're cookin' up."

Pearl smiled to reassure Sarah as the girl inched her way into the room to help. Years of teasing and harassment, coupled with a reclusive nature, made the girl shy to the point of awkwardness. When Lex smiled, Sarah blushed and hurried across the room to set the table.

Unused to dinner guests and with her nerves jangling, Pearl tried to make conversation. "Were you and your cousin successful at Oak Haven?"

"Yes. Well, Drake was. He'll pick up his horses tomorrow." Lex watched the two women prepare to serve the meal. "That's one fancy place, Oak Haven. Do you go there often?"

"My brother helps in the stables when there's trouble with a foaling." Proud as of a mother hen, she said, "Storm has a special touch with animals. Everyone says so." She added, "I've never been inside the house, only delivered bread or medicine to the back door."

Drake emerged from the bedroom in time to hear her. "You've never been inside that house?"

"No." She felt herself flush once more with embarrassment. How could she explain the situation at Oak Haven to strangers? Better just to avoid it altogether. "Dinner's ready. It's chicken and dumplings with vegetables on the side. If you gentlemen would like to wash up, there's a basin and soap by the pump. You'll find a clean towel on a hook by the door."

Pearl was glad she'd given Belle her evening meal earlier. The woman hadn't eaten much, but at least she gained strength and optimism each day. Although Evan needed quiet and lots of rest far away from this place, Belle needed so much more.

Unused to grown men, apparently very hungry men, sharing their meal, Pearl watched the food quickly disappear. Cooking was one thing she knew she did better than most, at least better than anyone else in Piper's Hollow. Only one biscuit remained and the apple pie vanished before her eyes.

As she poured another round of coffee for the men, Lex patted his stomach and grinned. "Ma'am, that meal made me happy all over. You're not just a good cook. You're a great cook."

Pearl felt another blush spread across her face as Drake pushed back from the table. She pressed a hand to her warm cheek. Good heavens, she'd blushed more this evening than in the past year.

"Thanks for the best meal I've had in a long time." Drake said and stood. He pushed his chair to the table. "There's something I need to discuss with you, ma'am. Privately. Mind if we step into another room?"

She knew her eyes widened. Had Evan already explained her plan? No, surely not. She gestured toward another room. "We can go into the parlor."

After glancing over her shoulder at the puzzled faces of the three people who remained seated at the table, she led the way. Although she and Sarah kept it spotless, no one had used the room since her grandmother's funeral three weeks ago. This was where Granny used to sit, where Granny received Pastor Upperly and the few neighbors who came to call.

Pearl hated being in the sitting room with the bitter memories it held. In her mind she still saw the rigid woman reigning from the high backed chair beside the sofa. For the few hours she had left her bed each day, Granny had sat here with a stony glare on her face. If infrequent visitors called, Granny filled their ears with tales of her supposed sacrifices and the heavy burdens she had to bear.

Sarah's mother, Roxie, had sometimes slipped over to visit Sarah in the early morning hours. Storm's grandfather, Tom

Black Bear, occasionally stopped by with fresh game or a story.

Evan was the only person who called on Pearl—unless someone needed her medical or cooking services. The sheriff preferred to sit at the kitchen table while he sipped coffee, complaining all the while her brew was too weak to deserve the name. The big kitchen eating area was hers, and where she kept her own rocking chair and one each for Sarah and Storm. That's the part of the house she felt home, that and her own bedroom.

Now Pearl sat primly on the red plush sofa, avoiding what she thought of as Granny's chair. She tugged the hem of her dress lower to hide the dust that clung to her bare feet. Then, to still the shaking of her hands, she folded them together in her lap.

While she searched her mind for a way to explain her plan, Drake launched into his own speech. "I've asked Evan and he, well, he thought it would be all right to speak to you about an idea I had."

Pearl watched Drake, mesmerized. Everything about the man fascinated her. His size dwarfed the small parlor, yet to her mind he was perfectly proportioned. He ran a hand through his hair and the thick locks fell back in place. She longed to touch them, to know firsthand if they were as silky as they appeared.

A tiny scar on his right cheek beneath his eye caught her eye. No other imperfections marred his skin. His suntanned face ended with a strong jaw now slightly shadowed by his day's growth of beard. She wondered what that stubble would feel like against her skin. Would it scratch or tickle? Warmth pooled in her abdomen and she scolded herself for her wayward thoughts.

His earlier confidence faded, and he suddenly seemed ill at ease. He paced the length of the small room and back. She watched the muscles rippling across his massive shoulders as he removed his coat and hung it on the back of a chair.

The fabric of finely woven pants pulled tight across his

thighs as he moved, outlining powerful legs. He clasped and unclasped strong hands which, from the looks of them, were no strangers to work. His every move spoke of a forceful man used to being in control.

She felt the familiar ball of worry tighten and grow in the pit of her stomach. Why would such a man help her and her family? How could she have been so foolish as to hinge her escape on him and his cousin? Only because she sensed time was running out did she even consider allying with him.

Drake raked a hand through his dark locks. "I don't know how to work up to this so I'll just say it out fast." As he faced her, he took a deep breath and blurted, "Willyoumarryme?"

She blinked once, then leaned forward. "What? What did you say?" Did she imagine he voiced those words?

After another deep breath, he spoke very slowly. "I said, will you marry me?" He held up his hand before she could speak. "You don't know me, but Evan will vouch for me. He and my grandfather have been friends for over forty years. He knew my father as well."

"You just met me, but you—you want me to marry you? To go to Texas with you?" She chewed on her lip, surprised his plan coincided so perfectly with her own. No. She looked at the handsome man who stood before her. His idea far surpassed her plan. "What about my family?"

"Oh." He must have forgotten about her family. "Well, they'd come too, of course." He tugged at his ear in thought. "We'd take Evan with us as far as Chattanooga and leave him with his daughter. Then we'd go to Texas."

Pacing again, he continued, "I live on a ranch only a few miles from town, but there's a real nice house in Kincaid Springs which belongs to my Grandpa. Our town's bigger than Piper's Hollow, and it's the county seat."

He stopped in front of her. "Kincaid Springs has shops and ladies' socials and all kinds of things to keep a woman occupied every minute of the day if she's up to it. Your brother and sister could go to school, have friends their own age."

Drake recalled the encounter in the sheriff's office early

that morning and surged ahead. "We have three churches and none of the pastors are anything like the one here. My grandfather, Robert Kincaid is his name, is the District Judge. My Aunt Lily Stephens, Grandpa's widowed daughter, lives with him."

"Why me? You don't even know me."

He shifted his feet and took another deep breath. "I hate lies of any kind and intend to start off being honest, but you might not like this part. I'll make it as brief as possible."

Drake pulled Granny's chair around to face her, but sat on the edge as if ready to jump up if his answer angered her.

As he leaned forward she caught his scent. She inhaled the blend of soap, sweat, horse, and something uniquely his. Using all her willpower she kept herself from leaning closer to imprint his fragrance on her mind.

"According to my father's will, I have to be married by the tenth of April or I lose my ranch." He spread his hands wide. "Everything I have. Every single thing."

When she made no move, nor spoke, he eased his hips back in the chair a little but still leaned forward, hands on his knees. "Now, it appears to me you and your family very much need to get away from this place. If you and I get married, we both gain something we need."

Her heart stopped beating. Of course, he didn't want *her*. He just needed a woman, any woman, to be his wife. No man like him would actually *want* a gangling giant of a woman to be his bride. Her pride wanted to scream for him to leave, to get out of her house and out of her sight. How she would love to throw something, to wallop that gorgeous head of his.

But she thought of all the marriage would mean, not just to her, but to her brother and sister. They would be part of a respected family, have decent clothes, attend school, have a chance at all she'd missed. They'd be safe.

She refused to think about the other part, about being a wife to the princely man who sat before her.

Common sense told her his offer was no more insulting to her than the one she'd devised. She needed what he offered, and she needed it well before the tenth of next month. Taking a deep breath, she willed herself calm.

"You're sure I can take my family. All my family?"

His eyes widened and he looked back through the open doorway to the kitchen. "How many people are we talking about?"

She also hated lies, but she refused to abandon her helpless new friend. "You've met my brother and sister. Well, there's also my, um, *our* cousin, Belle Renfro. You haven't met her because she's recovering from, um, from an accident. You see, she, um, she fell. Down some stairs in town, and hurt herself real bad."

What if he thought Belle would slow them down? She hastened to explain. "Oh, but she's lots better now, getting better every day. She won't be a bother at all on the trip." There, she'd said the lies and half-truths, though she couldn't meet his gaze as she did so.

"That's all? Four of you? You, your brother, sister, and this cousin?" He ticked them off on his fingers as he named them.

"Yes. Four of us." She sighed with relief. He didn't seem to mind her family. She smiled. No, he didn't even hesitate. Now his fingers drummed on his thigh, so she plunged ahead.

"We don't have many clothes, but there's my good feather bed, and our rocking chairs, my books, my herbs for doctoring, maybe a few other things. One wagon would do for all of us."

"All right. You, three family members, plus personal belongings and some pieces of furniture." He looked around, and she knew he liked nothing he saw there.

He frowned as his gaze roved across shabby furniture of a style too ornate for its setting. She slid her skirt aside to cover a worn spot on the red plush sofa. At least the dark wood of each piece gleamed with polish. He might fault Granny's taste, but not Sarah's and her housekeeping.

She hurried to reassure him. "None of the furniture in this room has sentimental value. We'd only want a few pieces from the kitchen and bedrooms."

With a nod, he said, "Fair enough."

She breathed a sigh of relief. He seemed willing to accept her family in the package. "When would we marry?"

He exhaled as if he, too, had been holding his breath. "Now, or in the morning on our way out of town. Then, I'll need to wire my grandfather the news right away. Guess there's a telegraph office in town?"

Panic swept over her. She shook her head in disagreement. "No, no. That wouldn't work. We have to be miles from here before anyone in town knows we're leaving." Remembering Evan's warning, she took a deep breath and softened her voice to explain.

"What I mean is, if anyone here knew how ill Evan really is or that the children and I are leaving, they'd appoint a new sheriff. Then they'd force Sarah and Storm to live with that awful Billy Joe Higgins and his wife. Please, don't let that happen."

The frown still creased his brow. "But you do agree you'll marry me and move to Texas right away?"

She knew he thought her request strange. Probably he still had no idea how important it was they escape the county before the pastor or his cohorts found out. Pearl stood and ran her hands down her dress.

"Yes, I agree, but until we're safely away from Piper's Hollow, it has to be just between the people in this house. Well, except for Sarah's mother and Storm's grandfather." She offered her hand. "Shall we shake on it to seal the bargain before we go back into the kitchen and tell our news?"

He took the hand she presented him and his warm touch sent tingles racing through her body. After a brief shake, he laced his long fingers with hers as they walked back into the common room. Together they faced Lex, Sarah, and Storm, each of whom looked puzzled.

Drake still held her hand as he pulled her close beside him. His other hand circled her waist, enclosing her in the protection of his arms. Suddenly relieved, she felt more protected than she had since the death of her mother over eleven years ago. It felt right, somehow, standing next to this man with her hand in his. The protective shell she erected around her heart cracked just a little. A small ray of hope seeped into her soul.

Lex stood when she entered the room. Such a small sign of honor made her more hopeful. Already these men treated her with more consideration and respect than she had ever been shown by people in Piper's Hollow. With a sidelong glance at Lex, Storm also stood, though he raised an eyebrow and shrugged.

"We have an announcement." Drake paused and cleared his throat before he continued, "Pearl has consented to be my wife."

She watched Lex's mouth drop open and his eyes widen in surprise. Storm and Sarah waited quietly, thoughtful as always, though they, too, widened their eyes in wonder. They had questioned her decision to leave with these men. That she planned now to wed Drake must have confused them. She faced her brother and sister.

"Drake has asked me to marry him and invited all of us to move to Texas with him."

Sarah forgot her timidity in astonishment and concern. "But what about Belle?"

"*Cousin* Belle is included in his invitation. After we take Evan to live with Mary Alice, we'll all live in Kincaid Springs. It will be a fresh start . . . for all *four* of us." She looked from Sarah to Storm for an answer, knowing her mind was already made up and assured of their consent.

From the door to Sarah's and her bedroom, Belle struggled to support her battered body against the frame. "Hallelujah, *Cousin* Pearl! Take this good man up on his offer before he changes his mind."

Belle's suggestion broke the tension, and they all laughed. Sarah rushed to help Belle back to bed. After a preliminary discussion, Drake took charge. His quick mind and no-nonsense questions and comments reassured Pearl she had made the right decision.

When it looked as if their arrangements were planned out,

Pearl took paper and her ink well from the drop front desk. "Will you two, along with Evan, witness the transfer of this house and our little plot of land to Storm's grandfather?"

Before he spoke, Lex shifted his weight and looked at his cousin. When Drake nodded, Lex volunteered. "Ma'am, I practice law in Texas. I could write that up for you so there's no loop holes."

"If you will—please." Pearl relinquished the duty. "It will relieve my mind to know it's all legal-like. Tom Black Bear is a good man who has helped us a lot over the years."

She paused to think her words out carefully, then gestured to herself and her two siblings. "We want Tom to have the house, land, and all the animals. Because he's Cherokee, we've worried about his being allowed to do so."

In fact, she feared someone might even loot and burn the house once they were gone. Now she could give one copy of the papers to Tom, then get other copies to the mayor and town council. She hated to think of the solid house her great-grandfather built sitting unused or in ruin.

The two men left the Parker home at dark, headed for the sheriff's house. They passed no one on their way. Once their horses were cared for and the men were inside the Cummins's house, Lex vented his anger.

He threw his bags on the kitchen floor and faced his cousin, arms crossed. "Are you serious about this marriage proposal?"

Drake dropped his saddlebags on the floor beside those of his cousin. "I'm dead serious."

"That woman will *not* fit in with Grandpa's life. He'll be mad as hell if you bring her and those other three into his house. Lord, I shudder to think what Aunt Lily will say."

"That's the idea." Drake smiled at the picture in his mind. "Besides, you saw her bravery when she faced those men in town. And think about how sturdy she looks. She'll breed big, healthy sons. She's cared for those two kids and that so-called cousin. Must be the nurturing sort who'll make a good mother."

"Brave, sturdy, nurturing—oh, and a hell of a cook. Those are good qualities, I admit, but think about this. Dammit, the woman goes barefoot and wears a ragged tent. Who knows when she bathes? Are you ready to consummate a marriage with her?"

Only the thought of his grandfather's reaction to the woman and her family fueled his enthusiasm. "Well, the house looked well kept, and she and the youngsters seemed tidy enough. She must put some value on cleanliness." He shrugged. "Besides, I can concentrate on her eyes. She has real nice eyes."

He recalled her long delicate fingers, the efficiently trimmed nails. The grip of her hand when they sealed their bargain was strong. For a moment he had forgotten to be angry, forgotten how much he hated the idea of a wife.

Unbidden, the memory of her fragrance leapt to his mind. The faint lilac scent lingering around her had tantalized him. He had wanted to touch her hair and cheek, lean close to take in her fragrance. Lilacs, fitting for a woman with her eyes. Thank God he restrained himself. The oddities of this place must have affected his mind.

Tension in Lex's voice snapped him from his reverie.

"And what is she supposed to concentrate on?" Easy going Lex seldom showed anger, but looked fit to spit nails tonight. "In spite of your talk about breeding with her, she's a woman, not a brood mare. She may not have been to finishing school back East like the women in our family, but she has feelings, damn it. Have you thought about what she wants out of this?"

Yes, he had wondered. He and Evan discussed it. "Away. Hell, she just wants away from this rotten place." He took a deep breath and reined in his temper. Quietly, he soothed his cousin. "You've seen this sorry excuse for a town, seen how she's treated here. Can you blame her?"

Five

With Evan still in her room, Pearl made a bed for herself on a pallet of quilts near the kitchen fire. Storm and Sarah were already washed and in bed and both her patients asleep before she allowed herself time to relax.

Lost in thought, she unbound her hair and brushed it until it shone. How wonderful it would feel to comb it into a pretty fashion without having to worry about attracting unwanted attention.

She filled a basin with the water she'd left warming on the big range. Using the kitchen table as her base, she set the bowl down and reached for the soaps she made. She might look like a ragamuffin, but she insisted on cleanliness and smelling nice.

She paused at the row of jars on a shelf, pleased she'd cooked off a nice selection of the special floral soaps she allowed as her one self-indulgence. Which one should she use tonight? Would it be rose, lavender, or lilac? The lilac again, she decided, and extracted a small ball of soap from a jar.

As she undressed, she started with her face and worked down. The touch of the wet cloth on her body and the cool air on her damp skin brought shivers of apprehension and wonder.

She bathed her breasts and felt her nipples harden when the air touched her wet skin. She moved down her torso in slow circular motions. How would it feel to have her husband touch her skin? Warmth pooled in her stomach and she hugged her arms in distress.

Oh, Lord, maybe she was wicked as Granny so often accused, as weak as her mother. But Mama had said she truly loved Pearl's father, that he brought her great joy until she learned he was engaged to marry another. They had planned to wed, but his parents chose a wealthy wife for him, not the daughter of a poor widow.

Pearl thought of the handsome man she soon would wed. Was it wrong to want that man's strong touch? Did he also want to feel her hands on his skin? Her face burned at the thought.

Evan and his wife were the only happy couple whose confidence she shared. She remembered the gentle way they touched, the soft smiles the two exchanged right up until Mrs. Cummins's death. What Evan and Pearl Cummins shared with one another couldn't be wrong. No, it couldn't be.

She recalled Drake taking her hand and pulling her to his side. It had felt right to have his arm about her waist, her hand in his. Tingles shot through her, almost as many as earlier when her fiancé touched her.

Her fiancé. Dear Lord, the gangly spinster actually has a fiancé. With a shrug she attacked the dirt on her feet.

Enough of your fancies. You'd best be thinking about how to get yourself and yours away from this place, not daydreaming such wanton thoughts.

She slept only fitfully in spite of the weariness that plagued her body. Her mind whirled with lists of tasks to be accomplished and fears of being stopped before they could escape, fears of what awaited her in Texas. Of one thing she was certain, it would be better than anything offered in Piper's Hollow.

Better for her, better for Sarah, better for Storm. She could not contain her smile, barely suppressed a giggle. Yes, better even for "Cousin" Belle.

Bitter memories roiled up to consume her. How happy she would be to leave this place forever. Yet sadness tinged that feeling. This home had served four generations of Parkers.

Strong and secure, the house could not be blamed for her grandmother's cruelty or the evil lurking in the community.

What waited in Texas?

Whatever awaited her, she hoped it would bring more happiness to her family than this place ever furnished any of them. And she hoped this house would be a safe dwelling for Tom Black Bear.

Last night Drake and Lex returned to Evan's home. What they would say should someone seek out Evan in the night, she could only wonder. With a sigh, she made preparations for the day's baking plus enough to keep them a day or two into the trip. She smiled, remembering how much the two men ate last night. Better pack a lot extra.

Silent as a wraith, Sarah slipped into the room. "It's early to start your baking."

Pearl gave her head a shake. "There's so much to get done today."

"Belle and I packed our things last night before we went to sleep. I'm so anxious to get away from here, but I'm a little sad, too."

Pearl placed her hands on her sister's shoulders and searched Sarah's face. How could she have been so selfish? "Oh, my poor dearest. I know you'll hate leaving Roxie, um, Rochelle. Remember, though, it's what she wants for you." Pearl bit her lip. Rochelle Jorgensen was known to most after the name of her tavern, Roxie's Place, but Sarah hated that nickname and its associations.

"Yes, I know it's for the best, but I hate to leave her here alone. Even though you've always been the one to take care of me, she's my mother. I know she loves me and she'll miss us."

"Rochelle will be fine, love. Remember, she's only waiting until we leave to go away herself."

"Do you think she might come to Texas, too?"

Pearl hated to quench the hopeful look in her sister's eyes, but she saw no point in holding out false assurances. "No, dear. Rochelle wants you to have a new start, and hopes for one herself. We'll all have a fresh beginning. Wherever she goes is bound to be better than here."

"I know, but I wonder if I'll ever see her again." The girl brushed away a tear and produced a trembling smile for Pearl. "Texas sounds nice the way the men described it."

"Yes, it sounds perfect for us. You can imagine how surprised I was to have Drake propose before I could offer to work for his family."

"Oh, Pearl, are you sure you should marry him? You don't even know him. He's truly handsome, but he might be mean to you. Look how handsome Quin is, and he's a horrible man."

"Quin's been nicer since I defended him against those kids. Remember when they taunted him about his mother's illness? That incident seemed to make a great change in the way he treats us."

"Only if there's no one else around to hear or see."

Pearl couldn't deny that fact. "Well, at least he's civil to us now. It isn't his fault his mother went mad, any more than it's our fault our father won't recognize us as his."

She longed to be truthful, to express her fears and misgivings about her engagement. Her sense of responsibility suppressed those thoughts and she donned a façade of calm optimism.

"Anyway, Drake seems very nice, for all that he is a bit bossy. Probably stubborn as a mule, too. And, Lord, doesn't he eat enough for two people? He's sure nice looking, though."

She hugged her younger sister. "His family are friends with Evan and Evan likes him, so how bad could he be? Besides, he truly needs a wife or he'll lose his ranch—even the house on it and all his cattle. We need to get away from here or who knows what will happen?"

Sarah still looked pensive. "I think there must be mean people everywhere. What if someone else tries to take us away?"

"With me married to a solid man like Drake Kincaid, no one can ever take you and Storm away from me. Since his cousin is a lawyer and his grandfather a judge, we'll be safe as bugs in a rug."

Sarah paled. "Oh, no. You can't marry for Storm and me."

Pearl hurried to correct her mistake. "Well, no, it's not just for you."

Keep your doubts to yourself. You're the older sister here.

"Evan thinks Drake is a good man and will be a good husband and father. Also, Drake didn't mind at all that I bring you and Storm with me, and his own cousin travels with him. He must like family around. Doing his grandfather's bidding to pay respects to Evan is the reason he came here in the first place. Besides, I want a husband with children and a home of my own in a nice, safe place."

Her brother slid down the ladder from the loft. "He cares for animals, too. That horse is powerful, in perfect condition, and very loyal to him. This speaks well for any man."

Pearl smiled at her brother. Trust him to judge a man by his animals. His cynicism had turned to admiration and excitement last night when he learned he could help move Drake's expensive thoroughbreds to Texas. "Ahh. So, now you approve of my decision?"

A sheepish grin spread across Storm's face and he tilted his head. "There are many advantages to this move."

Pearl patted Sarah's shoulder. "When I go in to town, I'll tell Rochelle about our decision. I'm sure she can slip over to see you before we leave." She turned to hug Storm. "And I'll ask your grandfather to come for dinner."

Storm stood lost in thought, then sighed and looked around the room. "I know we have to leave the animals. Thank you for giving them to Grandfather. He'll live well in this house. If ever my mother wishes to return, she will have a place here also." His eyes roamed the room with a look that seemed filled with regret.

"Yes, and your grandfather will take good care of everything." She touched his arm, then slid her hands to his thin shoulders. "I promise that if you ever regret our move, Storm, you can return and live here with your grandfather. But I hope you'll love our new home and want to remain there with Sarah and me."

All business again, she dropped her hands and scanned the room. "Now, we have a million things to do today, so let's get busy."

Pearl resumed working as she reviewed their plans with Sarah and Storm. "Drake said he'll bring the wagons and mules today. We'll have only one wagon for our things and a bed for Belle."

"I'll try not to be a burden on the trip." Belle's voice startled the three. When they turned, the dainty woman advanced slowly into the room. A rainbow of bruises mottled her pale skin and a long cut on her cheek almost reached an eye.

Pearl rushed to her. "It's so good to see you up and dressed. Are you certain you feel well enough, though?"

"I must gain strength for the trip." Tears welled in her brandy-colored eyes. She placed her hand on Pearl's arm. "Th-thank you so much for including me in your family."

Pearl reached for her friend to reassure her. "There, now. I could never leave you behind."

"You know, I could hear the two of you from the bedroom. When I heard that man ask you to marry him, I was so frightened. Oh, I know it's selfish, but I couldn't help it."

Belle closed her eyes and paled even more, her fingers tight on her friend's arm. Her voice lowered to a whisper meant only for Pearl's ears. "It wouldn't take another beating to kill me. If I had to go back to the life at Roxie's, I'd die of despair."

"You'll never have to. We'll all have a fresh start, just as I promised." She lay her arm across the small woman's shoulders, cautious of pressure on Belle's battered muscles. "Now, you take care. There's much to be done this day. I'd best get started to town."

After assigning duties to her brother and sister, Pearl left, laden with deliveries. One more day, and they would be safe, away from this place where sinister events plagued them. But, she wondered, could she ever feel truly secure? Would she ever feel as if she belonged, even in her new home with her own husband?

Drake urged the mules forward into the fading twilight. Pearl sat ramrod straight beside him, refusing to look back as the only home she ever knew disappeared in the background. In the wagon bed behind their seat, Belle sat on the feather bed ticking, pillows propped behind her.

Ahead Lex guided the wagon bearing Evan and their supplies. They agreed Evan must be in the lead wagon to prevent him inhaling dust. Though his pulse beat stronger, his breath still came in difficult rasps. Beside Lex, Sarah half-turned to wave a last good-bye to Tom Black Bear.

At the rear of their group, Storm guided the string of horses made up of the three men's mounts and Drake's four new mares. No one spoke. The only sounds were the creaking of wagons, jangling harnesses, the rattling of the cargo, and the occasional blowing of mules or horses.

Even with hope budding in her heart, she refused to relax her vigilance. Her glance darted to every tree and bush, every boulder. All the while she prayed no one rushed forward to stop their progress.

With each bump along the rutted road, Pearl jostled against Drake. Since the minute he held her hand the previous day, his presence made her nerves hum with awareness. This handsome man would soon become her husband. He had been kind, but remained distant.

Pearl stored the memories of their leaving. She inhaled the fragrances of the plants, woodsmoke from the cabin, even the plodding animals and their dust. As she bounced against her betrothed, she separated the unique scent of the man beside her to store it in a special part of her mind even as her eyes continued their vigilance.

He does not want to be married, is only marrying me to protect what he feels is already his. Will he take out his re-

sentment on me and my family? What could he be thinking now?

When they had ridden for almost an hour, she broke the silence. "Did things go well in town? I mean, did you have trouble getting the supplies and everything without being seen?"

"No trouble. We got the storekeeper to open up late in the evening by going to the back door. The letters we left for the mayor and the council members should get to them tomorrow. Also your letter to the banker asking him to send your money."

"And no one except Pete saw you?" She held her breath while she waited for his answer.

"Not that we knew. The alley behind the store was dark."

"That's good, then. Pete's dependable."

The man at her side made no more comments. She longed to know him, find out about his life and the one awaiting her. "Tell me about your home."

The full moon rising over the trees cast a silvery glow on his face as he turned his head to meet her glance. "What do you want to know?"

"Well, what do you raise there, besides horses?"

He looked surprised. "I raise cattle, not horses. The market is changing, though. Railroads mainly. Barbed wire is coming, and farmers."

She waited while he paused. When he didn't add more, she probed. "Then, the horses are for your pleasure?"

"What? No. I thought I might take some thoroughbreds and cross them with the range mustangs. Lots of ranchers do that. Breeds a tough animal that rides easy, moves fast."

"For use on your ranch?"

"Yes, but maybe also to sell—if I get lucky." He gave her a puzzled look. "You really interested in all this?"

Did he think she talked just to hear herself? She bristled. "Of course. You may take it all for granted, but it's new to me. I want to learn all I can about my new home."

"Sorry. I'm not used to a woman caring about the ranch.

Most of the ones I know only care about the latest fashion or the next social event."

"Hmph. Then maybe you've known the wrong women."

She thought he chuckled, but couldn't be certain.

"Yes, ma'am. I guess I have at that." He urged the mules forward, and she gave up trying to coax information from him.

Close to midnight they stopped to rest the animals and let the humans stretch their legs. Accustomed to walking everywhere, Pearl's muscles rebelled at the bouncing of the journey. Drake helped her from the wagon.

Their eyes met and he held her gaze. Her legs almost refused support. He continued to hold her waist and moved near. She thought he might say something. Or kiss her. Then Lex called something to him and the mood broke. Drake moved away with a shake of his head.

She watched him speak to his cousin and walk along the string of horses with Storm. Two thoughts occurred to her, each powerful and surprising in its own way. Drake was as affected by her as she was by him. And she wanted his kiss.

As agreed, they planned driving straight through tonight and all day tomorrow until evening. That meant only one night's camping before Chattanooga. The light meal she prepared required neither a fire nor a lantern.

Fearing a light of any kind might attract unwanted attention, she had planned the food carefully before their journey began. Portions of cold meat, cheese, bread and milk already waited, separated and ready to serve. She also served another pie made from her store of dried apples. With Sarah's help she set out the light meal near Evan's bed.

Lex handed a plate to Evan then walked to the other wagon. He helped Belle back onto the feather bed then fetched her a plate. They talked in quiet tones while they ate. After a half-hour's rest, they resumed their journey.

By the time dawn broke, Pearl felt they had traveled for days. Every bone and muscle in her body protested the rough movement of the wagon over the rough road. When they came to a low water crossing, Drake called camp for breakfast.

Turning to Pearl, he explained, "We're well into the next county. No one from Piper's Hollow has any authority here. We'll have a fire for coffee."

Lex helped Belle from the wagon as if she were a china figurine. Sarah rushed forward to help support her frail new friend. The women went into the bushes several yards away to relieve themselves, then returned to the stream to splash water on their faces and hands.

While the men watered the mules and horses, Pearl and Sarah cooked bacon, gravy, and biscuits. After they ate, Lex and Drake rolled in blankets and dozed while the animals cropped nearby.

Pearl watched Storm sit with his back against a tree, his gaze combing the area around their camp. In his arms he cradled his rifle. She went to stand beside him.

"Aren't you going to sleep, too?"

He shook his head. "I'll sleep next time. Then Drake will watch. We made a plan before we started."

"You think we'll have trouble?"

"Maybe not. If we do, we won't be caught off guard."

Neither Pearl nor her siblings had been this far from Piper's Hollow. To Pearl, the landscape looked much the same as the one they left. The trees, hills, grasses, even the rutted and dusty road.

One thing was very different. For the first time in her life Pearl tasted freedom.

By midmorning the next day, it seemed they had traveled for days instead of only hours. They now climbed the steepest hill of the journey. Belle and Evan were the only passengers in the wagons. Sarah and Pearl walked.

Occasionally, the wagons halted. Drake and Lex placed chocks to brace the back wheels so the mules could rest and blow. On this long hill, they had to stop twice for a half hour each time.

As they crested the hill and began their descent, the women

returned to ride in the wagons. The drivers had to brake almost constantly to slow the descent. Suddenly Storm shouted a warning.

A huge boulder rolled their way. Stones and gravel followed. The massive rock narrowly missed their wagon. Large stones slammed against the tail of the second vehicle. Pearl was almost thrown from her perch by the lurch of her wagon as rocks and gravel bombarded.

Behind them, startled horses screamed and reared. Lex turned the lead wagon to the side and set the brake. Within seconds he rushed back to help Drake.

"Everything all right here?"

Drake had already braked and chocked the wagon—not that it could move anywhere. Talus of the rockslide submerged one rear wheel and pushed against the planking sides. He raced with his cousin to help Storm quiet the horses. Pearl turned to help Belle, who sat coughing and waving away the cloud of dirt.

When the dust settled and the animals quieted, Storm spoke. "I saw a man up there." He pointed to a bush on the hillside above them. "Someone started this."

Drake and Lex exchanged doubtful looks before Lex spoke. "Might have been an animal. Or a shadow."

Storm took another step toward the men, shaking his head. "No. A man. I couldn't see his face, but he was there." He pointed again to the top of the bluff beside the road. "Right where the slide started."

Drake put a hand to the boy's shoulder. "Okay. We'd better check it out. Let's see what kind of tracks we find."

Before they left Pearl's cabin, both Drake and his cousin had belted on their handguns. Not the kind in Evan's little books about the West. Those showed drawings of gunfighters wearing double holsters all tied down and worn on the thigh. These were in a leather holster, but smaller and worn at the belt. Now the men grabbed rifles and each unfastened the flap securing his handgun in place.

"Lex, will you stay with the women in case someone has

a mind to make more mischief?" When his cousin nodded and took a stance beside the damaged wagon, Drake turned to Storm. "Let's go. You stay behind me."

The two slid and stumbled up the hillside. At the top, they disappeared from view. Pearl held her breath. It seemed they were gone a long time without a sound to reassure those who waited below. She comforted herself that at least there were no gunshots.

She shook her head and rummaged through the tools stored in the first wagon. "I can't stand the suspense of not knowing, of just waiting here. I'll get a shovel and dig out the wheel."

Lex addressed Belle. "You know how to use one of these?" He nodded at the rifle.

Belle nodded. "Yes. I'm a purty good shot."

He handed her the firearm. "You watch. I'll dig."

Evan called from the other wagon. "I'm watching, too."

Pearl and Sarah gathered stones and moved them aside while Lex dug. Each cast frequent glances at the ridge, but saw no one. By the time Drake and Storm reappeared atop the bluff, the wheel was almost free. A mess of rubble littered the roadside, but a wagon could pass.

A grim-faced Drake slid down the last few feet to the roadside. "Storm was right."

Lex looked astonished. "You don't mean it? Sonofabitch. Uh, beg pardon, ladies." He glanced at the women before he continued speaking to his cousin, "You saw someone?"

Drake shook his head. "Whoever did this is long gone. We found where they waited, though. Found the pole they used as a lever to start the slide. Looked like prints of two men."

Lex shook his head, as if he still couldn't believe what he heard. "Who would want to wreck our wagons? If they wanted to rob us, why not hold us up and take the wagons as well?"

Storm looked grave. "Not rob. Someone wants to hurt Pearl. Maybe Sarah and me, too."

"You believe this was directed at you and your sisters?" Drake no longer doubted Storm's opinion. The boy was sharp.

Drake's anger surprised him. Who would have the nerve to attack his horses and people in his care? Damned if he wouldn't like to get his hands on the varmints right now. Storm's voice brought his attention back to the moment.

"Lots of things happened lately. Started when Pearl's Granny died. Too many things to all be accidents."

"What kinds of things?"

Storm looked to Pearl, seeking reassurance. She nodded at him to continue.

"There was the fire in the barn. Smelled like coal oil. We got it out before the barn burned, but only because it rained hard. Two days later someone killed a chicken and put it in our well to ruin the water. One night someone tried to break in the back door, but I shot at him."

Belle added, "Those men in town wrecked Pearl's cart, too. Evan put them in jail for three days."

Drake looked from Pearl to her brother. "You think it was them? The men we saw in Piper's Hollow?"

Storm shook his head. "No. That fire was while the two brothers were in jail for another thing. So was the chicken." He looked at Evan and shrugged. "Those three cause trouble and stay in jail a lot, especially the Ainsworths. Mostly for little things, though, like too much liquor or causing a fight."

Sarah leaned close to her brother's ear. "Tell them about the men who followed Sister."

Drake heard her. "Men followed Pearl? What men?"

Pearl stepped between her brother and sister. "I'll tell them." She patted the shoulder of each, then looked at Drake and Lex. "It was the first of these incidents, I suppose. A couple of days after Granny's funeral, I helped Jenny Sinclair with her baby's birthing. She lives across the valley past Oak Haven and up the mountain, maybe two miles from home, um, our old cabin. It was late, way after midnight when I returned."

She crossed her arms and hugged herself against the unpleasant memory. "In all the years I've been healing, I don't think I've ever been afraid until then. I thought I heard something behind me and stopped to listen. A man stepped out in front of me and tried to grab me. It sounded as if another one moved up behind me." Though the sun shone warm on her now, she shivered as if chilled.

"I admit it really scared me. Instead of turning away, I pushed hard into the man in front and knocked him over. Then I ran. I know the paths well along there and I can run pretty fast—even carrying my doctorin' bag."

"So there were at least two men? Did you see their faces?"

She shook her head. "It was dark. I only saw the man in front of me. He had a sack over his head with holes cut for his eyes. It—it was frightening. After that, if I was out late, I just stayed all night at the sick folks' house unless one of their menfolk could see me home."

Storm nodded. "But that's when Evan insisted she carry our pistol with her. He taught her to use it years ago, but he made her practice again. She carried it so she could protect herself when she was out doctorin' people or delivering her breads and sweets."

"But why would they attack you?"

Pearl and her family exchanged sorrowful looks before she shrugged a shoulder. "We don't know."

Drake took Pearl's elbow and guided her back onto the wagon. "There's nothing to be gained standing here. Let's get underway. The sooner we get to Chattanooga, the better."

Why would anyone want to harm Pearl? As far as Drake could see, she had nothing of value. Did she hide some secret? He decided to talk to Evan once more.

Damn. What had he gotten himself into? All he wanted was a wife. No, he *wanted* to be left alone. He *needed* a wife. Then he picked one who came with a string of family members who included a woman of ill repute labeled as a fake cousin. To make matters worse, someone targeted all or part of this family.

Evan rode propped up so he faced the wagon in which Pearl, Belle, and Drake rode. He held his rifle across his lap. Drake noticed his cousin also left the flap of his holster unfastened and kept a rifle beside him.

Drake had thought himself indifferent toward Pearl and her family. That someone would attack them while they were in his care infuriated him. No one threatened him or his and got away with it. Surely they would be safe in the city of Chattanooga.

Drake hated to think what that slide would have done to his new mares. Well, he had to admit it wouldn't have done the people any good either if it had been a more timely hit. Did the criminals miscalculate or only mean to terrorize? With a sinking feeling in the pit of his stomach, he admitted his fears. He suspected lethal intent, but the culprits erred in their timing.

Pearl sat quietly with her hands folded in her lap. She half turned on the seat to meet his gaze. "This makes things very different."

"It certainly does. We'll have to be even more careful from now on."

She shook her head. "No. I never would have involved you and Lex if I had known anything like this would happen. I truly thought once we left Piper's Hollow we'd be safe. We never dreamed the trouble would follow us out of the county. This alters our agreement."

For just a moment, panic gripped his gut. "You gave me your word. You trying to get out of our deal?"

"I'm giving you a chance to do that. You need a wife, not a passel of trouble. You can leave us in Chattanooga. Mary Alice, that's Evan's daughter, can help you find a suitable wife."

"No. I don't scare so easily. Besides, if someone hereabouts wants to harm you, the further away you are, the safer you'll be. We'll continue on to Texas as we planned."

He saw her exhale, as if she had held her breath. Her features relaxed, though she didn't say more. So, she wanted to continue their bargain. Decent of her to give him an out, but Kincaids stuck to their bargains. And they didn't run scared.

Why would anyone target Pearl or her family? Was there some secret not even Evan knew? After mulling this over for several minutes, Drake turned his attention to Pearl and repeated his question.

"Any ideas why anyone would attack you or your family?"

Six

Pearl felt a flush spread across her face. She sat straight and tall, hiding the shame she felt. "You know people don't like us because of our being born outside marriage?"

Drake shrugged. "That's something you had no control over. Why would that make anyone want to hurt you?"

He had no idea what a gift he gave her.

Drake's simple dismissal of her illegitimate birth lifted a burden from her heart. Unsure what Evan told him, how much he understood of her life, she hoped he knew very little. If he knew her shame, he might shun her as others did, might refuse to help her family.

She couldn't explain it to him, so she said only, "Not everyone is as logical as you. Or as forgiving."

"What's this about people taking Sarah and Storm away from you? Could that have anything to do with the incidents?"

She shook her head. "I wondered the same thing at first. No, I can't explain why, but there's something else. Something even worse. Merline and Billy Joe Higgins didn't want Sarah and Storm out of any sense of looking out for their welfare. They wanted them living at their place as slave labor."

"Why them? Why not just hire someone?"

"Well, I don't think they can afford to hire anyone. Merline Higgins is ailing. I tried doctoring her, but without much luck. Mostly, I think, she's just plumb sick of Billy Joe. Who could blame her?" She paused, unsure of how much to tell.

With a sigh, she continued. "Billy Joe is a terrible, horrid man. Lazy and a bad provider. Since his wife is ill, I think he wanted Sarah for himself. I mean in—in his bed. The way he looked at Sarah when he thought no one saw him,"—she shuddered—"made me sick."

The revulsion she felt for Billy Joe caused her to shudder again and shrug her shoulders. She always felt dirty when he looked at her or Sarah, wanted to rush home and scrub herself.

"Before you came," she continued, "I decided we would run away with only the clothes on our backs before I'd let the Higginses get hold of Sarah and Storm. We even talked about putting Belle in my cart and taking turns pushing her." She turned to him and smiled. "Wouldn't we've been a sight to see?"

The smile he returned set her heart singing. Talking to her as if she were somebody, an equal, he offered her hope she might really find a fit life with this gorgeous man.

He gave the reins a flick and he said, "Might've worked. At least you had a plan. You have a destination in mind?"

"Yes. We were going to Memphis and wait for my money from the bank. Then we were going to Wyoming territory."

He gave her an incredulous stare before he asked, "Wyoming? That's a long way to travel. Why there?"

"I heard women are treated more as equals in Wyoming. And there're not many women in the state, so they're probably especially welcomed. Figured to give an eating place serving good meals a try."

He shook his head and chuckled. "You're definitely a good enough cook to have made a go of it if that's what you wanted to do."

She knew he laughed at her, thought both her and her idea crazy. Maybe so. Maybe going to Texas was just as crazy.

The little line appeared between his brows and the smile disappeared. "What about this Higgins fellow, though?"

She sat lost in thought again for a few seconds before she shook her head. "Oh, Billy Joe Higgins is too lazy to try anything as complicated as following us and creating a rock slide. It has to be someone else, someone smarter. I just can't imagine who."

"What about that preacher? He sure seemed full of right-eous indignation. So did that shrewish wife of his."

"That's just about an old slight." Her face heated. When Drake looked at her with his eyebrows raised in question, she forged on. But she looked straight ahead, avoiding his gaze. "He—well, he hates me for having the nerve to turn down his marriage proposal four years ago. Dessie Mae hates me because she knows he asked me before he proposed to her."

"Then I guess I'm lucky you turned him down."

She looked at him. "You guess? Hmph. Well, whether you are or not, I wasn't about to marry Fayne Upperly. That pompous, sanctimonious windbag."

He smiled then and looked as if he choked back a laugh. "I take it he didn't court you with flowers and such?"

"Court me?" She felt like hitting something—or some-one—at the memory. "He came to call on Granny regular-like each week. I hardly even spoke to the man, other than to bring him coffee and a slice of cake or pie—unless Granny asked him to stay for dinner. Then, out of the clear blue one day, he starts telling me how he's willing to overlook the sin I was born in and raise my station in life by marrying me. Can you believe the nerve of that man?"

"I can see the fellow has a way with words." She heard the chuckle he tried to hide.

She punched Drake's arm. Her instinctive action surprised her, but not enough that she missed feeling the hard muscle met by her hand. Never had she felt this comfortable talking with a man.

Fighting a laugh of her own, she said, "Oh, laugh if you will, but the man made me mad enough to eat a bug. Before I even had a chance to turn him down he told me that, of course, Sarah and Storm would have to live elsewhere, espe-cially with Storm being what he called a heathen."

"Silver-tongued devil. Good thing he's the only preacher in town or he'd be wanting for church members."

"Well, I fair gave his ears a good blistering. And I never set foot in his church again, 'cept for Granny's funeral. He never forgave me, though, so he's no Christian example, is he? In fact, I heard he preached against those born in sin lots of times. From pure spite, he kept people stirred up against us."

"Sounds like spite's the only thing pure about him. What about your father? Is he around?"

She met his gaze with her chin raised. "And what if he is?" With a shake of her head, she added, "No, it's not him. Again I can't tell you how I know, but I do. I just know."

Drake must have heard the finality in her voice, because he didn't press her. She couldn't discuss her father with anyone yet. Maybe she never would. Some hurts went too deep.

Pearl sat lost in thought as the wagon moved forward. The rock slide had caught her completely unaware. All these weeks she thought they would be safe once they escaped Piper's Hollow. Her only fear had been someone would try to take Sarah and Storm before they escaped the county.

Now trouble followed them. Bad trouble. Although she had no idea who wanted her dead or injured, she felt her fear quieting with the men alerted.

Dear Lord, who could be doing this to us? And why?

They camped well off the road, but in an exposed area. No one could approach them without being seen. The bright moon cast a silver glow on their campsite. A small fire lent warmth against the early spring's chill.

Drake took the first watch. Quiet and uneventful. Just the kind of night he usually liked, except this one also gave him plenty of time to think.

First came shock that anyone deliberately tried to kill Pearl or her family. Fury suffused him, but not just from that revelation. His anger sprang from the threat to what was his, in his care. He also thought about the wrongs suffered by Pearl and her family at other people's hands—and words.

A pair of violet eyes drifted into his mind's eye. But he

knew there was a lot more to Pearl than beautiful eyes, lots more than he suspected when he proposed to her. Trying not to think about the effect those violet eyes had on him, he admired the way she kept going in spite of whatever came her way.

It must have been hard for her to provide for a family all these years. Never complained on this trip either. Bossy woman, damn bossy. But she kept working, doing whatever had to be done.

Drake had been surprised when he and Storm came down the hill after the rock slide back there and saw Pearl and Sarah helping Lex dig out the wagon wheel. But he was realizing Pearl was not one to stand by and wring her hands when trouble came. Didn't he learn that the first time he saw her?

When he came back down the rock slide, she'd had her skirt tucked up to keep it out of the dust. The sight of her ankles set him thinking about the long legs above them. In spite of her tall form, she moved with grace and with no wasted motion. Pearl Parker was definitely a lot more woman than he'd first imagined. He shook his head to clear his traitorous thoughts. He damn well refused to feel anything for a woman he didn't want. If he couldn't have the kind of romance his grandparents shared, he wanted only a token wife. He'd give her his name, but not his heart. *Never his heart.*

Belle lay in the wagon unable to sleep while she waited for Pearl and Sarah to turn in on the feather bed with her. So many thoughts jumbled her mind she failed to hear Lex approach. She started when he spoke.

"Are you comfortable, Miss Renfro?"

"Why yes, thank you." Though she couldn't make them out in the dark, she knew his eyes must show the warm concern he had displayed throughout the trip.

"The road's rough. I know it must be hard to bear, what with you injured and all."

She thought he started to say more. When he didn't, she explained, "It's not as bad as I thought it would be. Pearl's feather bed's a nice cushion with pillows all piled behind me."

This man with the dark red hair treated her like a princess, bringing her things, talking to her each time they stopped. She knew he pretended not to see the bruises that still mottled her face, yet took such care when he helped her down from the wagon.

So much had happened recently to change her life. She had thought she would die, felt certain of it, even hoped for it until Roxie found her. Thank God Roxie got her to Pearl, and thank God for Pearl's compassion and knowledge of healing.

"I don't mean to trouble you, but I thought no one asked and, well, you might know some clue. Do you have any thoughts about who could have been responsible for that rock slide?"

"Law, wasn't it awful? But no, I can't imagine. You have no idea yet just how good a person Pearl is, or how mean spirited some of the people in Piper's Hollow can be." Thoughts of her own parents brought tears to her eyes. How mean and stiff-necked to throw away their own daughter over one mistake?

"What about you, Miss Renfro? What will your family think about you leaving so suddenly?" he asked, concern coloring his tone.

She panicked. How odd it must seem to him, but she could tell him nothing of the truth. Her own story would repel him. The soft look in his brown eyes would change from concern to disgust, a disgust she shared. Or would it become the leer so familiar to her from the men at Roxie's Place?

Please, God, no. Never that from him.

"My family is large and my parents haven't much money. They couldn't even give Pearl a few pennies to help with my care after the, uh, the accident." *Not couldn't, but wouldn't, even if they knew about her troubles.* "They'll be happy for me to have this chance to get away from Piper's Hollow." *They would be happy never to hear of her shame or see her ever again.*

She could die each time she remembered how trusting she'd been. Well, that innocence didn't last long, did it? Now she had another chance. She must not say or do anything to lose it.

His silence stretched into awkwardness, though he remained beside the wagon. She longed to continue the conversation but sought a safer topic. "It's a lovely moon, isn't it, Mr. Tremont?"

"Oh, please, call me Lex. Or Alexon. That's my name but no one ever uses it."

"All right—Alexon. If you'll call me Belle. Just Belle. My name is really Arabella Angeline, but I like Belle best."

"It suits you. I'll bet you were the belle of any ball you attended."

"Oh. Well, I never attended a party where there was dancing. My folks don't hold with dancing or drinking. We did have a piano, though." *Which Mama pleaded for years to get from tightfisted Papa.*

"And do you play?"

"Yes, mostly hymns." She had to learn any other songs when Papa was outside working. He wouldn't stand for any songs but church music in his house. But how he used to love to hear her sing. Sorrow clogged her throat and made her afraid to speak. What would Alexon think if she started sobbing over a discussion of the piano?

"Well, I know you need your rest while the wagon is still. I see your cousins heading this way to turn in. And I'd better get some sleep before it's my watch."

"Good night, Alexon."

"Goodnight, Miss . . . Belle."

She watched him walk through the silvery night and crawl into his bedroll. Such a kind man. Not at all the type she had known.

Other than her brothers, she had talked to few men before George came to work for Papa at harvest. Then he stayed around until after Christmas, calling on Belle. When the man she had thought dashing and adventurous asked her to run away with him, she thought he meant to marry her. Later he had laughed at her for being so stupid.

She left George then and went home, but they'd been gone two nights. Papa called her terrible names. He wouldn't even let her come into their house, wouldn't let her talk to Mama or her brothers and sisters. How could he be so vicious, so cold to his own daughter?

She knew Alexon's good manners would never let him behave so cruelly. But his opinion of her would change if he knew. Then he wouldn't speak to her again unless he made an offer for her services. Oh, God, if that happened, she would just die.

What's to become of me?

With a terrible sadness, she scooted to the edge of the feather bed to make room for her two new friends. Then, as she had done so many nights these last two months, she wept silently into her pillow.

At the crest of a hill, Lex stopped the wagon and motioned Drake to pull alongside. When the two sat parallel, Lex gestured to the sprawling town below. "There it is. Chattanooga."

The women cheered. Belle pulled herself up and sat on a trunk. She smoothed her dress and straightened her bonnet. "I'm not going into town lying in a sick bed."

Even Evan perked up when he realized he would soon see his daughter and her family. Moving slowly, he squeezed onto the seat beside Sarah. "Mary Alice lives only a few blocks from downtown."

The rutted road eventually became a main street. Pearl knew her eyes must be wide. "My goodness, I can't keep from staring. Never in my life have I seen so many people at one time! And look at all the kinds of buildings. Big and small and in between. It fair takes your breath away."

Storm called out, "Did you see that buggy? You ever see anything so fancy?"

Drake half turned and called to him, "It's called a surrey."

Evan directed Lex to turn first this way and then the other. Soon the wagon stopped in front of a bungalow set back from the road about fifty yards. A picket fence separated the yard from the street and a hitching rail stood by the front gate.

At the sound of their arrival, Mary Alice stepped onto the porch. When she saw her father, she called out to someone in the house, then ran down the front walk toward the visitors. Three children rushed out to follow their mother.

Pearl felt lost, awkward. The giggling Mary Alice she knew years ago had disappeared. Now a more dignified and matronly stranger stood in her place.

But the matron became a laughing girl when she reached her father. "Papa, Papa! At last you've come."

Pearl sat still and watched the happy reunion. Evan looked so happy. Finally. What a lovely sight.

Drake got down and came to her side to offer his assistance. He placed his hands on her waist. "Time to greet your hostess." When she stood beside him, he laid an arm across her shoulders and gave her a light hug. "Everything will be all right now."

She hoped he spoke the truth. Sarah came to stand on the other side of her sister as Lex helped Belle from the wagon. Pearl linked Sarah's arm with hers.

No doubt Sarah felt as out of place as she did, maybe more. She reminded her, "You probably don't remember, but Mary Alice loved playing with you when you were a baby. She moved here ten years ago when she married." She glanced over her shoulder and motioned for Storm to join them.

Having Drake beside her amid all the confusion gave her a strange sense of partnership with him. The group moved up the walk and into the home.

Mary Alice chided her father. "Papa, you're way too pale but it's so good just to look at you."

"And it's good to look at you. And my grandbabies."

"Hey, we're not babies. I'm gonna be ten at Christmas. Janie's eight." The eldest boy, named Evan after his grandfather, spoke up. "'Course, Danny's only five, so he's almost a baby."

"Am not." The youngest ran at his older brother.

Mary Alice intervened, separating the two boys with a skill that spoke of practice. "Young Evan, run to the shop and tell your father we have company. Then you come straight back, you hear?"

Drake stopped at the steps to the porch. "Ma'am, I reckon my cousin and I will go book hotel rooms for our group, if you'll direct us to the nearest place fit for young women."

A worried frown replaced the happy smile. Mary Alice looked at the crowd of people. Pearl knew that, in her mind, the woman frantically sought places for all these people to sleep in her small home.

The smile reappeared, but didn't quite reach Mary Alice's eyes. "You're all welcome here."

"Thank you, but we planned to treat the ladies here to a big dinner in town and let you get reacquainted with your father."

"Well, unless you have your heart set on it, I insist you stay with us. That is, if you men don't mind sleeping on floor pallets." She turned to her father, "Not you, Papa. We have a corner room downstairs away from the children's noise. We fixed it all ready for you, knowing you'd come when you could. I can see you need plenty of rest and some fattening up."

Drake waited until she turned back to him and nodded. "Thank you, Ma'am. Lex and I have our own bedrolls. There's also Evan's bed in the wagon, and Pearl's feather bed."

The bright smile reappeared. "Why, of course. We'll find a place for everyone. It's so exciting to have you all here." She touched her father's arm then leaned over to kiss his cheek, as if not believing he stood beside her. "Especially you, Papa."

Lex and Drake drove the wagons to the back of the house. After unloading Evan's bed and Pearl's feather mattress, they threw large canvas tarpaulins over the wagons to protect the contents from the elements.

Eventually the horses and mules were settled at the nearby livery. By the time Drake wired his grandfather of his up coming wedding, checked train schedules, and returned to the house, the women had dinner ready.

Michael Cooper arrived home to greet the visitors after closing his hardware store a half-hour early. When Mary Alice and Michael learned of the impending marriage, they insisted on hosting the event. Amid all the chaotic chatter, Drake watched the woman who sat beside him. Pearl seemed to withdraw into herself, even as she smiled at those around her.

As far as he could determine, these people were all related to Pearl. Through her Granny they were some sort of cousins. That meant they were not kin to Sarah or Storm. He had no idea how—or if—Belle was related to anyone here. But he was willing to go along with the story his bride-to-be spun for him about her so-called cousin.

"Now, Mr. Kincaid," Mary Alice insisted, "I know you're eager to wed my cousin Pearl, but you simply must wait a couple of days to marry. Pearl needs time to shop for a trousseau and make the wedding arrangements."

Irked at the delay, he agreed. "Our time here must be short. But, I guess two days won't hurt."

Mary Alice clapped her hands. "Wonderful. You can wed Saturday afternoon right here in the parlor. Oh, the new Excelsior Hotel has just opened. It would be perfect for your honeymoon."

Pearl, who seemed to blush a lot around him, went pale as the flour she used for her baking. Neither one had talked about a hotel or a honeymoon. Still, he supposed a woman expected that sort of thing. He tugged at the shirt collar that seemed suddenly to tighten.

"All right. I'll take care of the arrangements for our train tickets and the stock and the, um, the honeymoon. But come Sunday, we depart for Texas." Damn, he wanted all this wedding business over and done with so he could be on his way home.

Drake consulted with Michael about the stable, worried about his new mares. "What if someone takes a liking to them and steals them?"

Michael shared his concern for so much prime horseflesh

in a busy area. "You know you're welcome here. But, if it was me, I'd want to be close enough to keep an eye on those horses, especially at night. You know we'll look after your bride and her family."

Lex and Storm decided to go with him and sleep in the loft of the stable. Drake went to speak with Pearl before they left.

"I suppose you'll be coming to the house tomorrow to eat?" she asked.

"By lunchtime or soon thereafter." He took out his wallet. "You'll be needing money for your shopping."

She visibly bristled, drawing herself up like a prim spinster. "Thank you, but I saved out money from my baking in case we had to leave sudden-like. Which we did, of course."

"There's no need to spend your own money. I have plenty."

Damn stubborn woman. He'd never known a female to turn down extra funds for a shopping spree.

She repeated, "No, I'll make do with my own. Don't worry, I'll find something presentable to wear for the wedding and to meet your family. I don't intend to shame you."

Guilt nagged at him. How could he confess he wanted her less than presentable? How could he admit that's why he chose her? Well, mostly why he chose her. He looked into those violet eyes of hers and almost lost his train of thought.

Guilt forced him to add more bills to the stack. "But I'll leave this money with you. Things may be more costly than you imagine and you'll need at least two or three sets of clothes." He took her hand and placed the bills in her palm. Loathe to break physical contact, he closed her fingers around the money and cradled her hand in his. What had come over him, he wondered, giving away large sums of money and clinging to a woman he didn't want to like?

She looked at the funds and then back to him, her eyes wide. "Why, I haven't spent that much in all my lifetime."

His voice sounded brusque to his ears. "Well, you don't get married every day. Get whatever you need—or want. For yourself and the others." Reluctantly, he forced his hands to release hers.

"Mr. Kincaid, I don't wish to offend you, but I have to tell you again that I have my own money. Enough to do for me and my family."

Damn, was she always so bossy and stubborn? "Look, keep the money. If you need it, you'll have it and not be embarrassed. If you don't need it, you can save it for shopping another time. Don't forget, you've a lot of people to clothe."

She chewed her lip a second before nodding slightly. "Yes, you're right, of course. I was thinking only of myself. Sarah and Storm and Belle need better things to meet your people. We want to do you proud. I mustn't let my own pride stand in the way." She shoved the money into her pocket as if it were tainted. "I've never been to a real store, just Pete Hammonds's place back ho—um, back in Piper's Hollow."

He smiled at the thought of all she would experience for the first time tomorrow. "I think you'll enjoy yourself. Please, get Mary Alice something also. Maybe the whole family. After all, we're putting the Coopers to a good bit of trouble."

She brightened, lost some of her starch. "Yes, that would please Mary Alice and the children. And Michael won't mind."

He put his hands in his pockets and smiled. "There. Now, was that so hard?"

Chin up, her solemn gaze met his. "You have no idea how hard. But I thank you for thinking of us. Thank you for everything you've done."

"It's my pleasure." With surprise, he found he meant it. Strange how such a small thing made him feel so good. "It will please me even more when you remember to call me Drake."

A smile chased the shadows from her violet eyes. "Thank you, Drake." She raised herself on tiptoe and kissed his cheek.

The sensations that washed over him from that simple gesture caught him by surprise. Before he let himself pull her into his arms, he took a step back and gave her a slight bow.

"Then I'll wish you good night, Pearl." Feeling every bit a coward, he turned and left the room.

Young Evan accompanied them to the livery stable, to Lex's amusement. "Him being with us must have considerably lowered the noise level at the Cooper home, maybe that whole block of homes." It did nothing to ease Drake's frayed nerves. "Damn, the boy runs instead of walking, shouts instead of talking. By morning, I'll be questioning my desire for heirs."

But at bedtime, Storm quieted the younger boy by telling stories about horses. Soon Drake heard Lex's soft snore while Storm switched to a Cherokee myth. Young Evan laughed as he heard "Where The Dog Ran," the story of how the Milky Way came to be in the sky.

Drake wondered if someday he would be able to tell stories to his own son? Would that son have eyes of striking violet or plain gray? He drifted to sleep listening to Storm's soft voice paint word pictures for young Evan.

Early Friday morning noises roused the adults in the loft. The hostler opened the barn doors wide to the breaking day. Both boys slept, but Drake and Lex descended the ladder to talk with the stable owner about transportation and breakfast.

Storm soon dropped to the floor beside them. "Shall I stay with the horses or take the kid back to his house?"

Drake handed his future brother-in-law a handful of coins. "Stop by the baker's near here and get something to take the Coopers. Something to help with the food for today. You can keep the rest for sight-seeing later. Keep an eye out around the Cooper place until I get my errands done. I'll be back midday."

"Yes, I'll watch for a mischief maker." The twinkle in his eyes told Drake that Storm referred to young Evan.

"Thanks. We'll spell you in a few hours. I expect there's a lot for a young man to see in Chattanooga."

After breakfast at the nearby hotel, the men wandered to

the depot. Drake purchased tickets for his family, then made arrangements for a cattle car.

"We want the partitions for seven horses here," he told the railway agent as he sketched out a design on a scrap of paper. When his cousin raised his eyebrows at the number, he explained, "Evan sold me his paint for Storm. We'll pick up a new saddle later."

The agent assured him the stalls would be fitted immediately.

"Then, we'll want a small cabin partitioned off at this end for furniture storage and room for a man to sleep."

Lex grimaced. "Don't tell me. You're going to make me the stable hand." He waited for an answer with his arms crossed.

"No. Storm and I can take turns. He volunteered to do it alone. That wouldn't be fair, though he is damn good with horses."

"But it's his first train ride."

"Right. He'd miss seeing the sights. No windows in the cattle car."

"Well, I'll do my share. Fair division of labor and all."

The cousins walked through the bustling town, commenting on merchandise in store windows and enjoying the morning.

"You going to buy wedding clothes?"

"Me?" Drake planned only to show up and go through whatever tomfoolery the women arranged.

"Man, you have some responsibilities here."

Damn. There went Lex getting testy again.

"All right, all right." He hated the whole set up, but he gave in to his cousin's voice of reason. "Tell me, Counselor, what do you view as my part in this?"

"You need a new suit, inside to out. You need a ring, flowers, and a present for the bride. You must book the honeymoon suite. . . ." Lex looked set to continue his list, but Drake held up his hand.

"I'll get her a ring. Make the hotel reservations, will you?"

"After we get your suit fitted."

For a man of Drake's height and breadth, finding a suit

proved no easy task. It took several attempts before they were
directed to a tailor with a large staff. And a large price tag.
Drake endured what seemed tortuous hours of fitting.

When he received a pinprick as reward for fidgeting, he
asked the tailor, "Can't you hurry this up?"

Finally, the shop owner promised to have the clothes delivered to the Cooper home by noon the following day. He
even recommended a reliable jeweler three doors down the
street.

Whistling a carefree tune, Lex strolled toward the hotel.
With his jaw set, Drake stalked toward the jeweler's shop.

Lex arrived at the Cooper home around midmorning. Belle
sat at the piano in the parlor, playing what sounded like wedding music. How sweet and genteel she looked, even with her
bruises.

His first day in Piper's Hollow and accusations made by
the pastor's wife churned in his mind. The puffed up old
biddy mentioned Sarah and Storm, and a soiled dove being
harbored by Pearl. Belle had to be the woman accused as a
harlot.

With a sigh he shrugged off the knowledge. If she wanted
to be known as Pearl's cousin, why not? What did it matter
to him?

He ambled to the piano and rested an arm on the lid. "Are
you one of the bride's attendants?"

She looked down at her fingers. "Oh, no. I could never.
The bruises from my, um, accident still look so awful. But
I'm going to play." She met his gaze and offered a small
smile. "I think we're all in the wedding. Except maybe Mr.
Cooper and the children."

He leaned against the piano. "I understand from my cousin
that I'm the best man. Now, that's something I've been telling
him all our lives."

She rewarded him with another smile, genuine this time
and it lit her face. "And Mary Alice is the matron of honor.

Sarah is a bridesmaid, Storm is seating the guests. Evan is giving Pearl away."

Her voice held excitement for the first time since he met her.

"Will there be anyone here who's not in the ceremony?"

"Some. Mary Alice invited neighbors, and some distant relatives who live a few blocks away."

"Where's the bride?" He tilted his head as if to listen. "The house sounds deserted. Must mean young Evan is in another state."

Belle's tinkling laugh met his ears. "Storm's helping the children make a tree house out back. Seems he's as good with children as with horses. Mary Alice took Pearl and Sarah shopping."

He frowned. "Didn't you feel well enough to go with them?"

She looked down again. "Well, with all the doings of the wedding tomorrow and the trip the next day, I thought I should stay here and take it easy. But Pearl is bringing me something special to wear tomorrow. She measured me carefully."

He looked at the tiny woman seated in front of the window, his brain suddenly awhirl contemplating measuring each delicate part of her. Reining his thoughts in quickly, he scolded himself. None of that, Tremont. None of that at all.

To distract himself, he paced the room. "So, you're going to play? Will you sing also?" Turning toward her, he stopped. "I believe you mentioned you sing."

"Well, Pearl only asked about me playing." Her hands clasped and unclasped above the piano keys. "So, I've been practicing my playing. It's been a while since I tried."

"Would you? I mean, sing? Now. For me?"

"If—if you want me to. What should I sing?"

"You decide." He chose the large chair near the fireplace and sat.

Sunlight brushed glistening highlights into her chestnut hair and formed a halo. Her slender fingers touched the keys and coaxed a melody from the instrument. Soon her voice joined in song, softly at first, then gaining in confidence.

She sang like an angel. She played like an angel. She looked like an angel.

He leaned back, closed his eyes, and let the music enfold him. Good God in Heaven. How could he be so thoroughly attracted to a prostitute?

The children and Storm took a bucket of food to the tree house for lunch. Lex, Evan, and Belle waited to eat until Michael returned at one. The other three women came in soon afterward, laden with packages and full of chatter about selections and deliveries to come. As soon as they cleared away the food, the women, including young Janie, went upstairs to talk wedding. Michael escaped back to his store, looking grateful to be away from the prattle.

Over a hand of poker, Lex and Evan offered to corral the kids while Storm looked over the town. After only half an hour, Storm returned. The sullen look on his face left no doubt he had encountered trouble.

Evan asked, "What happened, son? You look fit to fight a bear."

He shrugged. "This man in a store said he didn't want Indians in his place." He shoved his hands into his pockets and hunched his shoulders. "I could pay. Drake gave me money."

Drake entered just as the boy explained. His eyes met Lex's. "Why don't we go out together and try another store?"

The boy shook his head. "Why? So I get insulted again? I'll stay with the horses. You always know where you stand with horses."

Drake reassured him, "Son, there's a rotten apple in every barrel. Don't let a bad one spoil your enjoyment of the others."

Storm tilted his head and peered at each of the men. "Is it always going to be like this? I thought if I got away from Piper's Hollow, people would give me a chance."

Drake spoke softly to the youngster. "Most will. Some won't. Let's try again."

Lex tossed his cards onto the table and stood. "Say, isn't it about time you started practicing corralling these grandkids?"

"You bet." The former sheriff made a wave of dismissal before he gathered the cards and shuffled them. "I've rested 'til I'm about ready to lead a revolt. You three look over the town. I'll tell the others to look for you when they see you." He dealt himself a hand of solitaire.

Drake peered into the kitchen. "I'll explain to them. That is, if they're around."

Evan gestured at the stairs. "They took a ton of packages upstairs. Haven't seen them since."

"I won't be a minute." Drake took two steps at a time.

In a few seconds he returned. "Trying on dresses or something. Never heard so much chattering and giggling. Told them not to wait supper."

Drake placed a hand on Storm's shoulder. "All right, Storm, where shall we start?"

Seven

Pearl tilted her head as she held an emerald traveling suit up to Belle. Sarah and Mary Alice looked on while little Janie played with a ribbon.

"It looks a perfect fit."

"Oh, it's the loveliest thing I've ever seen. Let me try it on right now." Belle wasted no time unhooking the dress she wore to slip into the new one. She twirled and preened in front of the mirror. "It's a perfect fit. How ever did you manage it?"

"There's unmentionables, too." Sarah sorted through the packages on the bed and handed a stack to Belle. "Here are yours."

Pearl reached for another dress in soft yellow. "This one is for you also. You and Sarah each get two." Embarrassed, she added, "I also got two skirts and shirtwaists for wearing around the house." She felt decadent for her selfish purchases, but she thought to make sure Drake had no reason to be ashamed of her.

"The seamstress hadn't hemmed the skirts, so they'll be long enough for Sister." Sarah hunted through packages. "One is blue and the other brown."

"Thank goodness. Pearl, I hope you'll burn those horrid things you've been wearing. What did you get for the ceremony?"

Belle held her delicate underthings as if they were worth a king's ransom. To Pearl's mind they were, but she had never purchased such things before. She sewed all her own under-things, and Sarah's. She smiled and answered her new "cousin."

"I'm so tall it was hard to find anything. The seamstress added another row of pleating to the hem and sleeves to make this fit my height." Pearl held up a lavender-blue dress. "Didn't she do a nice job?" She clasped the dress to her as she swished back and forth.

Belle nodded as if she approved. "I'm glad you found something so pretty for your wedding. You'll take Drake's breath away in that dress."

"Sister will look nice in her gray traveling suit, too. It will be delivered later." Sarah's eyes sparkled with excitement from their shopping trip. "The dressmaker will add another tier of pleats to the skirt hem. She's adding extra braid and an-other drape to the jacket. It'll be the perfect length for her."

Pearl unwrapped a package and held the contents up for Belle's inspection. "But the most amazing thing is these. This is the first pair of new shoes I ever owned."

Adding up in her head, the total she spent in one day made her dizzy. "I hope I guessed right for Storm. I forgot to draw around his foot like I did yours. And he has two changes of clothes he can use on the ranch."

She caressed the soft leather of her footwear with awe akin to reverence. Never had she even seen so many beautiful things as in the stores today. Never had she possessed any-thing so lovely as these. Oh, Lord. Never had she spent so much money.

Though she made the decisions hours ago, she still worried over each one. How right Drake had been. Prices were far more dear than she expected. Early in the shopping trip she realized her funds would not stretch to provide even mini-mal clothing suitable for a wedding and to meet her new family in Texas. Though it hurt her pride, she used some of the money Drake gave her. Even a queen wouldn't have used it all.

She kept careful count of each penny of his she spent.

When her money arrived, there would be enough to pay part of it back. How she would pay the rest she didn't know.

Maybe she could have chickens and milk cows at the ranch and sell the eggs and milk not needed by the family. Somehow she *would* repay him for everything spent for her family before the wedding. She'd be beholden to no man, especially a husband who didn't want a wife in the first place. Best not to dwell on that, she thought, and turned her attention to the others.

Sarah held up a dark blue traveling suit. "I'm wearing the pink dress for Pearl's wedding and this for the train on Sunday. We have hats and gloves to match our suits, too." She attacked a stack of round boxes to display their contents. "See? Your hat has pheasant feathers, Belle."

"Sit here, Pearl." Mary Alice slid a chair to face the cheval mirror. "I'm itching to experiment with your hair."

Pearl took the seat and frowned at her reflection. She knew her faults. Hadn't Granny pointed them out at every opportunity? Waist too small to be healthy for her frame, breasts too large to look respectable, legs too long to be graceful, and on and on. Apparently nothing about her pleased Granny.

Mary Alice loosened Pearl's braid and began brushing and sectioning off strands. "You have such beautiful hair. It's like liquid honey."

Pearl saw her own surprise reflected in the mirror. "It is? Granny always said it was too thick. She said it made my head look too large for my body."

"Nancy said a lot of things, as I remember, and none of them kind." Mary Alice's mouth made a firm line as she worked.

"It's true she often complained." Pearl nodded, forgetting to keep her head still. "I think her illness made her short tempered."

Mary Alice met Pearl's gaze in the mirror. "Oh, Pearl, you would say that. But I knew her when she was able-bodied, and she still had nothing good to say about anyone. With what she tried to do to you, I'd think you wouldn't be so kind to her."

"She was jealous of Pearl." Sarah's soft voice sounded firmer than usual.

"Sarah—" Pearl would have scolded her sister for speaking ill of the dead, but Sarah wouldn't be stopped.

"You know it's true, Sister. She hated Storm and me, but she hated you more. You're everything she wanted to be and couldn't. You reminded her of things she wanted to forget. She was a spiteful, hateful old woman, and I'm glad she's gone." Sarah's fists clenched at her side and she sank onto the bed, barely missing their new finery.

Belle pushed aside a box and sat beside Sarah. She put her arm around the girl and hugged her. "Now, don't be getting all upset on the eve of Pearl's wedding. That's all behind you now. Life will be grand from now on."

"That's true enough." Mary Alice nodded, a smile spreading over her face. "With a handsome brother-in-law to look out for you, how can life be otherwise?"

Pearl stopped chewing on her lip long enough to bite out, "I can certainly take care of my own family. All we needed was to get away from Piper's Hollow." She met Mary Alice's gaze in the mirror and instantly regretted her outburst. How soon she had forgotten the threats to her and her family, the desperation she felt to get away. "I'm sorry, Mary Alice. I shouldn't take it out on you because I'm nervous about tomorrow. And about the move to Texas, and . . . oh, everything."

The older woman stopped twisting Pearl's hair into ringlets just long enough to offer a reassuring pat on her shoulder. "Everything will work out fine. You'll see."

Pearl exhaled a deep sigh. Trouble followed her out of Piper's Hollow. Would it trail her to Texas?

Twenty-four hours later, Pearl gazed at the stranger staring back from the mirror. The lavender gown made her eyes sparkle and seem brighter, larger. She patted the ruching at her sleeve. Who would have thought she could look the lady?

Her fingers slid across the dinner dress' silky fabric to smooth the lace at the dropped waist. She never dreamed she would own anything so lovely. Feeling like a fairy princess, she wondered what her prince would think?

Thoughts of Drake brought her attention to the necklace and matching drop earscrews. The wedding pearls from her soon-to-be-husband were the perfect touch to the low-scooped neckline. Lovely pearls, beautiful dress, fancy hairdo, handsome groom. Today truly brought many firsts.

Her mind leapt ahead to the wedding night and she panicked. At separate times, Belle and Mary Alice had each explained what to expect tonight. She had trouble reconciling the different viewpoints with the few facts she knew. Better to think of other things for now.

Mary Alice had worked wonders with her hair. Most of it piled in curls on her head except for a cascade of ringlets down her right shoulder. She wore no veil or hat, but a ribbon matching her gown wove in and out of the curls. Having watched the procedure carefully, she hoped to re-create the style herself.

Sarah hugged her. "You've never looked so beautiful. Drake is so lucky."

She pushed down the anxiety and forced a smile. "I think I'm the lucky one. He's very handsome. Did Storm tell you how kind he was yesterday?"

Sarah rolled her eyes. "Endlessly. Every sentence of his starts with Drake said this or did that."

Mary Alice tucked a runaway ribbon back into Pearl's hair. "If you're ready, I'll signal Belle to start playing."

Pearl took a deep breath. "I'm ready. Lord, I hope I don't fall down the stairs."

Twenty guests crowded into the parlor on borrowed chairs and benches. Drake resisted the urge to tug the collar of the stiff shirt under his new jacket and waistcoat. He wondered why he let Lex and the tailor talk him into a new wardrobe. After all, it wasn't as if he actually *wanted* to get married.

Eager to get the ceremony over with, he greeted the minister and took his place at the front of a makeshift lectern fashioned from a fern stand. The sooner this farce started, the sooner it would be over. His cousin stepped into place beside him, oozing affable charm. Damn Lex for looking so cheerful anyway.

Belle started playing the piano and the voices in the room hushed, even the Cooper boys. Suddenly, the music changed to the familiar wedding music. Dressed in pale pink with a deep rose sash and bow, Janie Cooper carried a basket of flower petals, some of which she remembered to drop on the floor. Mostly she stared at her transformed home and guests, eyes wide with wonder.

Sarah looked a princess in her pale rose dress as she descended the stairs. What a beauty she would be one day. Mary Alice followed in soft pink, glowing and looking suddenly younger as she smiled at her proud husband.

Evan stepped from the dining room to wait at the last tread of the staircase. Belle's playing increased in volume and Drake heard the murmur of the guests. His gaze sought the landing at the top of the stairs.

His heart stopped.

No! How could this be?

The dowdy Amazon disappeared. In her place a regal queen descended the stairs. Hair swept back from her face flowed like golden honey into an elaborate river of curls. Her dress echoed the color of eyes bright as jewels.

His eyes continued their enchanted journey, touching on the single strand of pearls kissing the gentle rise of her bosom. He'd known the necklace was right for her the minute he saw it in the jeweler's window. Now he realized it was her translucent ivory skin complimenting the pearls rather than the other way around.

With her creamy skin, tiny waist, and slim hips, she more resembled a porcelain doll come to life than the hardy peasant he'd asked to marry him. Damn. How could he have misjudged her so?

Double damn. She deceived him, pretending to be homely and awkward. All the time she hid this beauty beneath uncombed hair and a dress like a tent.

Evan held out his hand, took hers, and twined it with his arm as she stepped from the stairs. Paler than he'd ever seen her, she met his gaze. A tremulous smile tugged at the corners of her luscious mouth. As she came toward him, he felt as if all the breath left his body.

Evan stepped aside to take his seat and Drake took her icy hand in his. He tried hard to focus on the minister's words, but they got all jumbled in his mind. He thought of the freedom this ceremony curtailed, the anger he still felt at this forced union. He even gave a fleeting thought to the woman who trembled beside him.

When the time came to repeat their vows, she gave her small bouquet to Mary Alice. He slid the gold band onto her finger as he repeated the words of the preacher. Her response came soft but clear. In minutes, they were pronounced man and wife.

Drake leaned forward to claim the first kiss from his bride. He intended only a peck, but seemed unable to pull himself away. Her soft lips were warm, pliant, and surprisingly welcoming.

Of their own will, his arms slid around her and he deepened the kiss. When he heard the murmurs and hoots of the guests, he broke away and stared at his wife. How had this happened?

Pearl snapped out of the trance which had held her all day. Now the ceremony became sights, smells, and sounds strung together in a blur. With no illusions about Drake's feelings, she expected nothing but his presence. She looked at the man who faced her, stunned by her reaction to his simple kiss. Simple? Maybe to another. Earth shattering to her.

That he also wore new clothes pleased her, and it touched her that he provided a wedding ring. How thoughtful of him. She looked at her hand where it lay on his arm. The band shone bright gold.

Her new husband stepped behind her to free his right hand for congratulatory handshakes. In a fluid movement, he slid his arm about her waist and held her close by his side. Anyone watching would think he treasured her.

Was he merely doing as his breeding trained him? Or, could it be he disliked the idea of this marriage less? She hoped so.

Guests surrounded them, surging and pressing toward food waiting in the dining room. Drake greeted each guest with an ease she envied, as if he went through this every day. In the short time she had known him, she noted little clues to his moods. The tightness around his mouth, the little crinkle at the corners of his eyes, the slight hunch of one shoulder, these all belied the smile on his lips. He was not as comfortable, or as confident, as he appeared. She wondered why that reassured her.

Somehow she managed a response to each comment addressed to her, but could remember neither a word spoken to her nor her reply. They finished with toasting and more good wishes, and the newlyweds left in a hired carriage.

With a huge sigh, Drake leaned back against the leather seat. "At last, we've finished with that." As if he regretted voicing the remark, he added, "It was a nice wedding, but too many people for me."

"Yes, it's nice to be on our way." She flushed, afraid he might think she meant the wedding night. "I've never eaten in a restaurant nor set foot in a hotel." Oh, no, she thought. Why remind him I'm a nobody who's been nowhere?

"Being such a good cook yourself, you'd have no need for a place to dine out."

His answer pleased her. "Thank you. Still and all, everyone likes to have someone else cook sometimes."

"And does anyone cook for you?" He closed his eyes and massaged the bridge of his nose as if to pinch off a headache.

"Yes, Sarah often does. Even Storm cooks once in a while, though he prefers a campfire to a stove. Cooking's a skill everyone needs at some time."

He laughed. "Yes, but I only cook when I'm so hungry my stomach isn't too particular."

The carriage stopped at The Excelsior Hotel. A uniformed porter rushed to help them. Drake handed over their bags, then turned to help Pearl. The niggling doubts of the past few days rushed to ball in her stomach. She felt ready to cling to the man beside her one minute, then run away in the next.

The desk clerk produced a key and they followed the porter. The clicking of her heels against the polished marble of the lobby floor ceased on the carpeted halls and stairs. Trying not to gawk like the bumpkin she felt, Pearl studied the reflection she and Drake made as they passed a long mirror. What a handsome couple, she thought.

When she stepped into the room, she stopped. She stood in a sitting room lovelier than any she could have imagined. Through a door to her right she saw a large bed. To her left another bedroom opened.

"Goodness. It's like a house, isn't it?" She peered around.

He chuckled. "Don't worry, there's no kitchen."

The porter lit the gaslight on the wall before he put their bags in the larger bedroom.

Not in all her lifetime could she have envisioned a place this grand. She walked to heavy gold brocade draperies tied back to reveal lace curtains at the windows. Pearl parted the panels to look at the street below.

She jumped when Drake placed his hand on her arm. "Would you like to freshen up or something before we go down for dinner?"

"No, I'm ready now."

Later, seated beside Drake in the dining room, Pearl looked at the line of silverware spread on the crisp damask cloth. She saw waiters hurrying by with foods she did not recognize. From a well deep inside her mind she recalled what Mrs. Cummins told her years ago. "When you don't know what to do in a social situation, watch those around you."

She smiled. Pearl Cummins never meant her to mimic the men at a table in the corner. One smoked a cigar and the other picked his teeth with the blade of his pocketknife. Her gaze sought other diners and found a family seated nearby. The mother moved gracefully and with certainty. Pearl watched how the woman handled each fork, each dish and glass.

Picking up her own fork, she said, "Goodness, I never knew it was so much work just to eat. I'm glad I don't have to wash the dishes here."

The meal passed with a few comments about the upcoming trip, the wedding guests, and other general topics. Too soon the meal was over and it was time to return to their rooms. With each step, she grew more nervous.

How would she know what to do? Would he want to touch her before they got into bed? What if she hated their coming together? Dear Lord, she wished this night were over.

Drake must have sensed her fear. When they stepped inside their rooms, he turned her to him.

"Don't be nervous. It will be all right. You go in and get ready for bed. I'll sit out here for a while."

Grateful for his understanding, she hurried into the bedroom and closed the door. From her bag she took her new nightgown and laid it out on the bed. Mary Alice told her not to wear anything under it, not even her drawers.

My word. In the store the nightie hadn't looked nearly so thin. Fabric almost as transparent as the lace trim mocked her. She slid her hand under the fine lawn of the gown.

As she suspected, she plainly saw her hand, picked out the gold band on her finger. She felt her eyes widen in alarm. Why, he'd be able to see . . . no, better just get on with her preparations. What could she do now but wear the blasted thing?

With precise movements, she turned down the covers the same amount on each side of the bed. She plumped up the pillows and replaced them side by side. The heat of a flush spread across her face with the thought of her and Drake between the sheets, heads resting side by side on the pillows.

Next she took out the gray traveling suit for tomorrow, shook it and hung it in the wardrobe. She lay the reticule, hat, and gloves on the table near the window. When everything was ready for morning, she stripped off her clothes.

What a relief to be out of that horrid corset. She couldn't bear thinking about putting it on again. Very carefully, she folded her dress and put it into the bag. She bathed with her lilac soap before she slipped into the sinfully thin gown.

Fumbling fingers unpinned her hair and brushed it. She would never be able to duplicate the style Mary Alice managed, but she would make a stab at something similar in the morning. Pausing to gaze in the mirror, she pinched her cheeks and rubbed a rose petal along her lips.

Drake paced the sitting room, as nervous as a green kid. He wished he was visiting Abby or Lulu at Dalton's Saloon back home. Those women knew all about sex and then some. No need for care or caution there. A couple of drinks, a quick tumble, relief, and he was on his way back to the ranch.

With a woman like Pearl . . . well, hell, he'd never been with a woman like Pearl. He liked women who knew what to do and expected nothing from him but a good ride and a few dollars. Now, though, he would have to lead the way, go slow, teach a trembling spinster the way to pleasure.

Anger overwhelmed him. Once again he railed against his parents and grandfather for forcing this upon him. Because of the ridiculous will he acquired not only a wife he did not want, but a whole damn family. That they seemed nice enough people was beside the point and made little difference.

Marrying her now ruled out any future marriage should he find a woman as right for him as Grandma had been for Grandpa. There'd be no happily ever after for him now. All he could do was make the best of a bad situation. Fury swept over him, setting off a myriad of protests.

He wanted no one, needed no one in his personal life. Dammit, all he wanted was to be left alone to build his ranch. He needed no interruptions, no outside obligations, no woman wheedling him to do this or that. Well, at least that part of his life was secure now. The ranch would remain his.

Right now he wished this night was over, that they were

home. And home meant him at the ranch, her and her kin in town with his grandfather. Damn, he might as well get this over with. He tossed his jacket and tie on the sofa and strode to the bedroom. Rapping twice, he opened the door. He stepped through the opening and stopped. The world seemed to halt with him.

Pearl sat at the dressing table brushing her hair. It fell to her waist in thick waves of dark gold. Candlelight danced across her ivory skin. Brush in hand, she half-turned to meet his gaze. As she did, the thin fabric pulled across perfect breasts, outlining the aureoles and nipples.

Anger melted into something else entirely. Heat pounded through his veins. Blood pumped to his groin. Just like that, he was harder than a flagpole.

She laid the brush on the table and rose as he crossed to her. Her hand reached out to him and he took it in his. Eyes wide with apprehension met his gaze.

Softly, her voice hesitant, she said, "You know I've helped birth babies. I pretty much understand the . . . the way babies get planted. Mary Alice told me some of what might come. It's just that, you see, I don't know what you expect of me or exactly how this coming together really works."

"We start with this." He pulled her to him and kissed her. As at the wedding, her soft lips welcomed him. Her arms hung at her side. She raised her hands to rest lightly on his arms as if for balance.

His mouth guided hers. Teasing, coaxing, his mouth sucked her bottom lip, nipped at it. Her arms slid around his neck and she leaned into him. He ran his tongue across her lips and broke the kiss. Looking into her eyes, he smiled at her. Raw hunger swam in those violet pools.

"Open your lips for me."

She obeyed and he renewed the assault of her mouth. His tongue thrust between her teeth, tasting and probing. A quick learner, she soon followed his lead. Low moans came from her throat or his.

He no longer cared who made the sounds, only that they

increased his desire. His hands sought her hips and pulled her into his arousal. Rocking against her pelvis, he rubbed himself against her.

His lips moved to her cheek then trailed to her neck. Her skin was soft as a babe's. When he was near her ear he whispered, "Can you feel what you do to me?"

"Yes." She nodded slightly and held him close.

"Do you want me to stop?" *Lord, he hoped not.*

She shook her head. "No. I like the kissing. It's different than I imagined, though."

"How?"

"I thought . . . I didn't know it would make my toes tingle and my stomach feel all warm and funny."

He almost lost any reserve he had right then. Trying to rein in his lust, he took a deep breath.

Forgetting he had ever been reluctant to perform his marital duties, he pulled her to him. She smelled like the spring lilacs in his grandmother's garden at the ranch. She smelled like home.

"There's more."

"I know. I'm not afraid of you. Well . . . at least, not very much." She burrowed against his chest. "It's just all so new and, well, awkward."

He took her soft face in his hands. "If I frighten you, will you tell me?"

"Yes." She closed her eyes and swayed into him. "More. Now." As she sought his lips, she thrust her pelvis against his arousal.

He almost exploded with the need to be inside her. His hand found the tie of her gown and released it. At his bidding the fabric slid from her and pooled at her feet. His lips trailed along her neck to her shoulders. When his mouth found her peaked nipple, she gasped. Her skin tasted as sweet as the honey her hair resembled.

Fingers raked through his hair as she held him to her breast. When he moved to the other orb and held the first in his hand, a moan escaped her lips and her breath came in quickening rasps. She arched back as if to give him better access to her breasts.

It almost defeated his intention to proceed slowly. He stepped away from her and fumbled with his shirt studs. In a fervor, he ripped open the shirt and sent studs flying. When he tossed the garment aside, he scooped her up as if she weighed no more than a child. He laid her across the bed and looked at her.

"You are so beautiful." How could he have ever found her plain?

"Thank you." She patted the bed beside her hip. "Aren't you supposed to be here with me?"

He laughed as he sat on the edge of the mattress and tugged off his boots. "Damn, you are the bossiest woman I ever met."

She sent an innocent smile his way. "It was only a question."

He stretched out beside her. "Like hell it was." He nuzzled her neck and his hand found her breast.

She moaned with pleasure, then asked, "Why am I the only one with no clothes on?"

"Another question?" He raised his head and smiled at her. His fingers twirled a strand of her silken blond hair.

A twinkle sparked in her passion-filled eyes and a smile tugged at the corner of her luscious mouth. "Yes, just a question."

"In answer to your *question*, I'll strip off the rest."

He eased off the bed and pulled the top covers from beneath her. A flick of his wrist sent them to the foot of the bed before he unfastened his britches. Her gaze remained on him as he rid himself of clothing.

When he lay beside her, he leaned on his elbow to let his eyes feast on her body. She looked at his manhood and he saw panic on her face. He rolled against her and nuzzled her neck.

"Don't worry," he reassured. "Everything will fit together very well."

"That's what Mary Alice said. It seems unbelievable."

She didn't look convinced, but she opened her mouth with no urging to accept his kiss. Her hands slid up his chest to caress his shoulders. The need surging through his body drove him to hurry. His hand slid between them to touch the nub of her femininity as his mouth possessed her breast. She moaned with pleasure and thrashed her head against the pillow. He slid his finger into her and discovered wet heat.

Although he planned to take more time, give her more pleasure, he could wait no longer to possess this unexpected treasure. He parted her legs with his own and slid a little ways into her. She sheathed him with moist velvet. He took her mouth with his as he began the first strokes, pumping against her. The resistance of her maidenhead broke and he paused for her pain to subside.

She thrust herself at him, her head twisting on the pillow, her eyes squeezed shut. He pushed into her again and again, driving himself to an ecstasy he could not have dreamed. She cried out as he burst with fulfillment. Never could he have believed such rapture possible. How could he have thought he preferred saloon women to this?

Rolling off her, he cradled her head to his chest. He stilled the trembling of his hands and stroked her body, reveling in the satin of her skin.

She pushed her hair from her eyes and sighed.

Sorry for any pain, he consoled her. "I know it hurt this time, but it gets better. I promise." Would it? To his mind nothing could be better than the rapture he just experienced.

In echo, she asked, "Better? That's hard to believe." She moved to her back and folded her hands across her stomach.

After seeing her that first day—walking barefoot on the dusty road, in a baggy drab dress and pushing that handcart—he had trouble reconciling that woman with the beauty who now rested beside him. He smiled to himself and drew a finger down her chest, in the valley between her breasts.

"Are you laughing at me? Did I do it wrong?"

"You were perfect." He kissed her chin. "I think you're probably the most beautiful woman I've ever seen. But I was remembering that first day I saw you. Where did you get that dress you wore?"

"It was Granny's." When he waited, she sighed and continued. "When I was twelve and had a good start on, um, filling out, Mama told me I had to be careful not to attract men. She warned me since I was born out of wedlock, men would assume I had no morals." She rolled her eyes. "It was something I'd already noticed."

He frowned. "Men made advances to you? Because your parents weren't married?"

"Yes, men of all ages, even then. I got my height and figure early, so I looked a lot older. More than Sarah, although she looks a lot like I did at her age. Only she's softer, sweeter."

He doubted that but offered no argument. "So you disguised yourself?"

"About then Mama died, so I took her clothes to wear. They were too large, but I soon grew into them. Then I started wearing Granny's dresses. I also put grease on my hair and kind of frizzed it out around my face. I bound my breasts so they wouldn't show so much."

"That's incredible. Weren't you uncomfortable?"

"Phfft. Not half as much as in that corset I wore today, I can tell you."

"Then don't wear it."

She leaned on her elbow to look him in the eye. "You truly wouldn't mind?"

"Of course not." He took her breasts in his hands. "That corset does push these beauties into a nice shape, though." He lowered her to her back and demonstrated his admiration.

Pearl thought nothing could feel as wonderful as making love with Drake. The pain was less than she expected, the pleasure far greater. When his arousal grew against her thigh, she gasped. At once heat spread from her stomach to the moist juncture of her thighs.

Belle told her to expect him to want more than one time. Pearl would never let Drake learn Belle knew so much, but she was grateful for the other woman's instruction. In the short time Belle worked at Roxie's, she learned things that surprised even Mary Alice after her ten years of marriage.

Drake moved from one breast to the other. She slid her arms across his shoulders and massaged his back, urging him onward.

She thought she would explode. The need overwhelmed her. The power of her desire astonished her. She clawed at his back to urge him to her. "More. Oh, hurry. Can't you hurry?"

Just before he lowered his head, he looked at her and said, "Darlin', we have all night."

Eight

As the landscape whizzed past the train window, Pearl savored the delights of her wedding night. Neither she nor Drake had gotten much sleep. Yet she felt truly alive.

At first she feared she had been too brazen last night in their lovemaking. With a smile she remembered her husband's reaction when she voiced her concern. He reassured her with some fairly brazen suggestions of his own and demonstrated their application.

But now her muscles complained of unaccustomed activities and her mind numbed from lack of sleep. The steady thrumming of the wheels against the track coupled with the rhythmic sway of the train soon had her nodding. Fighting to stay awake lest she miss some interesting part of the trip, she soon lost her battle.

Later, she started awake to find Drake missing and the engine lagging. The train continued to climb and she felt the further slowing of the engine as it labored up a steep incline. Through the window she looked down into a beautiful green valley.

In the seat ahead of hers, Sarah and Belle talked quietly. Lex dozed across the aisle. No matter, she had the little gun Drake gave her. To reassure herself she patted her thigh where the derringer rested in the garter holster Belle provided.

She rose and made her way to the privy at the end of the car. Afterward, she splashed a bit of water on her face to chase the drowsiness. The speed of the train increased with the downward slope of the track and she balanced herself against the sway.

When she stepped into the narrow hallway outside the toilet, a scratchy bag fell over her head and some sort of closure drew tight against her throat. Cloth muffled her screech of surprise. Someone with long arms and the strength of an ox imprisoned her flailing arms. She struggled, only to feel herself dragged to the vestibule at the end of the car.

Rushing wind tugged at her skirts. Dear Lord, would she be thrown from the train? She kicked furiously but her only reward was a grunt of pain from her assailant.

From close to her ear she recognized a familiar voice, "You won't get away this time, pig girl."

Jug? Jug Eggers? How could it be? After a lifetime of his taunts, she would know that voice anywhere. Why was he here? And why would he do this to her? Pearl used all her strength to fight him. The wind rushed at her. She felt herself pushed, propelled toward the flow of air. She must stop him and save herself. But how?

With a sudden spurt of strength, she twisted and shoved. She heard a scream. Her arms dropped free and she hurtled through space. Desperately, she flailed for any grip, anything to stop her fall from the train.

Drake gave Midnight a pat as he spoke to his brother-in-law.

"Things look great. If you need any help or get tired of this, come get me. I'll come back anyway in an hour or so. Then you can take a turn watching the sights."

He left Storm with the horses and walked through the two passenger cars separating the boxcar from the coach in which the rest of his new family rode. As he stepped across the last of the connecting vestibules, movement startled him.

The tip of a foot on the bottom step of the open rail surprised him more. Good Lord. He recognized that foot.

He leaned over the railing and peered around the side. Even with a rough sack over her head, he also recognized his wife.

She hung precariously from the outside of the train, both hands gripping the thin metal rail functioning as handhold for passengers entering the train. The tip of one foot balanced on the bottom step. Her other leg dangled, flung helplessly awry by the force of air pouring off the fast-moving train.

Bracing himself against the metal railing, he grabbed her and shouted. "Pearl! I've got you."

He pulled at her arm but her hands still clung to the metal lifeline. He ripped the sack from her head with one hand. With all his strength, he hauled her toward him. They crashed to the hard floor of the open vestibule, Pearl cushioned by his body. His arms remained around her. He moved his hands over her back, comforting her, checking her, reassuring them both of her safety.

She sobbed into his chest, "I couldn't hold on much longer. I thought sure I was going to fall."

"It's all right, honey. You're all right now." He sat up and pulled her onto his lap, rocking her as a mother does a babe. "Can you tell me what happened?"

Pearl recounted all she knew of her attacker. "The bag muffled my hearing, but I'm sure I recognized the voice. It sounded like Jug Eggers. But why would he be here?"

"Wasn't he one of those men you shot at the first day I saw you in Piper's Hollow?"

She nodded and clung to him. "Yes. The two Ainsworths are just no account hangers on. Jug is the mean one." She raised her head to meet his gaze. "Oh, my. I . . . I think he must have fallen off the train."

He pulled her head back to his chest. "You could have been killed."

His hand grasped the jute bag he had flung from her head. "This answers one question, the identity of one of the men who followed you in the woods." He fished her new hat from the bag.

"I thought then they wanted only to scare me. Maybe they intended to kill me then. Today he said 'this time' I wouldn't get away." She took the hat and straightened the cloth flowers.

"Are you carrying the derringer I gave you?" He brushed some dusty smudges from her face.

She nodded and raised her skirt to show him the garter holster. "It's right here. But I didn't have a chance to use it. And I dropped my new gloves and reticule."

He had laughed when she showed him the holster the first time. He wondered where she found it. Probably from Belle. A woman in Belle's line of work would know about such things. He had kept thoughts of his wife's make-believe cousin to himself.

Drake kissed the top of her head, then slid her from him so they could stand. "We'll look for them on our way."

Reluctant to let her go, he slipped his arms around her for a quick embrace.

As she slid from his embrace, she cried, "There they are."

Her gloves and reticule lay just outside the door to the washroom. He scooped them up and returned them to his bride. His hand found hers and they moved into the coach. She'd experienced a terrible ordeal. Wouldn't hurt her to have a little pampering for a change. Hell, even his heart still pounded.

Pearl sat and leaned her head back against the seat with a sigh. Sarah and Belle turned in their seat and their eyes widened at the sight Pearl made. She held her hat and her hairdo tumbled undone across her shoulders. He brushed gently at another spot of dust on her face.

Sarah asked, "What's wrong? Your jacket is torn and you look white as a ghost."

Drake massaged Pearl's hands. "Almost a ghost. Someone tried to push her off the train."

Both women cried, "No!"

Sarah asked, "Who would do such a thing?"

Tears swam in Pearl's eyes. She straightened in the seat and took a deep breath before she answered. "I think it was Jug. Jug Eggers. At least, it sounded like him."

The commotion had roused Lex. "You didn't see him?"

Drake held up the sack used to hood Pearl's head. Sarah and Belle gasped again, but Lex took it from his cousin's hand.

"Held oats for horses."

Drake nodded his agreement. "Yeah. The kind you find everywhere." Drake reclaimed it and tucked it into his jacket pocket. "We think the person who tried to push Pearl fell off the train himself." He stopped massaging Pearl's hands and worked up her arms to her shoulders.

Lex stepped to the aisle. "I'll find the conductor and let him know. If the fall didn't kill the man, he'll need doctoring. At least until he gets to trial."

A horrified conductor assured Pearl things like this did not happen on the Memphis and Charleston Railroad—especially not on his run. Muttering to himself and shaking his head, he bustled off to alert his coworkers. Lex left to let Storm know about the attack and warn him to stay on alert for trouble.

"Why would anyone want me dead?" She looked shaken and bewildered, like a lost child. Drake gently urged her head to his shoulder.

Pearl said, "I thought we would be safe once we left Piper's Hollow. Then there was the rock slide, now this." She snuffled into her hankie. "Oh, I'm so sorry. I never should have involved you and Lex. Truly, I thought we would be fine once we left Piper's Hollow. Now trouble's followed us. I'm so sorry."

"Pearl, it's not your fault. You've done nothing to merit this treatment." Damn, here she was apologizing to him when he failed his responsibility to keep his wife and family safe.

"There must be something I've done, but I just can't think what."

Sarah patted Pearl's shoulder reassuringly. "It's over now, Sister. I doubt Jug will be in any shape to cause us more trouble."

Belle added, "Whether he died or was only injured, at least Jug's fall will stop the attacks."

Pearl shook her head as she met his gaze. "There were *two* men that night in the woods, *two* men at the rock slide."

"Damn, how did Jug manage it?" Drake questioned. "He must have been watching from the next car this whole trip. The nerve of the bast—the man, coming after you in broad daylight. Sorry I didn't do a better job protecting you."

She wiped her eyes again, then smiled up at him. "You can't be everywhere. I know you and Lex have been on guard the whole trip."

He nodded, pleased that for once she forgot to be so damned independent. "And we'll keep watching, for all the good it did you today."

Drake sat beside his wife, trying to reassure her. Yet the day's events staggered him. He accepted full blame for the incident that almost ended in her death. The bottom fell out of his stomach with the memory.

Thank God he walked by when he did. In only minutes she surely would have fallen. The thought of anyone plunging down the mountainside made him physically ill. But for it almost to have been her left him spitless. He leaned forward and rested his head in his hands, elbows braced against his knees.

A week ago he didn't know her. For all that he bedded her, he barely knew her now. Bound to her by more than marriage vows, the passion they shared the night before burned in his memory.

Within the span of a few days, his life had forever changed in so many ways. He saved his ranch. Found a wife. Gained a large family. The possibility even existed that he started his own child in this woman beside him.

But he did not know her, the way she felt and thought. Hell, he'd misjudged her and her entire situation from the very beginning. Remembering the way he had talked to Lex about her when they first met made him feel small. Damn. He had a lot to learn about being a family man.

He leaned back and took her fingers back in his, stroking them with his thumb. She smiled and cradled his hand with hers.

Trying to soothe her and probe at the same time, he said,

"Pearl, there's got to be answers to this. Think back. Could this be from a grudge that started long ago?"

"I've told you about the only people who have grudges against me, and they wouldn't have done this. This started when Granny died. I don't see how her dying caused it, but it did."

"Maybe. Or it could be coincidence. Maybe the opportunity wasn't there before. Did anything else change about then?"

"Don't you think I've tried to remember?" She twisted her hands from his and wrung them in frustration. "Mean as Jug was, he wasn't bright enough to try something like this on his own."

Belle snorted. "That's the truth. The man was mean as a snake, but hadn't the brains of a flea. He definitely took orders from someone else."

Pearl chewed her bottom lip and tears filled her eyes again. "But why would anyone want to kill me? I've never hurt anyone."

Sarah kneeled on her seat and leaned over the back to pat Pearl's arm. "Of course you've never hurt anyone. You're a healer. You've helped most of the people you know."

"And many who were strangers," Belle added.

"Maybe it's someone you went to school with. An old grudge?" He knew he grasped at straws with that idea.

Pearl and her sister exchanged sorrowful looks before Pearl answered. "I didn't go to school, except for a few months. The kids made fun of me, chased me, and called me names. I refused to go back."

What a sad life she had led. He compared it to his own. Damn. "But you seem so intelligent and well-read."

She lowered her eyes modestly, a first for her. "Thank you. Evan's wife taught me. She had lots of books from when she was at school in Bowling Green." She raised her gaze to meet his. "You know, in Kentucky? Anyway, she taught me more than I could have learned at the little Piper's Hollow school."

Another piece of the Pearl puzzle clicked into place. "Did she teach Sarah and Storm also?"

She shook her head. "Mrs. Cummins died when they were small. She had given me a lot of books, though. I taught Sarah and Storm. They're both very bright," she added like a proud mother hen.

He had another idea. "Belle, could this have anything to do with you coming to stay with Pearl?"

Belle looked as if he had slapped her. He saw panic in her eyes so great it bordered on terror. Before she could answer, Pearl leapt to her defense.

"It has nothing to do with her," Pearl snapped. She inhaled and continued, "Belle only came to stay with us a few days before you showed up. This started earlier. It's directed at me. Or, maybe at my brother and sister and me."

Grasping at straws, he remembered an earlier encounter. "You know that first time I saw you in Piper's Hollow with your cart? Jug called you 'pig girl.' Could this have anything to do with that? What that was about?"

Drake watched Pearl blush red as a chili pepper.

"That—it's nothing. Nothing that's important now. Just what children used to call me years ago. It couldn't have anything to do with this."

Drake would have asked more, but Lex came back to the coach.

"Storm barred the door behind me. He won't let anyone in but us or the conductor." He laughed. "At that, I think the conductor will have to do some fast talking to convince that boy to open the door."

Drake sat lost in thought. He had wanted her to be unworthy of his attention or devotion, someone easy to ignore. Then, when he left her at his grandfather's, no guilt would plague him. This marriage was not working out as he'd planned.

No one overlooked the woman beside him. Lex's accusation back in Piper's Hollow haunted him. True, he first

regarded Pearl as no more than a brood mare. Damn. What an
ass he'd been.

She had her own fears and dreams. Did she include him in
her dreams? Hell, no. She only wanted to escape whatever
demons pursued her and get her family to safety. She accepted him as the means to that end.

And what did he want? His dream of the greatest ranch in
Texas flashed into his mind. That dream sustained him through
tough times, through times so hard many of his neighbors gave
up and moved on. He clung to his goal, but this marriage business presented a new set of problems. He trod foreign ground
here. New rules, new problems, new people.

Realization hammered at him. This woman also had
dreams, feelings, needs. So did each of the three people in her
family. He closed his eyes and leaned his head back.

Dear God, what had he done?

Sarah's question broke through his reverie. "Could I go talk
to Storm?"

Lex stood. "Sure thing. I'll go with you. Need to help you
between the cars and make certain there're no more masked
men waiting."

When he returned, Lex took Sarah's seat beside Belle.
Their conversation was too quiet to overhear. Drake thought
Lex asked for trouble there. He exhaled with irritation at himself. What right had he to criticize his cousin when he'd made
such a mess for himself?

Pearl watched the landscape change as the miles clicked
away. If not for the threat that hung over them, the trip would
be a wonderful experience. She struggled to sleep in her seat
without success.

Lex took turns with Drake so that one of them stayed on
watch throughout the night. It was too hot for comfort with
the windows closed, too dirty and breezy with them opened.
After the threat to Pearl, no one rested comfortably. By
morning, their group presented a bedraggled and weary-
eyed sight.

When the train slowed, Drake turned to her. "I'll go get the kids. We're changing trains here. From Memphis we'll be on one of the new Pullman Palace cars."

After a hurried breakfast in the station restaurant they boarded their car, the Fort Wilmington. Pearl gasped in surprise when she stepped into the car. Polished walnut with ornate inlays covered every wall and ceiling. Elegant brass lamps hung from the ceiling ready to light the evening.

"Palace car is a good name. It's as fancy as the hotel in Chattanooga. Maybe fancier."

"We were in luck," Drake spoke as he guided Pearl to an alcove of two pairs of facing seats upholstered in luxurious plush. "This is a new car. Seventy feet long and the latest of everything."

Lex helped Belle with her small bag. "We'll have a little more privacy from here on. And they'll bring us our meals here. Unless you'd prefer going forward to the dining car?"

"Law, no. Who'd want to leave this?"

Lex sketched a brief bow. "Drake will leave you ladies for a bit while I stand watch. We want Storm to see the ferry crossing of the Mississippi."

Pearl settled into her seat, pleased at the consideration Drake showed her and her family. They left Memphis and crossed the great river a few cars at a time on a large, low ferry. Sarah and Storm were just as excited as she and Belle. Lex rejoined them, saying he'd act guard from his seat.

Sarah asked Lex, "How can this boat support the train for such a long way without sinking?"

Pearl wondered the same thing as she saw the water lapping far too close for comfort.

"Don't worry," Lex assured Sarah and flashed a smile to the other women. "It's a little bumpy landing and joining the engine, but we're safe enough."

Maybe so, but Pearl thought she held her breath all the way across. Her stomach lurched as they navigated the long stretch of water, which was far wider than any other river they had crossed. Large paddle wheel boats, small crafts, and barges sailed up and down while the large ferry glided across. Reading about rivers certainly fell short of seeing one.

The trip left her more idle time than ever in her life. She felt lost without her baking, her healing, the animals, and her garden. She tried to sew, but the movement of the train left her with pricked fingers and unsatisfactory seams. After mending her traveling suit jacket, she gave up and put away her sewing box.

She missed having her house and her things about her. At least she had some of her favorites packed to ease her way in her new home. How she hoped that Tom found happiness and peace in the cabin she left, and that Roxie would find a happier place.

As if in answer to her own thoughts, Sarah sat beside her. "I wonder if Mama left Piper's Hollow yet."

Pearl took her sister's hand. "By now she's probably in St. Louis. I'll bet she has new clothes and a nice place to live."

She hated the white lie, but sought to ease Sarah's mind. "You know, that man Cal wants Rochelle as his partner in a prosperous saloon. Life will be much easier for her now." Lie or no, it brightened her sister's face.

"He came with her one day, Cal did. He seemed nice, not oily like some men who work in saloons. Mama said she'd write to me in Kincaid Springs as soon as she's settled."

"She'll have a better life." Pearl hoped she spoke the truth this time.

The rest of the trip passed without incident, but tension plagued them. Drake insisted neither Pearl nor Sarah ever be alone during the day. He escorted Storm to and from the horse car. Lex stuck like glue to Belle. Either Drake or Lex was in the coach at all times.

At night, while the women slept in cozy beds made from the chair seats, Lex and Drake stood watch. With the knowledge a second man might be involved, they feared another attack on Pearl or one of her family. Although they took turns napping during the day, anxiety and loss of sleep left both Lex and Drake exhausted.

People changed trains in Little Rock and Texarkana, but Drake somehow had arranged for the Fort Wilmington to travel all the way to Kincaid Springs with them as passengers. When it seemed they had ridden forever, Drake gave a shout, "Yee-haw! We're crossing into Texas now."

The newcomers all crowded against the window. To Pearl the landscape looked like that they'd seen for hours.

"How can you tell?" she asked.

A nod of his head indicated the window. "This is the Sabine River crossing. That's the state line."

"Been raining some," Lex said.

Murky water swirled below the bridge. Though not as large as the Mississippi, its width cut an impressive swath from Pearl's view.

"Is this what your ranch is like, this dirt?"

"No. Our area has soil that's darker. Grayish brown. Lots of limestone in the area."

"So, your rivers are brown?"

He laughed. "No, honey. Ours run clean and clear and cold. Lots of springs around, too."

His eyes sparkled when he talked of his home. The planes of his face softened, shaving years from his age and highlighting the love for his land. The train stopped at Dennison to let more travelers join or leave the coach.

Near Fort Worth, the landscape changed from woodlands to open range ribboned by trees and streams. It seemed to Pearl the sky became bluer, the sun brighter with each passing hour. Drake and Lex became more cheerful and restless with every mile.

Drake looked ready to dance as he leaned near. "The car holding the horses, this car, and a few others will be switched in Austin for the tap line to Kincaid Springs."

"What's a tap line?" she asked.

"Like a dead end, the train line runs out to Kincaid Springs but no further. Train turns around and goes back to Austin."

Lex overheard and nodded. "Can't say I'll be sorry to see the last of this train. It's been too long since we've seen home."

In spite of her fatigue, fear of the unknown gripped Pearl. She brushed at her mended traveling suit and adjusted her battered hat. Questions bombarded her mind.

What would Drake's family think of her? Would they accept her or think of her and her family as an unwanted burden?

Nine

The men helped the four women down the steps from the railroad car. "We'll see to the baggage later"—Drake looked around anxiously—"Grandpa and Aunt Lily will be here somewhere. Lex's parents, too. And Jorge and Vincente are supposed to come from the ranch to help with the horses."

Sure enough, a crowd of people stood at the end of the station platform.

"There," said Lex, nodding toward the depot as he guided Belle toward a distinguished looking couple.

Pearl picked out Drake's grandfather at once. He looked as she imagined Drake would in thirty or forty years, tall and straight with a mustache to match his mane of white hair. Drake waved and hurried his new family to meet the old.

Grandpa thumped Drake on the back and said, "Well, it's about time you got back, and just in time for your birthday." He took Pearl's hand. "This must be the new Mrs. Drake Kincaid. What a lovely woman you are, my dear."

In all her twenty-six years, no one ever called her "lovely." Pearl hoped he meant it and loved him at once for even saying it.

"Thank you, Judge Kincaid. I've heard a lot about you from Evan Cummins. And from Drake and Lex, of course."

"Now, now. Call me Grandpa." He gestured to all his new family, "All of you, call me Grandpa. We're family here."

Sarah chewed her lip and nodded. Storm looked terrified.

Belle looked as if she just grabbed the brass ring on the carousel.

Pearl smiled at the elder Kincaid. "Thank you, Grandpa. It's nice of you to welcome us."

"It's good to have you finally here. I'd love to see Evan again. We had some high old times in our day. Perhaps you'll fill me in on him later. Now let me introduce you to the rest of your family. Rosilee and Samuel Tremont are Lex's parents."

Pearl nodded to the couple, who smiled and exchanged pleasantries. Their eyes hardly left their son, and Pearl read the questions as they looked from Lex to Belle. Rosilee Tremont shared her son's auburn hair, but her eyes were the soft blue of her father. Samuel's stocky build made him seem larger than his son in spite of standing an inch or so shorter.

Grandpa turned to the red-haired woman by his side. "And this is my youngest daughter, Lily Stephens."

"Oh, my." Pearl couldn't suppress her surprise. "I do apologize, but I expected Drake's aunt to be an older woman." Realizing her gaffe, she added, "It's a pleasure to meet you."

Lily's tight-lipped mouth twisted open to bite out, "My age has nothing to do with anything. I take care of my father and run his household." Several inches shorter than Pearl, the woman would have been beautiful if not for the sour lemon twist to her mouth and hard look in her gray eyes.

Bewildered by Lily's snappish speech, Pearl stammered, "I'm sure you do a wonderful job."

Before she could apologize again, Grandpa broke in. "Lily was a late blessing to Katherine and me, born only five years before Drake and seven before Lex. When Lily lost her husband, my darling wife had fallen ill. Lily came to live with us to help out, and has ridden herd on me since Katherine's death."

While Pearl's mind whirled with all the new faces, Drake introduced Sarah, Storm, and Belle to his family.

The group moved toward two buggies and a wagon. Grandpa left servants gathering baggage into the wagon and the family walked toward the buggies. Drake excused himself to see the horses safely unloaded.

When Storm hesitated at the side of the buggy, Grandpa asked him, "What's wrong, son?"

"I should stay with the horses."

Drake shook his head. "Vincente and Jorge will help get them off the car and to the ranch. You don't have to help." He shrugged. "But you can stay if you wish. If it's all right with your sister."

Pearl recognized the look of longing in her brother's eyes. He hated crowds and loved horses. "Of course." She turned to her host and hostess. "Storm is gifted with animals."

"That's true," Drake assured them. "He cared for them most of the trip. Lex, why don't you go on with your folks to Grandpa's. Storm and I'll bring your horse round later."

Lex tipped his hat in a thank you.

Pearl's stomach tightened into a worry ball when she realized Drake intended her to go with his family while he remained at the station unloading the horses. She had to go with this waspish woman to her home. At least Grandpa and Lex's parents acted friendly.

Maybe it wouldn't be too bad. How long could it take to unload horses? Before she knew it, she would be in her own home at the ranch.

The ride to Grandpa's house took only a few moments, but Pearl liked the looks of the town. Most of the homes appeared neat, the businesses prosperous and well kept. People waved or nodded as the buggies drove by.

Her heart grew lighter and the worry lessened. This looked exactly the sort of place she dreamed. Surely they would have a fresh start here. Encouraged, she smiled and nodded at the people they passed.

Grandpa guided the buggy up a long, tree-lined drive. Ahead sat a huge building. Larger than Oak Haven in Tennessee. Large enough for a castle. Surely that couldn't be Grandpa's house?

But it was. A large porch hugged the front and sides of the

frame structure. Dormered windows on the roof above the second story indicated a smaller third story, including the peaked turret at one side.

Oh, God help her. She had no idea Drake's family was so wealthy. How could she have been so stupid? The clues were there. His clothes were from better cloth than any she had seen before. He always carried cash money and seldom asked the cost of things. The special cattle car for the horses and fancy sleeping car on the train must have cost the earth. She'd been so intent on getting her family safely away for a new start in life that she hadn't considered Drake's bank account.

The chasm between them widened. She remembered the list of expenses she had kept to account for every cent he spent on behalf of her and her family. How foolish it would seem. Those sums probably meant nothing to him.

They meant a great deal to her. A great deal.

A servant rushed down the sweeping front steps. Grandpa helped Lily from the carriage while the servant rushed to help Pearl.

As she passed them, Belle leaned near Pearl and whispered, "Looks like a hotel, don't it?"

Sarah, eyes wide with wonder, nodded and added, "Or a palace."

Her back straight, Pearl followed the others through the portal into the foyer. The click of their slippers on the marble echoed through the entry hall. The polished surface of a cherry table reflected the parasol and gloves Lily tossed there.

Sarah, eyes still wide in her pale face, grasped Pearl's hand tightly. Belle grew silent and looked around with a stunned stare. Pearl knew she must wear a similar expression.

Lily called to a maid, "Ellen, show our guests their rooms." She faced the three newcomers. "You probably want to freshen up. I've put you all in the same part of the house, overlooking the gardens. Dinner will be at eight."

Grandpa must have sensed their distress. "Now don't you ladies worry your heads. If they aren't here in time for dinner, Drake and Storm will be back by nightfall. You rest up a bit and come down when you're ready. We'll be gabbing in the drawing room."

Pearl felt abandoned and bewildered as she followed Ellen up the stairs. Thin as a brown-haired stick, the maid moved with a plodding gait. The other two women trailed Pearl, and not a sound came from their feet treading the thick rugs of the upper hall. Sarah and Belle were each assigned a room along the central hallway and Ellen indicated which would be Storm's chamber. The maid showed Pearl the room she and Drake would share at the end of the passage.

Not a room. A group of rooms. Ellen held the door for Pearl and said, "These be your rooms, Missus Kincaid. Your things will be along in a bit."

Tentatively, Pearl let her fingertips touch the pale blue moiré covering the walls. Imagine, cloth on a wall. And not a quilt, either, like folks back in Tennessee used to keep the cold winter winds out. All she could manage was a simple, "Thank you, Ellen."

Ellen made a quick inspection of the area, then gestured to the second room. "There's water in the pitcher on the chest there if you want to have a wash before you lie down. Or, the bathing room be at the end of the hall."

Their honeymoon suite in Chattanooga boasted a bathing room, and Drake told her Grandpa's house had two. She should have suspected his wealth then.

She wondered how she would find her way in this huge home. Panic prompted her to ask, "Will someone call us for dinner?"

The young woman's brow furrowed. "I s'pose I can come for you."

"Oh, yes, would you?" Lord, she hadn't meant to sound so desperate. She straightened herself and added, "I'd hate to be late for dinner my first evening here."

The maidservant left and Pearl waited a bit before she opened the door a crack. When she peeked out, she saw Sarah and Belle tiptoeing toward her. She gestured for them to enter and held the door wide.

Sarah fairly gushed in a breathy whisper, "Sister, you should see the room they put me in. It's like one for a fairy princess. It's all in shades of pink with a beautiful white counterpane on the bed and curtains hanging from the top."

Belle nodded. "Mine, too, 'cept it's green with a darker green coverlet and curtains. I never saw nothing so fancy." Her eyes widened as she revolved slowly. "Except this. Lordy, this is as big as most houses I've seen."

"I know." Pearl looked into a dressing room. Worry furrowed her brow. She sat in a silk upholstered chair finer than any she had ever seen. As she held her hands in her lap, it was all she could do to keep from crying.

Sarah rushed over and knelt in front of her. "Sister, what's wrong? Are you ill?"

She shook her head, afraid she would give in to the desperation chilling her blood. "Why would a man who lives in a place like this choose me?"

"Because you're special." Sarah, always a romantic, looked wistful. "He must have been attracted to you the minute he saw you."

Pearl shook her head. "No. Remember? He said he had to marry or lose everything. Why wouldn't he marry someone from here? Or someone who grew up the same way he did?"

With a wave of dismissal, Belle assured her, "Why worry about it? You're here, Sarah and Storm and I are here with you. Be thankful for your good fortune. Lord knows I am."

"I—I am, too. At least, I think I am. But I don't understand."

And she didn't. She mulled it over, trying to look at it from every angle. No matter how she viewed her situation with Drake, it made no sense.

Why did he choose her? Why not marry a beautiful miss from a good family with wealth? What madness possessed him to marry her instead?

Ellen knocked on her door to announce dinner, then hurried back downstairs. When the three women went down for dinner, they found Storm and Drake in the foyer beating the dust from their clothes.

Pearl rushed to Drake with relief. "Thank heavens you're back." Drat, she hadn't meant to sound critical—or so needful.

Drake gave her a puzzled look, then offered his arm.

She took his arm and asked, "The horses are all settled in fine?"

"Great. And Storm was a big help."

Her brother beamed. "Wait 'til you see the ranch. You won't believe how big it is." He would have said more, but their host came into the hall to greet them.

"Ah, good," Grandpa beamed at them. "We were just going in to dinner." He shepherded the group toward the dining room.

Light from dozens of candles in the massive chandelier danced across the spotless white damask cloth. More crystal and silver glittered at the place settings than Pearl had seen in the hotel the night of her honeymoon. Ten chairs were placed for tonight's guests, but the table provided ample room for a larger group.

Maybe she should have changed from her traveling suit. Lily wore an ice blue taffeta dress trimmed in lace. Her eyes inventoried the other guests, and she exhaled with relief that Rosilee Tremont still wore the same muted afternoon dress she had worn to the depot.

Once again she thanked her lucky stars for the training given her by Pearl Cummins. At the time it seemed like play-acting, for she never dreamed she would put those sessions to use. Now she found herself in a setting even fancier than Mrs. Cummins had imagined.

Lily fluttered about the room, imperiously delivering seating instructions. Drake helped Pearl with her chair before he took his seat down the table and across from her. She sat to the right of Grandpa, with Lex's father at her right.

Sarah, across from her, looked pale and worried. Further down the table at the prune-faced Lily's right, Storm looked ready to bolt. She smiled at him, hoping she conveyed more confidence than she felt.

Of the four from Tennessee, only Belle looked genuinely happy. Seated two chairs down from Pearl between Samuel Tremont and Lex, she faced Rosilee. Judging from her cheerful smile, Belle felt very pleased with their elegant surroundings and the company she shared.

Lily rang a bell and Ellen served bowls of soup. In a few minutes, a plump older woman Lily addressed as Polly carried in a large platter of beef and served each guest. Ellen followed with bowls of vegetables. When Pearl thought she could hold no more, Polly returned to serve slabs of cake.

Throughout dinner, Drake and Lex entranced their family with tales of the trip and threats against them—the rockslide, the attack on the train, and earlier attempts on Pearl and her home. Drake's eyes sparkled with mirth as he explained his first sight of her in Piper's Hollow. When he mentioned her violet eyes, his voice softened. Pearl's heart gave a flip, and warmth flooded her. Maybe, just maybe, he did find something about her special.

Lily gasped in shock at the description of Pearl firing her gun, but Lex's parents showed only concern for Pearl's safety and Grandpa slapped his leg with glee. Pearl like to have died of shame at Drake's vivid description of her attire and her gun. At least Drake and Lex described her bravery as something they admired. The other salve to her pride came when Drake and Lex described how she helped people on the train with her medicines.

"I reckon this is about the trouble on the train." Grandpa pulled a sheet of paper from his pocket. "Sheriff Liles got this wire yesterday." He handed the note to Drake.

Drake scanned the page, then raised his eyes to Pearl. "From the railroad investigation." He looked down the table toward Lex, "It's about the attack on Pearl. They found the body of the man who tried to throw her off the train. Broke his neck in the fall. Serves the sorry b—serves him right."

Pearl's stomach did a flip. "Was it Jug?"

"Yep. Had some papers on him. They think he killed a railroad brakeman and stole his clothes. That's why no one noticed him waiting for you."

Grandpa patted Pearl's hand. "So, maybe this terrorizing is all behind you."

Drake shook his head. "No, Grandpa. There's at least one other man involved. And we have no idea who he is—or where."

"You're in Kincaid territory now and we take care of our own. Things will be better from now on, girl."

"Thank you, Grandpa. I hope I don't bring trouble to your family."

"We're *your* family now. Don't forget that."

The evening passed tortuously slow for Pearl. She worried over each course served, over each fork and spoon she used. Glances down the table assured her Storm and Sarah shared her discomfort with the formality of the meal. Even Belle's smile looked strained by the end of the meal. Drake's every word or movement registered in Pearl's mind.

How she wished they were away from this elaborate setting and at the ranch where they would live. Perhaps then she could relax, could draw a deep breath without fear of embarrassing herself or her new husband.

Relieved when the meal ended, Pearl followed the others into the parlor.

Lex guided Belle to the piano. "Please, play for us. And sing."

"Sing?" Belle's hand flew to her throat. "Not for all these people. I couldn't."

"Oh, yes, my dear, do." Rosilee Tremont urged.

Lily clapped her hands in delight. "You sing and play? How lovely. Please serenade us."

For the next half-hour or so, Belle treated her small audience to a concert. Appearing hesitant at first, she soon lost herself in the music.

Pearl contented herself observing the other listeners. Drake appeared attentive, but the tiny muscle twitching in his jaw revealed his impatience. From Storm's wriggling,

Pearl recognized her brother's "I hate crowds" signs. Sarah sat with hands folded in her lap, a happy smile lighting her lovely face. Even Lily looked pleased, her face softening to let her beauty shine through.

Lex sat enraptured, his gaze never leaving Belle. Sam Tremont's concerned frown exposed his alarm for the blossoming relationship between his only child and a stranger from nowhere. Pearl knew Lex and his parents would be shocked, perhaps even angry and disgusted, if they knew Belle's background. Loyal to her new friend, Pearl hoped Belle would be spared heartbreak and censure in their new home.

When the Tremonts left and the other men excused themselves to discuss business, the women made their way upstairs. Pearl's heart beat faster with each step. When would Drake join her? They had not made love since their wedding night. Since that time they had not even been alone in a place that permitted intimacy.

The sisters bid Belle goodnight at her door. Sarah gave Pearl a tour of the "princess" room before they, too, said goodnight. The few steps to her own quarters seemed very lonely.

In a dressing area the size of her cabin bedroom, she hurried through her evening toilette and donned her nightdress. She didn't have a proper wrapper to cover her nightie, so she crossed her arms as she paced into the sitting room. She sat first in a dark blue velvet lady's chair, then tried the matching larger chair near the fireplace. She attempted to read, but the words made no sense to her agitated mind. After several minutes, she closed the book and resumed pacing.

When ten minutes passed, she lowered the wick of the sitting room lamp and moved into the bedroom. With care, she turned back the heavy blue coverlet and smoothed the bed covers. The bedside lamp shed the only light in the suite. It lent a soft glow to the bed. Pearl stood lost in thought.

Lily's slights of the evening still stung. Her questions about Pearl's education left little doubt she found her new relative inferior. When Drake explained about Pearl's baking, Lily's nose wrinkled in disapproval. When Lex commented on Pearl's healing abilities, Lily commented about backwoods primitive methods being outdated.

The woman acted as if Pearl and her family were intruders, inferiors. Pearl was not surprised to be treated as an outsider. In fact, she was used to it. The surprise came that Drake's own aunt treated her so and that he seemed not to notice. Not wanting to embarrass her husband on her first night here, she tolerated the snubs and digs tonight.

No matter. When they were safely on the ranch, they probably would see Aunt Lily only occasionally at family get-togethers. She supposed she could tolerate the waspy woman in small doses.

Pearl fluffed bed pillows, then tried the mattress. Over twice the thickness of her own feather bed, this one felt like a cloud. That realization upset her further. The years it took to save feathers and down for her own mattress seemed pointless now. Pride she had felt in providing what she thought of as her own fine dowry bedding seemed foolish in this luxurious room. Perhaps the ranch was not so lavishly furnished. Her bedding might be needed there. Hope seeped through to soothe her wounded dignity.

The lamp burned low. She climbed into bed. So far, marriage was nothing like she expected.

Drake paced in front of the window. Earlier Lex and Uncle Samuel had gathered Aunt Rosilee and left for their homes and Storm climbed the stairs to his bed. Aunt Lily pled her usual headache coming on and retired. By now Lex would be tucked into his rooms over the law office. Unless Aunt Rosilee and Uncle Samuel chose to stay in town with their son tonight, they would be well on the way to their ranch. From his wing chair near the fireplace, Grandpa's concern showed on his face.

Drake faced his grandfather. "You see why I'm worried not

just about Pearl, but also her family. Storm and I stopped by to see Sheriff Liles, but he can't be everywhere. I figure they're safer here in town where there'll always be people around. The Sheriff will keep an eye on things, too."

"You're making a mistake, Son. Your bride won't take kindly to being dumped here while you go off to the ranch."

"She won't mind. I can't leave her and her kin alone at the ranch with only Maria and Miguel to watch after them. I need all the hands rounding up the herd."

"That's where you're making the mistake. Hire more hands. Or let Vincente handle things a while longer. He's done fine rounding up cattle while you were gone."

"Now, we've gone over this, Grandpa. With all the changes in the wind, I figure this will be the last big drive from this area. There's too much riding on it. Bingham and Holsapple are counting on me to get their cattle to Kansas with mine."

"It's a hard place you've made for yourself. I think that girl up there deserves your first loyalty."

"You don't want her and her family here, do you?"

"I'm not anxious to have a bunch of people running in and out, making noise and disturbing my peace. No, you've got that part right, but one has nothing to do with the other. That girl seems right enough, and so do her kin. Appears to me you're letting her down right off."

"You're the one who insisted I marry. Besides, women prefer living in town."

"Your parents' will insisted you marry, not me. And don't judge all women by your mother. My Kate liked living at the ranch. It was me wanted her in town. I was mistaken."

The admission jolted Drake. "Mistaken? How?"

"She loved that old place. It was me wanted the finer things for her." He waved at hand at their surroundings. "I'm the one who mail-ordered this house brought in from Chicago."

Though the event took place before he could remember, Drake had heard that story more times than he could count. Brought in before the railway reached the area, material for it had come to the coast by ship. He could recite by heart how many days and how many wagonloads it took to get the lumber here from Galveston. He knew exactly how long and how many men were required to put the house together from the store-bought plans which accompanied the building supplies.

Drake surveyed the tastefully decorated room. He remembered that Grandpa hired a firm to decorate the place. "Grandma liked being wherever you were, but I know she took pleasure in this house and the gardens. She liked the teas and the parties and visiting with folks."

The older man leaned his head back and his mouth softened into a smile. "She did love being with folks, didn't she? And they all loved her." He straightened and his tone accused, "But she loved the ranch. She'd hate knowing her garden there went to seed like it has."

"That was because Mama hated the ranch and everything about it, and Papa went along with whatever she said. Until I was old enough, no one but you really cared about the place." He gave a disgusted snort. "You and the tax men. Now I never seem to have time for the flower garden or fancying up the house any."

"So, let Pearl perk up the house and oversee repairing the garden." He gave an impatient wave at his grandson. "This is all beside the point, son. The point here is, you're doing this girl wrong by leaving her so soon after bringing her here. She won't stand for it."

"Now that's where you're wrong. Bossy as she is, Pearl never complains. She makes the best of any situation and goes on. I hope the women in town don't teach her differently."

"You'll live to regret this, believe me."

"Maybe so, but that's what I have to do. With you, Lex, the Sheriff, and several others about town keeping an eye on her, Pearl will fare as well as if I were here."

"Looks to me like, if you're set on doing this, you could wait a bit. Lily will be wanting to give you a birthday party—some sort of big to-do introducing everyone to your new family."

Drake waved a hand in impatience. "Please, spare me that.

She can have some sort of party after I'm gone to introduce Pearl, Belle, and Sarah to the ladies. You know I hate those things Lily gives. I'll take a Mexican fandango to one of her stiff-necked formal affairs anytime."

"So, you're set on doing this? When do you plan to leave?"

"I'll be leaving on the drive in another week, ten days at the most. With so little rain this spring, if I wait another month there won't be enough grass for the last part of the trip."

Grandpa cocked an eyebrow in question. "You staying here 'til then?"

"Yeah. Reckon I am. Leastwise tonight and on the weekend."

Later, as he climbed the stairs, Drake caught himself grinning like a possum in a persimmon tree. Damned if this marriage business wasn't working out after all. No wasting his time going to the saloon. He had his own private stock, so to speak, right here at Grandpa's. And he hoped nothing dimmed the fire burning in her.

He had a momentary twinge of guilt for using his wife like a saloon girl before he went off to the ranch and his cattle drive. Was he being as unfair to Pearl as Grandpa had accused? He stopped mid-step, then shrugged his shoulders and continued up the stairs.

Naw. She had everything she wanted out of this marriage. A safe place to live, family with her, pretty clothes, places to shop, people to visit. Half the people in town were looking after her safety. She had everything she asked for and more.

He had his ranch and the privileges being married carried as well as responsibility for the safety of Pearl and her kin. And with her passionate nature, she'd soon have his baby growing in her. What more could any woman want?

His blood heated with the memories of the ardor they'd shared. Since their wedding night he had tried to deny the desire she aroused in him. But memories of the passion they'd experienced never failed to set his blood boiling. Would she welcome his touch? Would he ignite her desire again tonight? His manhood surged to life at the thought.

* * *

Pearl wakened suddenly, her heart pounding. A noise. She heard a noise, someone breaking into her house. The lone lamp offered a faint glow to the room. Thank goodness. With a sigh of relief she remembered she was safe in her room at Grandpa's house. She sat up and caught her breath.

Her husband stood beside the bed, one hand on the covers as if ready to crawl in. Soft light folded his body in planes of shadow and pale gold. All he wore was an apologetic smile.

"Didn't mean to startle you. Feet this large just naturally make a lot of noise. Specially when they trip."

"I tried to wait up for you." She covered a yawn with her hand.

"You're awake now. Can't say I'm sorry either." He stepped back and turned up the lamp's wick. "Come here where I can see you."

She scooted across on her knees. He motioned her forward, so she stepped to the floor and across the room to face him, wondering what to do with her hands and arms. She folded her arms across herself and felt a flush on her cheeks.

His strong hands slid up her arms to the ties of her gown. "I mean *really* see you, honey. There wasn't enough light in that hotel room." His fingers worked at the ties and her gown slid to the floor.

She felt awkward, not really sure it was proper for a man to see all of a woman, even his wife. Probably it was no worse than touching all of her. He'd certainly done that. She had done her fair share of touching, too.

But she didn't know what to do now, felt clumsy and ungainly. He solved her dilemma when he pulled her arms away from her body.

"You're a beautiful woman. Please let me see all of you."

He dropped her hands and made a twirling motion with his right forefinger. Slowly she pivoted for him, worried at what he'd see, what he'd think. When he touched the scar on her right buttock, she dreaded his next move, feared his questions.

"What's this? It must have hurt."

"It's ugly, I know. Just a childhood injury," she lied. The shame almost staggered her. He must never know her sordid secret.

"Not ugly, Pearl. Never ugly." He pulled her to him and softly kissed her brow. "You're a beautiful woman." His hands caressed her shoulders.

She buried her face in the soft hair of his massive chest. Relief flooded through her. Without thought she clung to his solid strength. Flesh against flesh sent heat racing through her body. The warmth pooled near the juncture of her thighs and desire flamed inside her. She craved his touch, wanted him moving inside her again.

His mouth sought hers, drinking her in as if from a long thirst. She leaned into him, felt his rigid need as he cradled her body to his. He broke the kiss, lifted her and strode to the bed.

After lowering her gently to the sheets, he lay beside her. His strong hands roamed her body as his warm breath fanned her ear. "I've wanted you so much. Needed you like this." He trailed kisses down her throat. "Say you want me, too. Say it."

She wanted to tell him how much she had needed him with her earlier that day to lessen her fright at this new place. But she didn't know how to say it. She needed to tell him how she fumbled and groped to say and do the right thing so as not to shame him before his family. Words would not come. Longing to tell him she craved his love and respect as well as his touch, she could not frame the sentence.

Instead, she said only, "Yes, I want you. I need you here beside me."

Pearl heard his low growl of approval. When he suckled her nipple, pleasure ricocheted through her. Her fingers sought his hair, pressing him to her breast. When his finger found her nub of desire, her hands grasped at his back, fingers raking a trail across his broad shoulders.

"Yes, this is what I needed. This and more. So much more." Tears stung her eyelids with the realization that she needed him in many more ways than he needed her. Only her pride prevented her telling him how much.

He reclaimed her mouth and his tongue merged with hers in a frenetic dance. He broke the kiss to confide, "I thought of you all through dinner. I wanted to be with you here, like this."

She felt the rush of happiness at his admission. Her hands grew more bold, taking pleasure in the feel of his skin beneath her touch. The taste of his lips, his tongue on hers sent shudders of desire rushing through her in ever increasing waves.

Her hands slid to his rigid phallus and she heard his quick intake of breath.

"Easy, honey, if you want this to last." His kisses trailed her neck and shoulders before he wedged his body over hers.

"I've already waited a lifetime." She pulled him to her.

She felt his shaft enter her and matched her tempo to his. Passion raged through them, driving them further and further in powerful harmony. She left earth, soaring through the night in a shower of exploding stars. In a haze of ecstasy, she heard herself call his name as he cried out to her. Together they descended, wrapped in each other and the haze of liberated desire.

He collapsed beside her, their bodies still entwined. His hands tucked her into him as he curled about her. Her head lay on his shoulder and his leg across her thighs. His lips brushed her hair and she heard his sigh of satisfaction.

Contentment filled her. Her husband. Soon they would be in their own home. Would he learn to love her? Maybe at the ranch. She snuggled into him and drifted to sleep.

Ten

"What do you mean, stay here?"

Pearl had wakened cocooned in the hazy glow following a night of intermittent lovemaking with her husband to find him dressing for the ranch. Then he dropped a bombshell on her.

"You know it's not safe for you to be on your own. Ranch is too isolated. You'll be safer here in town." Drake stomped his feet to settle each in the boots he wore. He retrieved a blue chambray shirt from his bag and donned it.

"For how long?" Pearl slid from bed and grabbed her nightgown from the floor.

"Well. . . ."

She whirled on her husband, confronting him, "You never intended for me to move to the ranch, did you?" She yanked her nightie on. No one could argue buck-naked.

"Don't get riled. Women hate the seclusion. You'll be happier in town. Things to do here and people about you." Drake shoved his shirt into his twill pants without looking at his wife.

She stepped toward him and pointed at her chest. "What do you know about what makes *this* woman happy?"

A crooked smile broke his face. "Aw, I know what makes you happy, all right. Didn't I keep you happy all night?"

She shrugged away the comment she thought he aimed to distract her. "Did you ask me which I prefer? No." She hoped her glare chilled his randy hide.

His voice softened, placating. "Pearl, be reasonable. We don't know who's tried to kill you and your family. Someone might be trailing you right now, waiting somewhere, and watching the house."

He met her gaze. That muscle twitched in his cheek, letting her know he was less than happy with this conversation. Well, that didn't bother Pearl in the least. Some things needed talking about.

He walked over and put his hands on her shoulders, then took a deep breath and continued, "Look, the sheriff and his deputy as well as several of the town's leading citizens will be looking out for any newcomer. I talked to the owners of the livery stable, the hotel, the mercantile, all the places I could think of where a newcomer would stand out. If any strangers come around asking questions, the sheriff will find out immediately. You and Sarah will be safer here."

"You're taking Storm with you?" She hugged her arms, sensing a lost battle.

"Yes, um, with your permission. I can't see him attending teas or shopping here in town. Besides, he's a big help to me."

Her head came up and her hands fisted at her hips. "And I suppose Sarah and I are just so much baggage?"

"Now, I didn't say that and you know it." He held up a hand, palm out, as if to stay her fury. "But you have no place rounding up cattle and getting ready for a drive."

"It's true we don't ride, but we could learn." She could learn anything, given a chance. She suspected no chance would come.

"There's no time to teach you. 'Sides, it makes the cowboys and vaqueros nervous to have women around the cattle. They think it's bad luck. And I can't leave the two of you at the house with only the housekeeper to help you."

She sagged in defeat. "Okay, Drake. I'll stay here for now, and I'll try not to shame you. But this is only until we know there'll be no more meanness against my family. Don't think you can keep me waiting too long," she warned.

His face broke into a smile of relief. "You'll see. By the time this is over and things calm down, you'll like this sweet life so much you won't be able to tear yourself away from Grandpa's house."

"Too much sweet gives a body a belly ache."

Ignoring that and stepping close, he kissed her on the cheek then nuzzled her neck. "I'll be sleeping tonight in a bedroll on hard ground. Give me a kiss to remember."

Something to remember. She'd give him something to remember all right. She raised her mouth to his, let him plunder with his tongue. Her tongue did some plundering of its own as she moved her body against him. When their kiss ended, the heat of passion darkened his eyes.

"When you're sleeping on the hard ground, all *alone*, you remember that, husband." Head high, she turned and walked into the dressing room.

As she washed and dressed, she remembered their conversation the night Drake proposed. He talked about his ranch, yes. But he had talked about her living in town. Never did he mention her at the ranch. She sank onto the velvet chair and held her face in her hands. Dear Lord, he never meant me to live at his ranch.

It's not a real marriage he wants. He wanted none at all. In reaching for freedom, she chained herself to one man. A man who never wanted her, who might never want her as his wife. Oh, but how she wanted him. As a husband, as a partner forever. Good Lord, what should she do?

Pearl had no idea how long she sat there. She wept until no more tears came, then went over and over in her mind the things her husband said about life here. How could he think she would ever prefer living with Lily and Grandpa, socializing with Lily's friends, and dawdling away her days instead of living with her husband in her own home?

She started when she heard a knock on her door. Belle and Sarah entered.

"Sister, I heard Drake and Storm leave. Belle and I wondered what we're supposed to do today?" The girl knelt in front of Pearl, her hands on Pearl's arms. "What's the matter?"

"He intends us to remain here indefinitely." She shrugged,

"We're supposed to go shopping for more clothes today, visit with Lily, and get to know the townspeople. He says we'll be safer here, too."

"Well, to be honest, I cain't say that makes me unhappy. I sure like this house," Belle said. "This here is the fanciest place I ever saw. I keep worryin' they'll find out who I am and make me leave."

"Oh, don't worry, Belle. They all seem to love you," Pearl assured her. In fact, Belle seemed the only one of their group Lily truly liked.

"I like it, too," Sarah's soft voice added, "But I'll go wherever you say."

"I know you would, dear." Grateful for her sister's loyalty, Pearl reassured her, "It looks as if we're here for a while, so you don't have to worry about leaving."

Belle's smile lit her face. "Still and all, I'm sorry he's upset you. But I 'spect he's right. We'll be safer here with lots of folks to watch for strangers up to mischief."

Pearl stood and exchanged her damp handkerchief for a fresh one she slipped into her pocket. Forcing a smile, she said, "Then let's go down and face Lily and Grandpa."

Pearl stifled a yawn and wondered how so many women could spend so much time talking about so little. She forced a smile for her hostess, Emily Potter, wife of the Presbyterian minister. The cheerful woman reminded Pearl of a plump banty hen.

"Do you play the piano, my dear?" Without waiting for an answer, she plunged ahead. "We lost our church pianist. She and her husband, that's Mr. Barker, left last week for California. It's been such a worry, finding another. Many of our ladies play," she cast a covert glance at Lily, "but not, ahem, not quite well enough for the church services."

"My cousin plays very well, especially hymns." Now what possessed her to say that?

"You don't say?" Relief flooded Mrs. Potter's care-worn

features. "Oh, Miss Renfro." She waved her hand to attract Belle's attention, "Miss Renfro, Mrs. Kincaid tells me you play the piano. Would you happen to be Presbyterian?"

Panic flickered across Belle's face, but Pearl smiled and nodded.

Belle smoothed her skirt as if deep in thought before she raised her eyes and spoke. "Well, yes, ma'am."

A murmur of approving chatter swept the room. But Lex's mother, Rosilee Tremont, remained silent. She peered over her teacup, her lovely face inscrutable.

Mrs. Potter hurried to take Belle's hand in hers. "Please play for us now, won't you?"

Reluctantly, Belle let herself be guided to the piano. "What shall I play?"

"Just the hymns you know. Ones you like." Mrs. Potter took a seat near the piano, looking eager as a child.

Belle's gaze flickered to Pearl's once more before she began playing. Soon she closed her eyes and the music flowed. When she ended, her audience burst into applause.

Mrs. Potter was the first to speak. "Do say you'll be our new church pianist, Miss Renfro, won't you?"

Belle looked at Lily, "Oh, you must ask Mrs. Stephens. I'm a guest in her home."

All eyes turned to Lily. Looking pleased to be the center of attention, even indirectly, she cooed, "Of course, dear Belle, you must agree. You play so well, it will be lovely to have your music at the church services."

"If you're sure it'll be all right, and if the church members agree, I will."

Pearl noticed Belle spoke slowly, each word chosen carefully to conceal her background. Apparently, the other women mistook her hesitant speech for shyness. She had watched Belle through the week deliberately mimicking Lily's mannerisms with a great deal of success.

If only I was as interested in these silly affairs, maybe I could fit in, too.

"You should give lessons, Miss Renfro," nodded Mayor

McGee's wife. "My Millie was just learning when the Barkers moved."

Lily nodded, "You could give them in our parlor. Have you taught anyone else to play?"

Belle flushed delicately, "Just my two younger sisters and a few friends."

The room buzzed as mothers vied for a lesson time for their sons and daughters. Emily Potter rushed to get paper, pen, and ink for Belle's lesson records. Pearl smiled to herself. Maybe Sarah would like lessons, too. Maybe she would take them herself. Teaching piano and playing for the church services would give Belle a secure position in the community.

If only I felt secure. Would that day ever come?

Drake returned to the house four hot, dusty days after his argument with Pearl. He and Storm still wore their trail clothes, slipping in quietly long past dinnertime after a stop at the water trough pump to wash. When they stepped into the kitchen to hunt for food, Polly heard them from her room next to the larder. Drake took in her rumpled gray hair as she belted a faded wrapper against her considerable girth.

"Polly, there's no need for you to get up. We'll do just fine for ourselves."

"I don't believe in hard-workin' men skippin' meals. I've saved somethin' back in case you two straggled in."

Grateful, they waited at the breakfast table until she brought them thick slices of bread, great slabs of ham, cheese, and buttermilk pie.

"Mmm, thanks, Polly." Drake wasted no time filling his mouth and stomach. "Better than we've had since we left here."

Storm swallowed. "Tastes like Pearl's bread."

"That it is," Polly confessed with a laugh. "Her pie as well."

Drake's head came up. "What's Pearl doing baking?"

"Yer askin' the wrong person, Mr. Kincaid. Though Miz

Kincaid do be better at bakin' breads and sweets than me, and that's the pure truth."

Damn. He wished he could ignore the prickles running up and down his spine. "Doesn't Aunt Lily mind?"

Polly sniffed, "It's not me place to question me betters."

Storm cleaned his plate and waited for his brother-in-law, nodding with fatigue. Drake finished his pie and stood up. He favored Polly with a kiss on her pudgy cheek.

She laughed and pushed at his arm. "Get away with ye now."

Drake said goodnight to Storm at the boy's bedroom door. He slipped into the suite he shared with his wife. No sooner had he shut the door and tugged off one boot than he heard Pearl stir.

"It's me. Storm and I got in a few minutes ago."

She lit the lamp beside the bed and came around to face him.

He tugged at the other boot then stripped off his shirt. He figured he better tread mighty soft here. "You been busy?"

She rolled her eyes. "I've been shopping with Lily twice, attended two teas, and been to dinner with the pastor and his wife. Lily's giving a party in a week, and there's a social after church this Sunday."

"So, I guess you're having a high old time getting acquainted with folks." He could have sworn he heard her snort, but thought he must be wrong.

"You've eaten?" She crossed her arms over her chest.

He didn't know if she was self-conscious or still angry— or both. "Yes, Polly fixed us something. Polly gave us some of your bread and pie."

When she bit her lip at the mention of her baking, he asked, "How come you were in the kitchen baking?"

She sat on the bed and raised her chin. "I'm used to having something useful to do with my time. I slipped down each morning to bake before your aunt got up." She leaned forward, as if confiding something to him. "Did you know she sometimes sleeps until after ten in the morning?"

"I'm not surprised. What does she think of your baking?"

He watched the emotions play across Pearl's face, saw the anger flare in her eyes.

"Today is the first she knew about it. She forbade me to go into the kitchen again. Said I'll only get in cook's way. And she says that ladies don't do m-menial work." She paused, then let him have it. "I'm used to being my own *boss* in my own home. But this isn't my home. I'm like a broken spoke on a wheel here."

Why had he thought Pearl would fit in with his spoiled and pampered aunt? Lily's most serious thought was whether her gown was prettier than that of any other woman in the room. He shook his head at his folly. Damn.

What a spot to be in. He wanted to ask Grandpa to keep a firm hand on Lily, but Grandpa would only say "I told you so." No. He'd have to let this ride a while and hope for the best.

"How are Sarah and Belle getting on?"

Pearl looked as if she might cry. "They're doing fine. Belle especially. She's giving piano lessons in the parlor each afternoon. And she's agreed to be the new pianist at the Presbyterian Church."

He couldn't contain his laugh, thinking of a soiled dove playing for Sunday services and giving piano lessons in his snooty aunt's parlor. He stripped off his pants and drawers.

"And what's so funny about that?"

Shaking his head again, he said, "Nothing, honey. I'm just glad Sarah and Belle are fitting in. Glad I'm here with you." He held her close, burying his face in her glorious honey-colored hair. Thank God she still smelled of lilacs. "Come let me make you glad, too."

"That's all for today. You did right nice, Millie." Belle smiled at the mayor's daughter before sorting through the sheets of music the child had brought to her piano lesson. "Practice this one for next week, just like we did it today." She walked the little girl out.

When she opened the door, she saw Alexon coming up the steps. "Why, Alexon, how nice to see you. Grandpa and Drake ain't, um, aren't here." She noticed Millie staring from Alexon to her, her eyes wide in curiosity. "Run along home now, Millie. Tell your mama you did right nice today."

Alexon smiled at the little girl and watched her skip down the walk. "May I come in?"

"Well, he—, um, heavens yes." She almost bit her tongue to call back the cuss word. For all that she worked at Roxie's for only a few weeks, she had picked up some bad habits. "Please. This is your grandpa's home. You have a sight more business being here than me."

This man made her so nervous. No matter how she tried to copy Lily's speech, being nervous made it more difficult. Like now. Alexon made her all jittery and happy at the same time.

"Shall we go into the parlor?" He pointed with the hat he held, indicated she should precede him.

She walked into the parlor, gliding the way Lily had shown her. She wanted to fit in like Lily. After all Pearl had done for her, and with Lily being so cold to Pearl, guilt plagued Belle.

"Won't you sit down. Law, there I go again, inviting you to make yourself comfy in your own grandpa's house. Should I tell cook you'd like a dri—um, refreshments?"

He sat on the sofa, his tan pants pulling taut across his thighs. "You make a lovely hostess, but no. Where are the others?" He patted the seat beside him.

Lordy, he wanted her there beside him. She sat, arranging her lavender calico skirt carefully the way Lily showed her. "The men are out, but Grandpa will be here soon. Drake and Storm might come in later. Pearl and Sarah are sewing upstairs and your aunt's resting." She folded her hands in her lap. "Um, shouldn't I get your aunt? Or, maybe get you a drink?"

"No. I came to see you." He smiled and tossed his hat on the table beside the sofa. With one swift rake of a hand, he repaired the hat's damage to his auburn hair.

"Oh." The world slowed. Time dragged slowly as panic rose in her throat. She heard the clock ticking on the mantel. What should she say? "Um, is something wrong?"

"No." His chocolate eyes softened when he smiled. "Belle, I've come to call on you."

"To . . . to call on me? Oh. Call on me." She heard the squeak in her voice, searched for something to do or say. He couldn't mean *call* on her. Not courting her. She saw the admiration shining from his eyes, the hopeful smile on his face.

Dear God, what should I do? What should I say?

"Should . . . should I play the piano for you?"

"Maybe later." He nodded at the open doorway to the terrace. "Would you like to walk in the garden?"

She leapt to her feet. Moving would be better than sitting here, her heart in her throat. "That sounds nice. Yes, let's do that."

Lex offered his arm and guided her through the door. "How are you getting along in our little town?"

"It may be little compared to some of those we came through, but compared to Piper's Hollow it's fair sized. In fact, it's just right."

"Mama said she saw you at Emily Potter's tea."

"Yes." She wondered what Rosilee Tremont thought about her. The woman was polite, friendly, sort of, but hard to figure. It was nothing Belle could put her finger on, but she sensed Rosilee Tremont looked too deep. "That was when they asked me to play for the church. Do you go to the Presbyterian Church?"

"Our family helped build it."

"Oh. Of course." Though his last name was Tremont, she knew his mother was a Kincaid by birth. Alexon Tremont had that Kincaid blue blood running thick through his veins. Why was he here with her?

He took her hand. "I have to go soon. My folks expect me for dinner this evening. Perhaps you'll come with me some day. It's only a short drive in the buggy."

"Maybe." What did she say now? "It . . . it's nice to see you.

Thank you for coming by. I'll tell Grandpa and Lily you were here."

He grabbed her other hand and pulled her around to face him. "Will you go to the social with me Sunday? After church?"

"Oh, my. What will folks think? What will your parents think?"

"They'll think I'm lucky to be with the prettiest, sweetest woman there."

"Alexon. I . . . I can't."

She saw the hurt flash in his eyes before he smiled. "Is there someone else you prefer?"

"Someone else? Oh, no. Heavens, no. It's just, well, I'm so new here."

"Ah, you want to protect your reputation?" His smile returned.

For once she could answer honestly. "No, I want to protect yours. And the people who live in this house. They've all been so nice to me."

He laughed. "Dear Belle, what did you expect?" Not waiting for an answer, he cautioned, "I won't be discouraged so easily. I'll keep asking you out."

"Thank you." More than you know, she thought.

Eleven

The next morning Drake tromped into the house and set a heavy box onto the large desk in Grandpa's study. Grandpa looked up from his newspaper, annoyance at the interruption written on his face. "What's that?"

"Don't know. Came in on the train. Addressed to me."

Storm, who had become Drake's constant shadow, said, "Someone tried to hold up the train just this side of Austin."

Grandpa folded his paper and stood, his interest piqued. "Well, I'll be damned. Catch 'em?"

Drake shook his head. "No, two men. Brakemen shot at them. Says he winged both varmints." He eyed the box speculatively.

Storm's excited voice finished for his brother-in-law, "But they got clean away. Nobody's found hide nor hair of 'em."

"Dangdest thing I ever heard of. What's this country coming to when the tap train from Austin gets held up?" Grandpa's attention returned to the letter nailed to the lid of the box. "Well, you gonna open this or not? If not, get the danged thing off my desk."

Drake pried the envelope loose with his pocket knife, taking care not to tear the paper. As he extracted the letter, a small key slid to the massive desk.

He scanned the missive's contents. "Well, I'll be damned. It's from the Piper's Hollow Bank. It's Pearl's money."

Storm looked at the box, as if to gauge how much money

would fit inside. "Too big. She don't have that much money. Only got $157.28."

Drake turned to him, "Would you ask her to come here? She should be the one to open this, not me."

The boy tore out of the office and soon reappeared with Pearl and Sarah trailing him.

Drake pulled his Grandpa's leather desk chair around for Pearl and handed her the letter. She unfolded the paper as she sat, and a frown puckered her brow.

"They sent it to me because you wrote we'd be wed." He wondered if his bossy, independent wife knew that—in Texas—a wife's money became her husband's when they wed. "But this is yours. The money from Piper's Hollow." He leaned a hip against the desk and watched as she read the letter.

Her expression changed from puzzled to incredulous. "But this says there were *two* accounts. How could that be?" She read further then looked from her sister to her brother. "Granny had a big account in my name. Someone put money in each year for most of my life. Except during the war and a few years after."

"Maybe your father," Drake suggested.

She put her hand to her mouth. Her eyes searched Storm's and Sarah's faces. An understanding seemed to pass between them. "Could it be?"

Grandpa picked up the key and extended it toward her. "Don't you want to see what's in here?"

She shook her head, "Drake, you open it. Please."

He obliged her and unlocked the box. As he raised the lid, both Pearl and Storm gasped.

Sarah peered around her brother, blue eyes wide in surprise. "My stars! How could there be so much? We only had $157.28 saved."

They took out bills and coins. Good U.S. money. Pearl referred back to the paper in her hand. "The letter says it's $7,657.28 in all." Eyes widened, she stared at the treasure. "It's a fortune."

Take 4 FREE Books!

We created our convenient Home Subscription Service so you'll be sure to have the hottest new romances delivered each month right to your doorstep — usually before they are available in book stores. Just to show you how convenient Zebra Home Subscription Service is, we would like to send you 4 Kensington Choice Historical Romances as a FREE gift. You receive a gift worth up to $23.96 — absolutely FREE. You only pay for shipping and handling. There's no obligation to buy anything - ever!

Save Up To 30% On Home Delivery!

Accept your FREE gift and each month we'll deliver 4 brand new titles as soon as they are published. They'll be yours to examine FREE for 10 days. Then if you decide to keep the books, you'll pay the preferred subscriber's price. That's all 4 books for a savings of up to 30% off the cover price! Just add the cost of shipping and handling. Remember, you are under no obligation to buy any of these books at any time! If you are not delighted with them, simply return them and owe nothing. But if you enjoy Kensington Choice Historical Romances as much as we think you will, pay the special preferred subscriber rate and save over $7.00 off the bookstore price!

* * *

Pearl sat at the small cherry desk in the sitting room of the suite she and Drake shared. Her mind whirled with questions about her fortune. Near at hand, her sister sat quietly.

Pearl dropped the bank passbook onto the desk blotter. "Did Granny hate me too much to give me the funds, or did she hope to provide for me?"

Sarah shook her head as if she, too, still found the whole idea unbelievable. "We'll never know."

Grandpa had accompanied Storm and Drake to see Lex. Probably to talk about the money, though they denied men ever gossiped. Lily and Belle drove the buggy to the dressmaker for a fitting of another of Lily's endless series of new gowns. Pearl looked at her own sensible white shirtwaist over her navy skirt and sighed. She could buy her own new gowns now if she chose. But did she?

For the third time since she and Drake returned from the bank that morning, Pearl picked up the passbook and stared at it. How should she use the money? It must be for something important, something to make a difference in her life and the lives of Sarah and Storm.

Sarah's lovely face flushed with anger as she removed a loose thread from her green calico dress. "Your Granny was a mean woman. That money was there all the time we scrimped and worried. She should have told you about it."

"She despised me and all the memories I represented." Pearl shivered at the thought. "I wonder, did she demand the money or did *he* offer it?" She couldn't bring herself to voice her father's identity unless necessary. He wouldn't acknowledge her, so she refused to acknowledge him even by speaking his name.

Sarah squeezed her sister's hand, "I think she asked him, blackmailed him. But she wanted to punish him for marrying someone other than her daughter, not to help you."

Suddenly the importance of the funds rushed at Pearl. Her head swam, the lovely room whirled in a blur of blue. She put her head down and took deep breaths. "Oh, Lord. Oh, Dear Lord," she wailed.

"Sister, are you ailing?" Sarah laid her arm across Pearl's shoulders.

"I didn't have to marry Drake to get away. All that time we had money." Tears threatened to flow. "If only we had known, we could have left Piper's Hollow years ago. We could have started our own business, any place we chose."

Sarah patted her sister's back. "Maybe Granny feared we'd leave her there alone. Heaven knows the woman never did anything to deserve the loyalty you gave her. She gave you nothing but her constant sniping and complaining."

"I could never have abandoned my own grandmother." No matter how much the woman deserved it, Pearl thought. "Oh, Sarah, I've made a terrible mistake." Tears overflowed and rolled down her cheeks.

"No, Sister. What about Drake? You saved him."

Pearl raised her head and sniffed. "What?"

"Remember? He had to marry to save his ranch. At least you helped him."

She shook her head. "Not really. He never wanted to marry *me*. Any woman would have been all right. It didn't have to be me."

"But it is, Sister. He *chose* you from all the women he knows. You said yourself he could have had any other woman. But he married you." Her voice softened, "And you're married to him."

"No, I'm bound by marriage vows, but I'm not truly married."

"You are. And he cares for you. I can tell by the way he looks at you. I see it when touches you."

Anger warred with confusion, hurt, and remorse. Anger won and spared no sensitivities. "Hmph. You're confusing caring with animal lust. Would a man who cares for his wife leave her stuck in town while he spends most of his time elsewhere?" She stood and paced the room.

"If he thought it was best for his wife, he would." Sarah

walked over and put a hand on each of Pearl's arms. "It is best, you know. We're both safer here."

"You don't understand. Didn't you hear me? I said he *never* intended for us to live at the ranch. Before he knew the trouble would follow us. Before we even left Piper's Hollow. He *always* expected us to stay here with Grandpa and Lily forever."

"But it's nice here. It's just the kind of place we dreamed about. Only better."

"Better? How can it be better finding the last few years of scrimping were needless? How can it be better knowing my own grandmother cared so little for me? After twenty-six years of being unwanted, how can being an unwanted wife be better?"

"We live in a beautiful home. We have everything we've ever dreamed of and more. I think Drake cares about you. It will take time for him to realize how much."

"Well, I'm tired of hearing Lily and her friends babble on and on about how many more suitable women Drake could have chosen. I'm tired of endless social prattle about nothing. I'm tired of being snubbed and criticized no matter how hard I try."

A concerned frown puckered Sarah's brow. "Oh, Sister. W-what are you going to do?"

"I don't know what, but I'm going to do *something*. And soon."

Only a few puffy clouds dotted the brilliant azure sky. Groups of people gathered in the park-like setting behind the church. Pearl saw Storm race along the creek with several of his new friends. Even shy Sarah huddled with two giggling young women.

Under a canopy of trees, Lily and Pearl took up their assignment watching the dessert table until the dinner bell rang. The wildflowers were in full bloom now. Spiky lupines Pearl had come to know as bluebonnets bloomed among a coral feather called Indian paintbrush.

Lily tilted her parasol and rearranged the desserts for the third time. Pearl had not missed the fact that Lily's new mint green silk dress and matching parasol looked more suited to a drawing room social than a church picnic. She also noted Lily took her duties at these church socials very seriously. Mrs. Potter plopped two cakes at the end of the table. Lily shot her a hard look for the careless placement of the sweets and set about to rearrange them.

Grandpa merely chuckled at his youngest daughter's ill humor and resumed talking to Pearl. "I had a letter from Evan on Friday. In all the fuss about your money, I forgot to tell you."

"Oh, I do hope he's feeling stronger." Pearl brushed a leaf from Grandpa's dapper Sunday suit.

"Yes. In fact, he mentioned that it's only due to your care he lasted long enough to retire to Mary Alice's."

Pearl shook her head in denial. "He would never have stayed in Piper's Hollow after his wife died if it weren't for me and my family. I feared he'd waited too long."

"He asked about you. Said to tell you he's still taking his evil tonic and drinking that blasted tea. His words, not mine." He smiled, proving he bore no ill will with his statement.

"Before we left Chattanooga, I showed Mary Alice how to make the tonic. Since it was her mother who taught me, she soon remembered the routine. You can bet she makes sure Evan takes it right on time and gets the proper rest and food he needs."

"Drake said you doctored folks back in Tennessee, and some of the train passengers, too. He seemed right impressed with your skill."

Pearl took immeasurable pleasure hearing her husband gave merit to her doctoring. "From Piper's Hollow it was a half day's ride to a trained doctor who had a drinking problem. I saw to most birthings, sewed up cuts, treated lots of ailments. Most people I helped, but some were beyond my knowledge."

He pulled at his mustache several minutes, twitching

around as if undecided about something. In a flash she knew what he wanted. Or needed.

"Is something bothering you, Grandpa? Something I might help with?"

"Well, um," he stammered. "I have this pain in my joints."

Lily caught this portion of the conversation and whirled to face her father and Pearl. "Really, Papa. Surely you're not consulting Pearl about a medical matter. You saw Doctor Percival about this."

"Doc said it's just cause I'm getting older and to live with it. Costive old fool."

Suppressing a smile, Pearl asked, "What kind of pain? I mean, is it worse when you're tired, when you first get up, when it's cold or wet? Do you have redness and swelling? Tell me exactly how and where you feel pain."

"Papa!" Lily looked ready to have a fit.

He patted her arm. "Now, Lily, you just tend to your sweets and such. This is between Pearl and me."

Lily's gray eyes turned stormy. "Well, if that's the way you feel." She stormed around the table to stand in front, letting the desserts form a barrier and giving her parasol a dizzy twirl.

Grandpa took Pearl's arm and pulled her toward the other side of the group of trees shading the tables. "Let's talk over here in private."

"Would you prefer to wait until we're home this evening?"

He pulled at his mustache again. "Maybe so. Or maybe in the morning before Lily comes downstairs would be best. You're up early like me."

"Okay, we'll talk then." She squeezed his arm.

"You're a good woman, Pearl. Drake's a lucky man." He patted her shoulder before he walked away.

She walked back to the table. Shooing a fly hovering over one of her pies, she thought of Grandpa's parting words. She hardly had time to ponder them before Lily returned to her side.

The parasol popped shut and Lily wielded it like an accusing finger. "So, you intend to continue this, this charade of being a medical person, right in my home?"

Pearl stiffened, held herself straight and still. If this woman thought she could intimidate her, she had another thought coming. "I don't pretend to be a doctor, but I am a healer and medical person." Head high, she faced her adversary. She knew herself competent, knew she had made a difference in many lives. "It's true I haven't been to medical school, or even to finishing school. But I studied for many years, with personal apprenticeship to a wonderful healer."

"Hmph. A witch doctor. A charlatan." Lily lay her parasol on the table and her hands fisted at each hip. "Why can't you just act normal?" She stamped her foot for emphasis.

Pearl stepped toward her adversary. "Normal for who? Lily, I appreciate all the things you've done to help my family and me here. But I don't want the same things from life you want. Please allow me to be myself, to find my own happiness."

"Look at you! I've seen you barefoot around the house." She poked a long finger at Pearl's ribs. "And if you won't wear a corset at home, you could at least dress properly for church and social functions."

Pearl took a step away from the woman. "Drake said I don't have to wear a corset. If my husband doesn't mind, why should you?"

"Because what you do reflects on me and my father. You're an embarrassment to us. Now you want to carry on with this horrid medicine thing. I won't stand for it."

Pearl pulled herself up to her full height, her back stiff. "I've tried to show you respect because you are, in a sense, our hostess. But the house belongs to Grandpa and, whether you like it or not, I'm Drake's wife. You are not the boss of me, Lily Stephens, and I won't let you bully me."

"Oh, you are such a common woman. Why Drake chose you when he could have had Pamela Hudson or Helen Morris, I'll never know. They're from such good families, and both are beautiful and refined. And there were lots of others right here he could have wed."

Pearl leaned into Lily's face. "So you keep telling me. But he didn't choose either of them, did he? No, he did not. In fact, he cared so little for the women you prize that he even left the state to find a bride." She pointed to herself. "And I am the one he wed, and you can't change that. You may as well get used to me, because I am a Kincaid and in Kincaid County to stay."

Lily gave a toss of her perfectly coifed head. "I'll never get used to you, as you so crudely put it. And I won't have you pouring who knows what down my father. Do you hear me?"

With that, Lily left Pearl and flounced across the church yard to visit with the Morris family. She saw the woman talking to Helen, saw Lily look over her shoulder at Pearl. No doubt she filled the girl's ears with stories of misfortune from such an ill-bred house guest and inlaws.

Pearl watched and wondered how she could have handled that situation better. She hated sounding rude, but refused to be a doormat any longer.

Drake appeared and slid his arm around her waist. "What's wrong, honey? You look mad enough to fight a bear."

"I think I just did." She rested her aching head against his solid shoulder.

"Ah, I thought that was Lily's dragon lady walk. What happened?" He cupped her chin to meet her gaze.

She hoped the tears threatening would not overflow.

"She doesn't approve of me. Thinks I should do everything like her. Dress like her, talk like her, walk like her. Think like her." She shook her head, feeling near tears. "I can't do it, Drake. I have tried, but I can't be like Lily."

"Honey, if I wanted a woman like Lily, I could have found one right here in town. She had a couple all picked out for me to choose from."

"Yes, she's mentioned how much more suitable either would have been."

He waved at a couple passing, then cradled his arms around her. "Please don't let her get to you this way. She's spoiled, I admit, but she's had a frustrating life the past few years."

"You mean nursing your grandmother?"

"That's only part of it." He signaled Sarah and the girl left her group of friends to hurry over. "Would you watch this table until folks are ready to eat? I'm going to steal your sister for a while."

Sarah smiled. Pearl knew the little romantic imagined some sort of lovers' escape. As they walked back into the trees, Drake found a log large enough for a seat. He used his handkerchief to protect Pearl's clothes when she sat down. He faced her, one foot on the log, an elbow leaning on his knee.

"When Lily was at school, she met Harold Vermillion at a party and fell in love. His family lived in St. Louis, but he was going to the university in Boston. They were engaged."

"But her married name is Stephens."

"Right. She and Harold had a spat. In a fit of temper, she broke the engagement and immediately married Wes Stephens. Wes was crazy about her, but hadn't the least idea how to treat her. She bullied him. Neither was happy. He was one of the first to enlist in the War."

"And that's where he died?"

"Yes, she was a widow before her twentieth birthday. But by then Harold had married a girl from St. Louis. Someone his parents chose for him, I believe."

"Oh, no. So neither was happily married?"

"Well, maybe Harold's marriage worked out all right, I don't know. By then Grandma was sick, so Lily sold her house and moved in with my grandparents. She was a good nurse for Grandma. And she keeps Grandpa's house running smoothly."

"But she's probably not happy? She's just filling up time."

"Yes, very well put."

"I've not heard her mention a man. Are there no men in her life here?"

"Aw, she flirts with them all. Fact is, I think she's been seeing Frank Worthington some, on and off. Never thought much of the man myself, so can't say I'm surprised nothing has come of it. I guess she's still in love with Harold. Or thinks she is." He took her hands in his and pulled her to her feet. "She can be difficult sometimes, but please cut her some slack."

"I know it's been hard on her, having a houseful of people thrust on her for an indefinite time. I'll try to get along. But two women used to being in charge cannot get along in the same house." She met his gaze. "I'll be no one's puppet. I am my own person."

"I'm finding that out." A bell clanged in the distance. With a kiss to her brow, he added, "Sounds like folks are ready to eat." He offered his arm and they strolled back to the group.

Belle enjoyed this social more than any event since she left her parents' home. In spite of declining Lex's invitation, she found him constantly at her side. Pleased with his attention, she didn't try to discourage him.

Everyone treated her with friendship and courtesy. Like she was someone special. Belle's stomach gave a lurch, though, when Rosilee and Samuel Tremont sat across the table from her and Lex. What would she say to them? What must they think of their son trailing around with a nobody? Oh, but she wasn't really a nobody anymore, was she? She was related to Drake Kincaid, staying with Judge Kincaid and his daughter.

Oh, God, sometimes she forgot she wasn't really Pearl's cousin, forgot it was all a sham. Just like the parts of her background she conveniently omitted or altered. She worried about herself, falling into her newly invented past so deeply. But this was her big chance.

Law, who was she kidding? More likely this was her *only* chance. She was not about to mess it up, no matter how many lies she had to tell to protect her position.

"How are you liking Kincaid Springs, Miss Renfro?" Rosilee asked.

Belle saw the question in the woman's eyes. She wants to know if I'm staying in Kincaid Springs or moving on. Will I stay or break her son's heart? Or both? She took a deep breath before she answered and flashed her sweetest smile.

"I love it here. There's so much to do and people are so friendly. Lily and Grandpa have been very kind."

"How do your folks feel about your move?" Samuel Tremont asked from across the table.

Oh, no. Personal questions when she had nothing to say about that part of her life that would make these people happy.

"Well, they're happy to see me in a better position." The lies bothered her less now. That worried her some, too. "My folks have a farm, but it's hard work supporting a large family. I still have three brothers and two sisters at home."

From her side, Lex joined in. "The soil there is shallow, Dad, and farming is far less prosperous than here. I expect it's even harder work as well."

Oh, no. Now sweet Lex defended her blend of lies and truth. How humiliating to have placed such a wonderful man in a treacherous position. His loyalty made it even more important that he never know the truth.

"Yes," Belle agreed. "My folks are doing all right for that area. I mean, they have plenty to eat and all, they just ain— don't have any cash money to spare."

Samuel Tremont nodded. "Working with land often keeps a man wealthy on paper with no coins in his pocket."

She exhaled with relief. "Yes, that's it. I should have known you'd understand. That's why Pearl gave me part of her money."

Lex looked worried. "I didn't know. What are you going to do?" His frown deepened, "You won't leave, will you?"

"Well, I had thought I'd move into the boarding house and look for employment. I thought I might even open a little shop, like a milliner's, but Lily wouldn't hear of it. She said I'm family and would insult her by moving out."

Thank God Lily took the attitude she did. Belle loved living in Grandpa's fine home, loved the parties and shopping, loved being a part of a large and happy family. She loved everything about the good life she led. Except the lies. The lies and the constant fear of discovery.

"So, now you're a woman of independent means?" Lex's warm brown eyes sparkled.

The wind ruffled his auburn hair, sending a lock across his forehead. What a kind and handsome man. She could spend a lifetime looking at his sweet face. She prayed he never found out about her life at Roxie's. That would be sure to send him running away from her.

"Hardly that," she said. "Though to me it does seem a fortune. At least, now I can buy my own things when Lily wants to go shopping."

Rosilee nodded. "And with my sister, that is often."

The women exchanged a smile before Belle continued, "And I have the income from my piano students."

Rosilee reached across the table to pat Belle's hand. "Yes, I've heard very good reports from Mrs. McGee. She says Millie is actually practicing without a fuss."

"Well, we talked about goals and rewards." Belle smiled and revealed a secret. "And I mentioned to Millie she would probably get a special new dress when she plays good enough for a recital."

The Tremonts laughed and Rosilee said, "You're a clever woman as well as a good teacher then."

"I hope so. I'm trying as best I can." If only they knew how much.

Drake looked at his wife seated cross-legged on their bed. He twisted his hat. Damn, he hated arguing with Pearl. This is the very reason he'd avoided marriage. This is what he remembered of his parents' years together. Battle after endless battle. All very civilized warring for them, of course. His own little battle here had turned plumb hostile.

"Pearl, I *have* to go. Our fortune and that of the Holsapples and Binghams depend on it."

"Why does it have to be you?" She extended her hand to

point at him. "Why can't the neighbors take their own cows to Kansas?"

"Cattle, damn it. Not cows. Six thousand head of cattle. Hell, you've met George Bingham and Otto Holsapple. George has a broken leg and Otto is as old as Grandpa and only half as hardy."

"What about Vincente? He managed while you were gone to Tennessee." She tilted her head. Glorious honey-colored hair swept across her full breasts. He struggled to keep his mind on business.

"There are too many people between here and Kansas who won't give him the respect he's due, just 'cause he's Mexican. If he didn't lose half the cattle, he'd damn sure get a lot less for them at sale."

She slid off the bed to stand with her hands on her hips, sparks in her jewel-toned eyes. "So, I'm just supposed to stay here and watch for boogers and beasties while I play second fiddle for Lily?"

"Aw, Pearl, you know this is for the best." He feathered a finger down her cheek and softened his voice. Knowing he spoke the truth lessened the guilt that burdened him lately. She and Sarah would be much safer with Grandpa. He'd do his damnedest to keep Storm safe with him. "Try to understand. Give me a chance to go this one last time, will you?"

He saw her tremble at his touch, heard the sigh. She dropped her hands to lace fingers demurely in front of her.

"Yes. I'll give you your chance." She raised her head, the light of battle still in her violet eyes. "And I'll be waiting when you return. But promise when you're back, we'll talk about making changes."

He smiled, relief flowing through him. "Sure enough. Now, come here and give me one of those 'remember' kisses of yours to hold me 'til I get back."

"Hmph. After last night I hardly think you're likely to forget you're a married man." She blushed.

Remembering the night of lovemaking they'd shared last night, he smiled.

"Just one more reminder, honey. Show me how much I'll miss you."

She melted into his embrace. Damnation. This woman was habit forming.

It was another hour before he left the bedroom.

Twelve

Paper stacks littered the top of Pearl's cherry desk. Whirls of writing and figures covered each page. Pearl turned a sheet of paper to share information with Sarah and ran an ink-stained finger down a column of numbers.

"You can see I've made estimates on all the costs. We'll have plenty of money left over in case of bad luck. With some bargaining on the building, the place should pay for itself in a year."

"Are you sure, Sister?" Sarah bit her lip, a worried frown creasing her brow. "It's true you're a wonderful cook, but lunch every weekday is a lot to take on!"

Pearl nodded. "Yes, but there're enough people in this town to furnish steady lunch trade. I counted up the number of potential customers. If only a small portion of them come in, we'll sell enough lunches to keep us busy. And bread and desserts to sell for people to take home."

After worrying with it for days, she had made her decision last night. She refused to sit around and dally time away, enduring Lily's sour temper and biting remarks. Drake had no intention of allowing her out on the ranch, so that left little outlet for her energies.

She planned a small restaurant to serve lunch to the townspeople. Near the front she wanted a bakery counter for her breads and pies. She didn't need a lot of profit. Being useful and busy meant much more.

"I've looked at the building—at least on the outside. It's a good price even if the owner won't come down. The size works for this purpose. I'm going to make an offer for it."

"What will Drake say? What will Grandpa and Lily say?"

Pearl sought to soothe her sister's fears. Poor Sarah worried too much about what others would think.

"I don't know. But I can't be like Lily, and I can't sit around and drink tea all day with a woman who hates me. They'll have to understand."

Sarah nodded. "At least you'll be free in the evening to have dinner with Drake and Storm when they return."

"Yes. That's what I thought. While Drake's working at the ranch, I'll work at our restaurant. When he's home in the evening, I'll be there with him."

Her sister exhaled and lay both hands on the desk. "When do we start?"

Pearl couldn't hide her surprise. "Sarah, I know you like the life we have now. Even though school will be out for the summer in another few weeks, I don't expect you to be a part of this."

The young woman's eyes widened and pain flashed across her face.

"How could you think I would do anything else?"

Tears pricked behind Pearl's eyelids. Yes, how could she have doubted Sarah's loyalty? No matter what her sister said in private, to the world she offered Pearl unqualified support. She reached across and patted her sister's arm, then gave it a little squeeze.

"Thank you. Of course, we won't make much money at first, but we'll be partners in any profits we earn."

"But you've already given Storm and me part of your money. I don't need more."

"If the money came from the person we believe, it is partly yours and Storm's anyway. And you deserve to be paid for your work."

"It was kind of you to give Belle some money. She feels so much happier knowing she has money to provide for herself. Will she work at the restaurant too?"

Pearl shook her head. "No. I spoke to Belle, and asked her to keep on with her lessons and playing for the church. That's what she wants, and I don't want her forced to choose between Lily and me."

"That would be unpleasant for everyone. But won't we need more help?"

"We'll look for someone else. People we both like—if you're sure you want to go into this with me." She leveled her gaze at the younger woman, giving her another chance to refuse. "You'd still have your schooling for now, so it might mean getting up earlier to help with the baking."

Sarah repeated without hesitation. "When do we start?"

Pearl slid a sheaf of papers into her desk drawer. "Let's go look at the building. We'll make a list of all we'll need and start laying in supplies."

Sarah's eyes sparkled. "Let's change into our traveling suits. We'll look more-business like."

In spite of her determination to be independent and methodical, enthusiasm bubbled up and overflowed. "And we'll take the buggy to get the key."

"Where is the key?"

Pearl watched her sister's face as she answered. "This might be a bit awkward. It seems the owner became afflicted with wanderlust last fall. He left Lex acting for him."

Sarah's eyes widened and her hand covered her lips.

"You want *what*?" Lex almost shouted as he rose from his chair.

Pearl hoped her voice didn't squeak at his incredulous reaction. "I'm probably going to buy the building. But first, Sarah and I want to look it over."

He stood leaning forward, hands braced on his desk. "Pearl, have you thought this through?"

"Yes. I've given it a lot of thought. I want to invest my money in a business. I want to be doing something useful again."

"Wait until Drake returns. Please. The man only left two days ago. He'll be back in another month—six weeks at the outside." He ran his hand across his face. "Look, I know Aunt Lily can be a pill, but surely you can let things ride until then."

She decided on candor and shook her head. "No, Lex, I have tried, but I don't think I can bear it much longer. I mean no disrespect to your Aunt Lily. She's used to being boss in her house and so am I. But we see things very differently."

"I know you do. But, please," he held up a hand to stay her, "wait on this—just until Drake comes back."

Pearl's spine stiffened and she squared her shoulders. "Are you refusing to show me the property?" She hated the fact that Lex had to be involved, but this was the perfect property for her business.

His warm eyes softened. Chivalry and breeding forced him to concede, as she had known he would.

"You know I would never do that. I just want you to avoid unnecessary conflict. I promised Drake to look out for you while he's gone. Guess I'm not doing a very good job."

"Oh, Lex. I don't want you to be caught in the middle here. But I'm determined to open a restaurant to serve lunches to the townspeople. With desserts for them to take home. And to have a place to make my medicines and continue with my healing if people need me."

He exhaled and his body slumped, as if accepting defeat.

"All right. If your mind is set on this, then at least I can advise you on the condition of the property."

Together, the three of them walked from Lex's office and across a vacant lot to where the building stood. A false façade along the front added height to the wooden structure. Every board needed paint. A creaking sign moved in the breeze, the lettering faded and indecipherable.

Grimy windows prevented seeing inside, but the key worked easily in the lock. Lex opened the door and stepped aside to admit the two women. Enough light filtered through the soiled glass panes to show dust motes floating on pale sunbeams. Dirty oilcloth covered tables dotted across the room, their chairs overturned on table tops.

Sarah clapped her hands and smiled. "Oh, Sister. This will be perfect."

The look Lex shot Sarah's way left Pearl with no doubt of his true opinion of the venture.

He crammed his hands in his pants pockets and scowled. "It needs scraping and painting, the roof needs repair, and a ton of soap and water won't get this dump clean. And who knows what's nested in the kitchen?"

Pearl moved slowly through the large room, her mind mulling possibilities. When she reached the kitchen, she stopped. "Heavens. That range is older than I am."

Lex tapped it with his boot. "Can you cook on that?"

Always shy on her own behalf, Sarah leapt to Pearl's defense. "She can cook on anything."

"We'll do with this one until a new range arrives." She smiled at her sister. "Let's order it today."

Lex ran his hand through his thick auburn hair. "Pearl, please think on this some more. Are you sure you have to do this now? The building will still be here when Drake returns, at least it will if dirt acts like glue."

"It has to be now. And I have thought about it. A lot." Pearl looked around the room and smiled. She opened a cupboard to reveal a store of pots and pans waiting for use. She took a pan to the back door and tipped the contents onto a clump of weeds. "But all the mice families will have to find other homes."

The look of surprise on Lex's face at her reaction to a nest of mice amused her. He probably expected any woman to scream and climb on a chair at the sight of a rodent. He should know by now she came from tougher fabric. She continued her inventory. Another cupboard revealed stacks of plates in all patterns and states of disrepair—most cracked or chipped. Not to be discouraged, she said, "This will do very nicely. There's a big pantry and a storage room I can use for my medicines and herbs. Yes, we want to buy this."

Lex tugged at his ear and refused to meet her gaze. "Is, um, is Belle going to be working here, too?"

Pearl smiled at the smitten man. "No. She's happy with her music. She enjoys life with Lily and Grandpa."

She saw relief wash across Lex's features.

He asked, "But won't you need someone else to help? At least with the cleaning?"

"Yes, Sarah and I will need another woman to help us with the cooking and serving and also someone for the heavy cleaning and washing. First we need help with the painting and such. Maybe you can recommend someone."

"I'll ask around and let you know. If you're set on this, we might as well go back to the office and draw up the papers. Oh, hell. Beggin' your pardon, ladies, but Drake's gonna kill me. O' course, first he's goin' to beat me to a pulp."

After signing the papers, Pearl and Sarah went back to their building and measured for curtains, tablecloths, and seat cushions. When at last they climbed into the buggy for the trip back to Grandpa's, they had ordered a new range all the way from Chicago, claimed all the spare table flatware in town, and bought three sets of stoneware dishes to be delivered to the new restaurant. The bolts of fabric they took with them in the buggy. They chose crisp white cotton for aprons, red and white checks for tablecloths and curtains, bright red for chair cushions.

When Sarah and Pearl stepped into the front entry of the house, they heard a couple of loud crashes from the kitchen. Lily's angry voice followed. The two sisters rushed toward the sounds.

In the kitchen they found Ellen and Polly wringing their hands and cowering against the wall while Lily poured Pearl's remedies into a large pan. From the amount splashed on the floor and the litter of broken containers, she had been at her pursuit for some time.

"Let's see how she likes this. Mixing up her potions in my very own kitchen. And after I forbade her practicing her spells and witchcraft in this town, shaming me in front of all my friends."

Pearl stepped forward and wrenched a bottle from Lily's hand. "That was to help your father's rheumatism, you selfish woman!"

Lily's eyes blazed fire in a fit of temper greater than any Pearl had ever witnessed.

"Selfish? Me? Why you common quack, you! What right have you to come in here and take over? This house belongs to me and my father. You're only a guest here because your husband doesn't want you."

"I'm here for the safety of myself and my family. Do you think I prefer being here to living in my own home?"

"You have no home. Drake has the ranch, but you can be assured he doesn't want you there. You're nothing to him, nothing more than a legal mistress."

Pearl stepped closer to the irate woman. "I married your nephew, but don't think that gives you a right to be rude to me."

"He only married you because he needed someone fast to save his ranch." Lily gave a toss of her head and tilted her nose. "Drake would never have chosen you for a wife if he hadn't been desperate."

Pearl knew Lily spoke the truth, but her pride would never let her admit as much to this bitter woman. Still, all her newfound pride and the pleasure of the day's activities fled. She sagged to a chair as Grandpa stormed into the room.

"What in tarnation's going on out here?" He stopped in his tracks at the broken crocks, bottles, and spilled medicines.

Lily whirled on her father. "This is your fault for encouraging her. For enforcing that ridiculous will my foolish brother and his snooty wife made."

"That'll be enough, Lily. You're too old for me to send you to your room. But if you know what's good for you, you'll decide to go there *right now*."

"Oooooh!" Lily stamped her foot before she ran out of the room.

Grandpa sighed and put his arm across Pearl's shoulder. "Come on into my study. You too, Sarah." At the door he stopped and addressed the frightened servants. "You get this cleaned up and get on with your other chores. Take tomorrow off to make up for the extra work."

He didn't wait to see their reaction, but ushered Pearl and Sarah ahead of him to his private sanctuary.

He helped a sagging Pearl into a wing-backed chair near the fireplace and indicated Sarah should settle nearby before he sat at his desk.

"I told Drake this wouldn't work. He seemed convinced otherwise. Any fool knows two bossy women can't live in the same house."

Pearl fought back tears of anger, frustration, and embarrassment. "I'm so sorry, Grandpa. I've tried not to be bossy. I never meant to cause you trouble."

"Now, don't go holdin' yourself too much to blame for this mess today. Lily's used to having her way. So are you. It doesn't take a mastermind to figure out you two can't live in the same house for long."

"There's more." Tears that had threatened overflowed. "Oh, Grandpa, please don't hate me."

Through choking sobs, Pearl told Grandpa about the restaurant and her new plans. She knew she could no longer remain under the same roof as Lily, so she told Grandpa the other part of her plan.

"It will only cause continual problems, my being here. I think it would be better if I move somewhere else, so Lily doesn't have to see me at dinner or in the evening. Don't worry. I'll find a house to live in nearby, but far enough that Lily won't have to see me."

"Now, you can't be doing that, girl. You can't go shaming Drake that way, no matter if he does need to have his backside kicked a good swift one. And there's your safety to consider."

"But, I can't stay here. You see that, don't you? I would like to live at the ranch, but I don't want to endanger Sarah and myself by moving into an isolated area."

Grandpa sat with his chin on his chest for a few minutes,

his fingers making a tent over his stomach. "Here's what I think we should do. I'll hire four men as body guards for the two of you if you promise not to separate in your coming and going."

Pearl stopped snuffling to consider his idea. "How will I get my repairs done? And then the cooking?"

"The men can ride into town with you each day when Sarah comes in to school. You'll have to stay all day and the men can ride home with you in the evening. They can take turns being on watch all night."

She wiped her eyes with her handkerchief. "And I can live at the ranch now? Make it our real home?" A great burden lifted from her heart.

Grandpa nodded. "Yes, girl, I believe you're the very one to do exactly that."

The next morning Pearl hugged Belle. "Don't worry. Lily loves having you for companionship and wants you to stay." She met her friend's gaze. "You know you're welcome to come anytime you change your mind, or to visit. But don't come without an escort—for safety's sake."

Belle wrung her hands. "I feel disloyal. After all you've done for me."

"There's no need. This is what I want, but it's not right for you."

"Thank you for understanding." Belle hugged her once more.

Lily was conspicuously absent from the parting, but Grandpa oversaw loading onto the wagon those things belonging to Pearl's family. The four men he'd hired were well armed and looked able. All four were so pleased to have the job that Pearl wondered what sort of payment they received from Grandpa. All but one had served as a lawman in some capacity.

Jeff Granger stood almost as tall as Drake. The middle-aged man had served as a Texas Ranger until a gunshot to his lung left him reluctant to take on those duties again. He seemed fit enough but liked to stay near Kincaid Springs. He vowed to Pearl he would never sleep on the hard ground again, nor camp out in all kinds of weather.

Beau Benton was a bounty hunter who looked every bit as dangerous as those he hunted. He wore buckskin clothing and his hair hung past his shoulders. In spite of his rough appearance, he was polite and offered the women a soft spoken greeting. Though a large man, he moved silently as a wraith.

Abe Kline was short and squat, but Pearl marveled at the strength he displayed when he loaded her trunk by himself. Also a bounty hunter, he had intelligent brown eyes and a friendly smile. He looked like a storekeeper in his collarless shirt and waistcoat.

Zed Isaacs was down and out, fighting the ravages of years of alcohol, and needed a job to stay out of jail. He was one of Grandpa's projects and coming along well toward staying on the wagon and out of the gutter. The lanky man walked slowly and seldom spoke. He was reported to be a perfect shot with pistol or rifle—drunk or sober.

Grandpa drove the wagon with Pearl and Sarah sharing the seat. They rode half an hour before he turned down a narrow road between large live oaks. As they rounded a bend, Pearl caught her breath.

Grandpa stopped the horses and pointed to the river gliding along tree-lined banks to their left. "That's the Pedernales River running there. Spelled wrong on the maps 'cause some Yankee fellow surveying it got it wrong. Folks who know pronounce it pur-duh-nall-ess."

Above them at the right, a house sprawled across a rise overlooking the river. Long, low and stretching across the hill, the square-cut stone merged with the landscape. A metal roof extended over the porch running along the front and as far on the sides as she could see. Her heart pounded in her breast.

"It's beautiful. The prettiest house I've ever seen." She blushed and remembered herself. "Your house is grand,

Grandpa. But this one . . . well, this one is perfect for this spot and for me."

"I built it, so don't think you'll make me mad by liking it." He clicked his tongue to the horses. "Of course, we started with just two rooms there in the center. Then we built on. Later Drake's father built on quite a bit, but his Amanda—that's his mother—never liked living here. They spent most of their life in town near Kate and me."

He stopped the wagon in front of the house. The door opened and a Mexican woman stepped out. "Señor Kincaid. How good to see you. Is all well with Señor Drake?"

"*Sí*, yes, Maria. This is Drake's wife and her sister, Sarah." He turned to Pearl and explained, "Maria has been house-keeper here for many years. She and her husband Miguel keep things going while Drake chases his cattle and horses."

The housekeeper bobbed to Pearl, and her face glowed with a beatific smile. Probably in her late fifties, her round figure and pleasing features made her look the aging madonna her name implied.

"Oh Señora, it is so good to meet you at last. Come, come, into your home."

Sarah and Pearl climbed down from the wagon and fol-lowed the glowing woman into the house. The guards checked through the rooms, against Maria's indignant protests in rapid-fire Spanish. Grandpa explained to the housekeeper about the need for extra safety while the men left to check the outbuildings. Then, the four guards could move into the bunkhouse and stow their gear where they would sleep.

Sarah had not spoken a word until they stepped into the house. "It's right for this place. This is a good house for you, Sister."

The native stone floor of the entry belonged to the original home. It now served as a large landing overlooking a massive room. A fireplace large enough to stand in ran along one wall. Facing her, doors opened onto a porch at the back of the house.

"Everything is in readiness for you, Señora Kincaid." Maria beamed at Pearl. "You have only to request and it will be done."

What a difference in the reception here and at Grandpa's. Calm descended on Pearl like a welcome cloak. She turned to Grandpa and asked, "Grandpa, do you want to show me through the house, or would you like Maria to do so?"

"You go ahead, girl. I believe I'll speak to Miguel about unloading that wagon. Might draft us some body guards to tote stuff." Grandpa closed the door behind him as he stepped onto the porch.

So far the house appeared spartanly furnished. No paintings or knickknacks to add warmth, nothing out of place, nothing to indicate anyone actually lived here. What furniture there was shone with polish, as did the floors. It was clean, and just a bit drab. She tingled with anticipation and contemplated the changes she could make.

Pearl stepped down to the main room and walked to the glass-paned doors. The house formed a large U-shape which enclosed a walled area.

"Oh, a garden." She noted the vegetable patch in the corner, and the neglected flower beds elsewhere. A fountain in the center no longer held water, but benches sat in place nearby beneath a large tree. It needed love and attention. She had both to offer.

Maria stopped beside Pearl. "I think when Señora Kate lived here it was *muy linda*, very pretty." She shrugged. "Señor Drake's mama hated this place. Now he has no time for the planning. He thinks only of business and building a great ranch. *Mí* Miguel is old now and has time only for the vegetables."

Sarah joined the other two women. "It could be lovely again."

Pearl nodded. "Yes, and there's plenty of room to grow my herbs."

"*Pardón?*" Maria's brow puckered.

"I need to grow herbs for my medical remedies."

Searching for the right explanation, Pearl didn't hear Grandpa return.

"Pearl is *la curandera,* Maria." To Pearl, he added, "That's Spanish for a folk healer."

Maria beamed and clasped her hands. "This is *verdad,* true, Señora? *Madre de Dios,* the Holy Mother of God smiles on us. We have great need."

She turned to Grandpa. "I see I must learn the Mexican language."

He nodded in agreement. "Yes, it would help a lot if you leaned the lingo. Drake speaks it like he was born to it." He laughed and scratched his chin. "Well, I guess he was, come to think of it. Maria took care of him when he was a baby."

Sarah came forward. "I'll learn with you, Sister."

"Wonderful. Will you show us the house now, Maria?"

Drake choked on the dust from thousands of cattle and swung around the herd. So far the trip had been routine. Storm, in charge of the *remuda,* waved as Drake rode by. That boy was a godsend, he'd say that. He turned his horse toward his brother-in-law.

"You eatin' again? Where do you get all the food?"

Storm shot him a crooked smile. "Fill my saddlebags with biscuits and jerky every morning. Cookie makes extra for me."

"No wonder you're growing like a weed. Time we get to Dodge, you'll be a foot taller." He noted the hem of Storm's denim pants already struck him several inches too high on his legs. The cuffs of his red shirt tugged tight and high above his wrists and fabric pulled taut across the shoulders and chest. "You better start wearin' the new duds Pearl bought you."

Storm paused with a biscuit almost to his mouth and looked at his clothes. "These are the new duds. Can't wear the others any more. Cookie says I'm havin' a growth spurt."

"Your sisters will be surprised when we get back." He thought about the two women, his woman in particular. "I guess they're enjoying themselves with the social life of Kincaid Springs about now. What do you reckon they're up to? A tea or shopping?"

"I think you'll be surprised. Pearl don't like that stuff."

Drake frowned. "What do you mean? Did Pearl say something before we left?"

Storm looked pensive for a moment and popped his uneaten biscuit into his shirt pocket. He licked his fingers and cocked his head at Drake.

"No need. I came to live with Pearl nine years ago, when I was five. I've watched her moods a long time. She tries always to get along, to be peaceful. But she has this certain place where she won't be pushed any more. Then she pushes back." He nodded his head. "She's 'bout to push back, do something. Make some big change."

"Like what? What the hell could she change about living in town? The women there seemed to do the same things over and over." Maybe that's what she hated. Hell, he thought women liked that sort of thing.

Storm shook his head and shrugged. "Don't know. But she'll do something. Maybe soon, maybe while we're gone. She won't stay in Lily's house, doing Lily's bidding."

"It's Grandpa's house." Damnation, how had his life gotten in such a mess?

Storm asked, "You sure Lily knows that?"

The kid had a point. Double damnation. He should have talked with Grandpa about keeping a tight rein on Lily. He sure as hell hadn't a clue how to keep one on Pearl. He wasn't even sure he wanted to.

Drake shook his head. "Naw, reckon Lily thinks she's queen bee. But what could happen? A little dustup maybe, soon over. After all, Grandpa and Lex are right there."

Storm raised his eyebrows in question. "You haven't spent much time with women, have you?" He cocked his head at Drake. "I lived with women all my life. My mother first, then my sisters and Pearl's mean old granny. Women don't think like men. You can believe me on this."

Storm should know his sister. All through the drive, Drake fretted about what Pearl might be up to. He imagined her tossing tea in Lily's face. Or telling the church folks the truth about her so-called cousin Belle. Or selling baked goods up and down the street from a cart with Lily chasing after her with a parasol.

Then he'd try telling himself Pearl couldn't get into any trouble right under Grandpa's and Lex's noses, especially with strait-laced Lily lordin' it over everyone. Part of him even tried to believe it.

One day flowed into another through the endless trip. Rustlers hit them twice and cut a hundred head after they crossed the Red River. They lost one of Bingham's men in that fight. Jayhawkers tried to keep them out of Kansas and forced a four-day detour. By the time Dodge City loomed on the horizon, Drake found only relief in the knowledge this was his last drive.

"Stay close to me, Storm," Drake cautioned as they entered the hotel. "This town has a surplus of mean hombres."

"Never saw a place like this." Storm wrinkled his nose. "Or smelled one."

"Ain't that the truth? This many cattle sure have their own perfume." Drake moved to the reception counter and checked them into adjoining rooms.

Storm slid the key into his pocket. "It'll seem odd to sleep in a bed tonight. But nice."

"Right. And I'm heading for the bathhouse and then to get a meal. You coming?"

"Sounds good to me." Storm examined a rip in his shirt sleeve. "I want to get some clothes I'm not bustin' out of, too."

After baths, haircuts, and a shave for Drake, the two dug into the biggest meal they could find. Drake had to leave part of his steak, but Storm cleaned his plate, finished Drake's steak, and had a helping of pie.

On the way back to their hotel they stopped at a mercantile and bought several sets of clothes for Storm. In the back room, Storm changed into a new pair of denim pants, gray shirt, and his new boots. Drake picked up a fancy shirt and added it to his own purchases for his family back in Texas. He had a bolt of fabric for Pearl and another for Sarah, handkerchiefs for Lily and Belle, and a money clip each for Lex and Grandpa.

"I needed something to wear home," he said to explain his new shirt as they left the store. "That meal and bath set real well with me. I swear I'm a new man."

"Smell like one." Storm cocked an eyebrow at him. "If you ask me, it's a big improvement."

A window display of women's things caught Drake's eye. He stopped in his tracks. "See that wrapper? That's just the color of Pearl's eyes." He put his hand on the door handle.

Storm stopped, but took a step backward. "You going in there? That's a woman's store, looks maybe like for fancy women."

"Gotta get that for Pearl. She doesn't have one. It'll look real nice on her."

A crooked grin broke across Storm's face. "I think you got it bad. Soon you'll find out how much."

He stopped, his hand still on the door knob. "What do you mean? Can't a man buy his wife a present?" What made this kid think he knew so damn much anyway? Especially anything about men and women business? He shoved open the door and stepped in.

Storm nodded and followed. "A man can, yes, if he is thinking of his wife often and sees something she'll like. Especially if being without her has made this man very grumpy."

As highly as Drake thought of his brother-in-law, he was coming to hate that almost inscrutable look on the boy. Let Storm play the stoic Indian. Hell, he'd buy his wife any damn thing he pleased.

Later, in the hotel room Drake called himself every kind of fool. He might have gotten carried away. All right, he definitely got carried away. He bought the lavender wrapper and a white one, two nightgowns of fine satin, some stockings, and a pair of earrings and matching necklace. He draped the necklace across his hand. The stones were the color of her eyes but they couldn't match Pearl's sparkle.

Hell, it was no big deal. He had lots of money, didn't he? Any man would want to spend some of it on his family. Hadn't he and Storm picked out gifts for Sarah and Belle and Lily, too? And Grandpa and Lex, Aunt Rosilee and Uncle Samuel. Storm was even mailing something to his grandfather in Tennessee.

It meant nothing. Just the sort of thing people did when they made a big sale. That's why the stores clustered near the stockyards. He sat on the bed as realization washed over him. He missed Pearl. Bad. No, not just the sex, though he sure as hell missed that.

No, he missed everything about his woman. And she was *his* woman. He missed the way she tilted her head and smiled at him. He held the necklace so the lamp glow caught the stones. And her eyes sparkling at him like brilliant jewels. And her sass. Lord, that woman had a mouth on her. He lay back on the bed and thought about all the things that mouth could do.

Storm's words haunted him. He had it bad for her all right. He wished he could be home tomorrow instead of the days and days it would take to ride back.

He sat up and put his purchases in his saddlebags. Ride, hell. In the morning he was catching the first train to Texas.

Thirteen

"Over here. Against this wall." Pearl had been drafting her body guards in their off duty time to help her remodel the ranch house. Now she instructed Abe and Jeff on placement of a large server for the dining room.

"That's perfect, thank you." She stood back to admire the room. "Doesn't it look nice?" Pearl set a pewter candelabra on the dark golden oak.

For days she had combed through the accumulation of Kincaid family furnishings stored here in the barn and in one of the outbuildings near Grandpa's house. Rosilee and Samuel Tremont opened their attic to her. Most things she found were too formal for the ranch setting. She salvaged a table here, a chair or rug there, until the large home now looked well furnished and inviting.

As the two men left, Sarah clasped her hands. "Oh, that looks perfect."

Maria nodded. "*Sí*. This house now looks like a home. Señor Drake will be so proud." She patted Pearl's arm and hurried back to her kitchen.

Pearl wondered if Maria was correct about Drake. What would his reaction be when he found she had not only moved in, but redecorated the home he loved and protected so carefully? She tried not to worry about it, but it lay always at the back of her mind. So many changes for him to come home to. What if he hated them all? What if he hated her for intruding on his sanctuary? Lost in thought, she stepped to the double doors of the veranda.

The garden also bore signs of remodeling. Piles of weeds and dead plants awaited hauling and burning where another guard, Zed Isaacs, worked with Miguel to right the neglect of years. Zed had thrown himself into the project with an enthusiasm surprising everyone. It seemed he knew a lot about gardening. His family had an estate with extensive gardens before the War and he supervised this garden as if it were the showplace his former home had been.

Still lost in reverie, she walked outside. Water piped from the river once again flowed through the fountain, thanks to an intricate set of wheels and chutes repaired by Zed. Pearl sat on a bench shaded by an ancient live oak and watched small fish dance through pads of the fountain's water plants. A gentle breeze tugged at her hair and cooled her skin. Peace returned to her each time she relaxed here.

In her heart, she knew Drake could not find fault with all the work she'd done. No, he might be angry she acted without his permission, but he would enjoy the result.

"Are you still nervous about opening the restaurant on Monday?" Sarah slid onto the bench beside her.

"Yes. It's only three days away," she answered, refusing to voice her anxiety about the changes at the ranch. "I know we have everything ready, but what if no one comes to eat there?"

"They'll come, if only out of curiosity. Everyone in town's talking about the restaurant."

Early Monday morning, after sending Sarah to school accompanied by Abe and George, Pearl opened the door to Kincaid Springs's new luncheon spot while Jeff stood watch outside. Pale yellow paint covered the building and dazzling white trimmed the molding at the green front door and each window. Flowers, still small but promising, bloomed in green window boxes.

Inside, bright light poured through sparkling glass framed by red and white checked curtains. Each table sported a spotless cloth over oil-cloth covered wood. Bright red cushions decorated each chair. Near the front of the room a long glass case awaited baked goods to be offered for that day. Not a speck of dust or dirt greeted the eye.

Before Pearl could put on her apron or Zed could take his sentry place in the corner, Rhoda Spiegel bustled in. "I just couldn't wait to get started. I've been watching for you."

The small woman removed the bonnet from her dark hair. Her brown eyes sparkled with enthusiasm as she tied a crisp white apron over her yellow dress. She moved without a wasted effort and seemed to have boundless energy. Pearl had Lex to thank for recommending the young widow.

Pearl had warned Rhoda about the need for safety and cautioned her about never being in the place alone. Dick Harrigan, another of Lex's contacts hired as kitchen helper, offered his help with any problems. Certainly the big, beefy man looked capable of handling any difficulty. Until all this trouble ended, though, she wanted no one left in the building after the guards left.

By eleven, they were ready for the rush of customers. And a rush it was. When they closed at two, they welcomed the respite.

"I think almost everyone who works in town came in." Pearl sipped her tea hoping for an infusion of energy.

Dick nodded as he poured hot water into the sink once again. "That they did. And they all liked what they found— even crotchety old Mr. Rockwell."

Pearl asked, "Which one was he?"

Rhoda rolled her eyes. "The sour lemon who asked for a second piece of pie because his first had a lump in it."

"It never!" Pearl straightened.

"Of course not, dear. He tries to cheat everyone. He wanted a free second piece of pie, so I let him have one today with a severe warning." She looked at Pearl and a frown creased her brow. "I do hope that's all right. You were so busy at the time I didn't want to bother you."

Pearl nodded. "Of course, you should use your judgment,

especially since you know these people so much better than I do. What did you tell him?"

"I told him that after today there would be no lumps in any pie, all the food would be perfectly seasoned and cooked, and he might as well plan on paying for whatever he ate."

Dick laughed and slapped his leg. "And what did the old grouch say to that?"

"He had the good grace to blush and said he'd have to see that for himself."

Pearl smiled. "So, I guess he'll be back?"

"You can count on it." Rhoda patted Pearl's hand. "His kind always come back."

Drake smoothed the wrinkles from his new shirt as the train rolled into the Kincaid Springs depot. "Let's go straight to the house, soon as we unload our horses."

Storm smiled at his brother-in-law. "I hope Pearl's been baking. I sure missed her cooking."

"Yeah? You don't look like you missed anyone's cooking. I think you gained twenty pounds and several inches."

Drake missed Pearl. He could hardly wait to see her, tell her about the trip and how successful he'd been. And to give her the presents. Most of all to get her alone in their room. He hoped she'd show him how happy she was to see him home.

Almost as soon as the train stopped, he and Storm were lowering the ramp from the boxcar where their horses rode. By the time other passengers greeted friends and relatives, he and Storm were hightailing it to Grandpa's.

They rushed into the house and Drake yelled, "Hello, anybody here?" He strode to the study. "Pearl? Grandpa?"

Lily flounced down the stairs. "Well, it's about time you showed up."

"Where is everyone? Where's Pearl?" He peered into the drawing room.

With a toss of her head, Lily dropped her bomb. "That woman you foolishly married no longer lives here."

He stopped cold and turned. "What do you mean, she no longer lives here? Where the hell does she live?"

"She and Sarah moved to the ranch three days after you left."

Drake didn't miss the "I told you so" look Storm shot his way before the boy asked, "What about the danger?"

"Papa hired four men to act as their bodyguards and to . . ."

Before his aunt could finish, Drake whirled and bolted out the front door and onto his horse, Storm following close behind. As fast as he could ride, Drake turned Midnight away from town and toward the ranch.

On the road, he slowed his horse and tried to think. Storm had been right, Pearl apparently got fed up with Lily. Why hadn't he seen it?

Maybe he should have made different arrangements for her before the drive. Damn, looks like a man could depend on his wife waiting for him. All she had to do was just bide her time. How hard could that be?

When the ranch house came into view, he slowed even more. It looked different.

Storm saw it too. "Things been fixed up some."

Drake noted the gate now hung straight, bright flowers bordered the walk and porch. A bushy fern stood on the porch near the rocker he liked to use of a summer evening. He dropped the reins over the hitching post and bounded up the steps. The door opened before he could reach it.

"Señor Drake, how wonderful you are home." Maria beamed her cheerful smile at him. "Señora Pearl will be so happy."

Inside the front door, Drake stopped in his tracks. Three people sat on a bench in the foyer, a bench that hadn't been there when he left. As he entered, they stood and nodded their heads in respect.

The eldest, a man he recognized as Vincente's father, spoke. "Welcome home, Señor *Jefe*, Chief. Your trip went well?"

"Yes, very well. Vincente brings our *remuda* and men back.

He and the rest of the men will be home soon." Feeling as if he overlooked an important factor here, he asked, "Is there something I can do for you?"

The three shook their heads in unison. "No, Señor *Jefe*. We wait for *La Curandera*."

Maria hastened forward. "Señora Pearl has helped so many with her medicines. People come from all over the county to see her. She lets them wait here until she can see them."

Storm said, "She likes to help people. Pearl's real good with her healing."

Close to snapping, Drake spoke slowly and clearly, "Maria, where is my wife?"

Surprise showed on the housekeeper's face. "Why, she is still in town at her restaurant, of course."

Hoping he hid his own surprise, he said, "I see." But he certainly did *not* see. *Not at all*. Her restaurant? What restaurant?

Still beaming at him, Maria continued, "At this time she's serving lunch to her customers. You can find her there, but she usually comes home about four with Señorita Sarah. Shall I find lunch for you and Señor Storm?"

"Yes, please." Storm said.

"No." Gesturing to his brother-in-law, he said, "You go ahead, Storm."

"Señor Storm, my Carlotta will find food for you if you will go into the kitchen. Or, you could come with us to see the changes in your home. Come, Señor Drake, let me show you the many things Señora Pearl has done for you." Maria tugged at his arm, leading him on a tour of his own home with Storm trailing along. "You see how she has used the pieces stored by your family to make this place welcome you. She has worked very hard."

He took in the rugs on the floor, the additions to the furnishings. He noticed little things like the placement of serving pieces on the buffet that used to sit in his mother's dining room—until she hired that fancy decorator. Drake had always liked that old furniture better than the ornate stuff the decorator ordered from all over the world. He wandered through the house taking in the changes as Maria chattered on and on reciting Pearl's virtues.

In the doorway of his study, he stopped dead in his tracks. The old rocking chair made from cattle horns stood waiting beside his desk. Though wood comprised the rockers and supported the thickly padded seat and back, a craftsman had used matched pairs of horns to form the legs, arms, splats, and a decorative fan across the top.

Maria smiled and patted his arm. "Ah, I knew that would please you."

"I thought Mother had it burned." Although he and his father loved that chair and laughed about the eccentricity of it, his mother had called it an abomination and refused to have it in *her* house.

Marie adopted her inscrutable mask. "It is possible Miguel misunderstood her. He stored it in a barn with other old furniture and covered it with heavy cloth to protect it." She shook her head. "Then, it seems, he forgot about it. But Señora Pearl found it. Oh, she laughed and laughed when she saw it."

"She—she laughed?"

"Oh, *sí*, yes. She said it was perfect for a rancher's home. I told her how you used to sit in it when your feet were barely long enough to touch the floor, how you would laugh at your longhorn chair."

Damn. Who would have figured her laughing? Just like he and his father had. Who could understand the woman?

Storm sat in the chair and gave a push to start it rocking. The boy had a silly grin on his face. With a shake of his head to clear his brain, Drake turned and left the room.

Every room showed Pearl's hand. Anger coursed through him that she had defied him. Lily had said Pearl moved here three days after he left. As soon as his back was turned, she deliberately went against him. She hadn't tried to wait out his trip as she promised. He should have sought out Grandpa or Lex. Where the hell were they when Pearl decided to move to the ranch?

He remembered about the body guards. That meant Grandpa was in on the move. Grandpa wanted Pearl here to begin with. Well, let's see how she liked it now that her husband was back. He stepped into his bedroom, oblivious now to Maria's commentary.

A five-fold screen in the corner caught his eye, the stained and painted panels depicting birds. He had no idea where she dug it up, but he recognized the Aubusson rug his grandmother loved. It had been discarded by his Aunt Lily after Grandma's death. The dark rose, violet, green, and browns were echoed in the new coverlet on the bed. There against the solid oak headboard of his massive tester bed lay fluffy pillows edged with ruffles.

Ruffles, on *his* bed. Now that was too much. Damned if Pearl hadn't changed his own bedroom. Moved her stuff right in. If he wasn't mistaken, that was even her blasted feather bed under the other bedding. Her rocker sat beside the fireplace, a basket of sewing on the floor nearby.

An extra wardrobe sat against one wall. He opened it to find Pearl's clothes hanging inside. Made herself right at home, didn't she? Well, it might be polite to let her live here, but he was a grown man. He didn't have to be polite, especially about his own home.

He caught himself. He guessed this was her home too. At least, the only one she had now.

A long buried pain gripped at his heart. Oh, God, what was he going to do?

This place had always been his safe harbor, his lone sanctuary against the cruelties of the world, a solitary solace. He couldn't let her in here, not the one place he felt safe. No, he couldn't let her—or anyone else—matter to him that much. He refused to let her into his heart, refused to open himself to the pain that might bring.

Something out back caught his eye. Gently, he tugged himself loose from Maria and walked to the window at the end of the room. He felt his jaw drop. In a daze he opened the door and moved onto the veranda—and stepped into the past.

He almost staggered to the bench beneath the tree he'd loved to climb as a child. Weak-kneed, he dropped onto the seat and stared around him. So many changes here, too. Compared to the way it looked when he left, he'd stepped into the Garden of Eden. He'd never noticed how bad it had been, not until now when he saw the difference care made. No wonder Grandpa wanted him to fix up the place. From the corner of the garden near the tall fence, Miguel stopped hoeing long enough to wave. Drake returned the greeting but made no effort to move from his perch.

He thought Maria had gone back to her kitchen, but she approached him from the house. Concern in her voice showed when she addressed him as she had when he was a boy in her charge. "*Mi Niñito*, my little one? Drake? Are you all right? Perhaps you should eat something, have a cool drink? Let me bring you something here in the garden."

"No, thanks, Maria." He stood, feeling several times his thirty years. "I . . . I think I'll go to town. I need to see my wife."

He and Storm agreed the boy would settle in at the ranch and stay safely inside the house while Drake sought out Pearl. His pride kept him from asking Maria how to find the restaurant. How hard could it be? How many new businesses could there be in town?

He spotted it right away. All neat and proper, just like Pearl would have it. Neat green lettering on a white sign announced *Granny's Lunches and Baked Goods*. Now why would she name her business after a woman who treated her so badly? Ah, he thought, because that's where she got the money, from her Granny.

Underneath the large print, smaller letters confirmed *Open Weekdays Eleven Until Two O'clock*. He glanced at his watch. One o'clock.

An hour to go until closing. What should he do? Should he rush in and demand to know what she meant, opening a place like this as soon as his back was turned? Should he drag her out and take her home? No, he'd slip in and wait to be noticed. She deserved to squirm a little before he laid down the law to her.

Then he saw Jeff Granger leaning against the corner of the building, rifle in hand. Drake nodded to the man and stepped in front of him. "How's it going, Granger?"

"Wondered when you'd get back. Lot of changes since you left." The man rolled a toothpick in his teeth.

Damn the man for his impudence. "Yep. I can see that. You one of my wife's guards?"

At the man's nod of assent, Drake added, "Any trouble?"

"Nope. Not yet." Granger smiled, and Drake caught the twinkle in the man's eyes. "Is there gonna be?"

He muttered, "Too soon to tell," and tipped his finger to his hat as he opened the door of his wife's establishment.

Inside, he stood with hands on his hips watching the buzz of activity. Men sat at every table. Zed Isaacs, stationed in a corner with a rifle across his knees, nodded at him but made no other movement. Pearl and another woman hurried back and forth carrying plates of food or taking away empty serving platters. Danged if there in another corner of the room didn't sit his own kin, Grandpa and Lex.

Although angry with her, he couldn't help but appreciate his wife's beauty. Pearl wore a crisp dark blue calico dress with a white apron to protect it. Her golden hair whirled in some sort of twist at the back of her head. She laughed and called over her shoulder to someone in the kitchen. He clenched his fists. Men joked with her, joked with *his wife*. Worse, she smiled and joked back. Where was her pistol now?

He nodded to the dark-haired woman and walked toward the woman he'd come to see, *his* woman. One by one, heads turned his way and the hum of conversation died.

He heard Grandpa say, "Lordy, we're in for it now."

Drake ignored everyone but his wife. He had him a fine head of steam building. And he could have held on to his anger—if about then Pearl hadn't spotted him and looked so danged happy to see him.

Her jewel-toned eyes lit with warmth and pure joy spread across her face. She was glad to see him. In all his life no one had ever looked so pleased just to see him. It hit him with a rush of happiness, warmed him all over. Then she bit her lip as if unsure what to do, unsure what he intended. That hit him just as hard.

She slid two plates haphazardly onto a table and stepped toward him. Suddenly he didn't give a damn about the other men in the room.

"Hello, honey." He stepped forward, swept her up in his arms and planted a kiss on her luscious mouth.

Hoots and cheers greeted his display. Her arms slid around his neck and she hugged him to her.

She broke the kiss, flustered and blushing. But she ran her hands over his chest and arms as if checking to make certain he was really there.

Seeing her again after all the weeks apart made him even randier than usual around her. All he could think about was getting her home and into his bed. What was it about this one woman that made his brain derail and him do all his thinking with his pecker?

"Thank goodness you're finally home. Is everything all right? Where's Storm?"

"Yes, everything's fine. He's at the ranch eating like he has a hollow leg." He looked at the plates she had carelessly deposited in front of two diners a few seconds ago. "Wouldn't mind eating myself. How about I sit here with Grandpa," he leaned near her ear to finish, "and you bring something to tide me over 'til I get you alone?"

She pressed him toward a chair, then ran her hands across his shoulders when he sat. "Yes, yes. Sit here. I'll get your dinner." She rushed into the kitchen.

From his seat across the table from Lex, Drake pinned his cousin with what he hoped was a blood-curdling glare. "So, you were gonna watch out for her while I was gone, huh? Keep her out of trouble?"

Lex held his hands up, palm out in supplication. "I told her you'd kill me, but only after you beat me to a bloody pulp first." He lowered his hands and shrugged. "She was bound and determined to do this. The least I could do was see it was legal and her investment protected."

Drake turned to his grandfather. "And your story?"

"The same, son, just looking out for her. Lily had one of her worst fits ever. Lordy, you never saw the like, screeching and carrying on. Poured out all Pearl's medicines and broke the bottles. There was no keeping the two in the same house after that."

"So, how long's this place been open?"

"This is her fourth full week." Grandpa looked around the busy room. "Doing real well. Busy people need a decent place to eat."

Drake snorted. "Looks to me like all the 'busy people' are men."

Lex corrected him, "No, sometimes ladies come in to eat. Lots come by for baked goods to serve at home."

As if to underline his comment, Mrs. McGee stepped inside and up to the glass display of cakes and pies. From the empty spaces, Drake guessed the case had held several times the number of desserts now tempting the clientele. The dark-haired woman waited on the mayor's wife.

Drake nodded to the front. "Who's waiting on Mrs. McGee?"

"Rhoda Spiegel. You remember, her husband was killed at the quarry this winter? Has three young kids."

"Yeah. Bad business. Tough on her. Who's in the kitchen?"

Grandpa glanced toward the open doorway into the preparation area. "Dick Harrigan. He does some of the cooking. Worked his way from Boston's bars to Texas doing whatever he found. Even worked as an assistant chef in some fancy Chicago hotel." He paused before he added, "He's also done some boxing. Promised to keep customers in line if necessary."

Lex leaned forward. "Things go all right on the drive?"

"We lost one of Bingham's men to rustlers." He tapped a

hand on his thigh, dreading relating the news to George Bingham. Thank the Lord, the dead man had no family, wouldn't leave another woman widowed. "Other than that, things went better than expected. One of our best drives."

Grandpa looked pleased. "That's good. Holsapple's going to need the money. His leg isn't healing up right. He won't walk again, or I miss my guess."

"Too bad, hate to hear it. But he'll have plenty of money now to hire someone to push him around in one of those fancy wheeled chairs."

Flexing his hand, Grandpa added, "I told him he should ask Pearl what to do to help his bones knit proper. That old fool doctor's no help. Thinks anyone past fifty ought to give up and die quietly."

Drake noticed his grandfather's gnarled hand looked less inflamed. The redness and swelling of his knuckles had all but disappeared. Grandpa sat straighter, his eyes shone clearer, sparkled more.

"You're looking fit and in the peak, Grandpa."

"Well, I'm feeling it. A sight better 'n I've felt in years, that's for durn sure. But I'm feeling guilty, too, if you want to know."

Surprised at the admission, Drake asked, "Why is that? Appears to me you should feel grateful your health has improved."

"Don't think I'm not. But, well, doctorin' me is what caused all the ruckus with Lily." Grandpa paused to tug at his earlobe. "You see, it was a tonic Pearl mixed up for me that set Lily off. If I hadn't asked for Pearl's help, the whole thing would have held off until you got back."

Drake shook his head. "Maybe. Storm didn't think so."

The other two men looked at one another then back to Drake with questioning faces, so Drake continued, "Storm told me on the trail that Pearl was . . . let's see, what did he say? Oh, yeah, he said Pearl could only be pushed so far, and she would be about to push back. I thought he was crazy, but he told me she would do something before we got home."

"He was right." Lex nodded. "Don't know how he knew, but he sure had her figured out there."

"He said it's 'cause he's lived with women all his life. Says they just don't think like men."

All three men shared a laugh before Grandpa admitted, "Yep, he sure enough hit the nail right square on the head there. Danged if he didn't."

Drake watched his beaming wife bringing him his lunch. The look of welcome warmed his heart again. It felt damn good to have someone to come home to, someone glad to see him. Maybe the changes at the ranch weren't so bad after all. What did he care if she dragged in old furniture and sewed on a few ruffles?

Pearl sat a heaping plate of roast beef, vegetables, and fresh bread in front of Drake. "It's nice to see the three of you laughing together again."

"It's good to be home," Drake grabbed her hand, realizing he spoke the trite phrase with his heart.

"Are you staying in town for a while? I'll be through as soon as Sarah's here from school."

She looked flushed, flustered. Like a girl with a beau. That welcomed him again. Damn, he wished he could take the pins out of her proper hairdo and spread it out across her shoulders. He wished they were alone.

He shook his head. "I'd better square up with Holsapple and Bingham. Got good news for them about the drive, but sad news for Bingham about one of his hands." Drake flashed a smile to conceal his regret at leaving this woman here while he fulfilled other obligations. "Reckon I'll see you later at the ranch, honey."

Pearl enjoyed dinner that night more than any meal in her life. She sat in her own home beside her husband. Her brother and sister sat nearby, looking almost as happy as she felt. At last they were a complete family. Pearl glanced at the guards sharing the meal. Surely they wouldn't need others watching over them much longer.

Drake and Storm had regaled them with all the problems faced on the drive and the glory of making a good sale in Dodge. She told them of all the work she had done getting the restaurant launched and her healing. Sarah even spoke about her schooling and the people she had met in town.

"I can't get over how much you've grown," Pearl said to Storm. "You look older, too."

Drake said, "He did a man's work. Ate like two men. Every time I saw him he was stuffing food into his face."

"It's true," Storm confessed with a smile. "Cookie made me extra. Said a growing boy needed lots of food. I wasn't about to turn it down."

"And the work?" Sarah asked. "Was it hard?"

Storm nodded. "Sometimes. It was hot and dusty, or wet and cold when it rained. Days were long and nights short. But I was with the horses and the men treated me as an equal, so I was happy."

"You did a man's work and kept the horses in top shape." Drake turned to Pearl. "Storm has a real gift with animals. But you told me that the first day we met."

After dinner the sentries excused themselves for their split duties and their time off in the bunk house. Pearl and her family moved to sit in the large room Drake called his parlor.

Soon Drake stood and yawned. "I'm bushed. Think I'll turn in. You must be tired, too, Pearl."

Pearl saw the knowing glance pass between Storm and Sarah, but she could hardly wait to be alone with her husband. "Yes. We had a very busy day, all of us." She rose and walked with Drake down the hall.

As soon as the bedroom door closed behind them, Drake swept her into his arms.

"I've waited too long for this," he said as he carried her to the bed and deposited her on the coverlet. He leaned down and planted a kiss on her lips, then broke it to work the buttons on her dress.

"So you missed me a little?" Pearl asked as she pulled his shirt from his pants and slid her hands up his chest.

She saw his breath catch as he closed his eyes and leaned into her hands. "More than a little. I missed you every night. Thought about you during the day."

His admission was balm to her tired body and food for her soul. Maybe there was a chance he could come to need *her* with him, not just need her body. She had missed him so much, missed that cocky grin he gave her and the way he called her honey.

Their movements became more frenzied, more hurried. Soon they both lay against clean sheets with their clothes strewn across the floor. Pearl had a few seconds to wonder about the large windows of their suite and the door opening onto the veranda. Thank goodness Maria had closed the heavy draperies when she changed the linens earlier in the day. Now, though the hour was not late, the only light came from the oil lamp on the bedside table. With a happy sigh, Pearl gave in to the pleasure of enjoying her husband and his lovemaking in her very own home. Time enough to worry tomorrow.

Fourteen

They lay wrapped in each other's arms. Tingles of pleasure radiated through Pearl's body. She reveled in perfect, if temporary, peace at last. Perhaps this man would grow to care for her. She dared not say the word *love*, even to herself. As her mind avoided it, her heart whispered it, yearned for it. *Love. Love. Love.*

Drake nuzzled her neck. "You've lost weight."

"A little." Another wave of pleasure swept through her that he noticed the few pounds she'd lost in his absence.

"You're working too hard." His hand smoothed over the curve of her hip.

"I wanted to get the house and garden ready before you came back so we could surprise you. It turned out to be a big job. When I arrived, it looked as if you only ate and slept here. I've tried to make it a home, some place you would find warm and welcoming."

"You succeeded. Even I can see that. You spent a lot of time choosing and rearranging things." He slipped a ruffled pillow under her head. "And making things, too. Must've had to work long hours to get it all done."

Pleased, Pearl smiled to herself. "I couldn't have done it without Sarah's and Maria's help. It was a lot, I guess, what with the opening of the restaurant at the same time. Then all the people started coming for my healing."

"Well, I think you've taken on too much. You're too thin

and look tired to the bone." He ran his hand down her rib cage and caressed a hip, as if to emphasize his comment.

His words hit her wrong. All her life people had criticized her. She hadn't realized how much she needed praise from this man until now. Reminding herself to keep a lid on her temper, she sought to answer his accusation with calm.

"Time is not so precious now that the restaurant is open and running smoothly. I'm lucky to have found Rhoda and Dick to help."

"When did you get this crazy idea for a restaurant, anyway?"

Crazy? Pearl bristled. She pulled from his embrace and scooted around to face him. "I wanted to put Granny's money to use. A place for people in town to have lunch seemed a good idea." Realizing her voice had risen, she softened her tone. No use letting others in the household know about this disagreement. "From the business we've had, I'd say it's a darn good idea."

Drake sat up and swung his feet off the bed. Pearl watched the muscles ripple across his broad shoulders and longed to pull him back, to reclaim the contentment of a few minutes ago.

He stood and reached for his pants. "Hell, you slavin' in town all day, only to return home to face a houseful of people waiting for your medicines—you call that a good idea?"

Pearl scooted up against the solid headboard of the bed and pulled the sheet across her breasts. "Usually there's not so many as today," she defended. "Sometimes no one is waiting to see me." Did he care she worked so hard, or did he resent the inconvenience to his schedule? She thought it more likely he resented the intrusion her businesses made into his life, the invasion of his home.

"What happens when someone is real sick? You can't safely traipse around all over the countryside. They can't come to the restaurant where food's being prepared, either."

Drake stepped into his pants and paced the floor beside the bed. Black hair spanned his wide chest and made velvet patches which narrowed and furred to a low vee in the soft light. She curtailed the desire that curled her belly and tried to concentrate on the subject, irritating as it was.

"No. Miguel and Maria have explained about the danger to our family. People seem to understand. They come here and wait. If it's an emergency, they send word and I fetch Sarah from school and come home early, or they come into town to see the doctor. Rhoda and Dick can manage the restaurant for a while without me."

"Well, it sounds crazy to me. You can't be in two places at once." He ran his hand through his hair again and faced her to accuse, "Pearl, why couldn't you have just stayed at Grandpa's and waited for me 'til I got home like you promised?"

She felt her heart break a bit. As she feared, he wanted her back in town. He wanted to control her life. "I *tried*. Believe me I tried."

When he made no answer, she continued, "Lily is so different from me, but she expected me to be exactly like her. I'm not. I can't be like her and there's no pleasing her."

She heard the pleading tone in her voice and bit back tears. "Drake, please try to understand. I can't be what I'm not."

"I'm not asking you to be what you're not." He spread his arms wide, palms up, his face a mixture of confusion and anger. "I'm asking why couldn't you have waited for me?" he bit out again. "It was only a few weeks."

"I *did* wait for you. But I waited in your home, not in Grandpa's." She raised her chin, hiding the tremble of her lips. "In *our* home. I married you, Drake Kincaid, not your grandfather. I belong here."

"With four armed guards round the clock?"

"It's far better than living in another woman's home where I'm criticized constantly, where I'm not wanted." She hugged her arms. "But I'm not wanted here, either, am I?"

He dropped his hands to his side and stopped pacing, his back to her. His hands flexed and the muscles across his broad shoulders moved as if he took a deep breath before he spoke again. The pause cut her to the quick. She caught her lower lip between her teeth. Would he deny it?

When he spoke, his voice was low with controlled anger. "Pearl, I didn't say that."

"But it's true, isn't it? You never intended for me to live here, did you?" She pulled the sheet up again and crossed her arms over her breasts. The urge to throw herself under the covers and bawl like a baby almost overwhelmed her.

He faced her but refused to meet her gaze. "I would have brought you here, soon as the trouble was over."

She heard the lie in his tone. "Would you?" She shook her head in disbelief. "Somehow I don't think so. I promised to be your wife in every way, Drake, and thought you meant to be a husband to me in every way. Now I'm not so sure."

"Yes, I would have." He sat on the side of the bed and faced her. She heard hesitation in his voice, as if he were unsure of himself. "It's true I didn't intend to at first. Hell, I was so mad at having to marry to keep the ranch I couldn't think straight." He pried one of her hands loose from the sheet she clutched and drew tiny circles on her palm with this thumb. "But, well, after I got to know you some, that changed. I wanted you with me then."

A terrible weight lifted from her shoulders. She felt years younger. "Thank you. You have no idea how much that means to me. I've spent twenty-six years being unwanted. It's important I'm wanted now."

"You are." He dropped her hand and stood. "But why did you have to get so all-fired messed up with this restaurant? Why didn't you bide your time at Grandpa's until I got back?"

"The restaurant makes me feel independent. I'm not used to taking handouts or orders from anyone. And I've already explained about Lily. I can't be her or Helen Morris or any of the other women she thinks are right for you."

"I didn't ask you to change who you are. But couldn't you have tried to fit in a little until I got home? Go to a few tea parties and listen to women prattle. How hard could that be?"

"A lot harder than you know." Frustration overwhelmed

her. How she would like to rail at him, beat her fists against his chest.

She slid from bed and grabbed the new silk wrapper he'd brought her from his trip. "If I'd known about Granny's money, none of this would have happened. I'd have been gone when you came to Piper's Hollow and you would have married someone else."

"And I suppose that's what you wish happened?" He stood facing her, his hands at his hips.

"I didn't say that. But we would never have met, wouldn't be having this conversation if I'd had money. It came too late to make a difference that way."

"And you felt compelled to rush right out and use the money? Why not invest it—or save it? Why not discuss your plans with your husband?"

"My *husband* was never available to talk with. Even before you left with those cows you wouldn't talk to me about things. A marriage should be a partnership, but you don't want a partner. You want to use my body and then tuck me out of the way until you feel the urge to take me out again."

"Now that is unfair. When have I ever made you think all I wanted from you was your body?"

"That's all you ever wanted. First you needed my body to meet the terms of the will. Then you wanted my body for . . . for satisfying your body. You never considered my needs."

As soon as she said the words, she regretted them. "No, that's wrong. You've been very considerate of my family and me, seeing we had everything we needed and all the money we could spend. But you missed an important part."

"And what would that be? I'm sure you'll tell me."

"Everyone needs a purpose. To feel needed and useful." And to be loved, she silently added.

"And it takes that stupid restaurant to make you feel useful? Damn, I wish that place would burn to the ground."

She couldn't suppress the gasp of shock at his statement. "Yes, it makes me feel useful, like I'm doing something to make a difference in this community. You stashed me in

Grandpa's house like some unwanted toy until you were ready to play again. You treated me like a . . . a mistress or a fallen woman instead of a wife! Oh, you gave me your name, but you didn't give me any part of yourself."

He waved an arm at her, fury coloring his voice. "You knew this was no love match from the start. You agreed to the terms, even set some of the conditions yourself. I gave you everything I thought a woman wanted. What did you expect from me?"

"I thought a husband would share his thoughts and plans with me, share his life. I thought, well, I thought if or when I married, it would be to someone who would appreciate me for who I am and appreciate things I did for him."

"Like putting ruffles on my bed, taking over my home?"

"I wanted to make this house into a real home."

"Well, you sure made it a home for yourself." He picked up a ruffled pillow and tossed it across the room. "Did you ever think I might hate ruffles and gewgaws? Did it occur to you that maybe I liked the way the place was?"

"Fine." She gathered the coverlet and the other pillows into a pile. "I'll get rid of everything I changed in here. By the time you come in tomorrow, it will be exactly like you left it when you went away. And that includes me. I'll move to your mother's old room. You can have your barren room back to yourself again, just the way you wanted it all along."

He advanced on her, anger flaring his nostrils and sparking from his eyes. He jabbed a thumb at his chest. "No, I'll move. You needn't bother!"

"Oh, yes. I'll bother. You want to live like a monk, you have my blessing." She grabbed her dress and petticoat as she swept through to the adjoining bedroom once used by Drake's mother. She kicked the door closed behind her with a final and very satisfying bang.

In the tiny Ainsworth cabin in Piper's Hollow, Burris stuttered, "Now, boss, don't be gettin' so riled. It warn't our fault

Jug fell off'n the train. We wasn't even there. We found out about him fer you, though, didn't we?"

The sharp retort from the third man in the cramped room came before Willard could add to his brother's explanation.

"That Parker bitch is to blame for his death." He whirled and pointed a finger at the brothers. "And you two fools! It's your fault you botched a simple train holdup."

"It wasn't so simple." Willard braced himself and faced his employer. "We both got hurt—real bad. Like to got caught or even killed. We wuz laid up with no one to help us 'til we could make our way back home." He glanced at his brother who leaned heavily on a homemade crutch. "Burris still has trouble walkin'. I thought he wuz gonna die from the infection."

"Some loss that would've been." The man banged his hand on the table and leaned toward Willard. "You two've ruined everything so far. You have one more chance. I want Pearl and those two brats taken care of—even if you have to burn down the whole damned town. And I mean I want them out of the picture entirely." The man threw money on the table and his eyes narrowed to slits. "Do you understand?"

"Reckon we do." Willard picked up the stack of cash and slipped it in his pocket. He'd count it later.

Sure he understood what the man meant, but he didn't like it. How had he gotten into this anyway? He only wanted to make some money and see a little of the world. Didn't seem any harm in that. Now he was supposed to kill three people he'd no cause to hate, and two of them were women. It didn't sit well with him, but he was too scared of this man to object. He'd seen the results of this man's anger before and he had no wish to be on the receiving end.

When the other man had left, Burris listened at the door before he limped over to his brother. "What're we gonna do?" he whined. "We ain't gonna kill 'em, are we?"

Willard rubbed his hand across his face. He wished he could just rub this whole business away. "I don't know. No, course not. Maybe we could rob Pearl and take off for N'Orlins like we wanted to in the first place."

"Bet he'd find us. Then he'd kill us 'stead of them." Burris nodded at the door, and fear of the man who had just left showed in his face.

Willard feared their so-called friend as much as Burris, but he didn't want to admit it to his brother. "Get some sleep. We got to leave fer Texas first thing in the mornin'."

"I sure wish we could just keep going, real far away. He gives me the creepies, that cold look in his eyes and all. It's like he don't got no soul, like he's just hollow inside." Burris burrowed into the ragged blankets of his cot before he asked, "Reckon why he hates Pearl so much?"

"I cain't figure it. She never hurt nobody. Even took care of Momma when we couldn't pay her nothin'. Helped make Momma's last days go easier." Willard wondered what Momma would think of her boys now. It hurt him to know they had let her down again.

Burris lay on his cot and scratched his belly. "Did you know Jug was s'posed to kill Pearl?"

"No. Reckon them two did lots of things we didn't know about. They wuz allus plannin' somethin'. S'pose it's just as well we didn't know 'bout all that other stuff."

"Seems like we oughta be able to get out of this here mess. Think of somethin', Willard. You're better at thinkin' than me."

"He'd kill us fer sure if we tried to cross him." Willard lay down and shut his eyes, hoping the whole situation would disappear. "What are we gonna do? We ain't never killed nobody. We cain't kill no women."

"'Sides, I allus kinda liked Pearl."

Drake leaned on the corral, one foot balanced on the bottom rail. With frequent comments to Storm, he watched the boy put the new bay mare through her paces. Storm had matured in the months since they'd left Tennessee. The confidence he showed with horses now spilled over into his relationships with humans.

Drake willed his mind to focus on training the mares brought from Tennessee. No matter how hard he tried, he couldn't shut out thoughts of his marriage. When he left for the drive, everything looked rosy. Everything went his way then. A couple of months later, he felt lost in chaos. How had things gone so wrong in so short a time?

Had he lost his one chance at a happy marriage? His and Pearl's relationship looked more and more like that of his own parents. For a while there at first, he had thought Pearl and he might make a go of it. Sure she was mad about staying in town, but he would have brought her to the ranch eventually.

Guilt surged in him. When would he have brought her here?

In retrospect, his desire to foist his new family onto Grandpa seemed petty and childish. The question of safety could have been addressed at the ranch. He could have hired more men to help. Perhaps then Pearl wouldn't have come up with the crazy idea for this restaurant.

Damn, but he hated that place. All those men ogling his wife and her waiting on them like a servant. Drake never would have thought to agree wholeheartedly with his aunt about anything, but he hated the restaurant as much as Lily did. Maybe more. He pulled out his pocket watch. Almost eleven.

"Think I'll go into town," he called to Storm. "Want to go with me?"

"No. I'll stay here." Storm patted the neck of the smart-stepping mare. "She's making progress and I don't want to lose her mood."

Drake stopped off to tell Maria he'd eat in town. Miguel and his grandson Javier watched for strangers and Storm would stay close to the house all day.

He mulled over his problem on the ride into Kincaid Springs. With no decision in mind, he stopped off at the office of his cousin and grandfather. Lex sat at his desk surrounded by law books and stacks of papers.

"Grandpa in court?" he asked Lex.

Lex nodded. "The Henderson trial's dragging on. Defense dredges up witnesses, prosecution discredits them. Got Grandpa out of sorts." His cousin gave him a sharp look. "You look a mite put out yourself."

"Do I?" Drake wondered how to answer. "Guess I'm not used to Pearl's businesses yet. People come to the house for her healing late into the night, then she's up and gone into town early for that blasted lunch trade."

"Good thing she vetoed the idea of serving food in the evening as well as noon."

Drake froze. "What do you mean?"

"Ah, she didn't tell you. People approached her to serve meals all evening. She told them she wanted to eat dinner with her own family, sit beside her husband each evening."

"Hell, she's so tired now she can hardly sit at the table by evening."

Pleasure she'd turned down the extended business hours and her reasons mixed with annoyance she hadn't bothered to tell him about it. But then, she was so busy they hardly talked any more. They didn't do a lot of things as much any more.

"Yeah. Belle said Pearl's lost weight and looks tired all the time."

"You still seeing Belle?" Drake tried to keep the censure from his voice, but he thought Lex asked for major trouble there.

Lex's gaze held a steel challenge when it met his. "More than that. Tonight I'm proposing to her."

Things were worse than Drake figured. His cousin had such high goals, a stringent moral code. Drake couldn't reconcile those with Lex's choice to marry a common prostitute.

"What about running for office? I thought you wanted to be governor some day. Somebody finds out about Belle's past and you're political career is finished."

"I still plan to run for office. But without Belle, it all means nothing to me."

"What if someone recognizes her? It only takes one man to ruin her new life—and yours."

"What are the chances of someone from that backwoods place coming through here, seeing Belle as she is now, and recognizing her? From clues I've picked up, I think she only worked a few weeks before she went to stay with Pearl."

Drake fixed his gaze on his cousin and leaned on the desk's front edge. "She ever tell you the truth about her past?"

Lex shook his head. "No. She skips a short time of her life when she's talking. Goes from her folks' farm to Pearl's and gets real nervous. Guess I should tell her I know all about her."

"No. Wait for her to tell you. Probably she never will."

"Yes, she will. I know she cares for me, hope she even loves me. I intend to find out tonight."

"I think she's taking advantage of everyone in our family, Pearl included. Didn't take her long to abandon Pearl for Lily."

"Pearl insisted she stay with Lily, continue giving her piano lessons at Grandpa's. Lily likes having her around. Gives her someone to go shopping and socializing with."

Drake snorted. "And order around." His aunt loved being the center of attention and Belle gave her a constant audience.

"Lily will have to find a new companion. I want Belle for myself if she'll have me."

"You told your parents?" He could only imagine his proper Aunt Rosilee's reaction to having a prostitute for a daughter-in-law.

"Yes." Lex met his gaze. "All of it."

Incredulous, Drake asked, "You told them about her being a soiled dove?"

"I did. Don't want them finding out from someone else someday."

"And Aunt Rosilee and Uncle Samuel approve of you marrying this woman?"

Lex stood to meet Drake's gaze. "Didn't ask them. Just told them how it is. They seem to accept my decision."

"You're making a big mistake if you ask me."

"I didn't *ask* you, any more than you asked me when you proposed to Pearl. I *told* you my plans."

"Yeah, well maybe I should have let you talk me out of mine."

Lex shook his head. "You misunderstood my objections. I didn't want to talk you out of marrying Pearl. She's the perfect woman for you. I wanted you to realize you tampered with lives other than your own."

"Yes, now I see that." Drake slumped into a chair in front of his cousin's desk. "Damn! How could I have been so cocky?"

"We all have our moments." Lex sat back in his desk chair. "I take it things are a bit, um, strained at the ranch?"

"More than a bit. Pearl hardly talks to me." He took a deep breath and confessed, "She's moved into Mother's old room."

"How'd you let that happen?"

"Hell, I don't know. We were arguing about that darn lunch place and her money and all the changes she made at the ranch. Before I knew it, we both got riled."

Lex shook his head in disbelief. "Sounds like you got some fence mending to do."

"She's gone all day, has people coming in all evening and sometimes during the night. I never have a chance to see her alone."

"Give her time to work it out. She's still finding her way in all this."

He might have known Lex would recommend being calm and thinking things over—his cousin's favorite course of action.

Drake flexed his hands before he shoved one through his hair. "I'm giving her time, but sooner or later she has to cut out something."

Lex smiled. "Don't worry, cuz. It won't be you she cuts out. In case you haven't noticed, the lady is crazy about you."

The statement came as a shock to him. No, he hadn't noticed, especially lately. She seemed to tolerate him only as the means to an end. With a bitter taste in his mouth, he realized that had been his attitude toward her when they married. Now she was giving him back some of his own. Life sure played some devilish tricks on a man.

* * *

Drake watched Pearl carry clean linens down the hall. Her braid swished back and forth across her hips as it had the first day he'd seen her in Tennessee. As then, she wore no shoes, but her new lavender print dress fit in all the right places.

He followed her into the master bedroom and closed the door with a quiet click behind him. She whirled and her eyes widened in surprise.

"Saturday is one of the few days you can rest a little. Don't we pay Maria's granddaughters to do that sort of thing?"

"They went into town with their parents. I thought I'd get this side of the house ready. Sarah is taking care of the bedrooms on the other side."

He looked at the stark room and wished he could take back the words he'd spoken so recklessly. She had removed all the changes she'd made the day after their argument. It had come as a shock to him when he came in the next night. She'd been right when she called it a monk's room. Once he'd seen the difference with the additions she'd made, it looked cold and empty by comparison. After he'd made such a fuss, how could he tell her he liked it better her way without seeming a fool?

He took the stack of linens from her and laid them on the bed. "Pearl, I've missed you. Missed having you beside me at night, missed talking to you before we drifted off to sleep."

A blush spread across her face but she didn't give. "You mean you've missed, um, missed our coming together."

He trailed his fingers along her jaw. "Yes, I've missed that. But I've missed the closeness we had. I liked having you near."

He saw her expression change, soften, but still she didn't yield.

"Did you?"

"I've been thinking over what you said. You know, about being partners and all?"

"And?" She met his gaze with questioning eyes.

He slid his arms around her waist, drawing her near. "I

guess I never thought about marriage that way. I can see that's the way Grandpa and Grandma were, though. They had the kind of marriage I always wanted."

"Not your parents?" At last she laid her hand on his chest.

The thought of his parents' marriage and how much his had come to resemble theirs sobered him. "No, never theirs. Mother was Amanda Drake, of the Boston Drakes, and never let anyone forget it. She hated Texas and everything in it, especially the ranch. Dad always gave in to her, but he resented it."

"How sad for them . . . and for you." She brushed her hand across his jaw in a sympathetic gesture.

He thought that summed it up pretty well. "Yes, sad. They wasted years with petty bickering. I don't want us to be like that. Can't we start over?"

She cocked her head at him, her jewel-tone eyes aglow. "What do you suggest?"

"Let's start with this," he said as he lowered his mouth to hers.

She tasted so good, like the cinnamon on the bread at breakfast and her tea and . . . just her. At first she remained immobile against his touch. When she returned his kiss, his hands roamed across her body, snugging her into his arousal. Her arms came around him, kneading places on his back that yearned for her touch.

His fingers found the buttons of her dress then pushed the fabric aside to allow access to her beautiful breasts. How he had missed touching her, her touching him.

She stilled his hands with hers. "Drake, have you forgotten you wanted everything about me out of this room?"

"That wasn't my idea." His lips trailed down her throat to a rosy orb. He heard her gasp of pleasure when he nipped her peaked nipple.

When he swept her into his arms and lowered her to his bed, she pulled him with her. His hands grasped at her clothing, pushing and pulling it aside. Blood boiled in his veins, his heart pounded so hard he almost missed the loud knock.

Maria's excited cry came through the closed door. "Señora

Pearl, Señora Pearl. The Gonzales baby is very ill. The family is waiting for you now."

Drake lay across Pearl and their gaze locked. With what appeared a mixture of regret and relief, she straightened his shirt and slid out from under him.

Her hands righted her clothing. "I'm coming, Maria," she called, and tucked errant strands of hair back into her braid. "I have to go. Maybe we could talk later about us being partners and our marriage and all."

"All right, we'll talk later. I can see a sick baby needs help now."

After one long backward glance, she left the room.

Drake let himself fall across his bed. Would he ever get his own wife alone in his bed?

Pearl and Sarah cleaned up the small room she used as a treatment room. "You go on and I'll finish here. Do something fun until dinner," she said to Sarah before she turned to Maria's granddaughter. "Thank you again, Carlotta, for interpreting. I'm able to understand more every day, but I don't think I'll ever get your language clear in my mind."

"Ah, but your speaking is much better now, Señora Pearl. Soon you will not need me."

Sarah and Carlotta left together and Pearl sagged into a chair. Her exhaustion left her ready to weep. As she lay her head on crossed arms resting on the table, Maria came into the room.

"Señora Pearl, you must rest more. You will endanger the *bebé* if you do not."

Startled, Pearl raised her head. "You know?"

"I have many children and grandchildren. I know the signs well."

"Please don't tell anyone. I haven't told Drake yet."

"He will be pleased. A man needs children to carry on his work, to help build his land, to keep him company in his old age."

"I—I wasn't sure how he would feel. I know he wants children, but does he want them so soon?"

Maria patted Pearl's shoulder. "You will make him very happy."

Pearl remained where she sat after the housekeeper left the room. Would Drake be happy? He hadn't seemed happy at all with her of late. What was she to do about this restaurant and her healing? She couldn't keep up with both much longer. Those early days in town and having nothing to do with her time seemed a world away.

The sound of buggy wheels outside made her body cry out for rest. Not another patient now, please. But the voice she heard greet Maria startled her. She rose and rushed to the entryway.

"Belle?" When the other woman threw herself into Pearl's arms, Pearl asked, "Whatever's wrong?"

Belle's sobs muffled her words. "I've run away. Please let me stay here until I can figure out what to do, where to go."

Pearl's eyes met Maria's gaze over Belle's heaving shoulders. Pearl guided Belle down the hall to a guest bedroom. With the door closed, Pearl led her friend to the bed before she asked, "Now, tell me what this is all about."

Belle sat, then hopped up and paced. "Lex wants to marry me." She dabbed at her tear-streaked face.

"That's wonderful. You make such a nice couple." Then she remembered Belle's past. "Oh. You haven't told him about Roxie's?"

"No. How can I? He has such high ideals and morals, such high standards. How could I tell him?" Belle whirled to face her. "Did you know he wants to run for office, wants to be governor of Texas some day?"

"I see. I think you should have told him, Belle. He'll think you don't care for him if you run away."

"But that's why I have to disappear. I can't let him ruin his life because of me."

Pearl felt decades older than her friend instead of a few

years. "That should be his decision, not yours. He loves you. The choice should be his."

Belle shook her head in denial. "No, no. Don't you see? He'd probably feel honor bound to go through with the marriage because he proposed, even if he changed his mind later. I couldn't bear knowing he was ashamed of me, or resented me."

"Deserting him is no better," Pearl reasoned.

"Yes it is. Better for him, at least. What if we married and my being with him ruined his chance at politics? I couldn't stand it. No, he'll find some woman from a good family who can help his career."

"What are you going to do?"

Belle held her self straight, her head back. "I don't know, but next time I'll hold out for love, even if it's nothing like the love I feel for Lex. I know I'll never trade my body for a price again."

"There's always a price." Pearl felt close to tears herself.

"You never had one."

Pearl looked at Belle with a heavy heart, "We all have our price. Yours has gone up considerably now that you know your true worth."

"And yours?"

Pearl turned away, unable to meet her friend's questioning gaze. "Mine just changed, is all."

"Oh? How?"

"I was willing to trade myself for security, for a safe place for me and my family."

Belle placed a hand on her arm. "And now?"

She closed her eyes and sighed. "Now all I want is him. All I want is Drake's love."

"But you have it."

"I'm not so sure and I have to know. I have to know."

Before I tell him about the baby, she thought. I have to know if he would stay with me without the baby. I couldn't bear to think we're still married only because of our child. How can I know what he really feels?

* * *

"She says she can't marry him, that she's going away." Pearl explained to her husband.

"And did she say why?"

Pearl wondered at the speculative look he gave her. She didn't know if he was angry or worried for her friend. "She did. She thinks he can find someone from a good family who can help his career. You know he wants to be governor?"

He stood with his hands in the hip pockets of his denim pants. "I know." He looked about to say more, but didn't.

"It's all right that she's here at your ranch for a little while, isn't it?"

She sure knew how to make a man feel small. "Pearl, this is your home, too. Of course, it's all right. But I don't think it's the answer to their problem."

"We'd better send the buggy back to Grandpa's. Lily will be needing it."

Drake turned as Maria summoned them to dinner. "I'll take care of it after dinner."

After they ate, Drake set out for town with Midnight tied to the buggy. Before he had driven a mile he met his cousin. Drake tugged on the reins to stop the horse and waited for Lex to reach him.

When Lex reined in at the buggy, Drake said, "Fine day for a ride eh, Cuz?"

"Is she still at the ranch?"

Worry lines pulled at Lex's face. His usually sparkling eyes were darkened as if from pain.

"If you mean Belle, yes. Though I haven't seen her. She's stayed in her room since she got there."

Lex's jaw jutted out, features set in stone. "Well, I'm going to see her, see what this is all about."

"You know what it's about." Drake felt obliged to add, "I hate to admit it, but guess I was wrong about her."

"How?"

"Seems she thinks you need to marry someone from a good family who can help your career."

"Hell! What right has she to decide for me? I know who I want to marry and how to manage my own damned career."

"You're preaching to the wrong pew."

"I'm going to settle this right now." Lex said and nudged his horse into action.

With a shake of his head, Drake turned the buggy around and headed back to the ranch. He wanted to see the outcome of this confrontation. Then he wanted a word with his wife about keeping secrets.

Fifteen

Lex dropped his horse's reins over the hitching rail before he stormed up to the door. Damned if he'd let Belle walk out on him with no explanation. He should have settled this last night.

He raised his fist but the door opened before he had the satisfaction of banging for entry.

"Hello, Lex." Pearl greeted him, "I thought we might see you today."

"I want to see Belle."

"She says she wants to be alone to think. She won't come out of her room."

When she hesitated, he pushed past her. "Then I'll go to her." He stalked up the hallway, opening each door along the passageway. "Belle," he shouted, "We're going to talk about this now. You might as well come out."

On the fifth try, he found her. She stood by the window, reddened eyes and tear-streaked face testimony to her state of mind. He closed the door behind him with a bang.

"How could you walk out with only that ridiculous note for me?" He wanted to shake her for the pain she caused him, wanted to pull her close and comfort her for her own pain.

"I did what was best." She turned from him and faced the window.

"How could it be best? I love you. I think you at least care for me."

He saw her shaking hands, heard her shuddering sobs. But she held her head high, still refusing to look at him. "You're a nice man, but I . . . I thought we were just good friends. I'm not ready to settle down yet."

Good friends, hell. "And what do you plan to do?"

"I think I might like to have a business for myself, like Pearl and Sarah have. I might even go back East."

She turned and walked to a chair at the other side of the room. She stood with her hands on the molded back finials.

He followed her. "Oh? Back East?"

"Yes, I kind of liked some of the towns we came through on the train. Memphis seemed real nice."

"And what about me? About us?"

He stepped closer, but she turned away and waved a hand in dismissal.

"Why, you'll be so busy with your political plans, you won't even notice I'm gone."

"Belle, I asked you to be my wife. Do you think I could want to be with you enough to propose and not miss you?"

"Well, law, I don't know. I thought maybe you just needed to be married, for the campaign and all. I'm sure there are lots of suitable women in town who would make a wonderful governor's wife."

She kept her face turned away from him.

"There probably are, but not for me."

"Don't worry, you'll find the right one. Lily and your mother will help you."

She seemed to be getting into her role now, he decided. She gestured dramatically with an arm. "As for me, I'm much more suited to a life of solitude. I think a millinery shop for refined ladies would be quite nice. Oh, and I'd keep up piano lessons wherever I settle, of course. I enjoy them, and playing in church."

"And what about marriage? A family of your own?"

"Maybe someday. When the right man comes along. For now, I need to see more of the world, experience life, and test myself. I do hope we can still be friends, though."

He wanted to hit something, hard. He wanted to beat his own head against the wall. Most of all, he wanted to hold Belle. He put his hands on her shoulders and turned her facing his chest. She stiffened but didn't pull away. Except for red eyes and tear-stained cheeks, her face presented a mask.

"Belle, I know about your past and why you were at Pearl's when we met. It doesn't make any difference."

In a flash, the mask crumbled into an expression of sheer horror. "No! No! You can't know!" She stepped back and peered into his face. "Oh, you do. You do know." Her hand flew to her mouth. She pulled away and ran to the door.

He moved fast and stepped in front of her.

She hid her face in her hands. "Oh, the shame of it. Dear God, just let me die now." Sobs wracked her body. "How did you find out? When?"

He caressed her shoulders. "I've known since before I met you. That sorry excuse for a preacher and his wife came to Evan's office the first day in Piper's Hollow. They complained about Pearl, mentioned someone living in her house."

She hit her fists against his arms. "Oh, I'll bet they did, those horrid, horrid people." As if realizing she struck him, she stopped the pummelling. She placed her hands on his chest and raised her face to his. "I never wanted you to know, you of all people."

"Of all people, I'm the one you should have told." He pulled her heaving form to his chest and kissed her hair. "That happened before we met. Only now and the future are important."

She leaned back to examine his face. "You . . . you've always known, and you were still nice to me?"

"You never gave me reason to be otherwise. It doesn't matter."

She pulled away and turned from him. "It *will* matter. Someday, someone will say something and you'll be embarrassed. Or you'll wonder about me and . . . and other men.

You'll resent them, and then you'll resent me. I couldn't bear that."

"I could never resent you. Don't you see I love you? I want to be with you always."

"Think how you'd feel if someone from Tennessee recognized me. What if your parents found out about me? What then?"

"Belle, they already know. I told them."

She sank to a chair and buried her head in her lap. "No. Oh, Dear Heavenly God. Not your parents, too. They were always so nice to me. What must they think of me now?"

"They think you're the woman I've chosen to share the rest of my life with. And they've chosen to be happy for me—for us." He knelt in front of her and cupped her chin with his hand.

The tears pouring down her face broke his heart. How could he convince her she meant everything to him?

"You can't mean it, Alexon. Not really. You can't still want me, knowing what you do. What about your career? What about politics?"

"Without you, it would mean nothing. With you by my side, we can accomplish anything we set out to do."

"I can't believe you still want me, that you can forget all I've done."

"I know that whatever you did, you had what you thought were good reasons at the time. Running from me is wrong. I won't let you go, Belle. I won't let you go now I've found you."

"I couldn't bear it if you regretted our marriage later. You're too much a gentleman to break a vow. I don't want you to feel trapped . . ."

He broke in, "How could I feel trapped when I'd be the luckiest man alive?"

"You say that now, to persuade me. But I've seen your face when other men flirted with me at church or parties. I thought then that if you knew about my past, you'd be angry with me or disgusted."

He touched her cheek where fresh tears slid.

"Oh." She shook her head in disbelief. "But I see now you did know. Now I wonder what you were thinking. Alexon, I promise I never encouraged those men. I was polite, but that's all." She turned her face away and shrugged a shoulder. "That's how it would be. You see, I'm defending myself already."

"Did I ask you to? No, I *never* doubted you, Belle." He rose and pulled her to her feet. "I won't promise not to be jealous when men are too attentive to you. But you have to realize that's natural for a man. We protect those we love. It has nothing to do with your past, just that I want you all to myself. You're a beautiful woman and draw men like bees to honey."

"Please, Alexon. Don't tempt me further. It's too late. I know you can find someone who'll be right for your career, right for the wife of an important man."

"I've found her . . . you're the one, Belle. Only you. I'm not leaving this room without you."

She searched his face. He watched hope spring into her eyes, saw the longing there.

"Can you mean it?" She touched his cheek with her fingers.

"I can and do. We belong together, forever." He claimed her mouth with his and set about proving his devotion. When they broke their kiss, he brushed a hand across her moist cheek. "Let me take you home. Grandpa and Lily are worried about you."

"Do . . . does Lily. . . ."

"No, Lily doesn't know . . . and it's none of her business. Grandpa has known all along. Seems Evan wrote about how Pearl helped a lot of people."

"Grandpa knows? He's never let on, and he's been so nice to me. And Drake must know, too. Oh, Alexon, what a kind family you have, and so unusual."

He needn't tell her about Drake's comments. Especially since his cousin had admitted he was wrong about Belle. "They're your family now." He looked back at the room. "Do you have stuff to pack before we go back to town?"

"Could . . . could we go see your folks? I need to explain to them—and you—about what happened to me in Tennessee. Best to get it over with and just tell it one time."

"Whatever you want. As long as we do it together."

The lovestruck pair drove away a few minutes later, Lex's horse tied behind the buggy. Pearl closed the door with a sigh.

"Isn't that nice? They make a lovely couple." She turned to find Drake glaring at her, hands fisted at his waist.

"Would you step into my study? I'd like a word with you in private."

She followed him into his personal sanctum. Why was he so solemn?

"Would you care to explain why you told me Belle was your cousin? Why you never told me about her previous occupation?"

Shock raced through her. He knew. How long had he known and how much? And how did he find out?

"It's possible Belle and I are related through her mother's people, even if it is distant. As for the other, how . . . what do you know?"

"Not nearly enough, thank you. I know she worked for Sarah's mother. I know she was beaten by a customer and almost died. I know you took her in to help her." The little tic at the corner of his mouth twitched, but he appeared calm otherwise.

"That's most of what I know. A man who'd worked for her father asked her to go away with him and she thought he meant to marry her. When he laughed at her, she left him. She never meant to be anything but a good girl."

Pearl paused in thought. "She *is* a good person, she just had some bad trouble. After she left the man, her father wouldn't let her come home and she had no place to go. I didn't know her then, or she could have come to my place right off."

"So, she went to Roxie's place instead?"

"No, not at first. She went to all the businesses in town asking for work. Then she tried the houses to see if she could clean or help for food. After that, she went to the church asking for help."

That got his attention. "The church? To that pompous ass and his stick of a wife who came to Evan's office?"

"The same. They told her she had sinned and had to bear the burdens of her mistakes. They wouldn't even let her sleep in the church or give her any food."

"The hell you say."

"She had no money, no place to stay, no food. That was in January and it was awful cold. She went to Roxie's last, because she was freezing and hungry."

Pearl knew how Belle hated telling her about that time, knew she wanted no one else to know. "I'm not saying she did right, but I can't say what I would do in the same circumstances. She was alone and scared. If she had gone to Evan he would have brought her to me, but she was afraid he would put her in jail."

"You should have told me the truth."

"It wasn't mine to tell. Belle made me promise to tell no one when she came. She was so ashamed."

"I'm your husband. You're not supposed to have secrets from me."

"Drake, I didn't even know you when I . . . when I lied. I'd spent days trying to keep Belle from dying and I wasn't about to abandon her. Then there just never seemed to be a way to tell without making it worse. I only wanted to protect Belle and get my family away from Piper's Hollow. I thought it would get us away from danger and save your ranch at the same time."

"Who beat her like that?"

Pearl shook her head. "She won't say. In fact, she seemed more frightened each time I asked, so I stopped asking. Whoever he is, he must have threatened her with worse if she told."

"I wonder if he's one of the men chasing you. Surely there can't be that many killers in Piper's Hollow."

"I wondered, too, but couldn't see how the two could be tied together. Even though we might be distantly related, I'd never set eyes on Belle until Roxie and Cal brought her to me a week before you came." She wondered about his knowledge of Belle's plight. "When did you know about her?"

"Before I met you. Remember Lex and I were in Evan's office when the pastor and his wife came to call. They complained about you harboring a harlot with impressionable youngsters in your home. Evan filled us in later."

She rushed to him. "Oh, Drake. You've known all this time and you still treated her like family? What a kind and generous man you are."

Across the room sat the ridiculous cattle horn chair she'd found in the barn loft. She smiled and visualized a pint-sized version of Drake rocking in that chair in a few years. Maybe things would be all right after all. Maybe he would welcome the baby when he knew. She hugged his neck and planted a kiss on his cheek.

"Now, hold on. I'm not through being mad yet," he protested, but his arms slid around her waist. "You should have told me all this a long time ago."

She leaned back to look into his face, her arms still around him. "You don't look so angry now. Are you sure you're not over it?" She kissed the corner of his mouth. The tic had disappeared, and she ran her tongue along his lips.

He mumbled, "Maybe I'll be mad later. Right now I seem to be plumb filled up with other feelings."

Willard shuddered even though the air was soft and warm. He felt a chill run up his spine and got a scary feeling. Lordy, he wished this was over and done with

Burris hunkered down in the predawn dark behind Granny's Lunches and Baked Goods. He worked at the back locks, making several scratches in the paint and on the brass.

Willard held a hooded lantern near the door. "Hurry up, Burris. Someone's goin' to see us if'n we don't get inside. The sun'll be comin' up soon."

"I'm hurryin'. This here's a good strong lock." The click of the mechanism brought a sigh of relief from both men.

Burris opened the door and both men slipped inside.

Willard sniffed. "Mmm. Don't it smell good in here. That Pearl is sure one good cook."

Neither of them had eaten a decent meal in days. They had to stay out of sight. He sure was hungry, and he knew his brother was too. It couldn't hurt to eat now they were here.

Burris's thoughts must have been heading in the same direction. "Bet they's somethin' good to eat left from yesterday. Let's have us a good breakfast 'fore Pearl gets here."

"Yep. Here's some pie. And lookee here, some roast beef and bread. We can make us a pack to take with us."

The two men gathered food on the large wooden table in the center of the cooking area. "Ep, ss hrs Prls brd," Burris said around a mouthful of food.

"How can you make a sound with that much food in your mouth? I cain't understand a word you're sayin'." Willard sliced off a slab of beef and slapped it on a chunk of bread.

Burris's Adam's apple bobbled several times as he swallowed before he spoke again. "I said, yes, this here's Pearl's bread. She allus did make the best bread I ever et."

"Guess we'll have good bread on our way West. We can stop long enough for her to bake."

"You think we can get her and that girl Sarah to come with us? I still don't think this is goin' to work."

Willard gave his brother a glare. "I told you they'll come when they find out it's that or be killed. Then that boy'll foller us and we'll get him too."

"Now, see, that's another part I don't understand. How do you know the boy will foller?"

"Why, he's an injun, ain't he? That's what they do. You know, track people and such. We'll just wait for him along side the trail. When he comes along, we'll grab him."

"If he's trackin' us, he'll know we're beside the trail, won't he?" Burris scratched his face and smeared blackberry pie filling across scraggly stubble.

Willard's annoyance with his younger brother grew. "Will you quit askin' so danged many questions and just let me do the thinkin'? You plum drive a body crazy."

"Don't get riled. I know you're the smart one and older and all. But I still don't see how this is gonna work."

Willard wasn't sure it would, either. Lordy, he was desperate. He didn't want to kill anybody, especially not women. Specially not women he had no cause to hate. He wanted even worse not to get killed himself. This was the only plan he could come up with to get out of this mess.

He thought the big basket on the top shelf might be good to take their food in. He raised his hand to reach for it. Burris thought he meant to cuff him and jumped back against the large old range. The oven door, with coals banked to keep them live overnight, was hot.

"Yeow!" Burris shot forward and into the table. "That stove near seared my backside." The table wobbled, the lantern tilted. Both men reached for it, but the lantern hit the floor and rolled. Oil spilled from the base and ignited. Fire spread across the floor.

Willard grabbed as much food as he could shove into the basket. "Shit, we got to get out of here fast. Run fer it."

Drake and Storm were rising from the breakfast table when Beau Benton rushed into the house. "Looks like the glow of a fire from town. Big one."

Drake threw his napkin down on the table and hurried toward the door. "I'll sound the alarm for the hands," he called over his shoulder. "Storm, could you help your sisters get ready to ride in?"

Both Sarah and Pearl were moving even as Drake spoke. They had everything in preparation for their day's work at the restaurant. From outside the house, pounding hooves sounded over the hum of men clamoring to get mounts saddled and away.

Soon Beau stuck his head in long enough to call, "The Judge sent a rider from town. Miz Pearl, it's your eatin' place what's on fire."

The four guards and the four members of the Kincaid family raced on the half-hour's ride to town only seconds behind the ranch cowboys. Even before they left the ranch, the glow of the fire and plume of smoke marred the early morning light. By the time they reached town, only a pile of burning timber remained of what had been Pearl's café. Townspeople who had worked with water brigades to keep flames from spreading to nearby businesses slowed their assault. The café had sat apart from other buildings and the flames had not engulfed any other structures.

Pearl shot out of the buggy as soon as it stopped. She rushed toward the fire, frantic to help. Drake tossed the reins over a post and rushed after his wife.

He grabbed her arms to prevent her charging into the foray of people in the line of firefighters. "Pearl, it's too late. There's nothing we can do."

"No, no. It's all gone. Our lovely restaurant." Pearl stared in disbelief at the pile of blackened rubble, tears pouring down her face. Smoke still billowed and occasional bursts of flames shot up.

Grandpa stopped work to come over to them, his white mane streaked with black soot. "Sorry, Pearl. By the time the alarm sounded and folks rushed over, it was too late to save anything. All we could do is try to keep it from spreading."

"Honey, I'm sorry." Drake put a comforting arm around her. "It's too damn bad."

The smell of the smoke sickened her. It wasn't the crisp odor of a campfire nor the familiar aroma of a cook stove.

This smelled of things that should never burn, her precious things charred beyond recognition.

Pearl's wiped at her tears and her senses tried to register the disaster. Her mind froze. All that work, all that time. Gone in an instant. In a haze, she saw Abe Kline step up to take a water bucket from Rhoda. The two exchanged a few words before Rhoda stepped away from the group of fire fighters and rushed to Pearl with a tearful embrace.

"Your beautiful lunch place—all gone. It's too awful to believe."

"Yet there's the proof." Pearl stared over Rhoda's head at the smoldering rubble.

"Oh, Pearl," Rhoda sobbed. "What will you do? What will we all do?"

Pearl knew Rhoda depended on her income from the restaurant, knew she needed that income to feed her family. A widow with three children and a mother to support had a hard time. The restaurant had been perfect for Rhoda. Pearl even sent left-over food home for the Spiegel family. Now what would they do?

Try as she would, no solution came to Pearl's numbed mind. She tried to grasp the hard work, supplies, and planning which had disappeared in only a few moments' time. She couldn't do it. Better to reassure Rhoda and leave the rest for later.

"Don't worry. I won't abandon you. We'll think of something." She squeezed her friend's shoulders. "Thank you for fighting the fire. Why don't you go on home now? There's nothing more to be done here today."

Dick Harrigan spoke to Abe, then moved toward the Kincaids. He stopped in front of her and Drake. The burly man was covered in soot and sweat. Already blisters covered his burned red forearms.

"I'm sorry as can be, Pearl. We'll build her back 'fore you know it."

At the sight of Dick's injuries, a well-trained portion of Pearl's mind took charge of her body. "Oh, Dick, your poor arms. Let me get some salve for you." She reached into the buggy for her medical bag, relieved to have something familiar to occupy her hands while her mind worked on the disaster. "How could this have happened? We've always been so careful."

Lex appeared, looking as grubby as Dick. "It appears someone set it."

Drake asked, "Are you sure?"

Both men nodded. Dick looked at Lex to continue.

Lex nodded toward the hotel across the street. "Real early this morning, a couple in the hotel's second floor saw a light in the back of the café. They thought some of you'd come in extra early 'cause they saw movement, you know, shadows moving around like people working. That wasn't long before they saw the flames."

She felt weak. What if someone was trapped under all that rubble? "Could anyone be . . ?" She couldn't voice the words.

Dick shook his head. "No need to worry 'bout that, at least. Old Mr. Findley was walking his dog near the trees. He saw the flames and what he thought were two men running out the back carrying something."

She finished bandaging Dick's arms and turned to her husband. "Thank goodness, no one was caught inside." Then the impact hit. Anger raced through her and she turned around. "So, they stole something and then started the fire. How dare they do this to us after all our hard work."

Sarah shook her head in disbelief. "What could we have had in there to make it worth this?"

"Maybe just someone passing through needed some food." Storm stared at the remains of his sisters' business and shrugged a shoulder. "Maybe the fire was an accident during the theft."

Drake cradled Pearl in front of him, her back to his chest and his arms crossed in front of her. "Could be. We'll probably never know. Whoever was involved is probably long gone by now."

With the fire controlled and dying, townspeople drifted to

their homes to clean up from their fight. Most extended con-
dolences as they passed, some stumbling with fatigue. Pearl
offered her gratitude for their assistance but her mind reeled
with her loss.

Drake thanked his ranch hands and sent them back to their
day's work. He nodded to Sheriff Liles. "Guess you heard
about the two men seen running out the back?"

"Yes, and I'd like to talk to you, especially to Mrs. Kincaid."

Grandpa gave Pearl's shoulder a pat. "Y'all come on to the
house." He turned to the sheriff, "Ben, can you join us there
or do we need to come to your office?"

The sheriff stood several seconds surveying the damage
before he answered. "You folks go on with the Judge and I'll
look around here a bit more, talk to a few people. I'll be along
after you've had a chance to recover a bit."

Lex stepped away from the Kincaids. "I'll go to my rooms
and get cleaned up before I join you."

Only fifty feet of open space separated the law offices of
Kincaid and Tremont from Pearl's former café. The sheriff
and Lex walked slowly toward the outside stair which led to
Lex's second floor living quarters.

Sheriff Liles gauged the damage to the offices. The fire's
intense heat had left blistered paint on the side of the two-
story building. Smoke still engulfed the space between the
stairs and the remains of Pearl's café. When a breezy gust delivered a column of smoke their way, the sheriff coughed and
waved his hand in front of his face.

"That was a close call for your place, Lex."

"Too close. I always meant to brick the outside of this
place. This has convinced me to get it done right away."

The new assault—whether intentional or accidental—left
everyone's nerves raw. When they reached the Kincaid home,
Jeff and Beau circled to the back while Zed and Abe took a
stand in front of the house.

Pearl had not set foot in Grandpa's house since she and Sarah left weeks ago. Whenever they had met in town or at church, Lily turned her face the other way. Pearl dreaded an encounter with her, and refused to involve others in what she considered Lily's pettiness.

Grandpa led the group through the entryway. "Let's go on into the study. I'm plumb tuckered out." When the maid appeared, Grandpa said, "Bring us some coffee and something sweet to go with it, will you, Ellen?" as he swept into his sanctuary.

Pearl sat near the hearth, barely registering that Drake and Storm carried extra chairs into the room or that Sarah sat near her. She wanted to curl into a ball, close her eyes, and sleep away this nightmare. Who could have set fire to her beautiful restaurant? And why?

Was it an accident caused by hungry travelers as Storm speculated? Somehow, she thought not. Somehow, she thought it had to do with all the meanness that followed her. Somehow, she thought it a sign there were more bad things to come.

Sixteen

Belle rushed into the room with Lily swishing regally behind her and grasped Pearl's hands. "Oh, Pearl, we saw that awful fire. I'm so sorry, so very sorry."

Before Pearl could answer, Lily added, "Serves you right. It should never have been there in the first place."

"Lily!" Grandpa bellowed. "You watch what you say."

Lily merely gave a toss of her perfectly groomed head. "Well, it's the truth. Pearl had no call to go into trade."

Pearl met the other woman's stare with a defiant glare of her own. "My restaurant served a lot of people in this town. They appreciated having a good place to eat lunch and a place to get fresh baked goods for their home meals."

"Hmph. Parading yourself in front of all the men in town. I'm surprised Drake permitted such a thing."

In vain Pearl fought the flush she knew spread across her face. Lily must have known Drake hated the restaurant. Probably everyone in Kincaid Springs knew. His declaration that he wished the place would burn to the ground came back to her. For a second, she almost wondered if he could have been the one to set the fire. Instantly, shame suffused her that she even considered it.

Drake stepped forward. "Pearl did a good job, Lily, and you've got no call to criticize her. She's the best cook I've ever seen."

"She doesn't have to cook for the public like a common

tradesman. After all, she is now a Kincaid and what she does reflects on us."

Grandpa held up a hand to stay his daughter's tirade. "Pearl has been a credit to the Kincaids in all she's done—the restaurant and her healing of the poor in this area."

Relief flooded Pearl. Grandpa defended her to his own daughter. "Thank you, Grandpa. You saying that means a lot to me."

Lily glared at her father. "Don't get me started on that so-called healing. As if that eating place wasn't bad enough."

The tic had started at the side of Drake's mouth. He took a step toward his aunt and his eyes hardened to cold steel. "Pearl has helped a lot of people with her healing, even saved lives. And if she wants a restaurant, then by golly, she can have one. In fact, if she decides to rebuild, I'll get the hands from the ranch to help."

Storm nodded his approval. "Wouldn't take too long, once the timbers cool enough to handle."

"We'd have to get all new furniture and make curtains and such," Sarah added, caught up in the idea. She reached over to pat Pearl's hand. "We could do that while the men rebuild. And the new cook stove will be here soon."

Lily stamped her foot, her fisted hands pummeling the air. "Ooooh! Doesn't anyone understand that place was an abomination? How can you calmly talk about rebuilding it, having it open again?"

Drake gave Pearl a half-smile then faced his aunt. "Not everyone sees things the same way you do, Lily. Not everyone can be like you. Not everyone even wants to."

Pearl rushed to her husband and buried her head on his chest. His arms came around her with soothing motions across her back. After all these weeks, he understood. He had been listening when she tried to explain herself to him.

Lily whirled on Pearl, her finger pointed in accusation. "You! You've turned my own family against me. I rue the day you set foot in this town." She gave a final stamp of her foot and rushed from the room.

Belle hurried over to Pearl. "Please don't let her upset you. She's really ill and Doctor Percival's not been much help. That's why I stayed with her instead of helping fight the fire."

"I had no idea." Pearl wondered how long Lily had been ill, not that illness excused her rudeness since they'd met.

"If you don't mind, I'll go check on her."

Pearl shook her head. "No, Belle, go ahead. Let us know if we can do anything."

Now that would be the day. Anytime Lily Stephens asked for her help, Pearl would faint dead away.

Lex entered in time to exchange a lingering glance with Belle. Sheriff Liles trailed Lex. His appearance to question Pearl forestalled any more thoughts on Lily's temperament or possible ailment. The lawman's grim expression sent a chill along Pearl's spine.

Grandpa stood and gestured to his chair. "You sit here, Ben. There's paper, pen, and ink pot on the desk if you need it for note taking."

Sheriff Liles lowered himself to the chair as if every bone in his body ached. He looked around the room, his gaze moving from face to face. "I'm treating this as arson against Mrs. Kincaid until I find out different."

Drake nodded. "Any new evidence?"

"Findley showed me where two men ran into the trees. Found where they'd cold camped, looked like two or three days."

Storm's eyes narrowed in speculation. "So, they wanted no one to know they were here? Maybe they're still around then."

"Have to assume they are," the sheriff agreed. "Mrs. Kincaid, I want you to start right at the beginning of all this trouble and tell me every detail."

Pearl looked to her husband. "How far back should I go?"

Drake helped her to a chair then patted her back and took a stand beside her. "When your granny died and the attacks on you started. Wasn't the first attack the two men in the woods?"

"Yes. That was the first time I felt scared. The first time I thought someone meant us serious harm." Pearl retold each incident before she met Drake. Storm inserted an occasional comment, but Sarah sat still and pale. When Pearl got to the rockslide, Drake added his comments. Sheriff Liles listened with a question here or there.

"But before your grandmother died, nothing like this happened?"

Pearl looked from her sister to her brother and then to her husband. Drake squeezed her shoulder and nodded to her to answer.

"We've always been shunned and teased because, well, we're different from the folks who lived around us. There was nothing dangerous, though, nothing that threatened our lives before Granny died."

The sheriff pulled at his chin. "So something changed when your grandmother died. Something about her death affected someone who wants to harm you."

Storm nodded. "I think it has something to do with the money, but I don't know how it's connected."

Sheriff Liles head came up. "What money?"

"Of course," Drake said. "Remember the first day I saw you? Those three men asked about your Granny's gold. How did they know your Granny had any money?"

Pearl shook her head and reached for Drake's hand. She felt lost. "I don't know. It was Jug who mentioned it. How could he have known when none of us knew?"

The sheriff raised his voice to repeat, "What money?"

Pearl explained about the funds she received after she arrived, and how surprised she had been.

"And you don't know where this money came from?"

Pearl hesitated. How much should she tell? Would Drake want the lawman to know about her parents not being married? She would die if he knew *all* the details about her birth, but she couldn't see how to tell about the money without letting at least the facts of her illegitimacy being known. She felt an encouraging hand on her shoulder and looked up to see her husband smiling down at her.

"It's all right, honey. Ben's a good family friend as well as the best lawman around. Tell him all you know."

Pearl sighed and told about the letter which came with the money. "We—Storm and Sarah and I—share the same father but each had a different mother. We think our father paid it to Granny so she wouldn't tell who he was. When she died, he didn't have to pay anymore. But we can't see how that has anything to do with the trouble. We didn't know about the money in the first place."

Grandpa looked lost in thought, but injected, "Maybe the person who paid didn't know your grandmother kept it secret from you. Maybe he thought you all three knew."

"Someone knew, someone told Jug," Drake said. "Would someone at the bank have told him?"

"I don't know." Pearl wracked her brain. How had Jug known about the money? She had thought him just talking, mouthing off with no facts to back his gaff.

"How many people work at this bank?"

"Most of the time only the owner, Mr. Norris, and his assistant, Ulis Young. Sometimes Mrs. Norris came in to help if Ulis was sick."

"It's a small place, Ben," Drake added. "I'm surprised they even had a bank."

Storm spoke up, "Wasn't much of one. Not much bigger than this room."

Sheriff Liles stood. "I believe I'll send me some wires. Get in touch with your friend who used to be sheriff there as well as the new man. Maybe the banker. You folks go about your business. You've got good men working for you."

When the sheriff had left, Grandpa took his chair again. "This is a big puzzle to me. Seems like we ought to be able to unravel at least a part of it."

"I've tried, Grandpa. Ever since it started, I've worried and worried with it." All her life Pearl had faced trouble head on.

Now she wished she could just bury herself in her husband's arms and all the trouble would go away.

"We've talked it over, lots of times." Storm gestured to his sisters. "We figured at first someone wanted us to leave Piper's Hollow, or at least scare Pearl away so Sarah and I would have to live with the Higginses. Then, when the trouble followed, we just couldn't figure it out."

"There's something we're all missing, something that connects all these incidents." Drake took Pearl's hands and pulled her gently to her feet. "For now, I think I should take my family home."

Pearl allowed Drake to guide her along and help her into the buggy, as if she didn't drive herself in that same conveyance twice every weekday. She watched woodenly as Drake tied Midnight to the back of the buggy and climbed in beside her. Like a giant rag doll, Pearl propped herself on the seat incapable of clear thought or sensibility. Sarah sat in the back seat as if she, too, were in shock.

For most of Pearl's life she had been the one in charge of her family's welfare, the one to take command and see that what needed doing got done. Even when her mother was alive, Pearl acted more parent than child. As Granny's health waned, Pearl's burden of family responsibility grew. Not that she questioned her role. In fact, she preferred commanding her own destiny and that of her siblings. Better to rely only on yourself and not be disappointed, better to control than be controlled.

What a surprise to find herself welcoming her husband's intervention. She had resented his earlier attempts to impose his will on hers. Now his firm, gentle grasp soothed her raw nerves. She recalled his statement to Grandpa. He said he would take his family home.

What a wealth of sentiment that expressed to her. The way he pulled her to him as he spoke, gathered her and Storm and Sarah as a unit to leave together. Maybe he did care for them all, not just find them a duty or burden to be borne.

She wanted to lie snuggled in her husband's arms and sleep for a week. How could she rebuild her restaurant plus treat the people who came for her healing when she could hardly hold her head up? The exhaustion plaguing her the past few weeks took its toll on her weakened defenses. She exhaled a deep breath and leaned against Drake.

He switched the reins to one hand and brought his other arm around her. "That was a mighty big sigh. Are you going to be all right, honey?"

"Yes, I'm sure I'll survive this. But it's a terrible disappointment to have all our hard work destroyed in one brief moment and not know why."

"Don't worry. We can rebuild it just the way you want it."

She turned her face up to study his. "You really mean that? I know you hated the restaurant."

"It's true I didn't like it. You worked too hard there. If that makes you happy, though, then I'll help you keep it."

"What made you change your mind?"

His face turned grim. "First, I was afraid you'd remember what I said about wishing it would burn to the ground." He met her gaze. "Ah, I see you did remember that."

She rested her hand on his shoulder. "Drake, I know you didn't set the fire."

"Well, I've had a lot of time to think about this lately."

He raised his eyebrows. She knew he meant while he slept alone. With Sarah in the back seat of the buggy and Storm riding close by, Pearl made no comment, merely nodded her encouragement for him to continue.

"I remembered what you said when we were leaving Piper's Hollow. About meaning to go to Wyoming because women were treated more like equals there, how you'd start a business there serving food. Remember that plan?"

She nodded. "Yes, but I didn't think you would."

"Then, later, you told me you wanted your—*our*—marriage to be a partnership."

"And what do you want out of the partnership?"

"I guess I'm still trying to figure that out. I'd say it's changed considerably since we met."

The ranch house appeared on the horizon. Never had it looked so good to Pearl. Maria and Miguel rushed to the buggy, concern written on their faces. Maria cooed over and cosseted Pearl and Sarah as she shooed them to bed for a rest.

Drake followed the women, but pulled Sarah aside before she went into her own room. Pearl paused to listen, comforted he remembered her sister's part in the restaurant.

"Sarah, will you be all right now? I know it's been a terrible shock for you, too."

"Yes, I'll be fine. You stay with Pearl," Sarah said as her eyes sought Pearl. "I've never seen you like this, Sister."

Drake gave Sarah's shoulder a squeeze. "I'll stay with her a while. She needs sleep and time. I imagine that would help you, too."

"I will take care of Señorita Sarah," Maria assured them.

Carlotta delivered a cup of soothing tea to Pearl then left the couple alone. Drake turned down the bed.

When Pearl had drained her cup and set it aside, Drake helped her slip into bed. He sat beside her, her hand in his. With his other hand he caressed her hair.

"Try to sleep now, honey. We'll have plenty of time to deal with all this when you wake."

Too weary and stunned to protest, Pearl slept.

Drake watched slumber claim his wife. Dark circles shadowed beneath her closed lids against pale cheeks. When had she lost that sunkissed glow he found so appealing? Hollows in her cheeks spoke of her lost weight.

Damn. How had they gotten their marriage in such a mess? He wanted her in his bed, wanted her in his life. He couldn't say when she had claimed a part of him, but knew she had.

No longer did he think of her as a necessary burden to retain his ranch, but as a person to be admired. And desired.

Now he had to deal with this new attack on her. A terrible knot gripped his stomach. What if the fire had been later? What if she had been at work and trapped in the blaze? What if she were the intended victim instead of the building?

Dear God, he almost choked for air. Best not even think about it, it must have been an accident. Or, maybe someone planned it as a scare tactic. If so, the plan succeeded. It scared the hell out of him.

With tenderness he hadn't realized he possessed, he tucked the sheet around her sleeping form. After a kiss to her brow, he slipped from the room. He vowed to find the men responsible for this. Damned if he wouldn't.

Lex stood at the window of his office, Belle's hand in his. In the three days it took the embers to cool, Drake had lined up both workers and materials. Now Lex and Belle watched Drake and his ranch crew, along with a few others, clearing away the rubble from the fire. Sarah trailed Pearl around the site before the two women went toward the mercantile.

Lily sat in a chair near another window, her patience apparently growing thin even for her. "Who on earth are all those people out there? I've never seen such a shabby lot."

Lex thought his aunt even more waspish than usual of late, but Belle explained away Lily's ill humor as some sort of mysterious illness. Women stuff, he imagined, and was not anxious for a discussion of what it entailed.

He didn't let go of Belle's hand to answer his aunt's complaint. "Some are ranch hands. Most are people Pearl's helped with her healing. They couldn't pay cash, so they and some of their family are giving time now to help her."

"That must make Pearl so happy, knowing she's appreciated," Belle said. "She's waited so long to be accepted."

Lex heard Lily's snort of disapproval. "Well, I don't appreciate her carrying on like she does."

Ill or not, he was tired of his spoiled aunt's constant harangues. She seemed to condemn anything Pearl did.

"Pearl's helped a lot of people with her healing. She's delivered babies, stitched up wounds, and cured ailments. Look how much she helped Grandpa." He turned to challenge the prune-faced woman. "Surely you don't resent her helping Grandpa? Would you wish him still in pain just to spite Pearl?"

Lily looked as if he'd slapped her. Lord knows, many times he'd felt like it, especially lately. He would never do such a thing, of course. This was the first time since they'd been grown he'd been less than polite to her.

"N—no. Of course, I'm glad Papa's better." She raised her chin, a defiant sign he recognized. "I don't think Pearl had anything to do with it, though. If you ask me, it's a wonder he didn't die from her treatment. It's a coincidence he got better at the same time he was taking her vile tonic and following her silly special diet."

Lex tried not to grimace in disgust. *I should give up.*

"Some coincidence." He gestured out the window. "And all those people out there had the same coincidence happen to them. Think about it, Lily. For once don't be so stubborn. Admit you were wrong about Pearl."

"I'll do no such thing." Her pale face flushed with anger. "She is just the most common woman."

For once, Belle stood up to Lily, though her voice remained soft and placating. "You have no idea how good a woman she is, Lily. She helped so many before she left Tennessee. She had a terrible hard life, but she never let it get her down."

Lily gave a toss of her head. "Hmph. Baking and doing her witch doctoring? How does that make her some downtrodden heroine?"

"For years she took care of an invalid grandmother who never had a kind word for her. When Pearl didn't marry the town's minister, he tried to turn everyone against her and caused her all kinds of trouble. She took in Sarah and Storm when she was only a child herself. And she's taken such good care them—and anyone else under her roof. She never turned a sick person away, even those who'd been mean to her."

"Hmph," Lily snorted again in apparent disagreement. She stood as if she were eighty-five instead of thirty-five. "Belle, we're not getting your trousseau fitted with you two standing there making calves' eyes at each other. Let's get to the dressmaker's and leave all that noise next door to my nephews."

Lex dropped a kiss on Belle's brow. How he looked forward to the time when they were married and could be together with privacy. For now, he bided his time with the promise of their approaching engagement party the following night and their upcoming wedding.

He walked the two women to the door. As they left, he cautioned, "Lily, think about what you've heard about Pearl. There's no need to resent her. She wants to be your friend."

Lily's only answer was a look that would freeze hell over.

A crown of curls topped Pearl's head and cascaded to dance across her right shoulder. Confident her lavender wedding dress met even Lily's inflexible standards, she smoothed a flounce of lace. As a peace concession to her husband's aunt, Pearl wore the blasted corset. She refused to cinch it tight, but its stays pushed and poked at her with every breath or movement.

Her fingers touched the amethyst necklace Drake brought her from Kansas. Choosing between the sparkling gems or the wedding pearls had been a tough decision.

At Grandpa's insistence, the party was being held in his home. Rugs and most of the parlor furniture had been cleared away to make room for guests' dancing across polished oak floors. Windows and French doors were open to the stifling summer heat. An occasional whisper of a breeze brought with it the scent of jasmine and roses from the garden.

Pearl stood beside her husband at the punch table. Guests chose either champagne or fruit punch from a table laden with delicacies. She pretended she didn't see Storm whisk away a champagne glass, and admitted to herself he was almost grown. It made her sad to think of either he or Sarah leaving home, so she pushed it from her mind. For now she was content Storm had friends his age, Sarah chatted with a group of her friends over punch cups, and the evening seemed to be going well.

Drake's raised voice carried across the room and most guests stopped talking to look his way.

"May I have your attention, please, folks? It's my privilege to announce the engagement of my wife's cousin, Miss Arabella Angeline Renfro, to my lucky cousin, Alexon Samuel Tremont." He raised his glass and nodded toward Belle and Lex. "We wish you the best, Belle and Lex."

The hum of congratulations collided with the clink of champagne flutes and punch cups. Belle glowed, but no more than Lex. Love radiated from them like a beacon. Trying not to stare, Pearl watched their every move. If only Drake looked at her the way Lex now gazed at Belle. She felt a sigh escape and hoped no one else noticed.

When she turned, she saw Drake staring at the couple, an inscrutable expression on his face. What could he be thinking? Did he wish for himself a wife whom he loved as much as Lex loved Belle? Did he wish himself still single? Did he wish he had never become involved with her and her family? She sighed again and ordered herself to stop worrying so much. Tonight was meant for pleasant thoughts and celebration.

The five musicians snugged into a corner of the large room struck up a tune and couples glided onto the dance floor.

Lily's lemon-sour face broke into what must have been intended as a smile. It fell short. Obviously the woman's illness still plagued her, and Pearl wondered what the ailment might be. Lily's once-perfect posture sagged. The waspish woman's deathly pale face looked drawn and tense. Her once fiery hair no longer shone, it's brilliant color was now dull as sweet potato pie.

For any other person, Pearl would make inquiries or even offer her help. She knew solicitations to Lily would be unwelcome and resented, so she held her tongue. She wanted no trouble with Lily, wanted to cause none for Grandpa with his daughter.

Pearl thought there must be at least two hundred guests. Soon she was drawn into the merriment and lost track of time. Near midnight, some folks started drifting away to go home. Pearl hated for the magic night to end, but fatigue pulled at her.

Only about fifty guests remained when Lily sank to the floor in a faint. Several women screamed. Pearl rushed to Lily's side.

Belle cradled Lily's head in her lap. "Her skin's cold as death and dry as paper."

"We need to get her to her room." Pearl's training took over. "Drake, could you carry her upstairs? Storm, see if Dr. Percival's still here."

"He left an hour ago. I'll go get him."

Grandpa stayed Storm with a hand to his arm. "No, I'll send someone. Rosilee, you'll have to take over as hostess for your sister. Pearl, you go up with Lily and take care of her. I'll get things going again down here and join you in a few minutes."

Drake carried Lily upstairs and Pearl and Sarah trailed close behind. The sound of Grandpa's reassuring voice followed them.

"Sorry, folks. Lily got a little too excited over the party. She'll be fine."

The musicians stuck up a tune and the hum of conversation drifted over the music.

In Lily's room, Pearl and Sarah started undressing their patient while Drake opted to wait in the hall.

Pearl fumbled with the laces of a fancy corset. "I don't know how she got this corset laced so tight. No matter what it does for your posture, no one can convince me corsets are healthy."

"How could she breathe?" Sarah lifted petticoats to work at Lily's stockings. She halted with her hands in mid air. "Oh, my goodness, the smell. Sister, come here." Sarah put her hand over her mouth and stepped back.

Pearl threw the corset aside and joined her sister. Blood soaked the tops of Lily's stockings and streaked down her calves. Pearl almost gagged at the putrid odor. "Ugh. Something serious is wrong here."

Together they slipped the sodden hose from Lily's legs and dropped them into a basin from the dresser. They worked off layers of petticoats, some streaked with blood. "You'd better get some clean bedding, Sarah. We're going to have to pad the bed to protect the mattress."

At the light rap on the door, Sarah slid out and Belle slipped into the room.

"Grandpa wanted me to stay at the party, but I have to tell you about Lily. She wouldn't let Dr. Percival examine her properly."

"Why?" Pearl asked, but she suspected she knew.

"I don't know. She told him about being so tired, but I don't know what else she told him. Of course, the problem today has been the heavy bleeding."

"Yes, the bleeding. I wonder how long it's gone on?" Pearl remembered the pale skin, dull hair. Changes like that took more than a few days.

"I don't know, but at least a couple of weeks. It seems to me it's not like her monthlies, lots more."

"Has she had pain?"

"Yes, at first. That was before the bleeding started, though. Or maybe when it first started. She had terrible cramping. So bad she could hardly stand up."

Lily's eyes fluttered and her gaze met Pearl's. At once anger sparked. "What are you doing?" She looked at her unclothed body and gasped, "What's going on here?"

Belle stepped forward. "You fainted at the party. Drake brought you upstairs."

Lily glared at Pearl before she spoke to Belle. "I won't have her poking at me or pouring any of her evil concoctions into me."

"We've sent for Dr. Percival," Pearl assured her, averting an argument.

"You get back to your party guests, Belle. I'm fine now." Lily tried to rise, only to fall back on the pillows. "Maybe I'll just rest here awhile."

Sarah returned, arms laden with bedding. Pearl nodded at Belle, motioning her to leave. Drake stood his post in the hallway, awaiting the doctor's arrival.

She couldn't bear seeing anyone suffer, so Pearl brought a cool, damp cloth to Lily. "Let me make you as comfortable as possible while we wait for Dr. Percival." She reached to wipe Lily's brow, but the woman rolled into a ball.

Drake's knock on the door alerted them to the doctor's arrival. Pearl gave Lily's shoulder what she hoped was a comforting pat. "Here's the doctor now to examine you."

Lily's eyes, when she met Pearl's glance, were glazed with fear. "No! I don't want to see him. I don't want to see anyone."

Lily's protests came too late. The doctor strode across the room and set his bag on the bed.

"Well, well. How's the patient?" He rummaged in the black leather satchel. "What brought on this spell?"

"I told you I've been extremely tired lately. I think I did a bit too much getting ready for tonight's party."

He nodded. "It was a grand affair. I was barely home when your father's man came for me. Now, let's see what's going on here."

The doctor's examination took only a few minutes. When he asked Lily about her monthlies and requested he be allowed to examine her, her face became a mask. "No, I'll not have you poking into me." She clutched the sheet to her and struggled to sit. "I tell you I just got too tired, but I'll be fine by tomorrow."

Dr. Percival pursed his lips, obviously reluctant to leave a patient in such distress. He looked at Pearl and asked, "Mrs. Kincaid, may I speak with you privately?"

After a glance at Sarah, Pearl followed him into the hallway.

"Mrs. Stephens refuses to cooperate with me for treatment. She's keeping secrets from me, so I've not been able to help her. Maybe she'll confide in another woman."

"Perhaps, but I doubt it will be me." Pearl shook her head. She couldn't imagine Lily confiding in her. If Lily sought anyone's confidence it would be Belle's. "You may already know she resents me, and she has a very low opinion of my healing."

"I've seen some good results from your efforts right here in Kincaid Springs. Bear with me and I'll see if I can convince Mrs. Stephens to become your patient. Lord knows I'm weary to death of uncooperative patients who won't follow my advice and then blame me when they don't get well."

Pleased with his endorsement, Pearl assured him, "I'll do whatever I can, whatever she'll let me do, but I don't think she'll even want me in the same room."

"Ask the Judge to come up and wait here by the door, then you come back into her room."

With Grandpa at his post in the hallway, Pearl slipped back into Lily's room. Lily and the doctor argued while Sarah stood nearby and twisted a handkerchief in her hands.

Dr. Percival reached into his bag and removed a large jar. Pearl recognized the leeches at once and suppressed a shudder.

Lily yelled and waved her hands, "Get those away from me. Get away, do you hear?"

"Very well. Calm yourself. I must speak to your father, but you're in no state to be left alone. Mrs. Kincaid, will you stay with Mrs. Stephens while I speak to the Judge?" He snapped his bag closed with finality and took it with him.

Pearl nodded and the doctor stepped into the hall and closed the door behind him. They heard Grandpa ask about Lily. The doctor's answer came as a shock.

"Is there any history of insanity in your family?"

Pearl heard Grandpa laugh. "There's some mighty eccentric folks in the Kincaid clan, but no outright madness."

"I believe Mrs. Stephens is suffering from nervous lunacy. She needs rest and close supervision. She'll have to be sedated for some time until her nerves can recover. I don't believe she needs to be institutionalized, but certainly she needs extreme quiet. No visitors, of course, and no excitement of any kind."

Lily's eyes widened and she let loose a scream. "Aaaah! Crazy? Crazy, am I? Get him out of this house. Out, I say, and right now."

The doctor opened the door long enough to say, "I'll bid you good night and leave you in Mrs. Kincaid's care."

With a muffled moan, Lily began weeping. She mumbled something unintelligible between sobs.

Pearl pulled a chair beside the bed and sat down. "I can't understand you. Stop crying and talk to me."

Lily stopped sobbing long enough to wipe at her tears. When their gazes met, Pearl was shocked at the despair she saw in Lily's eyes. Pearl leaned forward and took Lily's hand.

"What can I do to help?"

"Oh, Pearl, I've done such a terrible and foolish thing. I didn't want anyone to know, but I'm so frightened I'll die."

"Tell me what's wrong."

Lily glanced at Sarah and back to Pearl.

Taking her cue from her sister's nod, Sarah said, "I'll go down and make you some tea, Lily."

When they were alone, Lily said, "Don't let me die. I'm so frightened. Please Pearl, don't let me die."

"I can't help you unless you tell me what's happening to you."

"Something's gone terribly wrong inside me. It's a punishment, I know, but I don't want to die."

"Lily, you're not making sense. Start at the first and tell me everything."

"No, no, it's too terrible." When Pearl insisted, Lily covered her face with her hands.

Pearl moved to sit on the edge of the bed and took Lily's hands in hers. A terrible suspicion had formed in her mind. "All right, let me guess, then. It involves a man."

Lily's eyes widened with surprise. "How did you know?" With a heaving sigh, she confessed, "Yes. I was foolish—in so many ways. I let myself be seduced by that smooth talking Frank Worthington. I thought he really cared for me."

"And you found yourself expecting his child?"

Lily tugged loose from Pearl's grasp and covered her face with her hands once again. "Yes. Oh, dear Lord, how could I have been so stupid?"

"Did you tell him? About the baby?"

She lowered her hands, anger sprinkling color on her pallid cheeks. "He . . . he said he thought a widow would have known what to do to prevent a child. You see, it wasn't me he wanted, it was a widow's experience."

"That's despicable."

"And a mistake. I hadn't all that much experience. Wes and I were only together two months before he went to war and got himself killed, and that was over fifteen years ago. Anyway, when I spoke of marriage, Frank laughed at me. He said when he married it would be to a younger woman, someone like Helen Morris."

"Oh, how mean of him. What did you do?"

"The next part is even worse." She refused to meet Pearl's eyes. "He arranged for me to get . . . something from the wife of one of his workers. She's some sort of voodoo woman from down by New Orleans and knows all kinds of potions and spells. Frank said it would take care of our little problem." She opened the drawer of her bedstand and handed the remains of an herbal mixture to Pearl.

"That's all it was to him—a little problem. My reputation would have been ruined, my life a shambles. And think what it would have done to Papa. Oh, I would never have been able to hold my head up in this town again."

Pearl smelled the concoction and an even greater sadness fell on her. Lily must have been so desperate, must have felt so alone. "But it created other problems as well?"

"I . . . I've been bleeding for several weeks. Yesterday, I thought I was dying." Her sobs started anew.

"And you might have. This works by poisoning the baby. It sometimes kills the mother as well. The bleeding is because your body knows the baby is dead and is trying to get rid of it."

"Oh, Pearl, you must hate me. I've been so horrible to you, and now this."

"No. I'm a healer, not a judge."

"What . . . what am I going to do? What will you do?"

"I'll help your body finish what it's started, then I'll have to pack you inside to stop the bleeding. After that we'll build and purify your blood with herbs and a special diet."

She opened the drawer and replaced the packet before stepping to the door to ask Drake, "Would you bring up my medical bag?"

Drake handed the worn black leather satchel through the narrow slit of open doorway. "Got it right here, honey. Storm brought it up earlier. Thought I should have it handy in case you needed it." He planted a kiss on her lips as she took the satchel.

"Thank you." She forced a smile to reward his thoughtfulness. From the floor below music drifted up. The hum of voices was less now. Though it sounded as if the party continued, a few more guests must have left for their homes.

Drake cupped her face with one hand. "Lily all right?"

"Yes, she's going to be fine, just fine." She patted his hand and stepped back. "You go on back to the party. Enjoy yourself with Belle and Lex and let them know Lily's all right. Sarah will be back to help in a few minutes."

After she had closed the door, she set the bag of medical supplies on the bedside chair. No use soiling her favorite dress. She unfastened the garment and stepped out of it, then discarded her petticoats as well. Wearing only her underthings, she set about her work. "The sooner we get started, the sooner you can rest."

Seventeen

Pearl crept into the room she and Drake had shared on their first night in Kincaid Springs. Her husband lay with eyes closed, only a sheet over the lower half of his body. A soft breeze drifted through the balcony door and toyed with the bedside lamp flame.

The smell of death and decay had stayed with her after she left Lily's room. She dropped her clothing on a chair and stepped to the balcony. With her hands in the pockets of a wrapper borrowed from Lily, Pearl inhaled fresh air deep into her lungs. Floral scents floated on the night air but failed to erase death's stench from her memory.

She loved healing, most of it. Nothing ever prepared her for the death of a child—wanted or unwanted. As if the loss of a baby were not tragic enough on its own, the event resurrected old pain from her own life. How fortunate she, Sarah, and Storm were that their mothers had not used Lily's solution.

She heard the pad of bare feet on the floor behind her. Strong arms pulled her against her husband's chest.

"Too tired to sleep?"

She turned into his strong chest and the shelter of his arms. How wonderful it felt to place her cheek against his bare skin, to hear the strong beat of his heart beneath his muscled chest. "No, I think I could sleep for a week."

"Lily going to be all right?"

"Yes, I think so. She'll need a few days' rest."

"She sleeping?"

"Yes. Sarah's with her for now. I'll go back in a few hours."

He scooped her into his arms and carried her to the bed. "Want to tell me what's really wrong with her?"

She raised her head to meet his gaze. "You know I can't discuss something private about a patient, even if she is your own aunt."

He kissed the tip of her nose and stood her beside the bed. His gentle hands unknotted the wrapper's tie. He slid the garment from her before he lifted her onto the bed. After tucking her in as if she were a small child, he turned out the lamp and slid in beside her.

"I finally get to sleep with you and there's only a couple of hours left until daybreak. I've missed you, honey." He spooned himself to her and rested his head near her ear.

Pearl felt tears well. She'd missed Drake but hadn't known how to remedy the mess they'd made of their personal life. Afraid she'd burst into tears if she confessed, she patted his arm where it crossed over her rib cage.

"I think I figured out what happened to my aunt. Was it Frank Worthington?"

Surprised, she turned to face him. "You know I can't say anything. Please don't ask me to break Lily's confidence." She raised on one elbow.

"You don't have to say anything. If he weren't involved, you would have been quick to deny it."

"How much did you hear from out in the hallway?"

"Not much. Still, I can put one and one together. Damn, but I'd like to get my hands on him."

"Oh, Drake, you mustn't. Promise me you won't do anything to call attention to this whole thing. Lily would be even more devastated if anyone else suspected."

"I know you're right, but the urge is still there." He pulled her back beside him. "Go to sleep now before you're the one fainting from fatigue."

She sighed. "Drake?"

"What?"

"Thank you. For being there tonight, for waiting for me here."

Pearl awoke to sunshine and an empty room. She rushed to the balcony doors. The sun was a quarter up the sky. "It must be almost ten o'clock," she said to no one as she hurried to the dressing room. Someone had delivered one of her calico dresses from the ranch along with comfortable shoes and clean underwear. How could she have slept so long and so soundly?

She flew down the hall to check on her patient. Rosilee sat beside her sister's bed and smiled when Pearl entered the room.

"We all stayed over last night. I hated to leave until I knew Lily was really all right."

The terrible smell of last night had dissipated from the room. Fresh air whirled in through open windows and carried the scent of honeysuckle and roses from the garden. When Pearl's gaze met Lily's, her patient's eyes sent a silent pleading message.

"I've told everyone I just got too tired."

All signs of the previous night's ordeal had been removed by Pearl and Sarah. She surveyed the room now to be certain they'd overlooked nothing, but everything looked in place. "It's true she needs rest and quiet."

Rosilee looked guilty. "Oh, Lily. I should have helped you more with the party. You always seem to enjoy planning things and you do parties so well. I left all the details up to you."

Pleased to be the center of attention in a positive way, Lily actually brightened. "Nonsense. It's my own fault for letting myself get too tired. I can't imagine what I was thinking of to skip meals, but I wanted everything to be perfect. In a couple of days I'll feel as good as new."

"Well," Rosilee hesitated. "If you're sure, then Sam and I will go on home."

Pearl stepped forward and took the breakfast tray from her. "You go ahead. I'll stay today. Sarah wants to stay a few days to help Lily and Belle will be here when she can tear herself away from Lex. Where are Belle and Sarah now?"

"I sent Sarah to bed when I came in at eight. The Zimmerman's new house by the river is complete and they want to sell their house in town. Belle and Lex have gone to look at it. They'll probably buy it instead of living here or over the law office."

When Rosilee had gone, Pearl checked her patient. "Your skin color is already better. How do you feel?"

"The cramping has almost stopped but I'm still too tired to move. Even though I have no energy, at least the breakfast tray didn't make me heave this morning."

"Good, that's good. If there's nothing I can do for you now, I'll go down and talk to Polly about your food. The changes in your eating will help your body heal and build your blood, so please eat even if the choices are not your favorites."

She paused and went over the treatment in her mind. "There will be some teas, and one of my tonics you'll hate. If you'll follow my plan, though, you should be back shopping within a week, and a few weeks to a month should have you feeling as good as ever."

Lily twisted the sheet in her hands. "Pearl, I'm not good at this."

Misunderstanding, she agreed. "Of course not. No one should be good at being ill. The days of rest may be boring for you and the teas and tonic tiresome, but they'll restore your energy and health."

"No. I mean, I'm not good at apologizing. I've not done much of it."

"Oh," was all Pearl could say.

"I want to apologize to you, though. If you want me to do it in front of the family, I will."

"Heavens, it's not necessary, not at all."

"Yes, it is. I was disappointed Drake didn't marry Helen Morris."

Pearl saw Lily grimace at the memory.

"Isn't that a good one on me?" Lily shrugged and waved a hand in dismissal. "Oh, well, you know how I love arranging things. It annoyed me when Drake ignored my advice entirely and chose you. I see now he was right. You are the best one for him. And I see you're a healer, in every sense of the word."

"Thank you for telling me that. I know it was hard to have a whole family thrust on you from nowhere. Even though we want to live different types of lives, I want to be your friend. Please, let's put this behind us."

Lily smiled her thanks and nodded before she leaned back on her pillows, exhausted by the exchange. Pearl slipped from the room and headed toward the kitchen.

Ila Mae Vincent, pianist from the First Baptist Church, sat in Belle's place at the First Presbyterian Church piano. August sunshine poured in the arched window to bless the St. Andrew's altar cross and send golden dust motes floating across beams of light.

From the front of the church Pearl watched Belle glide toward the altar. The silk wedding gown colored like new spring grass rustled with each step. Yellow roses from the Kincaid garden mixed with daisies and early asters for the bridal bouquet. As she stepped into a golden ray, Belle's skin glowed with the luminescence of pure sunlight. Escorting her, Grandpa looked as proud as a new poppa.

Memories of her own hasty wedding flooded Pearl's mind. It had seemed grand to her at the time, much more than she had expected. She tried not to make comparisons. Drake and she had shared a unique situation nothing like this love match of Lex and Belle. Mary Alice's wedding plans swept them along like a tidal wave. Pearl had been grateful to Drake for trailing along in Mary Alice's wake without complaint. She smiled. Well, there were a few muttered complaints about delays in travel but he gave in to Mary Alice on every point.

How hopeful she'd been. Peace and stability seemed so near. How could she have known the terrible trouble would follow them and even increase in danger? How could she have known she would fall hopelessly in love with her husband? No, not hopelessly. She still hoped he would return her love someday. Every day she hoped and prayed for his love in any measure.

With a tiny shrug, she adjusted the waist of her new periwinkle blue dress. In a few weeks she would be unable to conceal her rounding stomach. Soon she must tell her husband of their baby. Her eyes sought him on the other side of the altar.

How handsome he looked standing beside Lex. Drake's strong shoulders were the broadest of any man she knew. Dark black hair shone in the light before it curled against his collar. The white of his shirt looked stark against his robust, suntanned skin. His soft gray gaze met hers and he smiled, as if they shared a secret. In truth, they shared many.

Lex stepped forward to meet his bride, his face alight with adoration. Pearl's heart broke a little in the radiance of the couple's love. She didn't expect Drake to care for her as Lex loved Belle, but she yearned for even a small place in his heart. Her longing for his love almost numbed her, blocking out the wedding, the crowd, the couple beside her.

Reverend Potter began, "Dearly beloved, we are gathered together here in the sight of God, and in the face of this congregation, to join together this man and this woman in holy matrimony. . . ."

If Drake could love her just a little, just for herself, she would be happy. Then she could tell him about the baby due this winter.

"Do you, Alexon Samuel Tremont, take this woman as your lawfully wedded wife, to live together after God's ordinance in the holy state of matrimony? Wilt thou love her, comfort her, honor, and keep her in sickness and in health . . ."

What would Drake say now if he knew? Would he feign happiness about the baby? No, surely he would be truly happy about a baby. He needed sons and daughters to carry on the ranch, to inherit the fruit of his labors. But how did he feel about her as the mother of his children?

". . . and forsaking all other, keep thee only unto her, so long as you both shall live?"

Did he see her as a person yet or just as an extension of himself and his life? Did he accept her because she could give him children and run his home, or because he thought her admirable and lovable?

"I, Arabella Angeline Renfro, take thee, Alexon Samuel Tremont, to my wedded husband, to have and to hold from this day forward, for better or worse, for richer for poorer, in sickness and in health, to love, cherish, and to obey, 'til death us do part . . .'"

She needed to know before he learned about the baby, before he felt bound to her by blood ties, before he knew they were truly a new family.

"Ladies and gentlemen, I present to you Mr. and Mrs. Tremont. Lex, you may kiss your bride."

The flurry of the rush from the church to the reception at Grandpa's home cut short Pearl's musings. She rode the crest of excitement carrying her along with the family. Plans were in place for the most elaborate event ever staged by Lily.

Two hours later Lex and Belle waved from their flower-bedecked carriage. "We'll send you postcards," Belle assured the crowd watching from the Kincaid veranda.

Lex shook his head. "We won't even think about you," he called. "You may never see us again."

Belle's tinkling laugh trailed them as they drove off to the train station.

Grandpa raised his voice, "There's plenty more food inside, folks. Let's celebrate until there's not a crumb left."

Most of the crowd followed him inside. A few stood in little groups of two or three to converse on the shaded porch.

Drake offered his arm to Pearl. "Are you pleased with the way this turned out?"

"Yes, and a little surprised."

"Me, too. Who would have thought staid, straitlaced Lex would fall in love with Belle? He's the one who always wanted to reason things out before he took a step, always the cautious one."

"And you were never cautious?"

"Sometimes. But I leapt right in when I met you, didn't I?"

"We both did some leaping then."

She was about to return his question to him, to ask if he were pleased with the way their union had turned out, when Lily interrupted.

Lily fanned her handkerchief in front of her face in an attempt to cool herself. "Lordy, these people are thirsty as fishes. We need more cider. You have any at your restaurant, Pearl?"

"Yes, a couple of barrels. I'll ask Dick to bring them over."

Drake held up his hand. "No need for him to do that on his day off. Not his family having this shindig. I'll take Uncle Samuel. We'll bring the barrels round to the kitchen."

Drake rushed off and Pearl spoke to her hostess, "It was a lovely wedding. Everyone is talking about the wonderful reception, too."

Lily flushed with pleasure. "It has turned out well, hasn't it? And don't Lex and Belle make the perfect couple?"

"Yes, they do." Pearl touched Lily's arm. "You're not overtiring yourself, are you?"

"No. Well, maybe just a bit today." Lily shrugged and waved her hand. "I'll have plenty of time to rest up next week at Aunt Victoria's in Austin. She always pampers me."

"Don't forget to take your tonic and teas with you."

Pearl laughed when Lily grimaced at the mention of tonic, but then Lily joined in the laughter.

Drake had tried to purge from his mind the look on Pearl's face during the wedding. She looked as if she were at a funeral through most of the ceremony. Did she regret their marriage so much? He regretted only the sad state of their union. Separate bedrooms, hell.

It had taken an hour of working up his courage and two fingers of scotch to get to this spot. He rapped softly on the door. When there was no answer, he knocked harder.

Pearl opened the door and he stepped inside the bedroom. "Is something wrong?"

"No. I . . . I want to talk to you. Need to talk to you. Private like."

She stood in the wrapper he'd brought her from Kansas, the one that matched her eyes. Her hair flowed down her shoulders in honey colored waves. In the soft lamplight her skin glowed. The extra rest she'd had while the restaurant was closed had almost faded the dark circles under her eyes. She was still too thin, but the bloom was back in her cheeks and her eyes often sparkled with their old mischief now.

"Come over and sit by the window. Maybe we'll catch a breeze."

He nodded at the open window. "Zed in the garden tonight?"

"Yes, he said I could leave the windows open. He's watching the house from the bench by the fish pond."

He stepped over and turned out the lamp then came to her. "Damn, I wish the waiting and watching were over."

"What did you want to talk to me about?"

He took her hands and met her gaze. "Pearl, it's not easy for me to say I'm sorry, but I am."

"About what?"

"It was wrong of me to criticize the changes you made. I knew it then but the words slipped out anyway. Maybe it was coming home to find you moved out here and then the business in town. All of it together sort of poleaxed me."

"I wanted to make a home for you. For us."

"Yes, I see that." He pulled her to him and nuzzled his head against her hair. The lilac of her soap clung to her. Thank God she still used that special scent. "Can we start over?"

Her arms slid around his waist. "That would be nice."

"I want you back in my bed. I don't care if it's this one or the one in the other room. I want us to be together again, to make love to you."

She pulled away. "Is that all you miss? Our coming together?"

"Honey, I sure as hell miss that, but, no, that's not all. Not by a long shot." He sighed and took a deep breath. Once before he'd tried to tell her and they'd been interrupted. Afraid there would be interruptions tonight, he rushed to say it fast or he'd never get it all out.

"I miss talking to you at night with our heads close together on the pillow, or your head on my chest. Making plans and talking about our day. When I wake in the morning, I miss finding you beside me. All day while I'm working, I miss knowing I'll be with you at night."

"I've missed you, too."

She rested her head against his chest. Her hands toyed with his shirt buttons and set his blood pounding.

His hands spread at her waist and his thumbs caressed her breasts. She raised her head to meet his kiss. He intended it to be soft, gentle. The time apart had increased his need and lessened his control. She returned his deepening kisses measure for measure.

Her fingers worked his shirt free and pushed it aside. He shrugged out of it and fought the knotted belt of her wrapper. His hands trembled with urgency. She pushed them aside and made quick work ridding herself of the garment.

Moonlight from the window cast a silver glow on her hair and skin. She stepped back and her eyes met his as she released the ribbon tie of her camisole. His breath caught in his throat. The depth of his feeling for this woman surprised him. How had she captured his soul?

She reached toward him, touched his chest, and all his thoughts vanished. He shed his boots and trousers. When he looked up she stood in the moonlight. Her bare body waited for him.

He closed the distance between them. "Oh, honey. Pearl.

Tonight the moonlight makes your skin match your name."
He led her to the bed and turned down the coverlet.

She lay down and patted the place beside her as she had
done on their honeymoon. Bossy woman! He grinned and
joined her. He wouldn't have her any other way. His body
stretched beside hers and he pulled her to him.

Her breasts beckoned to him, and he took a peaked nipple
into his mouth. She gasped and twined her fingers in his hair.
Each brush of his fingers brought a sigh that drove him wild
with anticipation. He entered her but grasped for control,
wanting the pleasure to last and build. Her body moved
against his in pleasured writhing. When she arched against
him and held her breath, it sent him beyond control, beyond
thought, into a world where only they existed.

The fury of their passion erupted and their bodies entwined
in love's frantic dance until their fervor crescendoed. He sank
beside her and cradled her in his arms. Drifting back to real-
ity, he longed for this merging of souls to last past a night of
lovemaking and into the sunshine. He wanted the closeness
of the moment to last forever, to remain after the heat of their
passion cooled.

His hands caressed her, soothing and loving until her rhythmic breathing signaled she slept. He lay sated and happy. A
breeze brought fresh garden scents and cooled his fevered
skin.

No woman had ever driven him as she had. No woman had
ever given of herself so freely. He loved her, needed her. How
could he make it any plainer?

"Careful. Don't drop the sign," Drake cautioned Storm and
Dick.

"How's it look?" Storm asked from atop the ladder. He
tested to make certain the hooks would hold, then released the
sign.

Dick stepped back to admire their handiwork. "Granny's

Lunches and Baked Goods is back in business. Leastwise, it will be, come Monday."

Pearl looked excited enough to dance a jig. She clasped her hands and sparkled up at Drake. "Doesn't it look grand?"

"And it's nice to have it all new at once," Rhoda added. "You won't miss the chipped dinnerware and dented pots and pans."

"And Lex's office will look all new when he and Belle get back." Storm gestured to the law office where Mexican stone masons worked with quarried limestone.

After Pearl's fire, Lex had expressed concern about all the important papers which might have been destroyed if the fire had spread. He said he figured limestone facing on his building and a new tin roof would make his building less vulnerable to fire or storm. By the time he and Belle returned from their honeymoon, the work should be completed.

"Well, let's get everything moved in." Drake grabbed a chair from the wagon and carried it into the restaurant. "These new tables and chairs are heavier than the old ones. Ought to last a long time."

New wood, varnish, and fresh paint smells combined to offer a potent blend. Windows sparkled, ready for the new curtains Rhoda held in her arms.

Abe and Zed carted furniture and fixtures while Jeff and Beau stood guard. How much longer would these men's protection be needed? Who waited where to harm Pearl? And why?

Drake met with Sheriff Liles frequently to go over Pearl's safety. The trail of two men who had camped near town led to Austin and disappeared. Every newcomer to Kincaid County had been checked out. Wires from Tennessee added no clues. Someone very clever plotted against his wife and family. So far Drake had been unable to stop them. Impotent rage seethed in him.

He had fought against those who would rob him of his land but he knew who they were, how they worked. Over dusty cattle trails he had fought rustlers, drought, and storms. Those he could see, could anticipate. How could he protect his family against a foe he could neither identify nor understand?

Pearl carried in a large basket. "I've brought lunch for us now that we have places to sit and enjoy our meal."

"We've got lemonade," Sarah said and set a box on one of the tables. "We washed these new glasses at home so we could use them for lunch."

Storm placed a large jar of lemonade beside the box and looked around the dining room. "Looks like before, only better."

Rhoda beamed at him. "Wait until we get the curtains up and the tables decorated. You'll see how much better."

Pearl contented herself unpacking the lunch and serving her helpers. He hated this place, but he loved seeing his wife so happy.

Drake figured the restaurant would be better than the other. Pearl had talked over changes with Sarah, Rhoda, and Dick before construction began. They had made a minor change here and there to make the building more efficient for their needs.

One of the changes Zed had worked out was for the roof. Instead of the flat roof with a false front facade, this building had a peaked roof and well-ventilated attic. They hoped this would deflect some of the sun's heat and offer a little cooling in hot summer months. In winter, wooden doors would seal off the ventilation grills to hold in heat. A trap door to the pantry made the loft space available for extra storage.

Drake walked into the kitchen and stopped in front of the new cookstove. What a huge monster. Pearl joined him.

"Isn't it beautiful?" she asked.

"Don't know how you can find that thing beautiful, but I'm glad you do."

"It is to me. See here, the bigger water reservoir on the side? This will make washing up much easier for Dick." She ran her hands along the top tray. "This warming tray will keep things warm without overcooking them. And the nickel plating makes it look so pretty."

Though he couldn't think of a cookstove as pretty, he would never tell her. "All in all, I guess things have shaped up pretty well." He took stock of the kitchen. Boxes of cookware and dishes still sat waiting to be uncrated. Even with clutter, the room spoke of tidy efficiency.

He felt her hand on his arm.

"Thank you for rebuilding this for Sarah and me. It seems lately I'm always thanking you for one thing or another." She slid her arms around his waist and leaned her head on his shoulder.

He caressed her back and nuzzled his face into her neck. He loved the smell of her, the feel of her. Just thinking about her sent his blood racing. Being this close raised it to a boil. "I can think of a better way to say thank you."

She pulled away and smiled up at him. Her amethyst eyes sparkled. "Right now we'd better get in there and get your plate filled before Storm gobbles your share of the fried chicken."

Eighteen

Willard lowered his spyglass and turned to his brother. The spyglass wasn't much use in the dark. Neither was his brother. At least the moon offered a little light. "They left a big barrel right by the window. We can use it to reach the roof."

"How's this gonna work? How're we gonna stay up on that roof all day in the heat with no food? What if we have to pee?"

"I'm tired of explaining this to you and I ain't gonna do it again. You pee real good right now and come on."

"I just took care of my business. I'm follerin' you."

"Make durn sure no one sees us." Willard bobbled from shadow to shadow in the dark. He hated to be out at this time of morning. Just before dawn was the darkest part of the night.

He reached the barrel and tested it for stability. They didn't need the noise of him falling. He didn't need the pain. Burris hobbled up beside him. His brother still limped from injuries received in their attempt at train robbery.

Seems like lately nothing they did turned out right. This was their last chance, though. He touched his cheek where a large bruise still stung as a reminder.

"Here, hold this steady while I climb up to that grill thing."

"Who's gonna hold it fer me?"

"You won't need it, Burris. For once will you just do what I tell you without making a fuss?"

Burris held the rim of the barrel and Willard stood on the

top. He pried the ventilation grill loose and turned it so it slid inside the attic space. It took three tries to make it into the attic. He just wasn't strong like he used to be.

When he was in the attic, he leaned down. "Now hand me up that there lantern."

Burris stretched up and Willard hooked a finger through the lantern handle. After he shoved the grill back in place, he inched his way to the trap door and lifted it. It was pitch black in the room below, but he knew this room had no windows. He lit the lantern and set it on the top of a pantry shelf before he dropped into the small room.

He wanted no mistakes this time. He stood a moment to get his bearings and latched onto the lantern. Quick as he could, he slid out the door into the kitchen and over to the back door. The new lock opened on the inside. He slid the bolt and opened the door a slit.

Burris crouched by the barrel.

"Get in here, fast."

"I thought sure you was stuck or somethin'. Now what we gonna do? Hey, can we have somethin' to eat?"

"No we can't have nothin' to eat. Are you crazy? Remember what happened last time?"

Burris rubbed his stomach. "I'm awful hungry. We ain't had a good meal in days."

"We'll have plenty to eat soon if we do this right. If we don't, we won't need food where we'll be." He locked the door behind his brother. "Now get on into that small room there. We got to get outa sight 'fore daylight."

Burris hobbled into the pantry and Willard closed the door behind them. He hoped no one was around to see the short flash of light when he had opened the door. He and Burris had to have a light to get up into the attic.

"Reckon they's any pies around? Pearl sure makes good pies."

"I reckon there might be, but we can't go looking for 'em. That big man will be here soon and we can't be down here when he comes."

Burris opened the door to a cupboard. "Well, lookee here in this tin cover. Here's two pies right here." Burris poked one. "Apple. With cinnamon."

"Don't get crumbs all over. Gimme that pie and I'll set it in the attic. We can eat it later." Willard took the pie from Burris and set it on the top shelf beside the lantern. "Come here and climb up now. I'll foller you."

Burris looked over the shelves. "They might be some meat and bread here someplace." He found a loaf of bread and thrust it at Willard. "We're gonna git hungry, smelling cookin' smells all day. You'll be glad I thought of this."

Willard considered his brother's words. Much as he hated to admit it, Burris might be right. He searched the shelves nearby and found fresh apples, crackers, and a jar of jam. "We can't take much or they'll notice, but I'll set this up here, too. Now, git up there."

When Burris had climbed into the loft, Willard straightened up all the containers overturned by Burris's feet. He climbed into the attic and leaned down to retrieve the lantern and food. That done, he slid the trap door back, but offset enough for a tiny peephole crack to the room below.

He and Burris put the food between them. They each had a canteen in preparation for the hot day to come. He didn't tell Burris, but he'd brought an empty can, too. He knew his brother couldn't go all day without some kind of chamber pot.

He heard the front door open and the sound of footsteps coming their way. Lordy, they made it just in time. "Don't make even one sound," he warned his brother.

What seemed like days later they heard the big man call goodbye to Pearl. That lady was leaving too. Now was their chance.

Willard removed the trap door and lowered himself into the pantry. Burris followed him. Quiet as mice, they opened the door. No one was in the kitchen so they tiptoed toward the dining room. Willard drew his gun and paused at the swinging door into the eating area. Behind him, Burris drew his gun too.

He heard Pearl say, "I'm finished here for today. We can leave as soon as I put away these accounts."

"I'll put them away for you, Sister."

So Sarah was in there with her and that guard fellow too. Willard broke out in a sweat and his knees got trembly. This was the hardest part.

That man in there knew how to use his gun.

Bad as he wanted to turn and run the other way, Willard pushed open the door and said, "Hold it right there and drop your gun."

The tall man looked like he might shoot his rifle, but Burris pointed his gun at Pearl.

"If you don't want Pearl shot, you better drop the rifle."

Pearl put her hands on her hips and glared at them. "Willard and Burris Ainsworth! What in the name of heaven are you doing here?" She looked mad enough to choke them. He wondered if she still carried that big old pistol in her pocket.

Burris spoke up. "We got to rob you Pearl, and take you and Sarah with us."

Pearl just rolled her eyes at the threat. "It's okay, Beau. I don't think they even know how to use those guns."

The man lowered his rifle to the table nearby, but he never took his eyes off Willard. Sweat trickled down Willard's spine and beaded across his forehead. His stomach clinched into a lead ball. Lordy, this wasn't going like he planned at all.

Pearl's sister stood quietly, her eyes wide in surprise, but Pearl shook her finger at him.

"You'll do no such thing. We worked hard for this money. And if you think we'd go anywhere with the two of you, you're very mistaken."

"You got to, Pearl." Willard explained, "We're goin' to Oregon, and we need money for a grub stake and we need you to cook for us."

The tall man Pearl called Beau looked at Willard and then

at his brother. "You two plumb loco? Drake Kincaid would hunt you down and make you wish you was dead."

No sooner had the tall man spoken than the café door opened. Drake Kincaid strode in and stopped. "You two? What the hell do you think you're doing?"

In a flash, that Beau had his rifle pointed at Willard's stomach and Pearl's husband had a handgun aimed at Burris.

"You'd better drop those guns or you're both dead men."

No use denying it, they were in big trouble now. Big trouble. He could almost feel the noose tightening around his neck. Now he'd gotten his baby brother in the same fix. He heard Burris's gun drop. With a terrible sense of dread, he dropped his gun onto the nearest table.

"We weren't gonna hurt Pearl or Sarah. We was protectin' 'em."

Pearl's husband stepped over and took the two hand guns. "Are you the two who caused the fire here?"

He should have figured they'd guess about that. "It was a accident. We didn't mean no harm."

Burris added, "We was awful hungry. Pearl's such a good cook an' all we was loadin' up some supplies. I backed into the stove and burned myself. It made me jump something fierce and I knocked over the lantern."

The explanation did nothing to soothe the two men they faced nor to ease Pearl's angry glare.

"You boys are going to the hoosegow." Drake stepped to the door and called to the other man. "Look what we've got here, Jeff. Let's take them to the sheriff."

Burris peered over his shoulder before he went out the door. "Pearl, do you do the cookin' for the jail?"

Pearl grabbed Sarah's hand and joined those escorting the Ainsworths to justice. As they walked the short distance to Ben Liles's office, conflicting emotions whirled in Pearl's mind. She hoped this meant an end to the waiting and watching, the guards, and being constantly on alert. Anger at the two dim-witted men warred with relief they had been caught.

She gave little thought to the Mexican stone masons working on the exterior of Lex's office next door to her restaurant. Something fought for her mind's attention, but she dismissed it in her hurry to keep up with the procession. She'd deal with it later.

Townspeople watched the parade go by—four guards, four Kincaids, and two rag-tag men in handcuffs. Ben Liles was making rounds and crossed the street to meet them. Some folks attempted to follow behind Zed and Abe, but were told to go about their business and let the law take its course.

"Zed, would you let Grandpa know what's going on and then join us at the sheriff's office?" Drake asked as he shepherded his family into the small building which served as jail and law enforcement headquarters for Kincaid County.

When they were all inside and Drake's explanation made, the sheriff leveled his gaze on the two Ainsworths. "All right, now, boys. You better start at the first and tell me what you've been up to."

"I got to sit down somewheres," Burris whined. "My bad leg is actin' up something fierce."

"What about your leg?" The sheriff didn't look convinced anything was wrong.

Burris rubbed at his thigh. "It still ain't healed up from when the train man shot me."

Willard yelled, "Burris, shut up." Beads of sweat gathered across his forehead.

Drake stepped toward the two brothers, "You were responsible for that attempted train robbery in April?"

"Don't say nothin'," Willard cautioned Burris.

"The more you talk, the less trouble you're in." Sheriff Liles pulled a chair over for Burris.

Burris slumped into the chair and let his chin sag to his chest. "I don't see what difference it makes now. We're gonna die anyway."

Grandpa and Zed slipped quietly into the office and Zed

took his stand by the door, rifle in hand. Grandpa gave Pearl's shoulders a hug before he sat in a nearby chair. His silent show of support strengthened her. She had family now, she belonged here. Dear God, she prayed they never found out about her secret.

"Now, fellas, attempted robbery is hardly a hangin' offense," Drake said. "You just start at the first and tell us everything that happened since the first time I saw you boys back in Tennessee."

Willard cocked his head at Drake. "When was that?"

"The first day I was in Piper's Hollow, you two and another man were botherin' Pearl. Called her names and she shot at your feet."

Pearl's anger warred with embarrassment at the memory of their taunts. Thank heavens Drake didn't know the reason behind them. What would her new family think of her if they knew? Would they find her as contemptible as the residents of Piper's Hollow?

The two brothers exchanged a cautious look. Willard spoke, "I reckon maybe I remember. You and another fella rode horses into town. Bought some horses from the Walkers, didn't you?"

"Let's have it. I want the truth and all of it." Sheriff Liles crossed his arms and shot his locally famous no-nonsense look to each brother.

"We was jus' protectin' Pearl and Sarah. Someone wants 'em and that boy," Willard nodded to Storm, "dead and buried. We figured if we got 'em away from here and disappeared, we'd all be safe. If nobody knew where we was, couldn't no one kill nobody."

Pearl fairly snorted with anger. "Protecting me? You call burning down my restaurant and then coming back to rob me protecting me?"

Burris's head bobbed in agreement. "Yep, that's right, that's all we was doing. Honest. We had to get the money, so we'd have a grub stake. But we was only protectin' you and Sarah and Storm."

"Who wants my wife and her brother and sister dead?"

Angry as she was, her husband looked angrier. He looked mad enough to spit nails so hard it drove them through a fence post.

Sheriff Liles held up his hand to stay further comment. "Let me ask the questions. We'll get to the bottom of this soon enough." He rummaged in his file drawer for some papers and set them on the desk before he took his chair. "Let's see now," his fingers tapped as he read through his notes, "We'll start with that rock slide—you two know anything about that?"

Each of the brothers shook his head and looked bewildered. Pearl thought the two probably were bewildered most of the time.

"How about that attempt to push Pearl off the train?"

The two looked at one another, then each looked at the floor and said nothing. Sheriff Liles pointed at Willard.

"What do you know about that?"

Willard jumped. "It wasn't us. We didn't know nothing about it."

Burris nodded. "We had to go back and get Jug's body is all. Didn't neither of us know what he done to fall off the train."

"Who asked you to get the body? Who sent you?" Drake yelled.

"I'm getting to that, Drake. I know you're keyed up 'cause of your wife being under attack, but you let me handle this or I'll make you leave. Understand?"

"Sorry, Ben. I'd like to choke the information out of both of these worthless coyotes, but I'll try to be quiet and let you get on with it."

His fists clinched at his side. Pearl slipped her hand under his arm. His body relaxed and he pulled her to him. Solid muscles enfolded her. She breathed in his scent and closed her eyes against the tableau before her. How she wished this were over, settled forever and she and Drake were home. Soon, soon the nightmare would end and she and her husband could get on with their lives. Burris's whimper caused her eyes to fly open.

The sheriff pushed the papers to the side and looked directly at Willard. "How about it? You tell us who put you up to this mischief, and it'll make things easier for you."

"No," Willard shook his head. "It'd make things worse, lots worse, 'cause we'd be killed dead for sure then."

"So this person's here—in this area?" Sheriff Liles leaned back in his chair, speculation playing on his face.

"Don't say nothing, Burris." Willard clamped his mouth shut and resumed his examination of the floor.

Another hour of questioning made no headway in getting further information from the two criminals. In disgust, the sheriff told them he was locking them up.

Kincaid Springs' jail had two cells, so each brother had his own space. As soon as the cuffs were off and the door slammed closed behind them, Burris sank onto his bunk and lay down. Willard sat on his bed and held his head in his hands.

"You boys think about this. We'll have another go at your story later."

Turning to the Kincaids, he added, "Don't let your defenses down for a minute. Keep those four guards with you all the time. My deputy and I will both sleep here until this is settled."

Drake nodded. "We'll come back in the morning, Ben. See what happens then."

The late summer sun beat down on the group headed to Grandpa's. Drake and Pearl walked side by side and Storm and Sarah followed with Grandpa trailing. Two guards walked in front of the Kincaids and two behind. After weeks of this routine, the townspeople no longer stared at the entourage. Most folks they passed nodded a silent greeting but a few called out a question about the two men in jail.

"Who in Piper's Hollow hates me this much?" Pearl asked herself, then realized she voiced her thoughts.

Drake shook his head. "First ask why? Who has anything to gain by your death?"

"The brothers are plenty scared," Storm added, deep in thought. "I can think of only one man besides Jug who frightened them so much."

"Who?" Drake almost barked the question.

"The great Quin Walker."

Pearl whirled to face her brother and bumped into Sarah. "Surely you don't think he's behind this?" she exclaimed as she steadied herself and her sister.

"Who else could it be?" Storm countered with a shrug.

Pearl shook her head in disbelief, but turned and continued her progress toward Grandpa's. "What could he hope to gain? And why now? Why not years ago?"

"You may never know the answer to that, honey. But Storm's right. Those two shiftless weasels are scared to talk. That means whoever the person behind this is, he's nearby. Near enough they're afraid he can get to them in jail."

Pearl stopped in her tracks. In spite of the August heat, a chill slid down her spine. "We need to go back and make them talk. Now. Before Quin, or whoever, gets to them."

The Kincaids huddled on the sidewalk planking. The guards, backs to the family's circle, continued their vigilance.

"Pearl's right," Drake said. "Whoever's behind this is mean as a snake. He may try to kill those boys or break them out of jail tonight. Could get ugly."

"I'd like to get my hands on the low life who put them up to this." Grandpa's pale blue eyes fairly sparked with anger.

"Let's go back and have another go at them." Drake took Pearl's hand as he spoke, leading her toward the jail.

Fear engulfed her. As much as she wanted to live, to continue her life with Drake in Kincaid Springs, she dreaded the approaching encounter. Too much pain lay buried in her past. Best to leave it there. Opening old wounds promised fresh anguish.

Sheriff Liles had bolted the door behind them and they had to knock to gain entrance to his office. Though he made them welcome, Pearl wondered how the wily lawman felt about their return.

"Ben, we want to have another go at those two skunks in there." Grandpa nodded toward the cells. "We figure whoever is behind this will shoot them soon as it's dark."

Burris sat up and whimpered. He looked to Pearl to have aged years in the few months since she'd left Piper's Hollow.

Willard jumped off his bunk and rushed to the bars of his cell door. "Don't let him shoot us. We was just trying to protect Pearl and her kin. Don't let him kill us."

Drake reached through the bars to grab Willard's shirt. He pulled the other man up against the metal and growled, "Then you better start talking and be fast about it."

"Tell him, Willard. You might as well tell it all," Burris whined from his cell.

Willard slumped in defeat. "I'll tell you, but you got to promise to protect us. We'll be dead 'fore mornin' if'n he knows I talked. And he'll still be after Pearl and them."

"Back off, Drake," Sheriff Liles cautioned. He stepped between Drake and Willard. "Start with who put you up to this."

"It was Quin Walker. The young one."

The admission stunned Pearl. "But why?"

Willard wouldn't meet her gaze. "Because of the money and the will."

Pearl stepped to the cell door. "Willard, you're not making sense. What money and what will?"

He looked up, "Why the money his daddy paid your Granny each year. Quin found out about it after she died. He was sure mad. Said he'd get even with you for having that tucked away in the bank all this time."

"But I didn't even know about it until it arrived here."

He nodded. "I reckon we knew that. Would have told him but he was too riled. A body cain't reason with him, 'specially not when he gets all het up."

Burris nodded. "Ain't good to cross him when he's riled."

Willard continued, "Then, he found out about his daddy's will, 'bout it includin' you and Storm and Sarah. Lordy, he went plumb out of his head. Said ever'body would know his daddy was your daddy too."

"People figured that out long ago. Surely he knew that," Pearl reasoned.

"No, and you couldn't tell him neither. He was fair crazy worryin' about it."

Burris limped over to the cell bars. "That's when he beat up that there girl at Roxie's place. Threatened to kill her and Roxie both if she told who did it."

Pearl's gaze locked with Drake's. So, Quin was the one who beat Belle.

Burris put out a grimy hand to Pearl. "It was him paid us to keep folks riled about your granny throwin' you away to the hogs and all."

No! She wanted to make Burris take back his words. Pearl shrank within herself. Her worst fears had come true. She looked at Drake. His disgust with her would end their chance at happiness. Who could want a woman whose own granny threw her away with the pig's slop?

Outrage suffused Drake's face, his gray eyes blazed in fury. "Her granny did what?"

Willard hesitated, but gave in. "You know. When Pearl was born without her momma being married, her granny tried to kill her so no one would know there was a baby. Threw her in the hog pen. Big hog like to have et her. Sheriff Cummins come along and saved her."

Pearl's world crashed around her. She saw contempt in Drake's eyes, saw the anger coursing through him. He would hate her now as much as the people she'd left behind. Her life here ended with Willard's and Burris's arrest. She should have known there were no second chances for the likes of her.

Burris nodded his agreement with his brother. "That's why she's named Fannie Pearl. Cause the hog bit her on the fanny and the Sheriff's wife was named Pearl."

"Our momma said it was like castin' pearls before swine in

the Bible." Willard explained, "She said sometimes people don't recognize their treasures."

The statement did little to salve her wounds. She turned and slipped from the office. Sarah called after her but she ran on. She wasn't aware of Zed following her to the buggy, but he was there helping her when she climbed in. With a snap of the reins she headed for the ranch as fast as the horses could go.

Back in the jail, Drake lunged at the cell door once more. "You mean you spread filth like that for money? How could you hurt someone good like Pearl?"

"You don't know how mean Quin is." Willard had backed into the far corner of his cell. "If'n we didn't do what he said, he woulda killed us long 'fore now. Or hurt us so bad we wished we was dead."

Burris's head bobbled like a chicken. "Sometimes he likes to hurt things—and people. He's crazy, but real smart. And he can track and hunt better 'n any injun."

"Is he the one who used an arrow to set our barn on fire?" Storm asked.

"I reckon it were him. Him and Jug was always up to something. Burris and me didn't know what all they did." Willard sat on his bunk. "We didn't want to."

"Damn you two! I could kill you with my bare hands," Drake railed at the culprits. "You put Pearl through years of pain, caused her untold sorrow, and all for nothing but a few coins."

"We was just tryin' to help her this time," Burris whined. "I allus liked her and she was real good to our mamma."

Drake felt a sturdy hand on his shoulder. Grandpa said, "Steady, son. You'd best go after Pearl."

Drake whirled and scanned the room. "Go after her? Where is she?"

Grandpa nodded toward the door. "She ran out a while back when those boys were talking. Zed went with her."

Drake rushed for the door. "See Sarah and Storm home, will you?" he called to the three remaining guards.

His family poured out of the sheriff's office behind him, but he hurried on. He let Midnight have his head and they raced toward the ranch.

All this time she had harbored the pain of her granny's misdeed. No wonder Sarah had nothing good to say about the woman in whose home she had lived all her life. No wonder Storm called her a mean old lady. Who would try to kill her own grandchild? He didn't call that mean—evil was a better word.

Memories of his own grandmother and the pampering she showered on him and Lex made a sharp contrast to what Pearl must have endured. Yet Pearl nursed the woman, took care of her all those years. Dear Lord, what kind of woman had he married? No other human would show such compassion, such care, as to nurture the very person who had tried to kill her, who daily found fault with all she did.

How difficult life must have been for Pearl. Difficult? It must have been hell. Yet with all that pain in her life she found a way to rescue Storm and Sarah and provide a good home for them. She even rescued strangers like Belle. And here in town, she provided Rhoda with a job and dignity, a way to provide for her children and aging mother.

And you. Don't forget she saved you from yourself.

All the things he ever said to her came hurtling back at him. All the things he left unsaid gouged at him. What must she think of him? He had been so careless with her, left her alone while he went off on his fool trail drive. He remembered his anger at her restaurant, how he told her he wished it would burn to the ground. Shame mingled with his fury as he drove Midnight on.

Why hadn't she confided in him, told him about her granny and her mother? Did she have so little confidence in him or did she think something she had no control over would matter to him? True, he was less than an ideal husband to start, but he thought he had improved enough to win her trust. Damn, he still had a lot to learn about this marriage business.

Nineteen

Miguel led the unhitched team from the buggy as Midnight raced into the barn. Drake tossed the reins to Javier and dashed for the house.

Maria opened the door for him, concern etched on her face. "Señora Pearl is very upset."

"Where is she?"

She pointed toward the bedroom. "*Pobrecita,* my poor one is crying."

"Pearl? Pearl?" He rushed down the hall and stopped at the master suite.

"Go . . . a- . . .way!" she sobbed.

He pushed against the door but it refused to yield. "Open the door."

"No. Leave me alone."

"Pearl, open the damn door now." When he received no response, he lunged with his shoulder against the wood. The thud of his body mingled with the crack of the door frame. Once more and the wooden framework split from the wall and the door tumbled inward with a crash.

Pearl screamed and jumped from the bed where, from the looks of the wrinkled coverlet, she had been lying.

"Get out. Go away." She pulled her carpetbag from the wardrobe and threw clothes into it.

"Where do you think you're going?"

"What does it matter? I'll be out of your life. You won't have to see me ever again."

He took the valise from her and set it on the floor. She moved as if to pick it up but he grasped her hands in his.

"Pearl, why did you run away from town? I know I was coming down hard on those two, but they wouldn't talk fast enough."

She turned her head away. "But when they talked, they told too much. You know everything now. I know the sight of me disgusts you."

"Honey, honey, what are you saying? Why would anything about you disgust me?"

She looked into his eyes, tears streaming down her face. "How could it not? It was bad enough when you just knew my parents weren't married and how the people in Piper's Hollow shunned me. Now you know my own grandmother tried to kill me, threw me in the hog pen like a piece of garbage. If Evan hadn't come along and heard my cries, I would have died. Granny hated me so much she wouldn't have cared."

It hurt him to see her so sad, to know how much she had suffered in her life. "How can you not know me well enough to see I was disgusted with your granny, not you? How can you think what she did has any reflection on you? You were a newborn infant, for God's sake! The actions of a mean old woman disgraces her, not you." He tried to pull her to him but she turned away.

"I come from bad stock, have bad blood in my veins. That's not the kind of woman you need for a wife, not the kind you wanted. How can you even stand to be in the same room with me now?"

He led her to her rocking chair and guided her to sit down. Kneeling in front of her, he took both her hands again. "Pearl, I admire you more than any woman I've ever known, and that includes my grandmother."

She stopped sobbing long enough to look at him and ask, "You . . . you do?"

"Yes, I do. You've taken care of others all your life, including the very woman who tried to kill you. Do you have any idea how rare and special a person you are?"

She pulled her hand from his and brushed at her tears. "Oh, Drake, I'm so embarrassed. The sheriff and his deputy, Grandpa, the guards, they all heard the Ainsworths telling about me. Someone will talk and everyone in town will know. What will they think?"

"Same as I do, you're a wonderful woman." As he handed her his handkerchief, the realization hit him for the first time how much she cared what other people thought of her. She'd kept those feelings hidden because the painful criticism hurt her through the years. She'd probably grown up pretending to the world that taunts and condemnation mattered not a whit to her. All the time she longed for praise and acceptance.

She dabbed at her eyes then gripped his arm. "D-don't think poorly of my mother. Mama didn't know what Granny had done until Evan came into the house with me in his arms. At least Mama wanted me and let me know she loved me."

He asked, "Why would your granny think she could get rid of you and not be found out?"

"She always pretended Mama wasn't expecting. Mama stayed at home the last four months before I was born so no one except those who came to the house saw her. Granny told everyone Mama had been sick with pneumonia and the medicine she took made her swell."

Drake shook his head. "Surely no one believed her."

"I reckon not, but Granny thought they did. Or maybe she thought if there was no baby they would come to believe it. When she took me to the hog pen, she told Mama I died."

"Sounds like your mama had a hard life."

"Oh, she did. Granny never let her forget her one mistake. Mama never did get over it. She loved my father, you see. As if Granny always harping at her wasn't bad enough, having him live so near with another woman was awful hard on her."

"And did he love the woman he married?"

"I guess maybe he did. He had told his parents he wanted to marry Mama, but they wouldn't hear of it. They had a wealthy woman picked for him, the daughter of friends. I think he and his wife were happy, though, until she went crazy."

Drake remembered the sorrow in Quinton Walker's voice when he spoke of his wife dying. If he didn't love her to start with, he must have come to love her later.

Pearl looked up in wonder. "Oh, Drake. I just realized the Ainsworths said our father recognized us in his will. Maybe he didn't hate us too much."

"Did he ever come see you or your mother?"

"No. He never even spoke to me, except one time. I was out playing by the road when he came by on one of his fine horses all alone. He tipped his hat and said, 'Hello, my beautiful little girl.' I was five, but I remember it clearly."

From the front of the house Drake heard a commotion. The aroma of pot roast wafted through the halls and reminded him Maria would soon have their supper ready.

"Sarah and Storm must have come home." Rising, he tugged on Pearl's hands, then pulled her into his embrace. After a long kiss, he brushed his fingers across her cheek. "No more tears, huh? Let's go have our dinner, my beautiful wife. Later, we'll continue this discussion and I'll show you just how beautiful you are."

They stepped on the fallen door and into the hall.

Though the air was thick with tension over the aborted abduction and the threat of Quin's presence, the meal took on a festive mood.

It seemed to Drake the need for constant vigilance was drawing to an end. "With the arrest of the Ainsworths, it's only a matter of time before Ben captures Quin and we can all relax."

"When all this is over," Jeff said, "I aim to take me a little vacation, maybe go up to Denver and look around."

"You been on vacation since you took that shot in the lungs six months ago. When you gonna go to work?" Abe asked.

"Me, I'm off to places and parts unknown." Beau paused with a faraway look in his eyes. "Been feelin' restless lately. Got me a stack of wanted posters and I aim to head West, maybe go up to Oregon."

Storm laughed. "The Ainsworths should have kidnapped you. That's where they wanted to go."

"What about you, Abe? What are your plans when all this is over?" Drake asked.

"Well, I believe I'll try my hand at finding a job in town."

"That decision wouldn't have anything to do with staying near the restaurant, would it?" Pearl asked.

Abe blushed red as a beet. Even Drake hadn't missed the way Abe hung around Rhoda, or the way his eyes followed her when they were in the same room. Some good-natured jeers were exchanged between Abe and the other three guards before Zed spoke up, nodding from Drake to Pearl.

"If it's all right with you folks, I'd like to stay on here and help Miguel with the garden."

"Miguel's told me many times you're especially gifted with plants," Drake said. "Did a great job on the fountain."

"There's lots more I could do. Believe I could make you a hothouse over in the far corner of the garden. You could have early vegetables if I started them in the winter. Might could even grow things for others."

Pearl put her fork down and looked at Zed. "Could you grow my herbs in a hothouse?"

"Yes, ma'am." He nodded, then paused in thought a second before he added, "Not all of them. Some don't take to cultivation. Most I could grow. Have to experiment some."

Drake looked from his wife to Zed. Talk about herbs and Pearl was all ears. "Zed, I believe you've got yourself a job as gardener."

Pearl smoothed bed pillows and lowered the bedside lamp. Nervous as she had been on her wedding night, she still couldn't believe Drake knew her terrible secret yet wanted to be with her. All her life she'd been shunned and criticized for the sins of her grandmother and mother.

Taunts about the hog pen kept her from attending school as a child. Later the same taunts kept her from having a normal social life. Once again she thanked God for Evan Cummins and his wife. She turned as Drake came through the door he and Zed had repaired earlier.

He strode across the room and swept her into his arms. Twirling as if she were no heavier than a child, he said, "My beautiful wife, let me show you how much I love you." He lowered her gently onto their bed.

She sat up. "You . . . you what?" Could her ears have deceived her? Did she really hear the words she had longed for all these months? Yes, all her life she had waited for this moment.

"I said, let me show you how much I love you." He lay down and pulled her into his arms. "Do you think you could ever come to love me back?"

"Oh, Drake." She nestled into him and slid her arms around his waist. "I love you so much. I have almost since we met."

"Then why did you try to run away from me?"

"I was afraid you'd be disgusted with me since you knew my secret, afraid you'd send me away. I couldn't bear it, so I thought I'd leave before you could ask me to."

"Aw, honey. I'll never let you go. Wherever you went, I'd have found you and brought you back. This is where you belong, this is your home."

His arms caressed her. She pulled his shirt from his pants and slipped her hands against his skin. He pulled her night dress over her head and tossed it aside.

"Let me look at you. I'll never tire of seeing you like this." His hands trailed across her skin, then his lips followed the same path.

At her breasts, his lips paused to trace the circles with his tongue before he found a nipple with his mouth and suckled her. When she thought she would die from the pleasure, he moved down along her ribs to her waist. Tugging her over, he kissed the scar on her hip before he let her roll back to receive his mouth on her abdomen.

As he ran his tongue along her navel, the babe inside her quickened.

Eyes wide with surprise, he asked, "What . . . what was that? What just happened?"

She touched his cheek, her other hand seeking her rounding stomach. "Our baby just kicked."

"Our baby?"

Thank God, he looked happy. He looked happy enough to burst. And proud.

"Yesterday was the first time I felt him move. You are pleased, aren't you? You look pleased."

"Proud as a coat with new buttons." His hands stopped their movement. He gazed into her eyes. "Honey, is this, um, can we still, um. . . ."

"Oh, yes. Let me show you," she said and pulled him to her. Her hand moved down the front of his pants and followed the length of his erection.

He raised and sat on the bed to shuck off his boots and pants before he rejoined her. "Now, where were we?"

She cradled his manhood in her hand. "Right about here."

"Ahh, I remember now." He slid his finger inside her and laved her breast with his tongue.

She lost all rational thought. From outside herself she heard her voice urge him, "Now, please, now. Come inside me."

He entered her and she wrapped her legs around him. As one they moved in timeless rhythm. Higher and higher they soared into the night sky. Showers of stars burst around them and they sank slowly to earth on a cloud of bliss.

They lay nestled together when Drake said, "Honey, I'm worried about you working so hard." He rested his hand on her belly. "Won't getting so tired hurt you and the baby?"

"It was supposed to be a surprise for you, but all this with the Ainsworths spoiled it. Rhoda is going to run the restaurant now and she's hired a woman to help her."

He planted a loud kiss on her lips and leaned over her. "That's great. I mean, I know you love the place, but you've looked so tired and you've lost weight."

"She and Dick will be fine without Sarah and me. I suspect

Abe will want to help her when this whole mess is over. They're sweet on each other, you know?"

"No, I didn't notice, not until supper. When's your last day?"

"Today. Rhoda will have Oleta Mae Witt helping her, and Oleta Mae's daughter Evie can come in if she's needed. I'll still do my healing. Seems like it takes more and more time."

"Yes, but I know it's your gift and it's important. You help a lot of people," he agreed. After a pause, he asked, "Honey, if the baby's moving now, you must have known for some time you were expecting. Why didn't you tell me about the baby before now?"

"I wasn't sure how you felt about me. Drake, I couldn't bear to think you'd stay with me because of the baby and not because you wanted me."

"Oh, I want you. In every way. Let me show you how much."

Sarah stood on the piano bench while Pearl made last minute adjustments to a new dress.

Sarah twisted to look down at her sister. "Isn't it exciting about Mama and Cal getting married?" Without waiting for an answer, she continued, "They love St. Louis, and their place, The Lucky Times Palace, is already showing a profit."

Pearl tugged on Sarah's skirt to make certain she had the fabric straight. "I know you're happy for them, but please quit wiggling."

"Founder's Day will be so much fun. Carlotta and I plan to put our boxes in the box lunch auction. I hope Jimmy Simms buys mine."

Around a mouthful of pins, Pearl said, "Sarah, if you want this hem to be even and finished in time for Grandpa's birthday celebration tomorrow, you'd better stand still."

"Imagine, us being related to someone famous enough to have founded a town and have a day named after him. Well . . . I'm almost related to him." Sarah ran her hands along the skirt pleats of her dark green dress.

"You are related to him. You call him Grandpa, don't you? And he calls you part of his family." Pearl pulled the remaining pins from her mouth and stuck them into the pin cushion on her wrist, then offered her hand to help Sarah down from the bench.

"Yes, and I think of him as my grandpa. I wish he really was my grandpa." Sarah clapped her hands in excitement. "I can hardly wait until tomorrow's Founder's Day celebrations. Carlotta and I are staying for the dance tomorrow night—that is, if you let me and if her parents let her."

"We'll all stay, so maybe Carlotta can come home with us if her parents plan to leave early." Pearl walked to the window and peered out. "I hope the weather clears up before then. It looks as if there's a bad storm brewing in the Southwest."

"Oh, no. I'll bet it makes Grandpa's joints act up."

Trust Sarah to think of that. She doted on Grandpa, and he apparently returned the feeling. Pearl had so much to do before the celebration honoring Grandpa tomorrow that she'd almost forgotten about the new batch of tonic she'd poured up last night. Grandpa would be needing it. Weather changes always made the soreness and stiffness in his joints worse.

Voicing her thoughts to no one in particular, Pearl said, "I need to get his tonic to him. It'd be a shame if he was all stove up on his birthday and couldn't enjoy his big day."

Sarah stepped forward. "I'll take it to him. I want to get green ribbon for my hair to match the new dress and enough to tie on my box lunch so Jimmy will know it's mine."

Storm came through the room in time to hear the last of their exchange. "I promised to help hang more banners in town. I could take Sarah with me."

The wind picked up and they heard the gusts whistle down the chimney and push at the windows.

"You'd better take your slickers. Sounds like you'll get caught in the rain. Would you like to take the buggy?"

"Yes," Sarah said. "You could drive me, Storm."

Pearl saw the twinkle in Storm's eyes as he bowed to their sister. "I am your slave, Princess Sarah."

Sarah gave his shoulder a playful shove. "And that's just as it should be."

Pearl readied a basket of bottled tonic while Storm harnessed the team to the buggy. When she and Sarah went outside, the wind molded their dresses to their bodies. Bits of sand and dust stung Pearl's face. She handed the basket to Storm, who set it in the floor behind the buggy seat.

"Mind you don't stay late. Stop in at the restaurant and have an early lunch if you want to, then come home. You can let me know how Rhoda's doing with my replacement."

"No one could ever replace you, Sister." Sarah called as they rode away.

Jeff rode in front of them and Beau trailed behind. Pearl would be so glad when guards were no longer necessary for a simple ride into town. With a sigh of resignation, she returned to the house and her preparations for tomorrow.

Quin watched from behind a massive live oak. Waiting here had paid off, boring as it had been. He loaded an arrow into his bow and waited until the buggy was at the turn in the road. He let the arrow fly and it hit the man in buckskins. Without a sound the man slid from his horse. The horse must have been well trained, because it stopped beside its fallen rider.

After waiting a few seconds to make certain the others did not come back around the bend to see what happened to this man, Quin rushed onto the road and checked his victim. Dead as a door nail. The arrow had pierced his heart. Grabbing the man under the shoulders, he pulled him to the side of the road. He went back and led the dead man's horse to the trees.

As a man who raised prime horseflesh, he valued horses far more than humans. Quin didn't want to endanger the horse by tying him to a tree in case there were predators about. Predators other than himself, he thought and laughed.

He dropped the reins onto the dead man's chest. Left loose, the horse would eventually be spooked by something and return home. It would be too late to save that bitch Pearl and her bastard brother and sister.

Quin mounted his own horse and rode across the fields. The time schedule he'd worked out required precision. As usual, he had proven his mind superior to this bunch of rough Texans.

They hadn't even realized he was a white man while he laid stone on the building not fifty feet from where Pearl's smart-ass husband directed the rebuilding of her restaurant. No one seemed to notice one of the Mexican stone masons had blonde hair and light skin. Of course, he'd kept his hat pulled low and hadn't washed the dirt from his face.

He got mad all over again when he thought of those two bungling Ainsworths. He'd laid it out for them, step by step. After all the instructions he gave them on getting into the restaurant, they still fouled up. This time there would be no mistakes because he was taking care of it himself.

When he reached the group of trees he sought, he dismounted and hid behind a large outcropping of rocks. Heavy clouds made it seem as dark as dusk even though it was morning. In the distance he saw the buggy headed his way. He waited until it was almost even with him before he stepped out.

"You two in the buggy raise your hands. You there in front, get off your horse and throw down your guns."

The man they called Jeff looked around. "Where's Beau?" he asked as he dismounted.

"If you mean the guy who was riding behind you, he's dead. *I shot an arrow into the air, it came to rest* . . . right in his heart."

"You killed Beau?" Sarah cried.

She looked about ready to bawl. Good. He wanted her plenty miserable before she died.

"Why?" that bastard injun asked. "He never did anything to you?"

"Shut up. When I want you to know something, I'll tell you." He waved his gun at the guard. "Stand over there by the rocks."

When the guard was in place, Quin pulled the trigger. The man dropped as Sarah screamed and started to get out of the buggy.

The injun pulled her back. "Stay here or he'll shoot you, too."

"That's right. You're pretty smart for an injun. Course your mama was smart, too. My daddy would of married her if I hadn't put a stop to it."

That sure got the injun's attention. He leaned forward, his face filled with wonder. It was worth letting him know that secret to see a reaction on the bastard's face.

"He would have married my mother?" the bastard asked. "He was willing to do this?"

"Yeah. Had to threaten to kill you and her father if she went through with it. Daddy wouldn't leave her alone, though. Kept pesterin' her 'til she left you with Pearl and took off. Daddy would have taken you then but I had a major fit. Told him I'd kill anyone he brought into our house 'cept quality folks, so he figured he'd leave you where you were."

Sarah put her hand on the injun's arm. "Oh, Storm, that's wonderful. He wanted you—and your mother."

"Cut the conversation and get down out of that buggy. Get out on this side and don't try any tricks."

He liked the way Sarah's face was pale and her eyes wide with terror. She looked at the guard on the ground and tears streamed down her face. The injun helped her out of the buggy, but now his face might as well have been a mask. Quin tossed Sarah a length of rope. The wind caught it and she had to pick it up from the ground.

"Tie up the injun, hands behind his back. Do a good job or you'll be sorry."

When Sarah had bound the bastard injun's hands, Quin did the same for her. From his pocket he whipped out a couple of bandanas and gagged each of the two.

"Now climb back into the buggy."

Quin helped them up into the buggy but took the reins for the team of horses and tied them to his own horse's saddle.

Being careful not to get blood on himself, he eased the vest off the fallen man and picked up the man's hat from the ground. He dragged him behind the rocks. Quin took his own horse into the trees.

"This will be my little disguise," he said as he donned the vest and clamped the hat onto his head. "With me wearing these and riding his horse, folks will think it's business as usual when they see us ride up to the Kincaid mansion."

Pearl checked the clock on the mantle. Three o'clock. Where on earth were Sarah and Storm? They were supposed to return as soon as they ate at the restaurant. She looked out the window, but they weren't visible on the road. Clouds boiled across the horizon. Lightning split the sky, but too far away for the thunder to be heard.

Drake and the hands were out rounding up the horses to bring them in closer to the barns. Abe sat in the rocker on the front porch, watching as sentinel, but she couldn't see Zed.

When she stepped onto the porch, Abe stood up. "I have to go into town to see what's keeping my brother and sister. Could you ask Miguel to saddle a horse for me?"

She pulled off her apron and scribbled a note for Drake explaining her concern for Sarah and Storm. She left the note with Maria and got her reticule, one of Storm's hats, and a slicker. She'd quit wearing her thigh holster now that she wasn't going in to town every day. As an afterthought, she strapped on the little derringer. By the time she went outside, Abe was waiting on his horse with her horse beside him.

"Can't find Miguel or Zed. Guess they're off lookin' at plants or something. I'd better get Javier to go with us?"

Pearl shook her head. "No, I've heard you tell about bringing in three bank robbers single-handed. If you can't protect me by yourself, then no one can."

They rode at a fast pace, eager to stay out of the approaching rain and to find Sarah and Storm. When they reached Grandpa's, Pearl gave a sigh of relief. The buggy was parked at the side entrance which opened near Grandpa's study. There was Jeff's horse tied near the team. Beau must be around back.

Abe and Pearl dismounted and hurried into the house. Pearl crossed the hall and knocked at Grandpa's study door.

There was a long pause, then Grandpa said, "Come in, missy."

Pearl and Abe looked at one another. Grandpa never called anyone "missy." Abe motioned her aside and opened the door. As he stepped into the room with gun drawn, a gun blast rent the air. Abe dropped to the floor and his gun slipped from his hand. Pearl stopped in her tracks.

Quin called, "Come on in, Pearl, if you want to keep this old man alive."

She slipped into the room and stared in horror. A Quin she hardly recognized had his gun pointed at Grandpa, who was tied to his desk chair. Storm and Sarah sat on the floor nearby, bound as well as gagged.

"I'm sorry, girl," Grandpa said. "I tried to think of a way to warn you."

"That's enough from you, old man," Quin said and brought the gun down hard against Grandpa's head. Grandpa sagged from the blow and looked unconscious. Pearl bent to see about Abe. As she knelt beside him, he moved his fingers enough to clutch at her knee. Quin couldn't have seen the subtle movement, so she must keep Abe from further harm.

She looked up and said, "You've killed him."

"Leave him and get over here. Kick his gun this way."

Pearl rose and gave the gun a shove with her foot before she went to Grandpa. He was breathing all right, but was out cold. Thank goodness. Maybe Quin would leave Grandpa and Abe alone.

Quin slapped her hard. "I said get over here, not check on the old man. Now turn around."

She refused to let him see how much the slap hurt. Glaring at Quin first, she turned her back to him. Roughly, he bound her hands.

"What are you going to do with us?" she asked before he gagged her.

"I'm taking you back to the ranch." His shrill laugh sent chills down her spine. "There's a line shack there where we'll wait for that husband of yours to find us."

She whirled. This time she couldn't keep the fear from her eyes. He laughed at her again. Clearly he had slipped out of the bounds of sanity.

"That's right. I aim to let him see what happens to you before I kill all of you. The three of you get moving to that buggy. It's time we left town."

Twenty

Drake came in for supper with an appetite big enough for ten men. He was bone tired from a day in the saddle after a night of lovemaking. He smiled. Damn, it was good to have things back to normal with Pearl. And she loved him. Truly loved *him*, not just the idea of being a Kincaid. The woman had loved him all along.

And Pearl was some woman. Best of all, she was *his* woman, soon to be the mother of his son or daughter. Damned if he wasn't going to be a father after all. All day he'd thought about Pearl and the baby. They'd be a real family, he and Pearl would be good parents. Not like his. For sure not like hers.

That reminded him he'd meant to ask Pearl about adopting Storm and Sarah. Probably ought to ask the kids how they felt about it, especially since they were near as not grown. He already found himself calling Storm "son." And that Sarah was sweet as she could be. He already thought of them as his family. Why not make it official? He'd talk to Pearl tonight after supper. If she agreed, they'd talk to the kids together.

Maria met him with a worried frown on her face. "Señor, perhaps it is only the worries of an old woman, but I feel something is very wrong." She handed him a note. "Señora Pearl left this for you."

He read the note. "When did the kids go to town?"

"Early this morning. Señora Pearl, she left three hours ago."

"Three hours? Did she have Abe and Zed with her?"

"Only Señor Abe. Señor Zed was with my Miguel in the back and they did not tell him they were leaving."

"Damn. Something must be wrong. Maria, I'm going to look for Pearl and the kids. If I'm not back in two hours, you send Zed to get the sheriff and send the hands to look for us."

Midnight had ridden hard all day, but the horse had the best tracking instincts of any mount Drake had ever owned or seen. He resaddled the horse and gave his neck a pat.

"Sorry, old boy. You deserve a night off, but we have to find Pearl."

He spotted Beau's riderless horse trotting down the road about five minutes later. He caught it and tied the reins to the back of his saddle. Slowing to watch the tracks of Beau's horse, he scanned the ground. Soon, he found the slain guard.

He dismounted and checked Beau for breathing. The man was dead, so he lifted Beau's body across his horse. He'd take him to town and look for any sign of Pearl or the kids. Drake found footprints where someone had waited in hiding, but no signs of other activity and no marks to help him locate his family.

Damn. He'd thought this would soon be over. Quin was playing out his hand or he wouldn't have attacked Beau. Drake wondered why there was no sign of a struggle, no other sign on the ground. How was Beau killed without some re-action from the others? Maybe they simply took off as fast as they could, heading for town and safety.

The danger for Pearl, Storm, and Sarah had intensified. Now his baby was in danger also. He had to reach them before Quin could carry out his plans. Wondering where they were now, he pushed Midnight forward.

Minutes later he saw a log in the road ahead. He drew his gun in readiness for an ambush. As he came closer, he saw it was not a log, but a man. Jeff Granger lay on his belly in the dirt.

Drake saw a trail where Jeff had crawled from behind the rocks.

He hurried to the guard and asked, "Where you hurt?"

"Same damn place as before. Leave me and go after them. He's got Sarah and Storm, said he killed Beau."

"I've got Beau with me, and he's dead. I was taking his body to town. Think you can ride Beau's horse?"

"He took a horse back behind the rocks a ways. Couldn't have made it that far. Thought someone would come along the road and see me."

Drake retrieved the horse. Quin must have brought it from Tennessee. It was a fine animal, too good for a murdering crook like Quin.

"Someone came along before I could make it out here," Jeff said. "Figured it was your wife. Ridin' hell-bent for leather."

When he helped Jeff mount, the man paled, but didn't pass out.

Drake asked, "Gonna be able to sit all the way to town?"

When Jeff was seated firmly in the saddle, he said, "I'll have to go slow. You leave me to take Beau in and you go after them."

"You're sure you can make it?"

Jeff made an attempt to sit straighter. "Yeah, I can make it. You get after those kids. Check the Judge's place first."

"Thanks, Jeff."

"Drake, watch out. That bastard's crazy mean. Shot me after he made me drop my gun, just like that. No telling what he'll do."

Drake saw Jeff's horse tied near the side entrance, but no sign of the buggy. He threw Midnight's reins at a hitching rail. Thunder rumbled and lightning flashed across the sky. This storm was going to be a frog strangler. Worse, rain would wipe out Pearl's trail if he didn't find her inside. He rushed into the house with his gun drawn.

"Help! In here," Grandpa called.

Drake was not prepared for the sight which met him. Grandpa was tied in his chair. Blood matted his white mane on one side. Above his left ear the bloody trail led to a cut on a huge lump.

Abe lay motionless on the floor. The man had bled buckets, but was still alive. Drake didn't know who to take care of first, but figured he'd better take care of his grandfather.

"What happened?" he asked as he cut the ropes on Grandpa.

"That crazy Walker fella came bargin' in here this morning with Storm and Sarah. The kids were tied up and gagged, and he soon tied me up, too."

"Didn't anyone check to see why you hadn't come out of your study all day?"

"Aw, the sonofabitch had me call out the door and give everyone the day off to get ready for the big celebration tomorrow. Didn't take them long to clear out, I can tell you. Then we sat and waited for Pearl to show up."

The bottom fell out of his stomach and Drake thought he might have to sit down. He forced himself to stay calm and went to check on Abe. Abe's breathing was shallow but steady. Drake grabbed the water pitcher from Grandpa's desk. He filled a glass for Grandpa, then poured a thin trickle on Abe's mouth and forehead. Abe moved his head.

Drake poured again, and this time Abe opened his eyes. He grabbed Drake's hand. His voice was so soft Drake could barely her him.

"Line shack. Your ranch. Waitin' til you get there to kill all of you."

"Has he hurt any of them?" Drake prayed the answer would be no.

Abe said, "Hit Pearl hard 'cause she checked on the Judge."

Damnation, he'd kill the bastard for that alone. Drake reined in his temper to handle the present situation.

"Grandpa, how're you feeling? Think you can get help for Abe here and tell the sheriff what's happened?"

"Yeah, I can fetch Doc Percival and find Ben. Before I do anything else, though, I got to go to the privy."

Abe raised his hand in farewell as if the effort took all his strength, but he whispered, "Careful. Man's crazy. He'll be watching for you."

There were three line cabins on the ranch, but Drake figured the best bet was the one without brush or trees for cover. The storm moved closer. A few drops of rain hit his face. He reached behind him and untied his slicker without slowing Midnight. When he turned off toward the line shack, he saw the ribbon tracks of buggy wheels. He'd chosen right this time.

The rain started in full force, lashing at his back. The cabin was an hour's ride. He slowed Midnight to pace him. No use killing his favorite horse and winding up afoot. Being on a horse across open prairie with lightning around was danger enough.

Inside the cabin, Pearl was in a panic. Just when it looked as if her life was working out better than her wildest dreams, Quin had to show up. Things had gone to hell in a hand basket from then on. She shuddered when she thought of the lives lost because of Quin. Poor Grandpa, she hoped he was all right and Abe was at least alive.

Forcing herself to concentrate on the immediate situation, she wondered what she could do to save Storm, Sarah, and herself? And her baby? She had to save Drake's baby.

At least Quin had taken off their gags. The rain would have erased all their tracks by now. She hoped Abe was able to tell Drake where they'd gone. Not for an instant did she doubt Drake would find her, but a little guidance to save time might mean their lives.

She saw Storm work at his ropes. Unless his were looser than hers, he was wasting his time. She moved her head to nod at her thigh, then twisted to hide her hands from Quin while she made a gun with her fingers behind her back. If only Storm understood she had her derringer in the little thigh holster. Not that it would be any use unless one of them could get loose and help the other two. She turned to look at Storm and he nodded he'd understood.

They had to be careful Quin didn't see their motions. There was no telling what he'd do if he thought they were untying each other. As if they could. Quin had tightened the knots so it would take hours to undo them.

Storm turned to Sarah and nodded toward his boot. She was so upset it took her a while to grasp what he meant. Storm twisted so his boot was near Sarah's hands. He nudged her with his foot. Pearl scooted in front of Storm and Sarah to shield them from Quin's view.

"What are you two doin' over there?" Quin asked.

He looked as if he would come over, but didn't move from his chair at the table. Lucky for them Quin Walker was as lazy as the day was long.

"Just trying to get comfortable," Storm answered.

"Try all you want. You're not gonna' be anything for very long."

It was dark now and rain and wind battered at the small cabin. A single lantern on the table shed the only light except for the occasional streaks of lightning outside. Quin played solitaire with a deck of cards he had carried in his pocket. His gun lay beside him on the tabletop. Nearby was a liquor bottle, and he took frequent swigs from it.

When he spoke again, it seemed to Pearl he talked to himself more than to anyone in the room.

"Before long, I'll be living high on the hog."

"Seems to me you always lived pretty high," Pearl said. She hoped her talking kept him from looking at Storm and Sarah.

"Higher than trash like you three, but not high enough. When my daddy dies, I'll inherit the whole thing with you three worthless shits out of the way."

"I didn't know your daddy was sick. Is something wrong

with him?" Pearl couldn't keep the surprise from her voice. He might be a bad father, but he was her father too.

Quin gave a horrific laugh. "Not yet. He's going to meet with a tragic accident when I get back, though. I'll be grief stricken, o' course. In fact, I reckon I'll be so broke up I'll sell out and move down to New Orleans to get away from the sad reminders of living there. A man with money can live real good down in New Orleans."

Pearl heard Storm whisper to Sarah, "Keep your hands behind you until I give you the signal." So, Sarah must have used Storm's knife to free him and he had done the same for her.

Quin frowned. "Say, you stop that whispering. You want to talk, talk loud enough for me to hear."

Storm spoke up, "We were just remembering things about Tennessee. We heard your mama was a real pretty lady."

Sarah scooted beside Pearl, her unbound hands still behind her.

Quin relaxed. "Well, now, that's right nice of you to say. She was pretty, and a real lady. Not like those sluts who bred you."

Storm moved behind Pearl and sawed through the binding at her wrists. Now they were all three able to move freely—if they could distract Quin so he didn't shoot them before they could overpower him.

Pearl asked, "What kind of card game is that you're playing?"

Quin looked incredulous. "You mean you don't know how to play solitaire?"

"Granny didn't hold with playing cards," she answered.

"Mind if I sit across from you and watch?" Storm asked. "I ain't never seen a deck of cards up close."

Quin pushed the chair out with his foot. "Might's well. Won't do you no good after today, but might pass the time 'til Kincaid gets here."

Storm eased himself into the chair, knife still in his hands. He started asking questions about the game. Quin took to the role of showing how smart he was at cards, and dealt a hand of gin rummy.

"I'll play your hand and you can watch."

Pearl moved so Sarah hid a portion of her body. She eased her skirt up and slowly worked the little gun from its holster. With the gun in her hand, she inched her hand back to her side. Using her other hand, she tried to slide her skirt back to her feet, but Quin looked up before she finished.

"Well, lookee here, injun. Your hand lost." Quin gave a high-pitched laugh and looked at her and Sarah. He frowned. "Hey, what are you doin' with your skirt hiked up like that? Giving me a little peep show? Damned if your legs aren't better lookin' than I would of thought."

He threw down the cards and grabbed his gun. "Now that I think about it, you prettied up a lot since you left Piper's Hollow. Let's see what the rest of you looks like. I might like a little fun 'fore your high and mighty husband gets here. I'd planned to let him watch while I used you and Sarah, but I can always have another go at you when he gets here." He walked with his arm at his side and the gun dangling from his hand.

Pearl brought her arm up and aimed the derringer at Quin. "Stop right there. Drop your gun."

"Against a one-shot toy like that. I don't think so."

"I also have a weapon, and it will pierce your heart as you say your arrow went through Beau's." Storm stood, revealing the knife he held in throwing position.

Without taking her eyes from Quin, Pearl said, "Sarah, get the ropes and tie them together until you get a piece long enough to tie up this sorry excuse for a human. Make sure the knots are tight. Quin, I told you to drop your gun."

Quin let the gun slide from his grasp and hit the floor. He stood facing Pearl and she saw the anger in his eyes. More than anger sparked there. Quin was truly insane and beyond reason.

"Well, well. So, you had a hidden gun and the bastard injun has a knife. I didn't think of that. Reckon you can use that toy?"

Pearl assured him, "I can and I will." Though she devoted her life to healing and saving lives, she knew she could shoot this man. Too many lives depended on her for her to fail.

He lunged at her. She fired, saw him jerk against the bullet's jolt and red spread across his shoulder. He bent to retrieve his gun and she kicked it away.

"I'll teach you to cross me, bitch," Quin said and backhanded her. "You saw what I did to Belle. That's nothing to what you're gonna get."

The force of his blow near knocked her head from her shoulders. She fell against the wall with a jarring thud though Quin held her arm firm.

"Have you forgotten about me? Do not touch my sister again or I will kill you," Storm said. "Pearl, step away from him and stand by Sarah."

"Not likely," Quin said and yanked Pearl in front of him. "All right, Sarah. Pick up that gun and hand it to me. You hold it by the barrel real easy like." He backed away, pulling Pearl in front of him.

Outside the storm's intensity grew. Lightning stuck nearby. Deafening thunder rattled panes of window glass and shook the room. An eerie glow lit the cabin.

Sarah picked up the gun. She chewed her lip in indecision.

"Don't give it to him. He'll use it to kill all of us," Pearl shouted above the storm. She elbowed Quin hard in the stomach.

He let out an "Oof" and eased his grip on her.

She kicked backward at his shins and he let go. The sudden release left her off balance and she fell at his feet.

Quin grabbed the gun from Sarah. His shove sent Sarah stumbling to the floor halfway across the room. He aimed the gun at Pearl. Before he could fire, the door slammed open. Drenched and dripping pools of water on the floor, Drake stood in the doorway.

"You took my family," Drake said. "I'm taking them back."

Quin fired at Drake. Drake's body twitched when the bullet hit his left arm near his shoulder. He didn't seem to notice he'd been hit, but returned Quin's fire. His shot caught Quin in the heart half a second before Storm's knife found its mark.

Pearl saw surprise spread across Quin's face, the astonishment when he looked down at his chest and saw the red stain spread, saw the knife protruding. He raised his hand as if to tug at the knife but his fingers only clawed air. He opened his mouth and his lips moved, but no words came. His eyes rolled back in his head and he slowly dropped to the floor.

Storm rushed forward to check him. "He's dead."

Drake clasped Pearl in his arms. He buried his head in her hair. "God, honey, I thought I'd lost you. I swear I couldn't live without you." He raised his head and said, "Good throw, son. I knew I could count on you to protect your sisters if you had half a chance."

Pearl tugged at his slicker. "You've been hurt. Let me see."

"I'm fine. It can wait 'til we get home," Drake said.

She pushed the slicker from his shoulders and it fell to the floor. Her trembling fingers pulled his shirt buttons undone until she saw that the bullet had passed through the flesh. Apparently resigned to her care, he ripped the sleeve from his shirt and sat on the edge of the nearest bunk.

Using the bandanas which had been their gags, Pearl made a pad and tied it around Drake's arm. As she worked, the realization hit her again that he might have been killed, they all might have been. She hated the thought that her own half-brother had been responsible for all the terror of the past few months. Even more, she hated that he now lay dead only a few feet away. The baby moved inside her and she thanked God for her own safety and that of her family. That safety came at a terrible price, but there would be no more guards around the clock, no more jumping at sudden noises.

Pearl slid her arms around Drake's neck. She wanted never to be apart from him again. "Oh, Drake, I knew you'd come for us. I was just afraid the weather would make you too late."

Drake kissed her tenderly. "Knowing he was crazy and had already killed, I was going crazy with worry myself." Without easing his hold on Pearl, he asked Sarah and Storm, "You two all right? Get over here and let me see you."

"I'm not hurt," Storm said. "Are you?" he asked Sarah.

"No, not really." She looked at Quin's body, then quickly looked away. "I wanted to shoot him, but I was afraid I would hit Sister instead."

"You did fine," Storm said and put his arm around her shoulders. He led her to Drake and Pearl, to be included in a family embrace.

Tears slid down Sarah's cheeks, and Pearl brushed them away before she asked Drake, "How did you find us?"

"Lucky for me, Abe heard Quin talking about where he would take you. Otherwise it would have taken me longer. Rain wiped out your trail."

"Abe's all right, then?" Pearl asked.

"I wouldn't say he's all right, he lost a lot of blood. He's alive, though."

"How is Grandpa?" Sarah asked. "Quin hit him hard."

"Mad as a hornet. Seemed pretty fit considering the lump on his head."

"You know Quin killed Beau and Jeff?" asked Storm.

Drake nodded. "The good news is, Jeff's alive. Last I saw him he was riding to town with Beau's body. That Quin was some shot with an arrow."

"My grandfather taught Quin the Cherokee ways when the Walkers lived with my people," said Storm. "Guess Quin forgot the lessons about using those skills for good."

Sarah glanced over her shoulder at Quin's body. "He was just plain evil, but I'm sorry it had to come to this."

"Me, too, Sarah," Drake agreed. "But he chose his path some time back."

As the storm's noise abated, they heard the thunder of horses. Drake went to the open door. "Howdy, Ben. Sure good to see you."

The sheriff and two of his deputies strode into the cabin. "Had a hard time keeping half the town and all your hands from coming with me." He stepped over and nudged Quin's lifeless body. "We could have stayed home and kept dry. That man's dead as they come—looks to me like he's been killed twice."

"Still glad you're here," Drake assured him.

"The Judge and Granger both came to see me, told me what happened. Kline was still at Doc's when we left town. Sure sorry you folks had to go through all this, but it ought to put an end to your troubles."

Sheriff Liles pulled the knife from Quin's chest and cleaned it on Quin's clothes before he offered it to Drake. Drake handed it to Storm, who took it and stood staring at the blade a few seconds before he slid it back into his boot.

The sheriff signaled his deputies. "Boys, load this fella across a horse. We'll take his body back to town."

"Rain's letting up some," Drake said to Pearl. "You want to wait here 'til the rain stops or go home?"

Pearl, Storm, and Sarah said in unison, "Go home!"

He smiled. "Right. I can't think of anything nicer than taking my family home. Let's go."

Pearl's Chicken and Dumplings

1 large stewing hen	1 teaspoon baking powder
2 cups flower	$^1/_2$ teaspoon salt
$^1/_2$ cup lard or shortening	*Optional:*
1 cup milk	sliced carrot and celery

Choose and prepare a nice fat hen. Cut it up, with the meat on the bone. Stew the chicken in a large pot with plenty of water. After the chicken has cooked, you may want to remove the bones so people do not have to deal with them when they eat.

Cook the chicken until it is tender (about an hour). You can put slices of carrot and celery in the broth as the chicken cooks. Season broth with salt and pepper. When the chicken is tender, cook on very low simmer while you make the dumpling dough.

To make the dough: Mix the flour, shortening, baking powder, salt and milk. Roll dough out thin and add more flour if it is not stiff enough. Cut it into strips about 1" to 2" wide. Keep heat low under chicken. Drop half of dumplings into broth, pulling strips of dough into pieces as you drop them. After about five minutes, push those dumplings to the side of the pot and drop in the rest of the dough in the same way. Cook another five minutes or so. Stir. Take a little fresh milk or buttermilk and drizzle it around the edges of the pot. Stir. Cook another ten minutes. Test to make sure dumplings are cooked through and serve.

Put a Little Romance in Your Life With
Georgina Gentry

<u>BOOK YOUR PLACE ON OUR WEBSITE</u>
AND MAKE THE
<u>READING CONNECTION!</u>

We've created a customized website just for our very special readers, where you can get the inside scoop on everything that's going on with Zebra, Pinnacle and Kensington books.

When you come online, you'll have the exciting opportunity to:

- View covers of upcoming books

- Read sample chapters

- Learn about our future publishing schedule
  (listed by publication month *and author*)

- Find out when your favorite authors will be visiting a city near you

- Search for and order backlist books from our online catalog

- Check out author bios and background information

- Send e-mail to your favorite authors

- Meet the Kensington staff online

- Join us in weekly chats with authors, readers and other guests

- Get writing guidelines

- AND MUCH MORE!

Visit our website at
http://www.kensingtonbooks.com